Outstanding praise for the novels of
Michael Thomas Ford!

WHAT WE REMEMBER

"Ford knows how to weave layers of witticism, cleverness, humor
and subtlety into a quilt of sorts—stirring up emotions that keep
you oddly secure in knowing you're not the only one who's
experienced them before."
—*Instinct*

CHANGING TIDES

"Ford bridges the gap between gay romance and mainstream fiction
in his latest. A deft sense of place and a handle on romance—both
Ben and Caddie's—that's neither sappy nor shallow will help set
this one apart."
—*Publishers Weekly*

FULL CIRCLE

"Summer isn't the same without hitting the beach, getting a sunburn
and devouring a deliciously soapy novel. Ford knows how to draw in a
reader with sex and sin."
—*Entertainment Weekly*

"A must read for every gay man. Older readers will be reminded of
where we've been and just how far we've come. Younger readers
will be made more aware of recent gay history. And all will have more
respect for what gay men have had to endure and how they've
managed to overcome it."
—*Envy Man* magazine

"An excellent summer read."
—*Dallas Voice*

"Ford's sprawling tale chronicles the highlights of gay history in the
latter half of the 20th century."
—*Metrosource*

"*Full Circle* stunningly succeeds as a great novel."
—*We the People*

"The characters' many brushes with homosexual history—Harvey Milk
trolling for votes in a gay bar, the unfurling of the first Rainbow flag,
the sexual energy of early ACT UP meetings—will resonate with
gay readers."
—*Publishers Weekly*

**Please turn the page for more rave reviews of the novels
of Michael Thomas Ford!**

LOOKING FOR IT

"An insightful and entertaining read about what we seek, and what answers we find within and without."
—*Booklist*

"Ford handles his broad, diverse cast with amazing ease, and demonstrates a natural gift for storytelling."
—*Bay Area Reporter*

"Give Michael Thomas Ford credit for giving us a group of identifiable characters who do *not* live in L.A., NYC, or Miami, but in a small town like those where most readers actually live. It's also nice to see these characters addressing realistic differences of generation as well as spirituality, in addition to the usual mix of looking for love, dealing with internalized homophobia and creating support systems through friendships and families of choice."
—*Instinct*

"Ford handles his broad, diverse cast with aplomb, and his knowing sense of humor and emphasis on the positive make this novel as warm and inviting as a group hug."
—*Publishers Weekly*

"Ford has a knack for bringing together characters of all ages who share a common desire of just wanting to be loved and happy. Of all the books I reviewed this past year, this one generated the most response."
—*We the People*

"A warm-hearted story about the importance of friendship and the miracle of connection . . . Ford's fluid prose and strong storytelling deliver charming credibility."
—*Outlook News*

"Few authors have bothered to represent gay life outside of the usual queer meccas, and Ford captures it perfectly . . . Readers expecting a repeat of Ford's far sunnier *Last Summer* will be in for a shock, but *Looking for It* is a stronger, weightier product that will have readers impatiently turning pages to see how things turn out."
—*Bay Windows* (Boston)

LAST SUMMER

"He effectively draws his readers into the wild world of Provincetown . . . plenty of page-turning drama . . . a winner."
—*Entertainment Weekly*

"Ford expands his repertoire with this brimful first novel about life, love and self-discovery over the course of a steamy Provincetown summer . . . a satisfying beach book—and a pleasant fiction debut for Ford."
—*Publishers Weekly*

"A made-for-the-beach page-turner, complete with characters twining in and out of one another's arms and destinies that may leave readers wishing for a wintertime sequel."
—*Booklist*

Books by Michael Thomas Ford

LAST SUMMER

LOOKING FOR IT

TANGLED SHEETS

FULL CIRCLE

CHANGING TIDES

WHAT WE REMEMBER

THE ROAD HOME

PATH OF THE GREEN MAN

MASTERS OF MIDNIGHT
(with William J. Mann, Sean Wolfe, and Jeff Mann)

MIDNIGHT THIRSTS
(with Timothy Ridge, Greg Herren, and Sean Wolfe)

Published by Kensington Publishing Corporation

WHAT WE
REMEMBER

MICHAEL THOMAS FORD

WHAT WE REMEMBER

KENSINGTON BOOKS
http://www.kensingtonbooks.com

KENSINGTON BOOKS are published by

Kensington Publishing Corp.
119 West 40th Street
New York, NY 10018

Copyright © 2009 by Michael Thomas Ford

All Kensington titles, imprints and distributed lines are available at special quantity discounts for bulk purchases for sales promotion, premiums, fund-raising, educational or institutional use.

Special book excerpts or customized printings can also be created to fit specific needs. For details, write or phone the office of the Kensington Special Sales Manager: Kensington Publishing Corp., 119 West 40th Street, New York, NY 10018. Attn. Special Sales Department. Phone: 1-800-221-2647.

ISBN-13: 978-0-7582-1852-0
ISBN-10: 0-7582-1852-4

First Hardcover Printing: June 2009
First Trade Paperback Printing: May 2010

10   9   8   7   6   5   4   3   2   1

Printed in the United States of America

CHAPTER I

1991

"They found him."

"Found who?" James McCloud mumbled. Jarred awake by the shrill voice of the phone, he had answered it instinctively. The voice on the other end of the line was vaguely familiar, but sleep tempted him back into its arms, and the question of who had awakened him seemed ridiculously unimportant.

"Dad," the voice answered.

James sat up, suddenly very much alert. "Celeste?" he said.

"They found Dad," his sister repeated.

"When?" asked James.

"Last night," Celeste answered. "Nate waited to tell me until they were sure. I just found out a few minutes ago."

A soft murmur distracted James, and he glanced at the sleeping form next to him. Charly had turned her head and appeared to be looking right at him. Her lips were slightly parted, and one delicate hand lay across her breast. He started to tell her who was on the phone, but a soft snore revealed that she still slept.

After slipping out of bed, James left the bedroom, shutting the door softy behind him, and walked to the kitchen, where he could speak at a normal volume.

"Where did they find him?" he asked Celeste.

"In the woods," his sister informed him.

James leaned against the counter. Dressed only in boxer shorts, he shivered in the chill of the apartment. The tile floor was cold beneath his bare feet, and he wished he'd grabbed his robe before leaving the bedroom. A glance at the microwave's clock revealed that it was nearly five. In a few minutes the alarm clock on his bedside table would give its electronic caw and Charly would reach across where he would normally be lying, looking for the snooze button.

"James?" Celeste's voice brought him back to the moment.

"Seven years," he said, still not quite believing the news his sister had just delivered. "It's been seven years, and all of a sudden he turns up?"

"Nicky Turner was digging a foundation for a new cabin," Celeste explained. "That's how they found him."

"Does Mom know?" James asked.

"No," said Celeste. "I don't think I can tell her."

James sighed. "What about Billy?"

Celeste gave a short laugh. "Who knows?" she answered. "Probably drunk somewhere, or high. I haven't seen him in a couple of days."

A flash of anger at his younger brother rose up in James's thoughts, but he blocked it out. Being upset with Billy wouldn't help. Not now.

"James," Celeste said. "There's something else."

James waited for her to continue. It was a long moment before she did. "He was buried," she said.

"What do you mean?" James asked. From the bedroom came the harsh *beep-beep-beep* of the alarm clock. He heard Charly's muttered curses, followed by a crash as she found the clock and knocked it to the floor. Its voice was choked off.

"I mean someone buried him," Celeste told her brother.

"That's impossible," said James. "He killed—"

"He was in a box," Celeste interrupted. "Someone buried him in a box."

James felt his breath leave him, and for a moment he could do nothing but stare at the window above the sink. Raindrops dotted the glass, forming thin trickles that ran down and disappeared over the edge of the sill. He heard the sound of footsteps, and a moment later Charly appeared in the doorway. Her long brown hair fell loosely around her shoulders, and she had put on James's Yankees sweatshirt. The too-long sleeves covered her hands, which she rubbed against her bare thighs.

"Who are you talking to?" she asked, rubbing an eye and pushing her hair away from her face.

"I'll come up," James said to Celeste, holding up a finger to let Charly know he was almost finished. "Don't say anything to Mom until I get there, okay?"

"Yeah," Celeste replied. "I guess I can put it off for a few hours. But don't be too long. This is a small town, remember?"

"How could I forget?" said James. "I'll be there as soon as I can."

He hung up and looked at Charly, who was now eyeing him quizzically.

"What's going on?" she asked.

"I have to go home," said James.

"Why?"

"Just some family stuff," James answered.

Charly crossed her arms over her chest and gave him the look he'd come to realize meant that she didn't believe for one second that he was telling the truth. Although he hated that she could see through him better than anyone he'd ever met, he also found her insightfulness arousing. For a second he thought about taking her back to bed. Then his sister's words came back to him. *Someone buried him.*

"Really," he said. "It's no big deal. But I have to go up there and deal with my mother. Celeste thinks she may have early Alzheimer's or something."

"Your mother?" said Charly. "Early Alzheimer's? You mean the woman who remembers my birthday even though I've never met her? The woman who once recited her grandmother's recipe for peanut butter fudge to me over the phone from memory after I told her how good it was? *That* mother?"

James nodded. "I guess she's been forgetting a lot of things lately. Anyway, Celeste thinks I should come up and talk to her about maybe getting herself checked out. It's not a big deal."

Charly continued to stare at him. James met her gaze, smiling and forcing himself not to blink. Finally Charly nodded. "Okay," she said. "I guess you'll tell me when you're ready. Go run off to the hinterlands. I'll be fine."

James stepped forward and drew her to him. He slid a hand beneath the sweatshirt, feeling her warm, smooth skin beneath his fingers. Bending down, he kissed her lightly on the mouth.

"It should just take a day or two," he said. "I'll be back before you know it."

He was relieved that she couldn't see his face as he spoke.

CHAPTER 2

1983

"Hello?"

Ada McCloud's heart pounded in her chest as she waited for an answer.

"Ada, it's A.J."

Ada couldn't hide the concern in her voice as she asked, "Have you heard from him?"

"No," A.J. answered. "I was hoping you had."

"I haven't," Ada told him. She hesitated before asking, "Do you think he's all right?"

"Sure," A.J. answered, but his answer came too quickly, and his voice had the air of false reassurance.

He's as worried as I am, Ada thought.

"He's probably just run off somewhere," A.J. continued. "He'll turn up."

"I'm sure you're right," Ada replied.

She was lying as badly as A.J. was, and both of them knew it. Yet neither would admit their falsehoods. A.J. knew as well as Ada did that Dan McCloud wouldn't just run off anywhere. The two men had been best friends since childhood, so close that Ada often wondered if there were things about her husband that only A.J. Derry would ever know.

"Don't worry, Ada," A.J. said. "And call me as soon as you hear from him."

"Same to you," said Ada.

She hung up and turned her attention back to the potatoes waiting on the counter. As she ran the peeler over the brown skin and watched it fall in strips into the sink, she tried to focus her thoughts on preparing dinner for her family. The water was on the stove, lightly salted and simmering. She would quarter the potatoes, put them into the pot, and bring the water to a boil. She would cook them until they were fork tender, drain them, and cube them before adding the milk and butter and mashing them, just as her mother had taught her. She would place them in the same bowl her mother had used, the one with the yellow and blue flowers.

She thought about how often this ritual had been repeated, how many times she had cooked dinner for her husband and children. She'd been married for nineteen years, twenty in October. That added up to thousands of meals. Yet as she drew the peeler over the potato in her hand she felt as if she were doing it for the first time. Her fingers trembled. The peeler slipped, and drops of red appeared on the white surface of the potato.

She turned on the water and ran it until it was ice cold before sticking her finger into the stream. It quickly had the desired numbing effect, yet she held her hand steady for a while longer, until she felt nothing.

She turned the water off and patted her hand dry with the dishtowel. She considered finding a bandage, but the cut was a minor one and had already stopped bleeding. Besides, she reminded herself, she had mother's hands. It was a term coined by her own mother to describe the tolerance to discomfort built up by any woman who spent years cooking for a family. Ada smiled to herself. It was true; it would take much more than a little cut to make her complain. The kids were always remarking on how she could immerse her hands in dishwater so hot it turned her skin the color of a boiled lobster. Even Dan—big, macho Dan—winced when he tried to help her with the after-dinner cleanup.

At the thought of Dan her smile disappeared and she was once more consumed with worry. Her husband had left the house two days earlier, presumably to go to work, but had neither come home nor contacted Ada. It was unlike him. Dan McCloud was a man who liked order. He had a fondness for watches and clocks, was always on time and always making lists of things to be done. He was not someone who just failed to come home.

Ada knew that Dan could take care of himself. He was, after all, the town's sheriff. In addition to knowing how to use the gun he carried, Dan had a cool head. He would never rush into anything without thinking his way all around it first and figuring out at least three ways to extricate himself should things go badly. His wife had never seen him panic, and despite the dangers that came with his profession she had seldom worried over him.

But somehow this felt different.

The children, she was only somewhat surprised to see, had not really noticed their father's absence. Now that they were all three teenagers they had their own lives, which intersected with those of their parents only occasionally. Because of Dan's job they had never been a family that sat down to breakfast and dinner together religiously. The fact that Dan had not made an appearance at the supper table the night before was not unusual, and Ada had answered the questions regarding his whereabouts by explaining that Dan was working.

Another day, however, and she would have to answer them truthfully. What would she say then? How do you tell your children that their father is gone but you don't know to where? She couldn't claim he was on a business trip, or taking care of some emergency out of town. They would know she was lying. Which left her with only one option: to tell them the truth. Only she didn't know what the truth was.

The banging of the kitchen door startled her. She turned to see her youngest son, Billy, entering. Billy had recently turned thirteen, officially making her and Dan the parents of three teenagers. Although she admitted to no favorites among her children, as the baby Billy occupied a place in her heart perhaps a step or two above those of his brother and sister. James, who at sixteen was a younger version of his father, had the McCloud look about him, with dark hair and stormy eyes. Her oldest, Celeste, favored her, being tall and thin, her hair a deep red and her skin the pale, freckled cream that burned easily and never tanned.

But Billy was the perfect mingling of Ada and Dan, proof of their union in physical form. Slighter than his brother, he was graceful without being delicate. His face was less handsome than James's, but arguably more beautiful. His green eyes sparkled when he laughed, and of all the children he was the one most likely to make Ada smile. Even now, in the midst of worry, his appearance was reassuring. There was, she thought, no question of Dan's safety when such a child was waiting for him to come home.

"The mail came," Billy said. He dropped it on the counter and sniffed the air. "Roast beef?" he asked.

Ada nodded. "It'll be ready in about half an hour," she told her son. "Go wash up."

Billy left, and Ada finished peeling the potatoes and cutting them into chunks. Dropping them into the now-steaming water, she turned up the flame beneath the pot. Dinner preparations completed, she picked up the mail. She took it to the table, sat down, and leafed through it. She took time to peruse the circular from Penney's and to examine the weekly grocery specials, tearing out the 2-for-1 coupon for the brand of peanut butter Dan liked. She discarded several pieces of junk mail from various organizations wanting money, and read with only slight interest a bulletin from the church the family nominally attended but to which they hadn't actively gone in a long while.

Maybe we'll go this Sunday, she thought. *It might be good for the kids.*

The last piece of mail was a plain white envelope. It was addressed to her. Instinctively she looked to the upper left corner for a return address, but found none. The postmark was dated the previous day. Who, she wondered, had sent her a letter? She slid her finger beneath the lip of the envelope and opened it. Removing a single sheet of paper, she began to read.

CHAPTER 3

1991

"Billy, eat your eggs."

Billy poked at the plate of scrambled eggs, then set the fork down and pushed the plate away from him. He took a spoonful of sugar from the bowl on the table and added it to the coffee in his mug. Stirring it, he tried to pretend he was somewhere else.

"Billy," his mother said again. "You already put four spoonfuls in that coffee. That's enough."

"I'm not a kid, Mom," he snapped. "For fuck's sake, I'm twenty-one years old."

"Don't swear," said Ada. "Not in my house."

"Mom, are you okay?"

Billy looked across the table at his sister. Celeste was sitting beside her husband, Nate. The two of them were ignoring him—had been ignoring him ever since their arrival half an hour ago.

"I'll make some more eggs," Ada said, starting to get up.

"Ada," said Nate. "Sit down. Please."

Ada paused, then returned to her chair. *Of course she listens to Nate,* Billy thought. His head hurt. Slipping a hand into his pocket, he sought the little plastic bag he recalled putting there the night before. It wasn't there. *Fuck me,* he thought.

"I know this is hard for you to hear." Nate's voice droned in Billy's ears. He closed his eyes, trying to block it out. He wanted to sleep. If he could only sleep, he'd feel better. He hadn't been to bed in days.

How many? He tried to count backward but couldn't remember if it was Wednesday or only Tuesday. That made a difference.

"You say they found Dan," he heard his mother say. Her voice was flat, as if she were discussing the laundry or the weather. "I heard you." She was silent for a minute, then began speaking again. "I knew he was dead," she said. "We *all* knew that. This just proves it."

"It's not just that, Mom," Celeste said.

Billy opened his eyes. He seemed to be looking at his sister through a haze. She was blurry, indistinct, a ghost. Her voice was coming from far away. He blinked, and the fog lifted like a curtain going up on a play. Celeste's face came into focus, and he stared at her mouth.

"What else can there be?" his mother asked. "You've already told me he's dead. Seems to me that's the end of it."

Billy saw his sister look at her husband. Nate leaned forward, placing his elbows on the table and folding his hands. "Ada, we didn't just find Dan in those woods. We found him in a box."

"A box?" Ada repeated. "What do you mean, a box?"

"Dan was buried inside a trunk," said Nate.

Billy sat up. "What?" he said.

Nate ignored him, speaking directly to Ada.

"Somebody put Dan into a box—a trunk, actually—and buried him on the land where Nicky Turner is building his cabin," he said.

"How would he get inside a trunk?" asked Ada. She gave a short laugh, as if she'd just realized that someone had played a joke on her.

"Dad killed himself," Billy said. "We all know that."

This time Nate and Celeste did look at him. Celeste in particular looked angry. By speaking about his father's death he'd broken the agreement that had existed between the members of the family since that day seven years ago. But he didn't care. Celeste could go fuck herself. Nate too. Especially Nate.

"He killed himself," Billy repeated. "How the fuck would he get inside a trunk and bury himself in Nicky Turner's lot?"

"He didn't kill himself," said Nate. "Someone else killed him."

Stunned, Billy looked to his mother. She held her coffee mug in her hands, and she was looking out the window. "That squirrel has been at the suet again," she said.

"Mom," said Celeste. "Did you hear what Nate—"

"I heard him," Ada interrupted. "But he's wrong. I have the letter."

"I wish I was wrong, Mom," said Nate. "But I'm not. Dan didn't kill himself."

Ada shook her head. "No one would kill Dan," she said. "No one *could*. He would never let them."

Billy coughed. He felt sick, as if he might throw up the coffee and eggs in his stomach. His chest hurt. He felt another cough coming on and tried to suppress it. But it was too strong for him, and he began hacking. His sister and his brother-in-law shot him annoyed looks but said nothing.

"No," his mother said decisively. "You're wrong. That must not be Dan in that . . . box." She said the last word softly, letting it die in the still air. "It must be someone else."

Celeste got up and walked over to Ada. Putting her hand on her mother's shoulder, she said, "It's Dad, Mom. He's wearing his uniform."

"How do you know what he's wearing?" Ada snapped.

Celeste looked across the table at Nate. Billy saw Nate nod curtly.

"I've seen him," said Celeste.

"You've *seen* him?" Billy repeated.

Celeste continued speaking to their mother. "I wanted to be sure before we told you. At first I didn't want to believe Nate, either. But it's him, Mom. It really is."

Ada's face crumpled. She began to cry. *That's the first time I've seen her cry since he died,* Billy thought. He wished he could go and put his arms around his mother. But Celeste had already claimed her.

"Why did you have to tell me?" Ada said. She looked up. "It was all over," she said. "I let him go. Now . . ."

She lowered her eyes once more. Billy saw her shoulders buckle as more tears came. *Say something!* he telegraphed at Celeste, who remained motionless with her hands on their mother's shoulders.

"What about the letter?" he said, looking at Nate.

"That's one of the questions we're going to have to answer," Nate answered. "It will all be part of the investigation."

Ada looked up. Her eyes were wet. "Investigation?" she said weakly.

Nate nodded. "There will have to be an investigation," he said. "Now that this is a murder case."

Ada slammed her hand on the table. "No!" she said. She pointed a finger at her son-in-law. "You leave this alone! Do you hear me?"

"Mom—" Celeste began.

"I said no," Ada interrupted. "There's no need to bring all of that up again. It won't change anything."

"But Mom," Celeste said, "if Dad was murdered, then Nate has to find out who did it."

"I don't care who did it!" Ada cried. She looked at Billy. "I don't care," she said, more softly.

It's all right, Billy thought, giving her what he hoped was a reassuring look. The fog had descended again, and it was difficult to concentrate.

"It's my job, Mom," he heard Nate say. "It's my responsibility to find out what happened to Dan."

"I know this is hard," Celeste told her mother. "It's hard for all of us."

Celeste looked at Billy. He realized that she wanted him to say something to back her up. But he was so tired. All he wanted to do now was go lie down and sleep. Just for a little while. Until his head cleared.

Shaking her head in obvious irritation, Celeste pulled out the chair between Billy and Ada and sat down. She took one of Ada's hands in hers and held it, her back to Billy.

"Mom, you have to be prepared for the attention this is going to get. Once people find out that Dad was murdered, it's going to get crazy."

"Don't tell them," Ada said. "They don't need to know our business."

"You know I can't do that, Ada," said Nate.

The room fell silent. Billy knew that his mother had accepted the situation, although something still didn't feel right. He searched his fluttering thoughts, trying to pin one down as if trying to catch a moth in a jar. Something bothered him, but he couldn't get his mind to stop tumbling headlong through space to figure out what it was.

"James is coming, Mom," Celeste said, breaking the quiet. "He should be here soon."

Billy heard himself laugh. *James,* he thought. *Of course James is coming. It's always James to the rescue.* He had the sudden image of his older brother galloping across the prairie on a horse, his white hat shining in the sun. He laughed again.

"What's wrong with you?" Celeste asked.

Billy looked at her. "Nothing," he said. "Nothing at all. I'll be fine. We'll all be fine. James will be here and everything will be *fine.*" He emphasized the last word, and saw his sister's jaw tighten.

"Billy, why don't you go get some rest," Nate suggested. "You look beat."

"Do I?" asked Billy. "Do I look beat, Nate? That's weird, because like I told my sister, I feel just fine."

"Billy," Nate said. His voice was heavy with warning.

"Fuck you," said Billy. "I'm not married to you. And if anyone doesn't belong here it's you. You're not family."

"I'm the sheriff," Nate replied. "And in case you've forgotten, your father and my father were best friends."

Billy nodded. "That's right, Nate," he said. "That's right. Thank you for reminding me about that." He tapped his temple with his finger. "I forget things sometimes, you know?"

"Stop picking on your brother, Celeste," said Ada.

"Pick on him?" Celeste objected. "He's the one who's—"

"Celeste," said Nate, stopping her.

"I'm sorry, Mom," Celeste said. "Maybe *you* should go lie down."

"Maybe," said Ada. "Maybe I will at that."

She stood up. Celeste steadied her. "Let me help you, Mom," she said.

"I'm fine, Celeste," Ada answered. "Just let me be."

Billy watched as his mother left the kitchen. As soon as she was gone, Celeste turned to him. "You're high, aren't you?"

"What difference does it make?" Billy said.

"For one thing, it's illegal," Celeste told him.

"Illegal?" said Billy. He laughed. "You've been married to that one for too long," he told his sister, indicating Nate with a wave of his hand. "And it wasn't all that long ago that neither of you cared about it being illegal yourselves."

"That was a little pot," Celeste replied. "What you're doing is a lot worse."

"Right," said Billy, nodding.

"Mom doesn't need you being fucked up right now, Billy," Celeste said.

"Maybe not," Billy agreed. He looked his sister in the eyes. "But maybe it's what *I* need."

Celeste shook her head. "Can't you arrest him?" she asked her husband.

"Both of you need to pull it together," said Nate. "This is just going to get worse."

"Don't worry," Billy told him. "Didn't you hear? James is coming."

"I'm serious, Billy," Celeste said. "Once this gets out, everyone's going to be looking at us. I don't want them thinking . . ." She stopped, and turned to look out the window.

"Think what?" Billy asked her. "Think what, Celeste?" he repeated when his sister didn't reply.

"You know what," Celeste said quietly. "You know what, Billy."

Billy stood up. He swayed slightly as his head pounded. "Here's a news flash for you, big sister. They already think it."

He made his way out of the kitchen and into the bathroom that was off the hall leading to the living room. After shutting the door behind him, he slumped to the floor and sat there, his back against the side of the tub. The tile in the bathroom was pale pink. It hadn't changed since he was a kid. Sitting in there with the door closed, it felt like being inside a womb, small and closed in and safe.

He shut his eyes. They'd found his father. His father who had supposedly killed himself seven years ago but who now it seemed had been murdered. It seemed like he should feel something—sadness, anger, rage, anything. Instead, he just felt numb. Not that that was anything new. He had perfected achieving a state of total disinterest in everything.

The throbbing in his head had subsided to a dull pain. Through the door he could hear the voices of Celeste and Nate, faint as the droning of bees. Beside him warm air blew up through the vent in the floor, the breath of the oil furnace hibernating in its basement cave. It felt good to be warm; he was almost always cold. But not here, in the pink bathroom, away from everything.

He curled himself into a ball beside the tub, his head resting on the mat. And for the first time in days, he slept.

CHAPTER 4

1982

It took him a moment to realize that the reason the shoe wouldn't go on was because he was trying to put it on the wrong foot. Once he figured that out, he easily slipped the red pump over the delicate toes and tucked the heel into the back. He repeated the process on the other foot. The shoes were pretty, much better than the white sandals he'd tried first. Those had not matched the dress at all.

Billy took the Barbie and laid her on the carpet. Turning his attention to Ken, he removed the flower-patterned swimming trunks and replaced them with a pair of tuxedo pants. The garish Hawaiian shirt was abandoned in favor of a shirt and jacket. Black shoes completed the outfit.

With both Barbie and Ken now appropriately dressed for an evening out, he held one in each hand. Turning them to face one another, he took turns providing them with voices.

"Thanks for asking me to dinner," Barbie said sweetly.

Ken nodded. "Thank you for coming," he replied, his voice deep and manly. "You look beautiful."

Barbie turned away, embarrassed. When she looked back at Ken she said, "Aren't you going to kiss me good night?"

Ken leaned in, his lips touching Barbie's. Billy watched them, envious.

The door to the room burst open, startling him and causing him to drop the dolls. Behind him, James stood in the doorway, his gaze fixed on the clothes scattered across the floor. Billy began to quickly sweep them into a pile.

"Jesus Christ, Bill," James said. "What are you doing?"

"Nothing," said Billy. "Just fooling around."

"I thought Celeste told you to keep out of her stuff," James continued.

"She doesn't even look at these anymore," said Billy. "She says she's too old for them."

"Well, she is," said James. "And so are you. Also, you're a boy."

Billy shrugged as he picked up Ken and Barbie and put them back into the plastic carrying case. "It's just a game," he said.

"A *girl's* game," James said. "And you're almost thirteen, for Christ's sake."

"Mom told you not to say *Christ* like that," Billy reminded him. "It's a sin."

"Whatever," said James. "Just put that shit away. Dad wants you to come help outside."

"Help do what?" Billy asked. He slipped the dolls' carrying case back into Celeste's closet, then shut the door.

"He's working on the car," said James. "He wants you to learn how to change the oil."

Billy stood up. "Why?" he asked. "Isn't that why they have garages?"

"Because a guy should know how to change the oil in a car," said James.

They left Celeste's room and walked down the hallway toward the living room. As they did, James put his hand on Billy's shoulder.

"You've really got to grow up, Bill," he said. "You're not a kid anymore."

"My name's Billy," Billy reminded him

"See," said James. "That's what I mean. Billy is a little kid's name. You should go by Bill."

"But I like Billy."

They passed through the kitchen, pushing open the back door and exiting the house. In the driveway their father was standing in front of the family car. The hood was open, held in place by the thin rod that Billy was always afraid would snap in two at any moment, bringing the hood down on his fingers or his head.

"I found him," James said to their father.

Billy waited for his brother to tell their father *where* he had found him. But James left it at that. Sometimes he wasn't a total jerk, Billy thought. But not often.

"Come take a look at this," their father said, waving both boys over.

Billy followed James to the car. He stood a little bit back, peering down into the tangled knots of unidentifiable metal pieces. He had no idea what any of it was, nor did he care. It was just a car.

"See this?" his father said. He held out a long, thin piece of metal. It was covered in slick black oil. "This is the dipstick. It tells you how much oil is left in the car."

Billy hadn't the vaguest notion of why he should care about such a thing, yet he nodded gravely. He watched as his father took a rag and wiped the stick clean. The oil on the rag was a greenish black, ugly, like the insides of a bug.

"You want the dipstick clean when you slide it back inside the engine," his father continued, demonstrating. "That way you get an accurate reading when you take it out."

He pulled the dipstick from its sheath and held it out toward Billy. "See those two dots?" he asked. "You want the oil line to be between them. What do you do if it isn't?"

Billy hesitated. He looked at James, who was biting his lip as if to keep from blurting out the answer. But the question had not been directed at him, and Billy knew his brother would not come to his rescue.

"Um, take it to the garage?" he tried.

His father shook his head. "Maybe if you were your mother, you would," he said, laughing. "Or your sister. But you, me, or your brother would just add a quart of oil."

James laughed along with their father, as if the two of them were sharing a joke that Billy didn't understand. Billy tried to laugh as well, but it sounded too loud to him, and he was embarrassed by his attempt. He saw James glance at him, and he felt his cheeks flush.

"Now you add oil to the engine," his father continued, seeming not to notice. "Here, you do it."

He handed Billy a can of oil. It was heavier than Billy expected. Then his father handed him a metal spout with a single sharp metal tooth on one end.

"You snap that onto the can," his father explained. "Try it. It's easy."

Billy pressed the metal tooth against the top of the can. Applying pressure to it, he was surprised when it easily pierced the top and clicked into place.

"Good job," his father said. "Now just pour it into the hole where the oil goes."

Billy waited for his father to show him where the hole was. He could see several possibilities. But his father didn't offer any help, merely saying, "Go on. It's easy."

Billy stepped forward. In order to look for the oil hole he had to put his head beneath the raised hood. He looked once more at the flimsy rod holding it open. It was hooked into a hole in the edge of the hood. *That could slip out,* he thought. He turned his eyes away from it, concentrating on finding the correct hole in which to pour the oil.

He knew that his brother and father were watching him. He knew, too, that James at least expected him to mess up. James was always good at everything, while he, Billy, was always doing things the wrong way. It was as if James had gotten all of the common sense, while Billy had been given all the imagination. James had very little of that. He was practical, where Billy was always dreaming.

"You need to—" he heard James say.

"Let him do it," their father interrupted. Then he said to Billy, "You can do it, Bill."

Now he's calling me Bill too, Billy thought. He wondered when he had stopped being Billy.

He chose the hole from which he thought he recalled his father removing the stick and tilted the oil can toward it.

"That's the radiator!" he heard James shout.

A hand reached for the can, knocking Billy's arm. The can flew from his grip. The spout fell off, and oil spewed from the gash in the top. It sprayed Billy's T-shirt with heavy, wet drops. A thick smell filled his nose.

"Shit!" His father's voice was loud, harsh with anger.

Billy whirled around and looked into his face. His father looked disgusted as he reached for the can of oil, now on its side and pouring its viscous contents all over the car's insides. Billy reached for the rag in his father's hand.

"I'll clean it up," he said.

His father snatched his hand away. "Just go inside and clean yourself up," he said.

Billy backed away. James moved in to take his place. Their father handed James the rag, and James began mopping up the results of the spill. Neither paid any more attention to Billy.

Turning, he ran not back toward the house but away from it. The oil-slick shirt stuck to his skin, and the smell made him want to throw up. He wiped his arm across his face, leaving streaks of oil behind that only increased the stench in his nose.

He ran down the block, past the houses of neighbors, some of whom looked up from their porches and yards as he dashed by. He ignored them, looking straight ahead. At the corner he turned and continued on. He had no destination in mind. He just ran.

After another three blocks he stopped, gasping for breath. His lungs burned and his heart pounded. Feeling that he might throw up, he pulled his T-shirt over his head and dropped it to the sidewalk. Staring at it, he realized that it was his favorite—the blue one with the *Tron* iron-on. Now it was stained with oil, filthy and ruined.

He started to wipe his hands on his jeans, then thought better of it. Picking up the shirt, he attempted to use the still-clean part of it to remove some of the oil from his skin. He succeeded only in smearing it around.

He sat down on the sidewalk, feeling the warmth of it soaking up through his jeans. *Goddamn James,* he thought. Why had his brother had to do that? Why couldn't he have just minded his own business? Their father wouldn't have let him pour the oil into the wrong hole. James had just wanted to be right all along. He *always* wanted to be right. No, he *had* to be right.

His anger at James wasn't the worst of it, having disappointed his father was. He still saw the look on his father's face. He was the cause of it, his inability to do something as simple as put oil in a car engine. James was right; at his age he should know how to do that. He bet every other guy at school did.

But he didn't. Just as he didn't know how to hit a baseball or put a worm on a fishhook or shoot a rifle worth a damn. These were all things his father had tried to teach him, and at which he had failed. He didn't understand how these things came so easily to other people— to his father and to James in particular. What was missing from him that he couldn't do them? What defect prevented him from being like everyone else?

His father had never said as much, but Billy feared that he was a disappointment to him. *But he has James,* he thought. *Isn't that enough? Why can't they just leave me alone?*

He thought sometimes that he must be adopted. Somehow he had been switched at the hospital with another baby, one who belonged to a family that was even now wondering how they had ended up with a boy they didn't understand at all. They were waiting for him to come back to them, anxious to give up the practical, boring son they'd gotten by mistake and welcome home the one they'd wanted in the first place.

Someday he would find them. Someday he would get away from this small town and the people who had gotten him by mistake and kept him prisoner. *Then James will be sorry,* he thought. *Then they'll all be sorry.*

CHAPTER 5

1991

The house looked the same as it had the last time he'd visited. Actually, it looked the same as it had the day he'd left for his first year of college five years before. The same red-and-white dishtowels—not the exact ones, but identical to their predecessors—were hanging from the rack near the sink. The same pig cookie jar was on the counter. The same yellow paint was on the walls.

Celeste, though, looked different. Her face was worn, her eyes tired. Her hair, normally tied back neatly in a ponytail, fell loose about her shoulders. When she hugged James, she rested her head against his shoulder.

"I'm so glad you're here," she said.

James held her for a moment. When she pulled away, Celeste sighed. "It's been quite a morning."

"You told her," James said. "I thought we agreed—"

"We had to," Celeste interrupted. "It was going to be on the news. We didn't want her to find out that way."

"So how did she take it?" asked James.

Celeste sighed. "About as well as you think she did," she answered. "She didn't believe us at first, but Nate finally convinced her. She wanted to go see the body."

"You didn't let her, did you?"

Celeste shook her head. "Of course not. Nate told her that I had already ID'd it and that it was at the morgue."

"It," James said.

"What?" asked Celeste.

"It," James repeated. "You called Dad 'it.' "

"The body, then," Celeste said. She reached for a pack of cigarettes that was lying on the table. After shaking one out, she lit it and took a deep drag.

"When did you start smoking again?" James asked her, going to the refrigerator and opening it.

"About twelve hours ago," his sister told him. "They're Nate's."

James removed a carton of orange juice from the refrigerator. He got a glass from the cupboard beside the sink, filled it, and sat down at the table, across from Celeste. "Has Billy made an appearance?" he asked.

Celeste blew out a stream of smoke and tapped the ash from her cigarette into an empty Coke can. "You could say that," she said. "He passed out in the bathroom. I told Nate to leave him there, but he insisted on carrying Billy up to his room. He didn't want Mom to be upset."

James shook his head. "Is he still asleep?"

"No," said Celeste. "He left about an hour ago. I don't know where he went."

"It's probably best he's not here," James suggested. "He's not going to be much help."

"James?"

The voice coming from the hallway was soft, almost fearful. James rose as his mother emerged from the shadows into the light of the kitchen. When she saw him her face lit up. "It is you," she said.

James allowed her to take him in her arms. She kissed his cheek, then held his hands as she stepped back to look at him. "You've gained weight," she said.

"It hasn't been that long, Mom," he told her.

"Over a year," said his mother. "Not even at Christmas. That girl kept you from me."

"Charly didn't keep me from you, Mom," James said. "In fact, she wanted to come. I had to work."

"Work," his mother said mockingly. "What's so important that you can't come see your family at Christmas?"

"I told you," James explained. "Senator Leland was trying to get a big environmental protection bill through the legislature. I had to work on it."

"Nonsense," his mother said. "Those eagles or marshes or whatever foolishness you're worried about could have taken a few days off for Christmas. I think you just don't want us to meet this girl of yours."

"Of course I do, Mom," James said. "And she wants to meet you. But that's not why I'm here."

His mother went to the refrigerator. "Let me make you some dinner," she said. "You must be starving."

"I don't want anything, Mom," said James. "I want to talk about Dad."

His mother began rooting around in the refrigerator, ignoring him. James looked at Celeste, who raised one eyebrow and lit a second cigarette. "Mom—" James began again.

"You don't like lettuce, do you?" she interrupted. "Or is that Billy who doesn't like lettuce? I can never remember."

"Mom, come sit down," said James. He got up and went to her, shutting the refrigerator door and taking her arm. "Let's talk about this," he said.

His mother allowed herself to be led back to the table, where she sat down. She looked at Celeste and frowned. "Put that out," she said.

Celeste obeyed, stubbing the cigarette out on the top of the soda can, then dropping it through the hole. Her mother took the can and placed it on the other side of the table.

"I know this must be a big shock," James said. "I think first we—"

"I'm going to go to bed," his mother said. "I'm tired, and I want to go to bed."

"But don't you think we—" James tried.

"No, I don't," said his mother, standing up. "I think we should let Nate do his job. After all, that's what our taxes are for. That and the roads." She touched James's shoulder. "I'm happy you're here. You know where your room is. I'll see you in the morning. Good night, Celeste."

"Night, Mom," Celeste answered.

James watched his mother leave. Celeste stood and picked up her coat from the back of her chair. "Like she said," she told James.

"What, I get here and everyone leaves?" he said.

"I've been here all day, James," Celeste reminded him. "It's your turn. I'll see you in the morning."

When Celeste had left, James locked the kitchen door and turned off the light. He then checked the front door and, finding it secured, carried his bag up the stairs to the second floor. His parents' room was the first off the landing, a location that had caused no end of consternation to James when, as a teenager, he had come in past his curfew. Now he was the one to stop and peer through the mostly closed door. His mother was in the bathroom that adjoined the room. He heard water running and the sound of teeth being brushed.

Celeste's room was next, on the same side of the hall as their parents'. Billy's and his rooms were on the other side, Billy's closest to the stairs and James's the farthest from it. The door to Billy's room was shut, and James did not open it, continuing on to his own room.

It was exactly as he'd left it. Stepping inside, time seemed to telescope backward, taking him to 1986. He was eighteen again, packing for college and anxious to be out of his parents' house. He was looking ahead, reveling in the possibilities, but also worried that his mother would not be able to handle things without him around to help.

"And here I am again," he said out loud as he dropped his bag on the bed and sat down beside it. The mattress squeaked in protest, and he suddenly remembered how self-conscious he'd sometimes felt when, pleasuring himself before falling asleep, he had worried that the sound would give him away.

He looked at his watch. It was almost eleven. Back in Seattle Charly would probably just have gotten home. Kicking off his shoes, he stretched out on the bed, flipped open his cell phone, and dialed her number. He half hoped he would get her voice mail, but she picked up on the third ring.

"Hey," James said. "It's me."

"Hey, me," said Charly. "How was the flight?"

"Okay," James told her. "I sat next to an accountant on the way to Chicago, but from there to Albany I had the row to myself."

"An accountant," Charly said. "How awful for you."

James laughed. "Yeah," he said. "So how was your day?"

"Tell me about your mother first," said Charly.

"Oooh, you're good," James said. "Here I thought I would be able to get away with not talking about me. I bow to your superior skills, counselor."

"I didn't go to law school for nothing," said Charly. "So what's going on? How's your mother?"

James hesitated. He had been going out with Charly for more than a year. He thought she might even be The One. Despite this, there was a lot about his family he had yet to tell her.

"It's not my mother," he said. "It's my father."

"Your father?" Charly repeated. "Your father's dead."

"Right," said James.

"Cancer, right?" Charly said. "I think that's what you told me."

"That's what I told you," James agreed. "But that's not quite the whole story."

Charly said nothing. James knew it was one of her lawyer tricks—keep silent until the witness gets nervous and starts talking. She often used it on him during arguments. He hated it, mostly because it worked.

"Seven—almost eight—years ago my father disappeared," James began. "A few days later my mother received a letter from him. He said that he'd been diagnosed with terminal cancer, and that he didn't want us to watch him get sick and die. So he killed himself."

Charly still said nothing. James could picture her face, composed and beautiful. He often wondered how witnesses could look at that face and not fall apart on the spot, it had that effect.

"They never found my father's body," he continued. "We had a headstone made, and there was a memorial service, but there's no body in his grave." He hesitated, knowing that Charly was waiting for his revelation. "Well, they found him."

"Why didn't you tell me that this morning?" Charly asked.

James cleared his throat. "I wasn't sure I believed it myself," he answered.

"But it's true?" said Charly.

"I think so," James said. "Celeste says so, but I haven't seen for myself."

"How is your mother handling it?"

"There's more," said James. "They didn't just find his body. It looks like someone murdered him."

"But the letter—" Celeste said immediately.

"I know," said James. "Get out of lawyer mode for a minute, okay? That's all I know right now."

"That doesn't make any sense," Charly said. She sounded frustrated, and James had to smile a little bit at the way she immediately started examining the evidence of the case.

"I'll find out more tomorrow," he said.

There was a long pause before Charly said, "Why didn't you tell me?"

"I already told you, I wasn't sure that—"

"Not about what's happening now," Charly interrupted. "I mean about your father killing himself."

"I don't know," said James. "I guess because it's not exactly a shining moment in my family's history."

"Nobody's family is perfect, James," Charly countered. "I wouldn't have thought any less of them—or of you—because of it."

"No," James agreed. "I don't think you would have."

"We've been over this before," said Charly. "If we're going to be together, you have to trust me."

"I do," James assured her. "I do trust you."

"I hope you really believe that," said Charly.

There was a long silence, during which James had to fight the urge to hang up. Finally, to his relief, Charly said, "Get some rest. You're going to have a hell of a day tomorrow, I bet. Tell your mother I'm very sorry and I wish her son had told me the truth."

"Very funny," said James.

"I love you," Charly said.

"Me too," James told her. "I'll call you tomorrow."

He clicked off and closed the phone, setting it on the bedside table. *I couldn't even tell her I love her,* he scolded himself. *After all of that.* He rubbed his eyes, suddenly exhausted. Why was he such a dick? Charly was right; he had to trust her if they were going to stay together. He couldn't keep hiding things from her. He had to tell her the whole story. The problem was, he wasn't sure he knew what it was.

CHAPTER 6

1982

The knock at the door was barely audible through the sound of the music. At first James mistook it for some odd drumming pattern. But when it came again, he realized that someone was trying to get his attention. He removed the headphones and called out, "Come in!"

The door opened and his father entered the bedroom. James was surprised to see him. His father seldom came into his room. Now he stood just inside the door, his hands in his pockets, looking around the room as if he'd never been there. James waited for him to speak.

"Dad?" he said after a long silence. "What's up?"

His father cleared his throat. "I want to talk to you about something," he said.

James groaned. "I know, I need to get my trig grade up," he said. "I'm working on it. Nancy's been helping me, and—"

"That's what I want to talk to you about," his father interrupted. "Nancy," he clarified.

"Nancy?" James said. "What about her?"

His father looked at him. "I think you should spend less time with her," he said.

James, confused, leaned back in his desk chair. "Less time?" he repeated. "Why? I thought you and Mom liked her."

"We do like her," his father said. "We just think things might be getting a little too serious."

James, turning the words over in his head, suddenly blushed. "Oh,

God," he said. "No. We haven't . . . I mean, we aren't . . ." He stopped, unable to say the words.

To his surprise, his father chuckled. "Not that kind of serious," he said. "Although I'm glad to hear that I don't have to worry about that either, at least not yet."

"Then I don't understand," James told him.

His father gave him a little smile. "You're young," he said. "Only fifteen. There's a lot of time for girlfriends."

"Okay," James said slowly. "But I *have* a girlfriend now."

"I'm not saying you shouldn't see Nancy," his father explained. "I'm just saying I'd prefer it if you didn't see her quite so much."

James shook his head. "I don't get it," he said. "What's the problem?"

"There isn't one. Yet." His father spoke slowly, as if he were working out in his mind just what he wanted to say. "I just want to make sure it doesn't become one."

"Why would it?" James asked. He was starting to get angry. His father was speaking to him as if he were a kid, not a teenager. Christ, he was almost old enough to drive. Why shouldn't he have a girlfriend?

"You're schoolwork hasn't been great lately," his father said. "You've stopped playing ball."

"I told you, I'm working on the grades," James argued. "And I stopped playing baseball because it takes up too much time."

"Time you're now spending with Nancy," said his father. "James, I know how you feel. Believe me, I do. That's why I know what's best for you right now. All I'm asking—all your mother and I are asking—is that you and Nancy take a break for a while."

"A break," James said. "For how long? A week? A month? What are we talking about here?" His voice had an edge to it, and he saw his father stiffen.

"Don't speak to me in that tone," he said.

"You're treating me like I'm Billy's age!" James said, his anger growing. "I think I can decide for myself what I should and shouldn't do."

His father's face reddened, and for a moment James was afraid of what might come next. But his father stayed where he was, and after a moment he said, "I'm sure you do think that. I know I did when I was your age. But in this case I'm asking you to do what I think is best for you."

"It sounds more like you're *telling* me," James replied. "What if I say no?" He was testing his father, and he knew he was dangerously close to going too far. But he was mad, and that made him reckless.

"I hope that you won't," his father answered.

The implied threat hung between them. James considered the possible ramifications of refusing. What could his parents do? Ground him? Take away his driving privileges? If they did, he wouldn't be able to see Nancy anyway, not unless he did it behind their backs. And if he got caught doing that, things would be even worse.

He really didn't have any option but to agree to his father's demands. But he wasn't going to do it happily. "Fine," he muttered, turning back to the homework on his desk.

"Excuse me?" his father said.

"I said fine," James repeated. "I'll tell Nancy I can't see her so much."

"You don't have to tell her," said his father. "She already knows."

James whirled around. "What?" he exclaimed.

"A.J. is talking to her," his father explained.

James could only stare at him. He couldn't believe what he was hearing. It was bad enough that his parents were asking him to break things off with Nancy. But her father telling her the same thing made it feel even more like they were being ganged up on.

"Did you guys have, like, some kind of meeting about this?" he asked. He knew he was speaking too loudly, too accusatively, but he couldn't stop himself. "I mean, what the hell, Dad?"

"Watch your mouth," his father barked. But he looked away from James's face for a second, and in that moment James knew that they really *had* planned everything out. It wasn't just his parents who were worried about him and Nancy seeing each other; Nancy's father was too.

"You don't trust us," James said, shaking his head. "You say this is all about grades and sports and . . . and . . . a bunch of *bullshit*. But what you're really afraid of is that we're fu—"

"That's *enough!*" His father's voice thundered through the room, startling James and stopping his heart. As his father advanced toward him James put up his arms, instinctively shielding his face.

His father stopped barely a foot away. James looked at the big hands, clenched into fists and held waist level. Unable to bring himself to look at his father's face, he instead listened to the heavy exhalations of breath—like those of an angry bull—that chilled his blood. He closed his eyes, praying that he hadn't said too much, and knowing that he had.

"I asked you to mind your language, James," his father said. There was an edge to his voice now, a sharpness that warned of imminent danger. James felt it slice across his skin, and his cheeks burned with fear and shame.

"I'm sorry," he said, his voice sounding to him like that of a child. He was embarrassed that he couldn't speak with more assurance, ashamed of how he thought he must look to his father. Daniel McCloud, he thought, would never back down so easily.

"I don't ever want to hear you talk like that again," his father said. He turned and moved away from James. But only when his father was once again standing near the door did the fear that choked James's voice release its grip and his heart resume its usual steady beat.

"Nancy will understand that this is what's best for both of you," his father said. His voice was flat, emotionless, and this frightened James almost as much as had the previous harshness. This was the voice of the town sheriff laying down the law. Usually it was reserved for strangers or those who had in some way offended Daniel McCloud's strict code of conduct. When it was turned on one of his own, it meant that he had ceased any attempt at negotiation. Whatever edict came next, James knew that he would accept it without question.

"You'll get your grades back up," his father continued. "And you'll rejoin the team. I'll speak to Coach Baker about that." He paused for a moment. "If your next report card is better, we'll see about letting you and Nancy spend more time together."

"Can I at least call her sometimes?" James asked.

His father nodded. "Occasionally. And you'll see her at school, of course. Church. Whenever the families get together. None of that will change. You just won't be spending so much time with her alone. Okay?"

It wasn't okay, not at all. But James knew enough not to say as much. He'd come very close to trouble, and there would be no second chances. He merely said, "Okay."

"Good boy," his father said. "And you'll see—you'll be a better man for this. One day you'll thank me."

"Sure, Dad," James replied. "Sorry I got so angry."

His father waved one hand at him, and James understood that whatever had threatened the peace between them had now passed. His father, having won, could afford to be generous with his forgiveness. James accepted it with relief.

"I've got to go into town for a while," his father said. "Want to come along?"

James very much wanted to go, to sit beside his father in the sheriff's department pickup and be seen by any of his buddies who might be hanging around downtown. But he sensed that his father was testing him, and so he chose the path of safety. "Thanks, but I have a lot of homework to do," he said. "Next time."

"Next time," his father agreed, nodding. He left the room, closing the door behind him and leaving James alone with his resentment.

James picked up the headphones and fitted them over his ears. Hitting the Play button on his tape deck, he leaned back in his chair and closed his eyes, Journey's "Stone in Love" filling his head and driving away the anger he felt toward his father. He silently mouthed the words, and when the guitar solo kicked in he turned the volume up as high as it would go.

The song was a favorite of his, and the album from which it came played almost continuously on his stereo. Nancy, too, loved the band. James had even bought tickets to their upcoming concert in Syracuse. He'd been planning on surprising her with them. Now, he thought, he might as well give them to one of his friends. But the concert wasn't for another two months. Maybe by then his father and Nancy's father would have calmed down about the whole thing. *And even if they haven't* . . . he told himself. He didn't allow himself to finish the thought. He knew what would happen if he defied his father that way.

Still, it would almost be worth it to stand next to Nancy while Steve Perry sang "Open Arms." He'd first kissed her while slow dancing to that song, at one of the Friday night school dances. Normally he hated those things. They seemed so babyish. But one night Nancy had persuaded him to go, and he'd agreed to make her happy. When she'd asked him to slow dance with her, he had almost been afraid to. But he'd done it, and in the middle of the song he had leaned down and kissed her. He still didn't know why he'd done it. Maybe it was the song. Maybe it was the way it felt to have his arms around Nancy, smelling her perfume and feeling her head on his shoulder. Maybe he'd just been crazy. But he'd done it, and Nancy had let him.

That was three months earlier. Since then, they'd spent more and more time together, nearly every afternoon and sometimes the evenings too. Mostly they worked on homework and talked. James liked talking to Nancy. She made him feel good. He'd even told her about how he wanted to go into politics when he was older. He hadn't told anyone else that. And Nancy didn't think it was silly at all. She told him she thought he would make a great congressman, or even a senator.

Why couldn't his father understand that Nancy was *good* for him? Sure, his grades had slipped a little, but he could fix that. And baseball wasn't the most important thing in the world. Honestly, he didn't even really like playing all that much. But his father had this idea—this image—of how his son was supposed to be. James had always known that he was expected to be what his father wanted him to be, even if it wasn't what *he* wanted to be.

But someone had to be the son his father wanted, and Billy wasn't going to do it. It was pretty clear the kid was hopeless when it came to things like sports. He was a good kid, and most of the time he didn't bother James too much, but sometimes James wondered how they could have come from the same parents. Celeste could be a pain in the ass, but at least he understood her. Billy he just didn't get. It was as if he were an alien or something. He just didn't fit.

Anyway, he had resigned himself to the fact that he was the one who had to fulfill his father's expectations. And it wasn't such a bad job, really. But sometimes he wasn't sure which part of him was real and which part was him being what his father wanted him to be. He thought he *ought* to know, but it wasn't always totally clear in his head. Sometimes he looked in the bathroom mirror and saw someone he didn't recognize at all.

When he was with Nancy, though, he felt like himself. She didn't care what his grades were, or how he'd played in a game, or anything like that. When he was with her they talked about other things—music, and movies, and what they wanted to do when they were old enough to get out of Cold Falls. And they both agreed that they *would* get out. Maybe to Albany, or even New York. Nancy made him feel like he could do anything he wanted.

But now she was gone, or might as well be. Now all he had was homework and baseball practice and trying to make his father happy. It wasn't much to look forward to. *I'll do it, though,* he promised himself as he opened his history book to the chapter on the Reconstruction. *If it means I get her back, I'll do it.*

CHAPTER 7

1991

Billy looked down into the empty glass he held in his hands, cradled like a wounded bird. It was empty, but he brought it to his lips anyway, tilting his head back and extending his tongue, searching for any last drips of vodka. Finding none, he slammed the glass on the counter and nodded at the bartender.

"Another one, Cory."

He watched as Cory took a bottle from the shelf and poured him another shot. As soon as the bartender pulled the bottle away, Billy picked up the glass and drank. He closed his eyes, letting the vodka slide down his throat. It was crisp and clear, pure liquid fire. He never drank the flavored stuff. That was for the queens who liked their drinks with little straws in them, who drank cosmos like a bunch of catty women. Billy hated those queens. They looked down on him, thought he was trash.

"You and everyone else," he said, laughing as he emptied the glass with one more swallow.

"What was that?" Cory looked over at him, a washrag in his hand as he wiped down the bar.

"Nothing," Billy replied, wiping the back of his hand over his lips. His skin was dry, his lips chapped. He felt as if he'd been walking through a sandstorm.

He looked at the bartender. How long had Cory been working at the Engine Room? He thought he'd asked him once, but maybe he'd just *meant* to ask. He meant to do a lot of things, but somehow they almost never got done.

Billy had been an Engine Room regular for less than a year, since the night of his twenty-first birthday. Before that they hadn't let him in, even though he'd tried plenty of times. Despite his father being dead for almost eight years he was still known as Sheriff Dan's boy. The bar's staff had been given strict orders not to let him in, as if somehow his father's ghost would come back and close them down.

Looks like they might be right about that after all, he thought, chuckling at his own joke. But he was legal now. He could do what he liked. And his father couldn't do anything about it.

His gaze wandered once more to Cory. The bartender was kind of hot. Tall. Not skinny like most of the cosmo-swilling queens. Shaved head. Dark eyes. *Yeah, he would do,* Billy thought. The place was nearly deserted. Maybe he should see if he could get Cory to fool around in the back.

"I'm sorry to hear about your dad," Cory said. He was chopping up limes, getting ready for the night's business.

Billy pushed his empty glass toward Cory. "Thanks," he said. "Let's drink to him, shall we?"

Cory glanced up. "Another one?" he said. Billy knew that what he really meant was, "Seems to me you've had enough." He was familiar with that tone, although he'd never heard it in Cory's voice. Cory had always been friendly.

"Yeah, another one. For the old man."

Cory hesitated for a moment, looking at Billy. Billy met his gaze, daring him to say no. Finally, Cory wiped his hands on a towel and brought out the bottle of vodka. As soon as he was done pouring, Billy raised the glass. "To Daniel McCloud," he said. "Best dad a son could ever want."

He drank half the vodka in one swallow, then set the glass on the bar. He knew Cory wouldn't give him another drink, so he had to make this one last. He looked at his watch. It was just after nine. He considered his options. He could wait a couple of hours and then go to his mother's house. Celeste would probably be gone, and James might be asleep. He could probably get up to his room without running into any of them. But they would be there in the morning.

That brought him to Option Two: going back to his own place. That solved the whole running into James problem. But he didn't want to go there. He didn't want to be alone. What he wanted was to be able to help his mother. The thing with his father was really doing a number on her. But now James was there, so nobody needed him. *Just like always,* he thought.

He lit a cigarette. Inhaling the first rush of smoke, he closed his eyes and relaxed into the buzz the vodka had brought on. He imagined his body filling up with smoke, pictured it seeping out from his lungs and wrapping tendrils around his heart, cocooning it. He liked that image. Like a butterfly. He sometimes dreamed that his whole body was cocooned, that he was waiting inside to be transformed. Into what, he didn't know. Something beautiful. Something different. Something better.

He was startled from his reverie by a touch on his hand. When he opened his eyes he saw Cory looking at him. "You okay?" the bartender asked.

Billy smiled at him. "Depends who you ask," he said. "What do you think?"

Cory looked at the half-empty glass in front of Billy. "Maybe you should go home," he said. "Get some rest. You look tired."

Billy reached out and took the glass. *Don't pity me, asshole,* he thought as he picked the glass up and downed the rest of the drink. He set the empty glass down and pushed it toward Cory. Then he got up and made his way to the bathroom.

Inside, he stood over one of the three sinks and looked at himself in the mirror. He ran his hands through his hair. When had it gotten so long? He couldn't recall the last time it had been cut. Now it fell almost to his shoulders. He leaned forward and looked at his eyes. They were still the familiar dark green, but now the whites were shot through with red. And his skin was even paler than usual, looking yellowish in the bathroom's harsh fluorescent light.

I look like a vampire, he thought. He curled his lips back, exposing his teeth and snarling. He laughed. He did look like shit. But he was still handsome. Beneath it all he still had the face of a boy; that boy just needed a good night's sleep and some sun. That would do it. Then he would be his old self again.

The door opened and a familiar face appeared in the mirror beside

Billy's. There was no mistaking Red, whose hair color gave him his nickname and who would have been identifiable anyway by the Tweety bird tattoo on his neck. There were more tats on his arms, all of them cartoon characters: Sylvester the cat, Speedy Gonzales, Foghorn Leghorn, Pepé Le Pew. There were more, but Billy couldn't remember all of their names.

"Hey, handsome," Red said as he came over and leaned against the sink. He reached up and pushed Billy's hair out of his eyes. "How's tricks?"

Billy pulled away from Red's touch. "Okay," he said.

Red cocked his head. "You don't look so good," he remarked. "Need something to make you feel better?"

Billy shook his head. "No," he said. "Thanks anyway." He turned on the water and ran his hands in it, as if he had just pissed and was now about to return to the bar. As he reached for the soap dispenser, Red caught him by the wrist.

"You're all shaky, man," Red said. "Let me help."

Billy tried to pull away, but Red's thick fingers encircled his wrist like a handcuff. He looked into Red's face. Red smiled at him, his upper lip rising in a sexy snarl and his blue eyes watching him hungrily. *God, he's beautiful,* Billy thought helplessly.

"Come on, baby," Red purred. "I've got what you need."

Billy cleared his throat. "I've got to get out of here," he said. "My mom. She needs me. She—"

"I heard," said Red. He put his hand on Billy's neck, massaging the sore muscles. Billy relaxed into his hold. "Shame about all of that."

"Yeah," Billy said, his voice hoarse. "Yeah, it's fucked up."

Red stroked the side of Billy's face with his hand. "So let me help you feel better," he said.

Billy shook his head. "I can't," he said. "I'm busted."

Red shrugged. "No problem," he said. "I know you're good for it." He paused. "Or maybe we can work something out."

Billy looked at the floor. The tile was dirty, streaked with footprints and littered with crumpled-up paper towels that had missed the trashcan. An empty condom wrapper lay beside Red's foot like the discarded skin of some tiny creature.

"Come on," said Red. He took Billy's hand and pulled him toward one of the stalls.

Billy allowed himself to be led. Red bumped the door open and entered, drawing Billy after him. When the door was shut and locked, Red reached into the pocket of his jeans and took out a small plastic bag. He opened it and poured several white rocks into his palm. "Down or up?" he asked Billy.

Billy rubbed his nose. "Up," he said. It was faster that way. If he swallowed the stuff he would have to wait twenty minutes, maybe even half an hour, for it to kick in. Snorting it would bring instant joy.

Red took a short piece of plastic straw from his pocket. Picking up one of the rocks between his thumb and forefinger, he crushed it into powder. He repeated the procedure with the remaining rocks, then swept the powder into a neat pile on his palm. Handing the straw to Billy, he said, "After you."

Billy took the straw and, inserting one end into his nose, leaned down and snorted half the powder from Red's outstretched hand. He winced a little as the crystal entered his nose, but gave several short snorts to draw it into his sinus cavity. He stood up and leaned against the stall door, closing his eyes. He heard Red snort the rest of the ice. Then, a moment later, he heard the sound of Red fumbling with his belt.

"All right, Billy boy," Red said. "Time to pay up."

Without opening his eyes, Billy turned around to face the door. He undid the buttons of his jeans and pushed them down to his knees. He felt Red's hands at his waist, then heard the sound of spitting. A moment later there was a sharp stab of pain as Red entered him. He clenched his teeth and leaned his forehead against his crossed arms, feeling the cool metal of the door against his skin.

Thankfully, the crystal was good and began to work quickly. Red's shit was always good, Billy had to give him that. He made it himself, and he was proud of his product. It was—mostly—worth the price he demanded for it.

Billy's head began to spin as his heart sped up. This was the moment he loved best, when the ride was just beginning and the anticipation was at its highest point. It always made him think of being on a roller coaster, poised at the very top of the first hill, waiting for that first sharp drop that made his stomach leap and caused him to shout with joy. As a kid, at the county fair each summer he would ride the coaster over and over, always sitting in the very first car, never getting enough of that rush, coming back again and again for the two weeks the fair was open.

Now he was once again climbing to the top of that hill. He saw himself let go of the bar that kept him safely inside the car, lifting his arms high above his head as the coaster's chain *chucked-chucked-chucked* beneath him. Then the sound stopped as the car crested the top. For one long, breathtaking moment he was looking down the other side, anticipating the fall, and then the car was hurtling down and his ears were filled with the delighted screams coming from his mouth.

The sound of Red buckling his belt brought him back. He reached down and pulled his pants up, wordlessly tucking his T-shirt inside and buttoning his fly. He unlocked the stall door and opened it, stepping out and going once more to the sink. Red followed. As he passed Billy he slapped him on the ass. "Hope you feel better," he said as he left the men's room.

Billy once again regarded his reflection in the mirror. "Yeah," he said to himself. "Yeah, I feel a whole lot better."

He washed his hands again, not wanting to leave the bathroom. When one of the other stall doors opened and a man emerged, he thought at first he was imagining it. When had the guy come in? Had he heard everything? Of course he had. How could he not?

The man came over to the sinks and stood beside Billy, washing his hands. Billy glanced at him and recognized the face. He tried to put a name to it.

"Greg," he said. "Your name is Greg."

The man turned and looked at him briefly. "Right," he said.

Billy stared at him for another moment, trying to remember. "You're from Syracuse," he said finally. "We did it once. In your car. You have a Beemer."

Greg turned the water off and drew a paper towel from the dispenser. He said nothing as he dried his hands.

"That's right, isn't it?" Billy asked him. "Greg. From Syracuse. You have a Beemer." He reached out and ran his hand over Greg's arm. "It was nice. I remember that. You were nice."

Greg pulled his arm away and moved toward the door. "I don't think that was me," he said. "Maybe someone else."

"But your name is Greg," Billy insisted. "Greg from Syracuse. And it was *nice!*" He shouted the last word as the man disappeared back into the bar, leaving him alone.

"It was nice," Billy said again, his voice now a whisper. "You were nice."

He turned to his reflection in the mirror. "He was nice," he told himself. "He was."

CHAPTER 8

1983

It was weird sitting on the couch between James and Celeste. It made him feel like he was a little kid. But A.J. Derry was in his father's chair, and his mother was in the other, leaving the couch as the only option. Billy crossed his arms over his chest, trying not to touch his brother or sister. Fortunately, they seemed equally uncomfortable, and each was seated as close to their respective ends of the couch as possible.

"Is this about Dad?" Celeste asked, voicing what Billy knew they were all thinking.

His mother looked at Mr. Derry, who sat on the edge of the chair, as if he knew he didn't belong in it. His hands were clasped and resting between his knees, and his face looked troubled. So did their mother's. Her eyes were red, as if she'd been crying, and her fingers pulled anxiously at her skirt, incessantly smoothing out wrinkles that weren't there.

"Yes," Mr. Derry said. "It's about your father."

None of the three kids said anything. Billy felt the tension between them as they waited for someone to tell them what was going on. They hadn't even talked about his absence among themselves. Billy had assumed that their father was just busy with work, and since neither James nor Celeste had said anything to make him think otherwise, he didn't understand the sudden change in mood.

"What about him?" asked James. "Where is he?"

Again their mother looked at A.J. Derry, as if only he knew the answer to that question. Billy couldn't understand why she wasn't speaking to them directly. It made him anxious, and he heard himself say, "Yeah, where is he?" in a voice he didn't recognize.

"Don't yell at Mom," Celeste scolded him.

"I'm not yelling," Billy countered. "I just want to know what's going on. Why is everyone acting so weird?"

"I got a letter from your father," his mother said quickly.

"A letter?" James repeated. "Why would he send you a letter?"

His mother sighed, and Billy saw that she was trying to keep from crying. Instinctively he rose from the couch and ran to her. "What?" he cried out. "What's wrong?"

"Billy," said Mr. Derry. "Please. Sit down."

Billy ignored him. "Mom?" he asked. "Where's Dad?"

His mother took his hand and held it, but didn't look at him. "Your father is gone," she said, her voice breaking.

"Gone?" James said. "What do you mean, he left?"

Billy felt his mother's grip on his hand tighten. She began to cry, loudly and haltingly. Billy looked at James and Celeste, who looked back at him with equally puzzled expressions. Not knowing what to do, Billy knelt beside his mother's chair.

"There's no easy way to say this," said Mr. Derry. He seemed to be speaking directly to James, not looking at either Celeste or Billy. "Your father killed himself."

Celeste gasped, while James said, "What? Killed himself? Why would he do that?"

Billy said nothing. Suddenly, he realized that he was dreaming. He had to be. He was not in his living room, holding his mother's hand while she sobbed. He wasn't looking at A.J. Derry, who had just informed him that his father was dead. He was asleep in his own bed, and he was having a nightmare. He just had to wake himself up, and it would all be over.

"He sent me a letter," Billy heard his mother say. Her voice sounded very far away.

No one said anything else for what seemed a very long time. During the silence Billy tried to make himself wake from the dream. He shook his head, but nothing happened. He closed his eyes, willing himself awake, but when he opened them again he was still kneeling on the floor, still holding his mother's hand, still waiting for someone to explain to him what was happening.

"Apparently your father had cancer." Mr. Derry was speaking again. His voice, too, sounded as if it were coming from another room. Billy had to strain to hear him. "We didn't know. None of us knew. In his letter he says that he didn't want us—you—to see him suffer."

"Where's his body?" asked James. "Have you found it? Maybe it isn't true. Maybe it's a . . . joke . . . or someone is trying to make us *think* he's dead. Have you—"

"We haven't found his body," Mr. Derry interrupted. "He doesn't say where he went. The postmark is from Utica, so he could have gone anywhere. I've sent his description and a description of his car out on the wire. Hopefully someone will have seen him."

"So you don't know that he's actually dead," James said. "He could still be alive."

A.J. sighed. "Of course we hope so, son," he said. "Until we find him, we certainly hope that he hasn't really done this."

"Maybe he was just *thinking* about it," Celeste said. Her voice sounded hopeful, and Billy found himself listening to hers above all the others.

"That's possible," said Mr. Derry.

"But you don't think so," James said. "I can tell. You think he really is dead, don't you."

There was a long pause. Then Mr. Derry said, "I've known your father a long time. I've never known him to say he was going to do something and then not do it."

"Yeah," James countered. "But you're talking about building a shed, or raising money for a new cruiser, or organizing a Boy Scouts outing. That's not the same."

Billy wondered why James was arguing with Mr. Derry. It was rude, and he knew their father wouldn't stand for it. But his mother said nothing, and Mr. Derry wasn't getting angry. It was as if James was saying everything they themselves were hoping was true.

"Like I said, I hope that you're right," Mr. Derry said. "And all we can do is pray that you are. But right now we have to go by what's in the letter."

Celeste began to sniffle. James looked at her, then turned away. His face was stormy, and Billy knew that another argument was coming. He stood up, dropping his mother's hand.

"No," Billy heard himself say. "He isn't dead." He looked at A.J. Derry, then at his mother. "You're wrong. You're *wrong!*"

He turned and ran from the room. He heard his mother call after him, but he ignored her. He pushed open the screen door in the kitchen and ran outside. The sun blinded him, but he ran anyway, unseeing. He was no longer dreaming. He was awake, and his heart was pounding. He thought he heard the screen door slam again, but he didn't look behind him.

He ran away from the house, not toward the street but toward the grassy field behind it. In the distance he saw the dilapidated old barn. The grass was long, and it whisked against his legs as he ran, closing behind him so that he was swallowed up by it. He ran until he was halfway to the barn, then fell into the grass on his back. He lay there looking up at the sun, his body cupped in the grass. He hoped no one had followed him, and he listened for the sound of approaching feet. When none came he stretched out his legs and arms, forming a star.

His father wasn't dead. Billy knew that. But he couldn't tell them how he knew, or even exactly *what* he knew. They wouldn't believe him. But he was sure of it. His father was gone, yes, but he wasn't dead. He might come back. He *would* come back. When it was okay, he would come back.

He gathered his arms and legs, curling into a ball. The grass beneath his cheek was scratchy, but he ignored it. In front of him a grasshopper clung to a piece of grass, looking at him with large, black eyes. He watched it with disinterest, listening to the sound the grass made as the wind blew through it. No, none of them would believe him if he told them what he knew. They would say he was making it up.

Still, he wished he could tell his mother. Out of all of them she was the one he wished he could tell, because she was the saddest. But he just couldn't. Not yet, anyway. Not until he could make them believe him. The problem was, he wasn't sure he would ever be able to do that.

He lay there for an hour or so, the feelings of frustration growing inside of him. The more he thought, the angrier he became. Finally, as the shadows of twilight began to sweep across the field, he got up. He made his way back toward the house, but halfway there he turned and veered in a slightly different direction. When he emerged from the grass he was behind a house some distance from his own. He walked through the backyard to the street.

It wasn't dark, and wouldn't be for another hour or more. But it was dim enough that he knew he wouldn't be easily seen. And part of him didn't care if he *was* seen. It didn't really matter. It wouldn't change anything. At least not yet.

He walked, making a handful of turns, until he was on the right street. Now he slowed, his determination fading slightly as he approached his destination. Then he thought of his father, and of his mother crying in her chair, and he moved on.

Finding a rock was easy. He took one from a line of them that edged a bed of pansies and hens-and-chickens. It was a large rock, heavy and smooth in his hand. It would do nicely. As long as he could go through with his plan, it would do.

The house was mostly dark. A light burned in an upstairs window and the porch was illuminated by an electric bug zapper that crackled occasionally as something flew into it, but there was no one outside. Billy smelled smoke, and the scent of meat cooking, but he couldn't tell if it came from behind the house or from another one.

The car was in the driveway. He walked up to it and stood looking at the window on the driver's side. Then he lifted the rock and threw it as hard as he could at the dark pane of glass. The window shattered with a satisfying sound, and tiny pieces of glass scattered across the front seat and fell onto the driveway. The rock itself landed on the seat, where it lay like a large, brown egg.

Billy looked toward the house, waiting for someone to come outside. When no one did he screamed, "Bastard!" at the empty windows. "Fucking bastard!" he yelled again, his voice cutting through the quiet.

He saw a light go on behind the door, and he turned and ran. Someone came out, and he heard a voice, but he didn't hear what it said. He ran more quickly, pumping his arms and barely feeling the pavement beneath his feet. *Fucking bastard,* he thought to himself as he ran back toward home. *You stupid, fucking bastard.*

CHAPTER 9

1991

It was hard for Celeste to believe that Adam was five and Mary was soon to be four. It seemed to her that she had been pregnant only a few months ago. Now she was getting Adam ready for kindergarten. And it was proving to be something of a battle. She wanted him to wear jeans and a long-sleeved shirt, but he was insisting on shorts and a T-shirt with a Transformers picture on it. She decided to compromise on jeans and the T-shirt.

"Okay," Adam said doubtfully. "But no jacket."

"Deal," Celeste agreed. "Now go downstairs and eat your breakfast. I'll be down in a minute."

She watched her son run off, listening to his little feet as they thudded down the stairs. Why were boys always so loud? Nate was the same, always banging around. Girls were so much quieter. *So much easier,* she thought as she looked around Adam's room. It looked as if a tornado had recently swept through, strewing toys and books and clothes everywhere. She'd cleaned it just the other day, and it had taken Adam approximately fifteen minutes once he'd gotten home to undo two hours of work.

She shut the door to his room. She would deal with the mess later. Right now she had to make sure Mary was dressed. Adam, being more stubborn, required more attention in the morning. With him at the breakfast stage of the daily ritual she could now turn her attention to her daughter.

"How do I look?" Mary asked as Celeste entered her room. She was standing in front of the mirror, admiring her outfit of pink corduroy pants and a white sweater. She'd even combed her hair, although not terribly well, and put it into a lopsided ponytail.

"You look beautiful," Celeste assured her, slipping the elastic from her hair and picking up a brush from the dresser. "You just need a little tweaking."

Mary giggled. "Tweaking," she repeated.

A minute later, Celeste and Mary entered the kitchen, where they found Nate and Adam seated at the table. Adam was eating cereal; a glance showed Celeste that it was of the brightly colored variety.

"I thought I told you no Froot Loops," she scolded Nate. "Oatmeal, remember?"

"I couldn't find it," Nate answered without looking up from the paper. "Besides, the box says this has vitamins and whatever."

"The 'whatever' being about six cups of sugar," said Celeste. "And you don't have to deal with him when he's all wound up, or when he crashes and starts whining."

"I want Froot Loops!" Mary announced, eyeing her brother's bowl.

Celeste sighed. She knew she couldn't let Adam have the cereal without giving Mary the same. That would involve at least half an hour of fighting, and she didn't need it. *Let their teachers handle them,* she thought as she poured some cereal into a bowl and added milk from the carton on the table. As Mary began happily to eat, Celeste poured herself a cup of coffee from the pot on the counter, then sat across from her husband.

She wanted to talk to him about what was going on, but not in front of the kids. Mary might not be old enough to understand exactly what was being said, but Adam was. Even though neither of them had ever known their grandfather, Adam would pick up on the fact that something was wrong and that it involved his family. She had to wait until they were at school.

Nate folded the paper and set it down. "I was thinking," he said. "Do you know anyone who might have wanted your father dead?"

Celeste darted her eyes at her children, both of whom seemed not to have heard their father, then glared at Nate. He waved a hand at her. "They don't know," he said.

"Know what?" Adam piped up.

"Nothing," Celeste said quickly. "Your father was talking about someone else."

"Uh-uh," Mary said. "He was talking about *us*. Right, Daddy?"

Nate laughed. "You're pretty smart, aren't you?" he said, patting Mary on the head.

"Who's dead?" Adam asked. When no one replied, he looked at Celeste. "Who's dead?" he repeated.

"Um," Celeste said, trying to decide how to proceed.

"They're going to hear about it," said Nate. "You can't hide it forever."

Celeste frowned. She didn't want her kids exposed to something so awful. Even if it wasn't their grandfather they were talking about, the subject was way too morbid for them to be discussing. But now Nate had forced her past the point of no return.

"Do you remember how we told you that Grandpa McCloud is dead?" she asked.

Adam and Mary both nodded. "He died a long time ago," Mary said. "'Fore we were born."

"That's right," Celeste said. "Before you were born. Well, when he died we couldn't find his body."

Adam laughed, startling her. "What'd you do, lose it?" he asked.

Mary joined in the laughter. Celeste had to remind herself that to them her father was just a name. They didn't understand yet what it was to lose someone they loved. They hadn't even suffered the death of a pet. Still, their callousness disturbed her.

"No," she said, remaining calm. "We didn't know where he was when he died. But now we do. We found his body."

"Where?" Adam asked.

"He was buried in the ground," Celeste answered.

"Who buried him?" Adam continued.

Celeste looked to Nate for help. He was the one who had gotten her into the situation. Now she wanted him to help get her out of it.

"We don't know who buried him, sport," Nate said. "That's what we need to find out."

Adam nodded, apparently satisfied with the answer. Or maybe, Celeste thought, it was that the explanation had come from Nate and not from her. Adam always took what Nate said as the truth, while he questioned her on almost everything. Nate often joked that their son was almost certainly going to grow up to be a cop like his father and grandfather. Celeste, although she said nothing, hoped for exactly the opposite.

"See?" Nate said to her. "No big deal."

"We're telling you about your grandpa because you might hear people talking about him," Celeste said, ignoring her husband. "And if you hear anything you don't understand, we want you to come ask us, okay?"

"Sure," said Adam, shrugging.

"Mary?" Celeste said. "Do you understand?"

Mary nodded.

"Good," Nate said. "Now go brush your teeth. Amy will be here in a minute to take you to school."

The kids left the kitchen, obediently going upstairs where, Celeste suspected, Mary would brush her teeth and Adam would begin playing with some toy. As soon as they were gone, she turned on Nate.

"Thanks a lot!" she snapped. "I wasn't going to say anything to them."

"You said yourself, they're going to hear people talk," Nate replied. "They might as well know now."

"They don't even understand," said Celeste. "We might as well be talking about a movie they saw on TV."

"They'll be fine," Nate assured her.

A knock on the door ended the argument as a teenage girl came in. "Hey," she said. "Are the tinies ready?"

"Hi, Amy," Celeste said. "Just about. I'll go get them."

She was relieved to get out of the kitchen. She was still mad at Nate, and going upstairs to get the kids gave her a few minutes to calm down. As she'd suspected, Mary was ready to go, but Adam was in the middle of a battle involving action figures from three recent movies. It took her five minutes to get his teeth brushed and his backpack loaded.

When the three of them returned to the kitchen, she could tell that Nate had told Amy about the finding of Daniel McCloud's body. The girl looked at Celeste with a pained expression, although she said nothing. *That's the look I'm going to see for the next couple of weeks,* Celeste thought miserably.

"You guys ready?" Amy asked Adam and Mary, her voice betraying no sense of the pity Celeste had felt in her look.

The kids kissed Nate good-bye, then came to Celeste for hers. She hugged them each tightly, telling them she loved them, then watched as they followed Amy out to the car. Amy had been Nate's idea. She was a neighbor girl, sixteen or seventeen, a junior in high school. Nate had suggested they pay her to drive Mary to preschool and Adam to kindergarten and then pick them up in the afternoon when her own school let out. That way Celeste had one less thing to do. Celeste had been hesitant at first to surrender her children to the care of someone else, but it had worked out fine, and now she was more than happy to have the extra help.

"I want to ask you something," Nate said when they were alone. He added some sugar to his coffee and stirred it, while Celeste waited impatiently for him to actually ask the question. It was a habit of his that irritated her, and she suspected it was the same thing he did when he questioned suspects at work.

Finally he spoke again. "Can you think of anyone who might have wanted to kill your father?"

"No," she said instantly.

Nate looked up at her, his eyes fixed on her face. Again she imagined what it would be like to be sitting in a chair across from him being interrogated about a crime. For a moment she forgot that she was speaking to her husband.

"I mean, I'm sure there were people who did," she continued. "You know, people he'd arrested or made trouble for. They were always making threats. You know how that is."

Nate nodded as he sipped his coffee. "I mean *really* want him dead," he said. "So badly that they might have actually done it."

Celeste sighed. "He never talked about that kind of stuff," she said. "He didn't want us to think his job was dangerous. Really, you're probably better off asking your dad. He was his best friend."

"I will," Nate said. "I just thought maybe you could think of anyone Dad might not know about."

"Like who?" asked Celeste.

"Like someone who isn't a criminal," Nate said. "Someone maybe nobody would think of under normal circumstances."

Celeste shook her head. "No," she said. "Everybody loved him."

She drank her coffee, thinking about Nate's question. It was true that everybody loved her father. He'd been a favorite in town, and his death had saddened just about everyone.

"Sometimes it's not obvious," Nate said. Celeste looked at him. "Who might want someone dead," Nate elaborated. "Sometimes it's the person you least expect, or someone no one even knew that the victim was associated with."

"You know pretty much everyone in town," Celeste reminded him. "If you know someone who wanted him dead, it'll be news to me."

She returned to her coffee. Could there, she wondered, be someone who hated her father so much that he wanted him dead? *He or she,* she corrected herself. *It doesn't have to be a man.*

Suddenly her blood turned cold. Her fingers gripped the coffee mug tightly, and she couldn't even swallow what was in her mouth. It was as if her muscles had frozen and she were paralyzed. But her brain continued to function, and as it did a scene played out in her mind. It was one she hadn't thought of in a long time. Now it returned in startling clarity.

No, she told herself. *That has nothing to do with this.*

It couldn't. It simply wasn't possible. Yet the more times she replayed the memory, the more she couldn't help but wonder. *What if it did happen that way?* she asked herself. The idea was too terrible to even consider.

Just as suddenly as it had come upon her, the paralysis left. She swallowed the coffee and blinked her eyes. Across from her, Nate had resumed reading the paper. He hadn't seen the moment, didn't know what was running through her head.

She struggled with whether she should tell him what she was thinking. Part of her wanted to. But another part told her to keep her secrets to herself. *It would just cause a lot of trouble,* she argued with herself. *And you know that's not what happened.*

She wanted to believe that. Oh, how she wanted to believe it. But she *had* seen something. And if that something was related to her father's death, didn't she owe it to him to tell Nate?

Nate put the paper down. "I should get to the station," he said, standing up. "You're going to your mom's, right?"

Celeste nodded. "Yeah," she said. "I'll be over there."

Nate came around the table and kissed her. "It's going to be all right," he said. "I promise. Try not to worry."

"I know it will," said Celeste. "I just worry about Mom."

"Well, this is a big shock for her," Nate reminded her. "For all of us. Just give her time."

"You're right," Celeste agreed.

"I'll call you later," Nate told her as he picked up his hat and jacket and walked out. "If you need me, you know how to get me."

"Just dial 9-1-1," Celeste repeated automatically. It was their little joke, one that still made Nate laugh whenever she said it.

Celeste listened for the sound of the car door shutting, then the engine turning over. She didn't move from her spot as Nate pulled out of the driveway. For a long time she remained still, the coffee growing cold in the cup. Her thoughts were haunted by the memory dredged up by Nate's question.

"You're right," she said as if Nate were still at the table. "It's a big shock. To all of us."

CHAPTER 10

1983

Celeste looked at her watch. It was almost two in the morning. *They're going to kill me*, she thought as she eased open the front door, praying that it wouldn't squeak and betray her arrival. They almost never used the front door, preferring the one in the kitchen, and she'd chosen it because it was closer to the stairs. With a little luck she could make it upstairs without anyone seeing her. Probably everyone would be asleep anyway, but her father sometimes kept odd hours. And he was the one she least wanted to run into.

To her immense relief the door hinges didn't squeak. She peered inside and, finding the living room empty, slipped inside and gently pushed the door shut behind her. She had a clear shot to the stairs, and had one foot on the lowest step when she heard someone say, "Did you think I wouldn't find out?"

It was her mother's voice, angry and clear. Celeste turned, ready with an excuse, but found herself looking at empty space. Her mother wasn't in the room.

"Well?" She heard the voice again. This time, having had a moment to collect herself, Celeste realized that it was coming from the kitchen.

"You don't know what you're talking about, Ada." Her father. And he sounded angry.

Instinct told her to go to her room and forget about what she'd heard. After all, *she* was the one coming in well past midnight. If she was caught she would get the grilling of her life, and she doubted her parents would buy the explanation that she and Paul had been watch-ing a movie at his house and fallen asleep on the couch. They didn't much like Paul as it was; if they suspected that she and he were, as her mother said, "doing" something, then all hell would break loose.

Again she started up the stairs.

"Don't tell me I'm imagining things, Daniel," her mother said. "I saw the way you looked at her."

Celeste paused, and this time curiosity got the better of her. She turned and walked slowly toward the kitchen. If she remained in the living room but kept close to the swinging doors that opened into the kitchen she would be able to hear everything clearly. And if she got caught, she could always pretend she'd come down for a glass of milk. This was, she knew, a bad plan, but she could probably fudge her way through if she had to.

She crept close to the door, stopping and leaning against the wall just outside the kitchen. She didn't dare sneak a glance inside, but from her vantage point she could see through the door slats. Her fa-ther was seated at the table, still dressed in his uniform. Her mother was invisible to her, and Celeste assumed she must be standing by the refrigerator, which was on the other side of the room.

"Ada, you're making a whole lot out of nothing," her father said. His voice was weary, as if the argument had been going on for a long time.

"Am I?" her mother countered. "Are you telling me nothing ever went on between the two of you?"

Her father sighed. "All that was a very long time ago, Ada. You know that."

Celeste stiffened, shocked to hear her father's words. Had he had an affair? It certainly sounded like it. She held her breath, waiting to hear more.

"I want to believe you, Daniel," her mother said. "I do. But I . . ." Her words trailed off.

"But you don't," her father said. "Just say it. You don't trust me."

"Don't put words in my mouth," her mother countered.

Her father gave a short, sharp laugh. "I'm not putting them there," he said. "They're already there. You're just afraid to spit them out."

There was the sound of something being dropped into the sink. *A coffee cup,* Celeste thought vaguely. It was followed by the sound of running water. Then her mother said, "This is getting us nowhere. I'm going to bed."

The sound of feet coming toward the doorway sent Celeste scurrying for the stairs. She got there just as her mother pushed open the kitchen doors. Moving as quickly as she could, she stayed just far enough ahead of her mother that she wasn't seen. As Celeste opened the door to her bedroom, her mother reached the top of the stairs. Celeste shut the door and leaned against it, her heart pounding.

Afraid to turn on the light lest someone see it underneath the door, she undressed in the dark. She wanted to brush her teeth, but the bathroom was a dangerous walk down the hall, and she didn't dare risk it, at least not until she was fairly certain that her mother and father were asleep.

But she hadn't heard her father come upstairs. *Why would he?* she asked herself. If he and her mother were having a serious fight, chances were he would either sleep on the couch or go to the station and sleep there. He'd done it before, although Celeste had never heard her parents fight over something as serious as what she'd just heard them discussing.

Pulling a T-shirt over her head, she got into bed and lay in the darkness. The moon was near full, and once her eyes adjusted to the darkness she could actually see fairly well. Above her desk the members of Duran Duran stared down at her with their sexy pouts. The giant stuffed bear Paul had won for her at a carnival sat in a corner, his enormous head tilted to one side and one of her bras draped across his shoulder. It was all familiar and comforting.

Yet she was distressed by what she'd heard her parents talking about. Was her father really having an affair? She couldn't imagine it. Not that she thought about it a lot—or ever—but the idea of either of her parents having sex was kind of repulsive. They were her *parents.* She just couldn't imagine them naked, fumbling around the way she and Paul sometimes did. She especially couldn't imagine them doing it in the bedroom right down the hall from hers.

She pushed the image out of her mind and returned to the question of whether her father was cheating on her mother. From the sound of things, he might be. Then again, her mother sometimes blew things way out of proportion. Maybe she was doing it again.

I don't know, Celeste argued with herself. *That didn't sound like their usual fights.* Of course, cheating was a little more serious than her father forgetting an anniversary or not calling when he was going to be late. This was major. Like divorce major. Or take the gun from the bedside table and shoot someone major.

You're being dramatic, she told herself.

She rolled over, hugging her pillow as she thought about her night with Paul. She thought she might be in love with him. No, she *knew* she was in love with him. After all, she'd let him be her first, and she wouldn't have done that with someone she didn't love. And he'd been so gentle with her. It had hardly hurt at all, and even though she hadn't come, it had felt wonderful lying in Paul's arms afterward.

She wished her parents liked him more than they did. She knew they both hoped she would break up with him and date someone more suitable. *Suitable.* That was her mother's word, the one she'd used when she'd suggested that Celeste was too young to date seriously. "I'm sure Paul is a lot of fun," she said. "But you shouldn't settle on one boy. If you do, you won't find someone suitable."

"Suitable for what?" Celeste had asked her.

The answer, of course, was to marry. But Celeste wasn't thinking about marriage, at least not in any real way. It wasn't like she was picking out a dress or making a bridesmaid list or anything. She was just enjoying being in love with Paul. If she married him, she married him. It wasn't like when her parents were her age and you had to marry the first guy you slept with. *Or marry him just so you* could *sleep with him,* she thought.

But what if she and Paul did get married? She tried to imagine them living together, maybe having a couple of kids. She couldn't really see it. Then she tried to imagine Paul was cheating on her. She did know what that felt like. Her last boyfriend, Gary, had cheated on her with that whore from Elksville. Susan. He'd met her at a keg party. He'd said it was just a one-time thing, and Celeste had forgiven him. But then she'd found Susan's coat in the back of his car a few weeks later, along with a used rubber, and Gary had admitted to seeing her again.

Paul wouldn't do anything like that. He cared about her too much. *But what if he did?* she asked herself. *What would you do?*

With Gary she had been mad enough that she'd spread a rumor that he had a really tiny dick. The truth was she hadn't liked him enough to really want to hurt him (at least not physically). But Paul was a different story. If she found out Paul was cheating on her, she wasn't sure what she would do. Could she really get mad enough that she would try to kill him?

She'd seen it happen. A year earlier her father had been called to a trailer just outside of town. A man had stabbed his wife to death with a kitchen knife, then shot himself in the head with a shotgun. Only he'd missed, and the shot had blown off half of his face and not killed him. When he finally healed to where he could talk, he'd told the cops that he'd killed his wife because she was sleeping with his best friend. He'd meant to kill the friend, too, but the guy had run off somewhere. They never did find him, but it didn't much matter. The husband was in jail anyhow.

Celeste didn't think she could do something like that to Paul. Nor did she think her mother could ever do it. Then again, the man who now had half a face was also the father of two beautiful little girls and a deacon at his church. In every article about the killing, his neighbors said they couldn't believe he had done such a thing because he was "such a nice guy."

Suddenly she was worried, not so much that her mother might kill her father but just that their marriage might be unraveling. It wasn't like they were the perfect American family, but they were pretty happy. She always felt sorry for her friends whose parents had split up, and even though she didn't always get along with her mother and father, it was reassuring to know that they loved her and loved each other.

It was just a fight, she told herself. Her mother was just overreacting to something. In a few days she would forget all about it and things would be back to normal. That's how it always was.

She realized suddenly that she very badly had to pee. She tried to ignore it, but eventually she resigned herself to the fact that, without going, she would never get to sleep. She threw back the covers, got out of bed, and opened her door. The hall was dark. No light came from downstairs, and the narrow space beneath her parents' bedroom door was dark. She breathed a sigh of relief. Whatever had caused the fight, it now appeared to have passed.

She padded down the hallway, the rug soft beneath her feet. At the bathroom she stepped inside and shut the door before turning on the light. Cursing the male members of her family, she lowered the toilet seat, pushed her panties down, and sat. Immediately she felt better as the pressure on her bladder lessened. *And I can brush my teeth,* she thought. Her mouth tasted like beer and Paul. She blushed at this last thought, but it also made her happy.

She was tearing some sheets from the roll of tissue when she heard the muffled sound of someone crying. The bathroom was between her room and her parents' room, and she knew from experience that people in either room could hear what was going on in the bathroom and that in the bathroom you could hear noises coming from either of the bedrooms. She'd once heard James playing with himself and had teased him mercilessly until he'd threatened to tape-record her using the toilet and play it for all of his friends.

She knew that what she was hearing was her mother crying. It was loud enough that Celeste thought her mother must really be sobbing. Hearing it made her sad and self-conscious. Was she supposed to go in and comfort her mother? Should she just go back to her room and pretend she hadn't heard anything? If she flushed the toilet or ran the water, her mother would likely hear it and know that someone was listening to her.

She decided not to flush. James and Billy were always forgetting, and if anyone noticed they would blame one or the other of the boys. But she still wanted to brush her teeth. They felt funny, and she knew her breath would be horrible in the morning. After pulling her panties up, she opened the medicine cabinet and looked inside. She took out a bottle of mouthwash, opened it, and took a swig. As she swished the liquid around in her mouth, she recapped the bottle and put it away. After a minute she leaned down and spit the mouthwash into the sink, getting as much right into the drain as possible. The rest she wiped up with some more tissue, which she crumpled up and threw into the wastebasket beneath the sink.

Behind the wall her mother was still crying. The more Celeste listened, the more she wanted to knock on the bedroom door and see if her mother wanted to talk. But she just couldn't. It was her mother who talked to *her* when things went wrong, not the other way around. Her mother was the adult. What could Celeste possibly say to her that would help?

She put the toilet seat back up to make it look more like one of the boys had been in there. Then she turned off the light and opened the door. Again she walked quickly to her bedroom, away from the sound of her mother crying. The air was chilly now, and she got into bed and pulled the covers up. She was tired, and although what she'd seen and heard that night still troubled her, her thoughts turned to her own romantic happiness. After a restless twenty minutes she had forgotten all about her parents' marital difficulties and fell off to sleep to dream about being with Paul in a sun-dappled glade. His strong hands caressed her breasts, and as he kissed her he whispered in her ear. "Everything's going to be all right."

CHAPTER 11

1991

"Mom, I need to talk to you about something."

Ada looked at her daughter. Celeste had arrived only minutes before. James was still asleep, and she had no idea where Billy was, but she was making breakfast anyway. It gave her something to do. She'd been up since four and was tired of the novel she'd been reading, so she'd finally gotten up and come downstairs.

"What about?" she asked Celeste.

"Dad," Celeste replied.

"I don't see that there's anything to talk about," Ada told her. "Not until Nate comes up with something." She had, since the day before, accepted the truth about her husband. They had found his body. This was upsetting, but there was nothing she could do about it. What was done, was done. Now she just had to let things play out as they would.

"I don't mean about finding him," Celeste explained. "I want to ask you about something that happened a little before he disappeared."

Ada turned up the heat under the griddle. "Well, ask then," she said.

Celeste looked uncomfortable. Ada, keeping her eye on the pancakes on the griddle, waited for her to continue. Finally Celeste said, "One night I came home late. I heard you and Dad talking in the kitchen. Arguing, actually."

Ada turned one of the pancakes over. "What were we arguing about?" she asked, examining the bottom of the pancake to see if it was truly done. "Probably money. Seems like we were always arguing about money."

"No, it wasn't money," Celeste said. "It was about a woman."

Ada turned around. "A woman?" she said, and laughed. "Why on earth would we be arguing about a woman?"

"That's what I was hoping you could tell me," said Celeste. "It sounded to me like you were accusing him of having an affair."

Ada returned her attention to the stove, where the first pancakes were almost ready to come off. "I can't imagine what you're talking about," she said. "Your father never had an affair."

"I didn't think so," said Celeste. She sounded relieved. "But I distinctly remember you saying something like 'I see the way you look at her.' Also, I heard you crying in your room later that night."

Ada slid the spatula under a pancake and transferred it to the waiting plate. "Well, you were a regular little Nancy Drew, weren't you?" she remarked.

"Mom, I'm serious," Celeste countered. "I know I'm not making it up. I was right outside the kitchen. I heard what you said."

Ada added two more pancakes to the plate, then took it to the table. Setting it in front of her daughter she said, "And what were you doing coming in so late? Let me guess—out with Paul Lunardi? I never did like that boy."

"Well, yes," Celeste admitted. "I was. But that's not what we're talking about. I want to know who you and Dad were arguing about."

"We weren't arguing about a woman, I can tell you that," Ada said. "Your father was as faithful as a hunting dog. I don't know what you heard, but you heard wrong. Which is what you get for snooping around in the first place."

She went to the cupboard and returned with a container of brown sugar, which she set on the table. Then she opened the refrigerator and took out a bright yellow plastic lemon. "As I recall, you and your brothers prefer this to maple syrup," she said as she handed the lemon to Celeste.

Celeste smiled at her. "That's right," she said as she spooned brown sugar onto her pancakes. Then she removed the cap on the lemon and squeezed juice onto the sugar, which melted and formed a sticky glaze. "I forget why we started eating them this way."

"I don't remember either," Ada said. "Probably some foolish idea of your father's. All I know is that once you started I couldn't get you to go back to plain old syrup."

Celeste took a bite of pancake and made a face. "Too much lemon juice," she said, reaching for the brown sugar.

Ada resumed cooking. *James should be down in a minute,* she thought. *He'll save me from this foolishness.* She hoped that Celeste had forgotten the initial topic of conversation, or would at least be distracted enough by the pancakes so that Ada could change the subject. The current one was not to her liking.

"I'm sorry I brought up the thing about Dad," Celeste said from behind her. "I guess I must have heard wrong."

"That's all right," said Ada, relieved. "It was late. You were tired. Who knows what we were arguing about."

There was a long pause. Ada heard the click of a fork against Celeste's plate and the sound of chewing. She concentrated on making more pancakes. She already had a dozen stacked on the plate. *If James doesn't get down here soon, these are going to be cold,* she thought. *I should go wake him up.*

"Mom, have you thought about who might have wanted to kill . . . to see Dad dead?" Celeste asked.

"Of course I have," Ada answered. "What do you think I spent most of the night doing?"

She lifted the last pancake from the griddle and put it on the plate, which she in turn slipped into the oven. She turned the temperature to low so that the pancakes would stay warm. She hoped they wouldn't dry out. Then she sat down at the table.

"And what did you come up with?" Celeste asked.

"Nothing," said Ada. "Apart from the usual suspects. The people he put away. Any one of them could have done it. I think we have to assume it was one of them."

"You don't think it could be anyone he knew?"

"Who do we know that could do something like that?" Ada snapped. She knew she sounded angry, and she laid her hand on Celeste's. "I'm sorry. It's just that the idea of anyone we know doing such a thing . . ." Her voice trailed off as she found it impossible to say just how much the thought upset her.

"I know," said Celeste. "This sounds horrible, but I preferred thinking that he killed himself. At least having cancer is a reason."

"It was selfish of him," Ada said. She was surprised to hear herself say it. She had thought it often enough, but she'd never said anything like it in the presence of her children. Now that she had, though, she found herself continuing. "He robbed us. I could have taken care of him. He took that away from me."

Celeste put her fork down and looked at her mother with an unreadable expression. "I never knew you felt like this," she said.

Ada stood up. She didn't want her daughter looking at her the way she was. She didn't want anyone feeling *sorry* for her. "Well, I do," she said. "For a long time I hated him for what he did. I couldn't understand it, even with the letter. Now, well, I just feel, I don't know—guilty—I guess. For being mad at him all those years."

"Oh, Mom," Celeste said. "Don't. Don't beat yourself up. You didn't know. None of us knew."

"No," Ada said. "I suppose we didn't. But I can't help what I feel." She took a dishrag from a hook beside the sink and began to wipe the counter. "I just have to live with it," she said.

"Good morning."

Ada turned to see James standing in the doorway. He was dressed and looked freshly showered. For a moment she thought she was looking at a young version of Daniel, the resemblance was so close. When James stepped forward to give her a hug, she recoiled as if from a ghost. But when he touched her, the spell broke and she was once again looking at her son. She smiled and said, "Sit down. I made you pancakes."

James accepted a plate from her. "Any sign of Billy?" he asked as he began to eat.

"No," Ada said. "I thought he might be in his room. He stays here sometimes when he thinks I need looking after."

"More like when he needs looking after," Celeste commented. "He's got his own place," she informed James. "Over on Larson, above the liquor store."

"How convenient," James remarked.

"Now you two stop talking about your brother that way," Ada demanded. "He's a good boy. He's just a little troubled is all."

She saw Celeste raise one eyebrow, but no retort followed. She was angry again, at James and Celeste for speaking about Billy the way they were, and at Billy for not being there. She liked it when they were all together, even if the children didn't always get along as well as she would like. They were still a family, after all, and they needed to stick together. *Especially now,* she thought.

"I'll swing by his place later and see if he's around," James said. "First I want to talk to Nate."

"About what?" Celeste asked.

"The case," said James. "That's why I'm here, remember?"

"Sure," Celeste said. "But you might want to let him come to you."

"Why?" asked James.

Celeste stood up and took her plate to the sink. Ada watched as she ran water over it and set it in the plastic dishpan. As soon as Celeste moved away, Ada took up the plate and washed it properly, with soap and a sponge.

"Look," Celeste said to James. "Try to remember that Nate's in charge here, okay?"

"What's that supposed to mean?" said James, clearly irritated.

"It means don't walk in there acting all Mr. Big Shot," Celeste explained.

Ada rinsed the plate and set it in the drainer. As she folded the dish-towel James turned in his chair to look at her. "What is she talking about?" he asked.

Ada shook her head. "I'm not getting in the middle of this," she said. "You two work it out. I've got things to do."

She left her children in the kitchen and went upstairs to her bed-room. Shutting the door, she sat on the edge of the bed. On the dresser was a photograph of Daniel, smiling and young. It had been taken not long after their wedding, while they were vacationing in Maine.

"What are you looking at?" she demanded of the picture.

Celeste had upset her more than she'd let on. Much more. She'd lied to her daughter. Of course she remembered that night. She re-membered every word of the argument, and could have reenacted it perfectly had she wanted to. Discovering that someone else had over-heard her and Daniel horrified her. That it was one of their children made it even worse.

Why had Celeste chosen that night, of all nights, to come home late? And why had she waited until now to let her mother know that she'd heard? Ada realized that her hands were curled into fists, and she forced herself to relax. It was all right. She'd said the right things. Celeste almost certainly believed her. *But what if she doesn't?* she thought. *Then what will happen?*

Again she looked at the photograph of her late husband. "You had to come back, didn't you?" she said. "You couldn't stay gone."

She put her face in her hands, but she didn't cry. She breathed deeply, calming herself. Why was it all falling down on her? She'd worked so hard to pretend that everything was fine, that *she* was fine. And for some time she had actually believed that she was fine. Now, thanks to Nicky Turner and his idiotic cabin, her life had been turned upside down.

"Damn it, Daniel!" she said. "I laid you to rest. Now I have to do it all over again."

From out of nowhere she heard her own voice. "Are you telling me nothing ever went on between the two of you?"

She closed her eyes and saw Daniel. "All that was a very long time ago, Ada."

She remembered the expression on his face, how his eyes had looked away from her. It was the only time she'd seen him unable to face her. She had hated him for that, hated him because she knew it meant that he was lying. She remembered, too, lying in the very bed on which she now sat, sobbing and waiting for Daniel to come in and tell her that everything was all right. But he hadn't. He'd left her there, alone with her misery and her hatred.

She opened her eyes. The room had changed since then. It was a different color, and the bed was covered with a new quilt. She'd given all of Daniel's clothes to the Goodwill, and the scent of his aftershave no longer lingered. It was her room now, and hers alone. Yes, it had been a long time.

"But not long enough, Daniel," Ada said. "Not long enough."

CHAPTER 12

1982

Ada nodded her head, listening to Evelyn Burnham's description of the last Garden Club meeting, but out of the corner of her eye she was watching her husband as he talked to Bess Kunkel. Soon to be Bess Derry. She couldn't believe A.J. was actually going to marry the woman, but at least that meant she would be off the market. *Not that that would ever stop her,* Ada thought.

"The dahlias are absolutely *huge* this year," Evelyn said. "And the roses, oh, you should see the roses. The Mary Pickford I put in two years ago is just gorgeous."

"Do you remember when we were in high school and we found out Bess was stuffing her bra?" Ada said, interrupting Evelyn's rambling account of her garden's progress.

Evelyn stopped talking and thought. "You know, I do!" she said. "It was in Mister Reagan's history class. She raised her hand to answer a question, and Bobby Dugan saw the tissues sticking out." She laughed. "That was a laugh riot."

Ada jerked her head toward Bess. "I think she might still be at it," she said, pulling a face and feigning surprise.

Evelyn glanced over, then turned to Ada, laughing. "You're terrible," she said. "But I agree that those do not look like the ones God gave her."

Satisfied to have drawn Evelyn into a dissection of Bess's faults, Ada continued on. "I don't remember her being a blonde either," she said. "And I think her roots will back me up on that."

Again Evelyn laughed, and again Ada felt pleased with herself. *Two in a row,* she congratulated herself. She sipped her gin and tonic and stretched out on the chaise. A mosquito landed on her exposed arm, and she slapped it away. "Damn bugs," she said. "You'd think A.J. would have set out some citronella candles."

They were in the Derrys' backyard, a wide expanse of grass that, like most of their properties, bordered on wilder fields on the edges of the forest that surrounded Cold Falls on its westernmost side. A.J. had built a barbeque pit, and it was around this that the guests sat. Several picnic tables nearby were loaded with food. Ada's contribution was a green Jell-O salad in the shape of a fish. She had filled the mold halfway and let it set before adding a can of fruit cocktail and the remaining gelatin, so that when the fish was turned out of the mold and set on a plate it appeared to be filled with something it had eaten. Ada was thrilled with the effect and had added it to the assortment of salads and baked dishes with no small amount of pleasure. It was, she thought, one of the most ghastly things she had ever seen at a potluck.

Bess, however, was thrilled with it. She had exclaimed over it for several minutes, assuring Ada that it was one of the cleverest things she'd ever seen and demanding to be told how it had been done. "Those cherries look just like little bugs!" she cried, shaking with laughter.

Daniel had quickly abandoned Ada for the fire pit, where he and the other men were helping A.J. with the all-important cooking of the meat. It never ceased to amaze Ada that men who couldn't be counted on to boil water or fend for themselves with a refrigerator full of food at their disposal could suddenly transform into master chefs at the merest whiff of lighter fluid. But she didn't mind, especially if it meant she got to sit with a drink and wait for dinner to be ready.

But now she was annoyed. Bess had broken the husbands-only-at-the-pit rule. While Ada and the other ladies sat a respectable distance from the smoke, Bess was right there in the middle of the men, laughing at their jokes and drinking beer straight from the bottle. Once or twice she'd even pushed the cook aside to take over grill duty, and no one seemed to mind.

"I don't know what A.J. sees in her," Ada said. "Rebecca would roll over in her grave if she saw this."

"Are you sure you're not just sore because Daniel dated her before he dated you?" asked Olivia Peabody, who was seated to Ada's right and, like most of the women present, had attended the same high school as Ada and Dan.

There were several muted laughs, which Ada ignored. "I'd forgotten all about that," she said. "Did he really go with her?"

"Oh, you know he did," said Anne Wiley who, Ada now recalled, she had never really liked. "Don't you remember how mad you got when Daniel told you that he couldn't give you his class ring to wear because he'd lost it, but then it turned out he'd given it to Bess when they were going out and was too shy to ask for it back?"

"She did give it back, though," Evelyn said. "I remember. It was right before prom. She gave it back and Daniel gave it to you, but you refused to wear it because Bess had."

Ada nodded. The story was true; she *had* refused to wear the ring. She'd even broken up with Dan over it, for about forty-eight hours, forgiving him just in time for him to take her to the spring formal. But she never had worn the ring, and she'd never asked him what he'd done with it. She supposed it was in a box somewhere along with his letterman jacket and his various awards.

"You can't still be mad at her over *that*," said Anne. "Heavens, that was more than twenty years ago. You got Daniel. What more do you want?"

"Oh, I'm just teasing," Ada said, laughing a little too loudly. "I'm *glad* she and A.J. are getting married."

And she really was glad, but not because she was happy that A.J. and Bess had found one another. She didn't for one second believe that Bess could replace A.J.'s late wife in any way. Rebecca had been a wonderful woman, beautiful and kind and full of life. That she had died so suddenly and so horribly—murdered by an intruder—was unforgivable. Ada loved her daughter, Nancy, almost as much as she did her own children. Although Dan disapproved, she was happy that Nancy and James were dating.

Then Bess had returned to Cold Falls, after leaving it nearly twenty years before, claiming to have landed a modeling contract in New York. No one had heard from—or of—her since, and Ada had almost forgotten about her. Then one day she had run into Bess at the supermarket. It had taken a moment for her to remember the striking woman appraising the melons, but when Bess had turned to her and smiled, Ada had recognized her instantly. She'd greeted Bess coolly but Bess, seeming not to notice Ada's lack of enthusiasm over their meeting, had acted as if they were old friends. Ada had listened politely as Bess filled her in on her life over the past two decades: only minor success as a model, a marriage to a handsome man with a gambling problem, a foray into nursing, a divorce, and now a return to the city of her childhood.

And then there was Nate. Nate, who if he resembled his father at all confirmed Bess's claims regarding the man's beauty. Tall and dark, he was as quiet as Bess was loud, as if somehow—thankfully, Ada thought—the father's genetics had battled Bess's and won. Ada liked him immediately and forgave him his parentage because he seemed equally as embarrassed by his mother as Ada was. For his sake she had invited the two of them to dinner, hoping that Nate and James—who were about the same age—might become friends.

Regrettably, that had not happened. The boys simply had very little in common, and after a few perfunctory remarks about music and video games they had lapsed into typical teenage silence. Daniel and Bess, however, had chatted endlessly. Ada had endured it, with steadily mounting irritation, until finally she'd reminded Dan that he had to be at the station early the next morning.

They'd had words that evening, with Ada accusing Dan of making her uncomfortable with all of his talk about high school. He, predictably, had been bewildered, asking her why she had invited Bess over in the first place if she didn't want to be reminded of those years. Unreasonably, she had refused to discuss the situation any further, which only made Dan more confused and her more angry. They'd gone to bed not speaking, the first time in their entire marriage that they'd done so, although in the morning Ada had pretended that nothing was wrong, and Dan had, certainly with no small amount of relief, gone along with it.

It wasn't long after that that Bess and A.J. had begun dating. At first Ada had hoped that it was just a distraction on A.J.'s part. He hadn't dated since Rebecca's death. He blamed himself for not having been there when the house was broken into, but the truth was that he had probably saved both his own and his daughter's lives. He'd been chaperoning Nancy's class trip to Hershey Park when the break-in occurred, and although his presence in the house may have scared away the intruders, it was more likely that he and his daughter would have died along with his wife. Rebecca had been killed by a shotgun blast to the head while she slept, and the house had been emptied of cash, jewelry, and things that could be sold for quick money. It was most likely the work of drug addicts looking for a quick score, and Rebecca had been a casualty rather than a target.

Why it should be Bess who had shaken A.J. from his depression was something Ada could not understand. Perhaps it was because she reminded him of a happier time in his life. Perhaps, because she was the opposite of Rebecca, A.J. could be with her without feeling like he was making love to a ghost. Or, she supposed, he might really love her, although she found this difficult to believe.

At any rate, they were getting married. They'd set a date in October. Daniel was to be the best man. Ada, to her relief, was not asked to stand up beside Bess. That honor was going to Bess's sister, Louise, who had also left Cold Falls many years before and was now living somewhere in Minnesota. She was a few years younger than Bess, and Ada did not remember her at all.

"Come on, girls. We've got some hot, juicy meat for all of you."

Ada looked up to see Bess standing over her, tongs in hand. She snapped them together—*clack, clack, clack*—and laughed. "Up and at 'em, Ada. I've saved you a good one."

Ada swung her legs over the side of the chaise and stood up. She reluctantly followed the other women over to the barbeque, where Bess was now handing out chicken and hot dogs and hamburgers, loudly exhorting everyone to eat as much as possible. When she turned to Ada with a piece of chicken held in the tongs, Ada shook her head. "That's too much for me," she objected.

Bess instead dropped the chicken onto Dan's plate. "Here you go, Danny," she said. "I know you can handle it. You always were a breast man."

Dan laughed, and Ada stared at him, disgusted. Without waiting for Bess to offer her something else, she stormed over to the picnic table and began heaping a plate with macaroni salad, baked beans, and chips. Dan, coming up behind her, glanced at the plate and asked, "Aren't you having a hamburger or something?"

Ada snorted. "I've had enough 'something' to last me the rest of the night," she said. "But you apparently haven't."

"Whoa," Dan said, touching her arm. "What's going on here?"

She pulled away from him. "That woman is what's going on here," Ada replied. "That loud, vile woman you all seem to think is so fascinating."

"Bess?" said Daniel. "You're upset about Bess?"

"I'm not upset," Ada told him. "I just don't like her."

"This isn't about high school, is it?" her husband asked. "Because that would just be ridiculous."

"No, it isn't about high school," said Ada. "But even if it were, why would that be ridiculous?"

"How about because it was a million years ago?" Dan suggested. "And you and I have been married for what, eighteen years?"

"Nineteen," Ada corrected him.

Dan shook his head. "What is it with women," he said. "You can't let go of anything."

Ada, who was scooping ambrosia onto her plate, set the spoon down. "What exactly should I be letting go of?" she asked.

"You're jealous," said Dan. "Plain and simple."

"Of Bess Kunkel?" Ada said. "You think I'm *jealous* of Bess Kunkel?"

Dan, apparently not sensing the dangerous territory into which he had just wandered, nodded. "You always have been. Ever since that business with the ring." He picked up a chip and put it in his mouth. "It's okay. I get it. I mean, look at her."

Ada felt her hands shaking. She set her plate on the table and stepped back. "If for one second you think that I am jealous of that tramp, then you don't know me at all, Dan McCloud."

Dan looked at her, clearly shocked. He said nothing as Ada continued.

"And if you think *that* is something worth going after, then be my guest. Apparently you haven't gotten over her after all."

She realized that several people had overheard the conversation, but she didn't care. *Let them hear,* she thought. *Better yet, let them talk.* She knew they would, and she hoped Bess would be humiliated. But secretly she feared that *she* was the one who would be humiliated. When Olivia, or Anne, or even Evelyn heard what she'd said to Dan, the rumors would start. "Did you hear? Ada thinks something is going on between Dan and Bess!" She could hear it now, the whispers and the giggling, the stares and the exchange of knowing looks.

Maybe, she thought, she had made a grave error in being so open about her hostility toward Bess. She should have kept the matter private between her and Dan. Instead, she'd broken the cardinal rule of domestic life and aired her laundry in public. True, not many people had heard, but enough had that what little spark she'd ignited would soon grow and spread.

Dan was looking at her strangely, as if he'd never seen her before. She didn't like the look in his eyes, which were filled with both hurt and anger. Suddenly she wanted to be at home, where it was safe. She couldn't stand the idea that she was being looked at, that she was being judged. She felt vulnerable, and frightened, and she didn't like what she had become. All because of Bess.

"I'm not feeling well," she said. "I think I should just go." She turned and saw Anne looking at her. "My stomach," she said vaguely. "Don't worry. I'll be fine."

She stumbled away from the picnic tables, away from the fire and the laughter and her husband. She waited for Dan to follow her, but he remained where he was, watching her run into the darkness. And as she ran she heard the sound of Bess's voice, laughing as if she'd just heard the greatest joke in all the world.

CHAPTER 13

1991

James pulled his car into the station parking lot and parked in a space at the far end. It was a habit from when his father had been sheriff; you left the spaces nearest the door for the officers. It surprised him that all these years later he still instinctively followed that unwritten rule.

The station itself had changed little. The cinderblock walls had been painted a light blue instead of the gray that James remembered, but otherwise it looked the same. He pushed open the front door and went inside. Again, it looked much as it had in his father's day. A few new pictures had been added to the Wall of Honor, but the counter in the reception area was still worn yellow and the air smelled like a combination of lemon polish and leather. Or something like that. James had never been able to accurately describe the odor, but the moment it hit his nose he remembered it clearly.

He started to walk down the hall to where he knew Nate's office was, but he was stopped by a young woman wearing a brown uniform. "I'm sorry," she said. "You can't go back there."

"It's okay, Gwen." Nate emerged from his office and waved James toward him. "Come in," he said.

As James had expected, the office was the one his father had occupied. It still held the same desk, and the same battered file cabinet stood in the corner beneath the window, with what very well could have been the same dead plant in a pot sitting on it. Nate took a seat behind the desk.

"This is weird," James said.

"What?" Nate asked. Then he nodded. "I forgot. You haven't been here since your dad died."

"No," said James. "I think Celeste was the one who cleaned out his stuff. Mom couldn't do it, and Billy and I didn't want to. We were kind of assholes about the whole thing."

"It was hard for everyone," Nate said.

"And now here you are," said James. "Who would have thought?"

Nate grinned. "Not me," he said. "I was all set to get the hell out of this shithole once I graduated. I had big plans. I was going to go to California and be a rock star."

"So what happened?" James asked him. "Why'd you stay?"

"Well, your sister for one thing," said Nate. "Other than that, I really can't say."

"I guess some places you just can't get away from," James remarked.

"You did, though," said Nate.

James nodded. "So far," he agreed. "But here it is, sucking me back in."

"Sounds like you're doing pretty well for yourself," said Nate. "Celeste says you're working for a senator now."

"Just a state one," James replied. "It's not Washington, DC, but it's a step in the right direction."

"All that stuff is too complicated for a boy like me," said Nate. "I leave that to you college guys."

James didn't respond. He had the feeling that Nate was mocking him, but he didn't take the bait. For one thing, he'd promised Celeste that he wouldn't. For another, it wouldn't do him any good. He needed Nate.

"So what's happening with Dad?" he asked. "Anything to go on?"

Nate shook his head. "Nothing firm yet," he said. "But we're working on it."

"What are your thoughts about it?" James said, hoping to draw Nate into conversation.

"Don't really have any as of yet," his brother-in-law replied. "I was hoping you might have some."

"Me?" James said. "No, I don't. I mean I assume you've already run a list of the people Dad helped put away. But that's got to be a couple hundred. I guess then you'd try to narrow it down by cross-referencing it with the threat file. I assume they still have that?"

Nate nodded. "It's still around," he said.

"Anything helpful in it?" asked James.

"Just the usual 'you'd better watch your ass' letters," Nate answered. "We don't get as many now that every scumbag on the planet has access to e-mail. But at least we can trace those more easily. Most of them have AOL addresses. I don't know why."

"Did any of the letters you *do* have give you anything?" said James.

"There were three that I pulled," Nate told him. "Two were written by guys who were already back in prison at the time Dan disappeared. The third one wasn't signed, so we don't know who wrote it. So I guess that would be another big no."

James leaned back in his chair. "That's not much to go on," he remarked.

"I'm sorry to disappoint you," Nate said.

James looked at him. "I'm not slamming you or your people," he said. "I'm just saying it's frustrating."

Nate said nothing. Instead, he tapped his fingers on the desktop for a moment, as if trying to decide what to do. Finally he said, "Have you heard anything from Nancy?"

James, shocked, said, "Nancy? No. Not for years. I didn't think anyone had."

"We haven't," said Nate. "I just thought maybe she would have contacted you."

"I don't know why you'd think that," James said. "I mean, you're her brother. If she was going to contact anyone, I would think it would be you."

"Half brother," Nate reminded him.

"She hasn't even contacted her father?" James asked.

"Not that I know of," said Nate. "But she always was a weird one."

James bristled at the comment. He wanted to contradict Nate and say that Nancy had been anything but weird. But Nate was sort of right. Nancy had begun to act strangely. *Right around the time she broke up with me for good,* he thought. It was something he had never understood, then or now. Apparently, Nate wasn't able to tell him anything he didn't already know.

"So what happens next?" he asked.

"I'm working on a few things," said Nate. "Right now I'd like to keep them to myself, if you don't mind. It's nothing personal—I just don't want anything to get out that might jeopardize the investigation."

"Who would I tell?" James asked, incredulous. He couldn't believe his brother-in-law would think he might reveal information to anyone.

"I'm not saying you would," said Nate. "At least not on purpose. But you know how it is—someone accidentally mentions something to someone, who mentions it to someone else. It's best just not to say anything for now."

"Jesus Christ," James muttered, shaking his head.

"Hey, I'm just doing my job," said Nate. "Your dad would have done it the same way."

No, James thought. *My father would have had answers by now.*

He told himself to calm down. There was nothing to gain by getting into something with Nate. It would just upset Celeste and make it more difficult to get information when Nate did have something. Still, he was reminded why the two of them had never gotten along particularly well. Nate had been stubborn back in high school. He simply hadn't changed. *Not that you have either,* he reminded himself.

"Okay," he said, standing up. "Well, let me know what I can do to help. I'll be at the house."

Nate stood as well. "Will do," he said. "Thanks for coming in."

James left the office. Nate didn't follow. As he was walking down the corridor, James heard someone call his name. He turned to see a tall, rather heavy, balding man walking toward him.

"Frank!" he said, delighted to see the deputy.

Frank reached him and, without hesitating, gave James a bear hug. Laughing, James clapped Frank on the back. "It's good to see you," he said as Frank released him.

"You too," said Frank. Then he looked solemn. "I'm really sorry about your dad," he said.

"Me too," said James. Frank Despirito had been his father's right-hand man when he was sheriff. James had always liked him. "So," he said, unable to resist. "How do you like the new boss?"

Frank grinned. "He's not your dad," he said.

James suppressed a laugh. Then a thought came to him. "Hey, you have time for a cup of coffee?" he asked.

Frank nodded. "Do cops like donuts?" he responded. It was a line Dan McCloud had coined to express agreement, and hearing it again made James feel at home in the station for the first time since he'd walked through the doors.

The two men left the building and walked the two blocks to the

Over Easy, a diner popular with the town's heavily blue-collar popula-
tion. At a little after nine in the morning it was fairly empty, the regular
customers having long since left to begin work. James and Frank settled into a booth near the front window.

"Morning, boys," said the waitress.

"June," James said. "You're still here?"

"Where the hell else have I got to go?" the woman replied. Easily
70, she had gray hair cut short, and her blue eyes sparkled. Her mouth
moved from side to side as she chewed on some gum, and the lipstick
she wore was a garish shade of pink. "How are you, sweetie? It's been
a few years."

"It has," James agreed. He was amazed that June still looked the
same as she had when he was a kid. She seemed never to age. His father had always joked that it was because inhaling all the grease from
the kitchen had preserved her, like a mummy.

"Sorry about your dad," June said, putting her hand on James's
shoulder. "He was a good guy."

"How'd you hear about—" Frank started to ask.

"People talk," June said, cutting him off as if she'd expected the
question. "I hear things. What'll you fellows have?"

"Just coffee," James said.

"Two," said Frank.

June left to get their coffees. Frank looked at James and shook his
head. "Small town," he said.

"Well, we knew word would get around," said James. "I'm sure everyone working at Nicky's cabin went right home and told their wives."

June returned, carrying two mugs and a pot of coffee. Under her
arm she had a folded-up newspaper. She set the mugs down and handed
James the paper as she poured the coffee. "Front page," she said.

James opened the paper and took in the headline: BODY OF LOCAL
SHERIFF FOUND 8 YEARS AFTER ALLEGED SUICIDE. He scanned the article beneath it, then looked up at Frank, who was watching him. " 'The body
of former Cold Falls sheriff Daniel McCloud was found earlier this
week at the site of a construction project near Pollard Lake. McCloud
disappeared in 1983, and a letter received by his wife, Ada McCloud,
suggested that he had committed suicide following a diagnosis of terminal cancer. With the discovery of his body, which was reportedly
found inside a locked trunk buried at the site, the disappearance has

been reclassified as a murder by current town sheriff Nate Derry, who happens to be McCloud's son-in-law.' "

James put the paper down. "So much for keeping it quiet," he said. "How come he didn't tell us this was going to hit the paper?"

Frank raised one eyebrow. "He doesn't tell us much," he said. "He likes to be the one in charge."

"I noticed," James said.

"How's Ada handling it?" asked Frank.

"Pretty well, considering," James answered. "She was kind of a mess at first. Didn't want to believe it was him. I can't blame her. We all thought this was behind us."

Frank set his mug down. "You know, I never believed that he killed himself," he said.

"Why?" James asked him.

"I don't really know," Frank answered. "Just a feeling." He laughed. "I always hated it when Dan said shit like that. But it always turned out he was right."

"Who do you think did it?" said James, asking the question that had been on his mind since he'd invited Frank to have coffee with him.

"Hell if I know," the deputy said. "We dealt with so many creeps over the years, it could have been any of them." He looked up at James. "Sorry," he apologized. "I don't mean it to sound like this is some John Doe we're talking about."

"It's all right," James said. "I know." He looked out the window as he drank his coffee. As he watched the sidewalk, Nate came around the corner, walking briskly toward the diner.

"Here comes the boss," James informed Frank, who followed his gaze and groaned.

"I guess I should be going," he said, standing up. "It's good to see you, Jimmy. Give my best to your mom."

"I will," James told him. "Thanks, Frank."

He watched Frank leave the diner. Outside, Frank waved to Nate, who stopped to talk to him. He seemed to be excited about something, and moved his hands around as he spoke. James saw Frank glance quickly toward the window, then look away.

What's that about? he wondered. He was tempted to go and ask, but something in Frank's expression seemed to warn him not to. Had Nate learned something new? If so, why didn't he come in and tell

James what it was? His reluctance to include James in the investigation was irritating, but there was nothing James could do about it.

When he looked out the window again, Frank and Nate were gone. They'd left in a hurry, so whatever Nate had wanted to tell Frank must have been important. James was tempted to stop in at the station again when he went for his car. But he knew that was a bad idea. *I'll find out soon enough anyway,* he thought as he drained his cup.

CHAPTER 14

1982

James wished it would rain. It had been blisteringly hot for almost a week, with no breeze to cool things down, and the fan he'd set up in his room did nothing but push the warm air around. The only relief was swimming, which he and Nancy were now doing. They floated, side by side, in the dark water of Pollard Lake. Nancy made him hold her hand, as she was convinced that something living in the lake's depths would rise up to eat her. She and James had watched *Jaws* on cable the night before, which didn't help matters.

Nancy was the one good thing about the summer. Having raised his grades following his father's order not to spend so much time with Nancy, James had been allowed to resume the relationship, although not without a warning: should it become a "problem" (what, exactly, constituted a problem had not been defined) he would have to stop seeing her again. This annoyed him, but he tried not to think about it. They were together again, and that was what was important.

James kicked his legs gently, maintaining a float, and looked up at the sky. It was flat and cloudless and, despite the vivid blue color, not at all soothing. The sun, so bright it hurt his eyes, baked everything it touched. James had already turned a bright pink, and he knew he was heading for a major sunburn. He made a note to apply sunblock when he and Nancy got out.

"I'm getting tired," Nancy said. "Let's swim in."

She let go of his hand and headed for shore. She was a good swimmer, and she moved quickly through the water. Deciding to play a joke, James swam after her. When he had closed the gap to within a few feet, he dived, kicking hard and driving his body down and forward. He rose right beneath Nancy, and as he did he reached up and grabbed one pale white leg.

Nancy screamed and beat at the water with her hands as James's head broke the surface. He caught her hands and pulled her toward him, kissing her lightly on the mouth. "It's just me," he said.

She hit him lightly on the head. "Jerk," she said. "Don't ever do that again."

"Okay," said James. "I'm sorry."

"Promise," Nancy insisted.

"Promise," said James, trying to look sincere.

"You're such a liar," Nancy said. She put her hands on his shoulders and pushed, dunking him under the water. When he came back up she was halfway to the beach.

She was getting out when he caught up with her. As she exited the water, he admired her body, barely covered by the brightly flowered bikini she wore. Where he burned in the sun, Nancy turned a golden brown. Her hair, normally a dark brown, had lightened to a beautiful reddish color that brought out the gold flecks in her chestnut eyes. She was thin, but not too skinny, and had the fit body of the runner she was. Looking at her, James was completely mesmerized. He felt like a clumsy, lumbering dog next to her, and the fact that she wanted to be with him both surprised and delighted him.

Nancy walked up the beach to where they'd spread out their towels. Taking another towel from the large bag she'd packed for the afternoon, she dried her hair and lightly wiped her skin. As James approached, she tossed the towel to him so that he could do the same. Then she removed a bottle of suntan lotion from the bag and popped it open. After squirting some of the creamy liquid into her hand she applied it to her arms, legs, and neck while James watched. He realized to his embarrassment that he was becoming hard, and quickly looked away, concentrating on drying himself off.

"Here," Nancy said, handing him the bottle. "Do my back."

James groaned inwardly as Nancy sat down on one of the towels and turned her back to him. Touching her was not going to help matters any and would almost assuredly make things worse. But he couldn't very well say no, and so he knelt beside her and poured some lotion into his palm. He touched his hand to Nancy's back between her shoulder blades and hurriedly wiped the lotion across her skin.

"Not like that," Nancy complained, turning to look at him. "Really rub it in."

James gritted his teeth and did as she asked. Despite just having emerged from the lake, her skin was warm beneath his fingers, soft and yielding to his touch. He traced the delicate mountain range of her spine, covering as much of her as he dared, stopping only when he reached the edge of her bikini bottom. The skin there was lightly fuzzed, and he longed to touch the valley of her buttocks.

"Thanks," Nancy said, breaking his concentration. "Now I'll do you."

I wish you would, James thought as he handed Nancy the lotion. His mind was swirling with images he couldn't get out of his head, and the straining in his swimsuit was unbearable. He prayed that Nancy wouldn't notice, and he kept his hands in his crotch in an attempt to hide his excitement.

"Oh no you don't," Nancy said, and for a second James thought she had somehow read his mind. Horrified, he started to apologize. But then she continued. "You don't get lotion. You get sunscreen."

She traded one bottle for another, and a moment later James felt something cold squirt on his back. He shivered as goose bumps rose on his skin.

"Sorry," Nancy apologized. "I thought it would be warmer." Her hands massaged James's back, applying the sunscreen. He tried to think about something else—cars, algebraic equations, the order of the planets—anything to keep himself calm. To his horror, he wasn't succeeding.

"That's good," he said, leaning forward and away from Nancy's touch.

"But I didn't get it all," Nancy objected.

"It's okay," said James, picking up a T-shirt and slipping it over his head. "I'll wear this. It'll be fine."

Nancy shook her head but didn't argue. She slipped the sunscreen back into the bag, removed two cans of soda and set one in the sand beside James's towel, and stretched out on her own towel. James continued to sit up, his arms wrapped around his knees, as his erection slowly subsided. When it finally disappeared he lay down on his stomach on his towel, just in case it should happen again.

They were not the only ones on the beach. The unrelenting heat had brought many people to the lake in search of something that would cool them off. The entire expanse of sand was dotted with towels of various shades, most of them occupied by bathers whose bodies glistened with the sticky sheen of sweat mixed with lotion. Most wore sunglasses, and to James it felt as if he were looking into the eyes of a hundred big, pink insects.

"My dad and Bess are going to the movies tonight," Nancy said, popping the top on her Mountain Dew and taking a sip. "Do you want to come over and watch TV?"

"Is Nate going to be there?" James asked.

Bess Kunkel and her son, Nate, were a recent complication in his relationship with Nancy. Well, Bess wasn't, but it was because of her that Nate was. Bess had recently returned to live in Cold Falls after being away for a long time. James wasn't sure how long, but she'd left before he was born, so it was at least fifteen or sixteen years. His parents had gone to school with Bess, and from the way his mother talked about her, she'd kind of been the school slut, although his father said that James's mother just didn't like Bess and that she was really a nice woman.

James didn't really care one way or the other about Bess. Nate was a different story. His mother had invited Mrs. Kunkel and Nate to dinner once, and it was obvious to James that she wanted him and Nate to be friends. He didn't know why, since it was equally obvious that his mother didn't like Mrs. Kunkel. Anyway, he hadn't much liked Nate. They didn't have anything in common, and he found Nate kind of weird. He couldn't say why, but there was something about the kid that creeped him out. He was too quiet, like he was hiding something. After that one dinner he hadn't said more than a few words to Nate, and usually only at school, where they had a couple of classes together.

Then Nancy's dad had started dating Mrs. Kunkel. James was surprised, as Mr. Derry hadn't dated anyone since Nancy's mother had been killed. At first James worried that Nancy would be upset, but to his surprise she seemed happy that her dad was seeing someone. She said it was about time. Plus, she really liked Bess Kunkel. She said Bess was funny and that she made her father laugh.

Nate was another story, at least as far as James was concerned. He didn't like that having Bess in her life meant that Nancy also frequently had Nate in her life. The two families were spending more and more time together, and sometimes when James went over to Nancy's house he found Nate there too.

"No, he won't be there," Nancy said, answering his question. "He doesn't live with us, you know."

"One of these days he might," James said. "You said yourself that your dad really likes Mrs. Kunkel."

Nancy nodded. "He does," she said. "It wouldn't surprise me if they got married." She grinned. "Then Nate would be my stepbrother," she said. "And you would have to like him."

"No, I wouldn't," James snapped, and the smile disappeared from Nancy's face.

"I'm kidding," she said. "Lighten up. But really I don't understand what you have against him."

"I don't know," James admitted. "There's just something about him I don't like."

"Oh, that's a great reason," Nancy teased. "What will you do if *we* get married and he ends up being your brother-in-law."

James grimaced. "Don't even say that," he told her. "And who says we're getting married?"

"Relax," Nancy said. "We can just live in sin. I don't need a ring."

James laughed. "Tell that to my mother," he said. "I'd like to see her expression when you do."

Nancy slapped him on the butt. "Smart-ass," she said. "Seriously, though, you should be nicer to Nate. He's had it pretty rough. You know his dad left them when he was a baby, right?"

"I heard something about that," said James. "Do you know why?"

Nancy shook her head. "I don't think he knows," she answered. "His mother almost never talks about him."

"So why'd she come back here?" James asked.

Nancy sighed. "I guess it's the last place she felt at home," she said. "She knows a lot of people here."

"That's exactly why I want to *leave*," said James.

"As long as you take me with you," Nancy told him. "I'm not going to hang around here and work at the Stop & Save for the rest of my life."

James reached out and took her hand. "I'll save you from that," he said.

"My hero," Nancy said, laughing.

Then they lay there in silence, just holding hands. The sun traveled across the sky enough that it wasn't directly over them, and the heat abated somewhat. James closed his eyes and thought about what he and Nancy had just said to one another. He knew she was kidding about the whole getting married thing. So was he. But what if they *did* end up together? It wasn't such a ridiculous idea. They were too young now, of course, but what about in a couple of years, after they'd graduated from high school? His parents had been married around that age. Lots of people were.

He tried to imagine himself married. What would it be like? He saw himself standing in a church beside Nancy. She had on a pretty white dress, and he was holding her hand, just as he was at that moment in real life. A minister was saying something, but James didn't hear the words because he was looking at Nancy's face. Then, abruptly, he pictured the two of them in bed. They were naked, and kissing. He was touching Nancy's breast, and she had her hand between his legs.

He felt himself stiffening again and tried to block the image from his mind. He and Nancy had never done anything like that. Not that he hadn't *thought* about it. He thought about it a lot. He'd spent many nights thinking about it while he jerked himself off. But so far all he and Nancy had done was kiss. They hadn't even talked about doing anything else. *Maybe we should,* he thought.

But what if he wasn't good at it? What if, when the time came, he didn't know what to do? He'd seen a couple of porn magazines (his friend Jack Samuelson had stolen some *Hustler*s from his dad's collection, and he and James had looked at them), but he still wasn't quite sure how to do it *right.* He wanted it to be good. And it wasn't like he could ask his dad about it. "Hey, Dad. I want to do it with your best friend's daughter. Got any advice?" He chuckled at the idea.

"What's so funny?" Nancy asked.

He'd forgotten that she was right there next to him. Suddenly he was ashamed of his thoughts. "I was just thinking about a joke Jack told me the other day," he said. "But it's not that funny."

"Tell me," Nancy said.

Shit, James thought. Now he had to think of a joke. But he couldn't remember a single one. He racked his brain, trying to come up with something.

"Okay," he said. "What do you call a boomerang that doesn't come back?" It was the only joke he could remember, and it was one he'd learned when he was maybe four or five, from his grandfather.

"I don't know," Nancy said after a few moments. "What?"

"A stick."

Nancy groaned. "*That's* what you were laughing about?"

"Hey," James objected. "It's a classic."

A moment later, the sky suddenly darkened. James turned over and looked to see big, dark clouds rolling over the lake. A cool breeze swept across the water, rippling it, and then a low grumbling of thunder rang out. All across the beach people stood up, gathering their things and calling to children who were still splashing in the lake.

"Look," said Nancy as she folded her towel and stuffed it into the bag, "your joke was so bad even God is groaning."

James helped her pick everything up. Then they ran toward the shelter of the closed-in area where the picnic tables were, reaching it just as the rain began to pour down. It hit the corrugated metal roof, drumming loudly over their heads.

"Now what?" Nancy asked.

"Celeste isn't supposed to be here until four," James told her. Because he wasn't yet old enough to drive by himself, he still depended on his sister or his parents to take him places. It was annoying, and made him feel like a kid, but there wasn't anything he could do about it until his sixteenth birthday arrived in a couple of months.

"We could walk," Nancy suggested.

"In this?" said James. "We'd freeze." As much as he'd been wishing for rain, now that it was here he felt almost too cold.

"Maybe there's someone who could give us a ride," Nancy said. "Let's look in the parking lot."

It was a good suggestion, and James agreed. Darting through the rain, they scanned the lot. As they were looking, they heard a horn honking. A car emerged from the rain and stopped in front of them. The window rolled down and Nate stuck his head out. "Hey!" he called. "Get in."

James hesitated, but Nancy took his hand and pulled him toward the car. She opened the front passenger side door and got in, while James got into the back.

"Thanks," Nancy said to Nate.

"No problem," he replied. He didn't look back at James.

As Nate pulled out of the lot, James asked, "What are you doing out here anyway?"

"Oh, you know," Nate answered. "Just driving around."

James didn't respond. He found it more than a little weird that Nate had shown up at the beach. He wasn't a beach kind of guy. *It's almost like he was following us,* he thought. *Like he was waiting.*

"I'm just glad you were there," said Nancy. "James and I owe you one. Big time. Right, James?"

"Right," James said dutifully. He looked up and saw that Nate was staring at him in the rearview mirror. He had an unreadable expression on his face, a mixture of what seemed to James to be hatred and triumph. It made his skin crawl, and he looked away.

"Right," he repeated. "We sure do."

CHAPTER 15

1991

Billy removed the white plastic cap from the bottle and looked inside. He'd already checked it three times, but he kept hoping there might somehow be a pill he'd overlooked in the bottom. He turned the bottle over and tapped it on his palm, then tossed it onto the floor, where it rolled under the coffee table.

He wondered what had happened to all the Valium. He couldn't have taken all of them already, could he? He'd just gotten the prescription filled a week or so ago. At least that's what he remembered. Maybe it had been longer.

He took a sip from the can of beer in his hand. It was almost empty. He drained it and went to the kitchen in search of another one. Opening the refrigerator he looked inside. Good. There were four beers left. They would get him through the night if he spaced them out. Still, he really wanted something heavier.

The phone rang, and he thought about answering it but didn't. After four rings his machine came on. "This is Billy. Leave a message," he said along with his voice on the machine. "Maybe I'll call you back," he added. "But probably not."

"Billy, it's Celeste. Again." His sister's voice was sharp. She was mad. But wasn't she always mad when it came to him? It seemed to him she'd been mad at him since, oh, about 1985.

"Look," Celeste continued, "you really need to call me back. James is here, and we need to talk about Dad. Call me, okay?"

She hung up. Billy took one of the beers from the refrigerator and returned to the living room. He went to the machine and deleted Celeste's message, just as he'd deleted the previous three she'd left in the past twenty-four hours. He would call her back tomorrow, he thought. Maybe. If he felt like it. Really, he didn't care if he saw James. They had nothing to say to one another.

As for the thing with his father, he didn't know how to feel. It was weird, that was for sure. Other than that, he didn't know what anyone expected from him. James and Celeste could handle things. *I'd just be in the way,* he thought. *I'm better off staying here.* Although he did feel a little bad about not talking to his mother. He knew it must be hard on her.

He popped open the beer and downed a third of it in one long gulp. Why hadn't he asked Red for some more crystal the other night? He thought about calling him, but he didn't have enough money anyway. He could always make a trade again, but he didn't want Red to get tired of him. After too many times, they always moved on. He'd learned that lesson the hard way.

He turned on the television. He didn't care what was playing; he just liked the noise. He could never really get into a show anyway. His attention wandered, and by the time the episode ended he couldn't remember what had happened at the beginning. But sometimes he could watch the sitcoms. He didn't have to pay attention to those, and mostly he got the jokes.

The one on right now was one he'd seen before. He recognized the main character, even though he couldn't remember the guy's name. He'd been in something else—a movie. What was it? Something about a little girl and ghosts. No, not ghosts. *Poltergeist.* That was it. The little girl with the white hair. There had been a midget in it too, at least she looked like a midget. James and Celeste had taken him to see it, about a year before their dad disappeared.

Before he was murdered, Billy corrected himself. *Before someone killed him.*

Anyway, the guy from the sitcom had been in that movie. He played the father. Billy thought he was kind of hot: big, hairy, a regular guy. That's what he liked, regular guys. Too bad the ones he found either just wanted to fool around on their wives or were only interested in one-nighters.

He finished the beer while watching the rest of the show. He hadn't a clue as to what was going on, but the hairy guy had taken his shirt off in one scene, and that had done it for him. Now a new show had come on, and he couldn't follow it. He flipped around the channels for a while, but there was nothing on that he wanted to see. He wished he could afford cable, but he'd had it disconnected a few months ago. The money he saved bought him a couple of bags of weed, which he thought was a much more useful way to spend his money.

Thinking about weed, he decided to smoke a little. That would bring him down some. Not as much as a couple of Valium would, but enough that he could maybe sleep. He actually had to work in the morning, and he couldn't afford to be late again. His job at the comic store paid shit, but it was enough for him to have his own place (well, with the help of his mother, who always slipped him a couple of twenties when he visited), and mostly his boss didn't care if he was stoned some of the time. But he *did* mind if Billy was late, and he'd already been late two or three times this month.

He got up and went into his bedroom. Kneeling on the floor, he looked under the bed for the shoe box he kept there. He found it and brought it out. Removing the lid, he riffled through the contents. It contained odds and ends: creased and dirty bills, several condoms, a plastic Wonder Woman figurine, the passport he'd gotten for a never-taken trip to Paris, a half dozen scraps of paper with names and phone numbers scrawled on them. The bag of weed he could have sworn was there just a few days ago was nowhere to be found. He did find one loose joint, crushed and wizened as a mummy, which he removed.

He was putting the lid back on the box when he saw the photograph. It was buried under a pile of buffalo nickels (his grandfather had given them to him when he was seven), only a corner of it visible. Billy swept aside the coins and pulled it free. *Where did you come from?* he wondered. He hadn't seen the photo in years, had assumed that he'd thrown it out or lost it as he'd thrown away and lost so many other things.

He sat down on the floor, the box beside him. Straightening out the joint, he lit it with the lighter on his bedside table and inhaled. The weed *was* old, but it was better than nothing. He held the smoke in his lungs for as long as possible, then exhaled. After another two tokes the familiar comfortable floaty feeling began to creep over him. Only then did he pick the picture up again and look at it more closely.

In the photo a young man stood in front of a car. It was a Mustang, probably 1974 or '75. The body was cherry red, the top red and white.

The young man was tall and ruggedly handsome, with sandy brown hair, a mustache, and goatee. He was wearing a plain white T-shirt and faded jeans, and the arms crossed across his chest were well muscled.

It was actually only half of a photo. It had been torn down the middle, and the right side had a jagged edge that stopped just shy of the man's body. He and the front end of the car were intact, but the back end was missing. Billy flipped the picture over. On the back, written in blue ink, was "Paul, summer 1982." The writing was not his, but he recognized it. It was his sister's.

"Paul," Billy said, taking another hit from the joint. "How you doing, buddy?"

He held the photo close to his face and looked at Paul. On Paul's face was a confident smirk, as if he knew the person taking the photo found him terribly attractive. Which was true. Billy remembered vividly holding Celeste's Kodak Ektralite and looking through the viewfinder at her and Paul. He'd been so nervous, afraid of screwing up the shot, that he'd made them stand there while he took shot after shot. Paul had finally gotten fed up with him and taken the camera away. When the pictures came back from the drugstore, Billy had waited until Celeste was out for the night and stolen one from the packet. He'd ripped it to remove her from the photo.

Paul Lunardi. Billy hadn't thought about him in some time. He returned the picture to the box and replaced the lid before sliding it back under the bed. He took one last puff on the joint and crushed it out in the ashtray that was already overflowing with cigarette butts. Then he returned to the living room, drained the remaining beer from the can he'd left there, and sat down on the couch. He turned the TV off. The noise, normally comforting, was suddenly irritating. He wanted some quiet for a change.

He heard voices outside and went to the window to see what was going on. Living above a liquor store, he often witnessed fights between the drunks who came in search of late-night refreshment. There was also the occasional illicit transaction—sexual or otherwise—that he watched from above, unseen by the participants. But mostly he just overheard the conversations of passersby or people who happened to stop on the corner while waiting for the light to change.

This time the voices belonged to two young men. They were both handsome, probably in their early twenties. They stood with their hands in their pockets, waiting to cross to the other side of the street and talking in loud voices, the way people did who didn't know they were being observed.

"Dude, that girl was fucking *hot,*" one said to the other. "You totally should have nailed her."

The other laughed. "Nah," he said. "She talked too much."

"So what?" the other replied. "Once you have your dick in her mouth she'll shut up."

The light changed and the two of them crossed Larson Street, most likely heading to the bars that catered to the town's younger crowd, many of whom came from the nearby college. Billy watched them go, envious of their carelessness. He was the same age, yet he felt decades older. He couldn't remember the last time he'd gone somewhere with the anticipation of having a good time. For him it was all about killing time, passing the minutes and hours and days as painlessly as possible.

He thought again of Paul Lunardi but pushed the image of Paul's face from his thoughts. Thinking about Paul would get him nowhere. Still, it was strange that he'd found the photo now, particularly after the events of the past few days. "Everything happens for a reason," he said. He laughed, picturing his mother saying it as she often did whenever she heard someone complaining. It was her answer to the difficulties of life, he supposed. Blame God. Or whomever.

His laugh turned into a cough, and he found himself doubled over as he tried to breathe. He struck himself in the chest, hard, several times and the coughing stopped. He brought up a wad of something thick and sticky, which he spit into one of the empty beer cans. He'd been having a lot of coughing fits lately, and he hoped it wasn't something that would require a visit to the doctor. Visits to the doctor always ended up being far more complicated than he wanted them to be, especially when every doctor in town knew your family and knew not to give you certain prescriptions you might ask them for. Fortunately, there were other ways to get them, but they ended up costing a lot more.

He looked at the clock. It was after midnight. He had to be at the store by ten, but he knew that he wouldn't even begin to get tired until around three or four. Despite the alcohol and THC coursing through his veins, he was still too wired to sleep. Not that sleeping ever made him feel any better. He usually woke up more exhausted than he'd been when he went to bed.

He went to the kitchen and got another beer. On the way back to the couch he picked up a comic book he had left on the kitchen table. It was the first installment of a three-part Batman story. Although all twenty copies the store got had been pre-sold, Billy had kept one for himself, enraging the twentieth customer to come in and claim his copy. He'd pacified the kid with a hard-to-find Spectre book, which he'd later informed his boss had been shoplifted during a particularly busy after-school rush.

He stretched out on the couch and opened the comic. He was careful not to smudge the ink, using his shirt to wipe his hands of any moisture from the beer can and holding the crisp pages by their outer edges. His care came not from any concern he had about returning it to the store in pristine condition (he had no intention of giving it back) but purely from love. He had always adored comic books, ever since discovering his father's collection of vintage Batman titles. Since becoming hooked on those, he had dutifully purchased each month's issue, all of which he preserved in plastic sleeves in a series of boxes that were housed on the top shelf of his closet.

He turned to the first page and began reading. Instantly he was lost in the story, which centered around the theft of ancient Indian shaman artifacts. As he read, Billy forgot everything—his family, his problems, his unhappiness. He became once more that five-year-old boy sitting on his bed surrounded by stacks of comics yet to be read. Everything was possible, and the creatures of his nightmares could be banished by a hero in a black cape.

He read slowly, savoring the words and the accompanying art. He made the twenty-two pages last as long as he could. By the time he reached the last one, his eyes were heavy. He closed the book, rested it on his chest, and closed his eyes. Within minutes he was asleep.

CHAPTER 16

1982

The strange smell was getting stronger. Billy sniffed again—it was definitely smoke, but it was also sweet. He hoped the grass wasn't on fire. That would be dangerous, and he didn't know how to put it out. He would have to run and get his father, or James.

He was close to the old barn. He'd been warned by his parents never to play there, but he did anyway. Most of the kids did. The loft was still filled with hay. The older kids had broken some bales open and thrown the hay on the floor in a tall pile. You could jump out of the haymow and into the pile; it wasn't that far, and although the hay dust made Billy sneeze he liked the feeling of falling.

He reached the barn door. It was closed, but he pulled it open easily and looked inside. The sweet smell was really strong, and the air was kind of hazy. He heard noises coming from the loft, and someone giggled.

"Hello?" he called out. "Are you okay?"

"Shit," said a male voice. "Someone's here."

A girl's voice answered. "Relax. It's just some kid."

Billy walked to the wooden ladder that connected the ground floor with the haymow. He climbed up, peering over the edge. A blanket was spread across the floor, and his sister and Paul Lunardi were sitting on it. Paul had his shirt off, and Celeste was pulling her T-shirt over her head. Billy saw a brief flash of her breasts as she yanked the shirt down.

"Billy!" Celeste said. "What the fuck are you doing? You know you're not supposed to come in here."

Billy didn't answer her. He was looking at Paul. He'd never seen him with his shirt off. Paul's chest was covered in hair. A thick trail of it snaked from his belly button down to the waist of his jeans, the zipper of which was open. The head of Paul's dick poked up through the opening. Paul, following Billy's gaze, looked down. Then he looked back up at Billy, grinned, and slowly zipped his jeans up, slipping his hand inside to adjust himself. The outline of his dick was visible through the tight denim.

"Hey," Billy said, his voice cracking despite his attempt to sound cool. "What are you guys doing?"

"Nothing," Celeste said. "Just hanging out."

Paul brought a cigarette to his lips. The tip glowed as he sucked on it, and a moment later Paul blew out a cloud of the sweet-smelling smoke. It drifted through the loft, making Billy cough.

"You want a hit?" Paul asked him, holding out the cigarette.

"Stop it," Celeste said, taking the cigarette from Paul's hand. "He doesn't even know what it is."

"Maybe it's time he found out," said Paul. He crooked his finger at Billy. "Come here," he said. "Give it a try."

Billy climbed the rest of the way into the haymow. He stood up, not sure what he should do. He wanted to go to Paul and sit beside him. But Celeste was glaring at him, and he knew from experience that making her mad usually ended badly for him.

"That's pot," he said. "Right?"

"Smart kid," Paul replied. "You ever try it?"

Billy shook his head. He knew about pot, of course. After all he was almost thirteen. And he knew kids his age that smoked it. But he'd never tried it himself, and this was the first time he'd even smelled it. It actually didn't smell very good, and he couldn't imagine smoking it. He'd tried regular cigarettes a couple of times and had always felt sick afterward.

"Don't give him any, Paul," Celeste warned her boyfriend. "All I need is for him to come home high. My parents would kill me."

"He's not going to narc on us," said Paul. "He's cool. Right Billy?"

"Um . . . yeah," Billy answered. "It's cool, I guess."

Celeste groaned. "Fine," she said. "Whatever. But I swear, Billy, if you say anything to Mom and Dad—or James—I'm going to make your life fucking hell."

"Don't be such a bitch," Paul told Celeste. "You're always giving the kid a hard time."

"Yeah, well, you don't have to live with him," Celeste retorted. "I've gotten into trouble one too many times because of his big mouth."

Paul laughed. "You mean you've gotten into trouble because you don't know how to lie good," he said.

Billy laughed with him, earning him a nasty look from his sister. He liked how Paul teased her. He liked how Paul was standing up for him. He'd never paid much attention to Billy before, but now he was talking to him as if they were good friends. Plus, he was going to let him try pot. That was cool.

"Come on," Paul said. He held the joint out to Billy. "Take a walk on the wild side."

Billy approached him. He reached out and took the joint from Paul. As he did, his fingers touched Paul's, and he felt a weird kind of tingling in his stomach, as though electricity had passed between them. He held the joint the way he would a normal cigarette and brought it to his mouth.

"No, no, no," Paul said, reaching out and stopping him. He took Billy's hand and showed him how to hold the joint between his thumb and forefinger. "Now inhale and try to hold the smoke in your lungs as long as you can," he instructed Billy.

Billy put the end of the joint in his mouth and breathed in. Immediately he started coughing. It tasted terrible. He started to return the joint to Paul, but Paul waved it away. "Try again," he said. "You just have to get used to it."

Hesitantly Billy tried again. This time when the smoke started to burn he forced himself to endure it. He didn't want to look like a baby in front of Paul, and he also wanted to show Celeste that he was as cool as she thought she was. Her accusations had stung him, but now he had a chance to redeem himself and show her up.

When he could no longer stand it, he opened his mouth and let the smoke out. He was surprised that only a little bit exited his mouth.

"Good man," Paul said, clapping his hands. "That was one major toke."

Billy closed his eyes, wondering what he should be feeling. He knew that pot was supposed to make you feel good, but apart from his lungs feeling like they were on fire he felt nothing out of the ordinary.

"Just wait a minute," Paul said, as if he knew just what Billy was thinking. "It'll hit you."

Billy waited. In the meantime he gave the joint back to Paul, who took a hit and handed the joint on to Celeste. Billy watched her inhale. Suddenly, everything started to get a little swimmy, as if the floor were tilting. He laughed.

"There you go!" Paul exclaimed. He reached out and patted Billy's leg. "Now ride it, baby!"

Billy closed his eyes. He felt as if he were floating. It was weird, but also fantastic. He laughed again. Then he felt someone nudging his hand, and he opened his eyes to see Paul handing him the joint again. This time he took it eagerly, and when the smoke filled his lungs he almost enjoyed it.

He wasn't sure how many hits he took from the joint. Time went all funny, and all he knew was that he and Paul were talking and laughing. Paul told a joke—something about a woman whose tits were so big she couldn't see her feet—and to Billy it was the funniest joke he'd ever heard. Even Celeste seemed to be having a good time, although for some reason she seemed to fade away, leaving him alone with Paul. He kept stealing glances at Paul's chest and found himself wanting to touch it. He wondered what it would be like to kiss Paul and feel his mustache against his face.

For Christ's sake, he thought. *What are you, a fucking queer?* He laughed at the idea. He wasn't a fag. He was just stoned. The pot was making him have weird ideas.

He looked over and saw that Paul and Celeste were kissing. Paul was on his back, and Celeste was straddling him. Paul's hands were underneath her shirt, and Billy could see them moving over his sister's back.

His feelings of happiness dimmed a little. He didn't know what to do. Should he leave them alone? It was embarrassing watching his sister make out with her boyfriend, but at the same time he couldn't stop staring at the two of them. Also, he wasn't sure he could stand up. His legs felt like lead, and his head was spinning. He was afraid that if he got up he would just fall over.

All of a sudden Paul turned and looked at him. His eyes fixed on Billy's, and then he winked, as if the two of them were sharing a private joke. "We need to get you a girl, buddy," he said. "There's nothing like fucking when you're high. Is there, baby?" he added, kissing Celeste.

"I wouldn't know," Celeste replied. "I'm still a virgin." She and Paul laughed, and Paul rolled to one side, pushing Celeste off him so that their positions were reversed and he was on top of her.

"I can take care of that," he said, thrusting his crotch against her. "Maybe we can teach little Billy a thing or two."

"Pervert," Celeste said. "Get off me."

Paul did, and Celeste sat up. She started to pick hay from her hair. "Haven't you corrupted my brother enough for one day?" she said, giggling.

"Hey," Paul said, "I might as well take the whole McCloud family with me to hell, right?"

Billy leaned back against a hay bale. Paul was a lot nicer than he'd thought he was. He knew his parents didn't like that Celeste was dating him. He'd heard his father telling his mother that Paul had been arrested a couple of times for getting into fights and doing some other stuff. Stealing, maybe. Billy couldn't remember exactly what it was. Anyway, they didn't want Celeste hanging around him.

And as far as they knew, she wasn't. Paul never came over to the house, and Celeste never talked about him. She even sometimes went on dates with other guys. Billy wondered what Paul thought about that, and if he went on dates with other girls besides Celeste. If he were Celeste, he thought, he wouldn't like that.

"What time is it?" Celeste asked, interrupting his thoughts.

Paul looked at the watch on his wrist. "Almost five," he said.

"Shit," Celeste muttered. "Mom will be making dinner. Billy, come on. We've got to go." She picked her sneakers up and began putting them on.

Billy stood up. The floor tilted under him, and he fell against a hay bale. He laughed. He wasn't sure why it was funny, but it was.

Celeste looked at him and groaned. "I knew this was going to happen," she said. She looked at Paul. "I am so fucked."

"Relax," Paul told her. "He just needs some fresh air. Once he's outside he'll be fine."

Billy laughed again. "I don't think I can go down the ladder," he said.

Paul jumped up. "Then you'll just have to take the elevator," he said.

Before Billy knew what was happening Paul had picked him up and walked to the edge of the haymow. A second later, Billy was falling through space. Then he landed on the pile of hay below and was looking up at Paul's face.

"How was the ride?" Paul called out.

"Great," Billy said. "You should try it."

Paul jumped, spreading his arms and legs so that he was flat on his stomach. Billy watched him plummet toward him. He closed his eyes, anticipating the pain of having Paul fall on top of him. But Paul landed beside him. One arm was across Billy's chest, and Paul's face was burrowed in his neck. Billy felt warm breath on his ear and Paul's beard scratched his shoulder. Then Paul was standing up.

"First floor," Paul said. "Power tools. China. Ladies' lingerie." He reached down and pulled Billy to his feet.

"Nice," Celeste said as she came down the ladder. "First you get him high and then you try to break his neck. You really want to end up in jail, don't you?"

"Hey, it's not such a bad place once you get used to the ass rapings," Paul told her.

Celeste kissed him and handed him his T-shirt. "You're an asshole, you know that?"

Paul nodded. "So I've been told," he said as he got dressed.

The three of them exited the barn. Billy found that Paul was right—the fresh air did help, at least a little. He still felt a little dizzy, but he could walk. He actually felt good. Really good.

"Remember," Celeste said as they walked through the field. "Not a word about this. To *anyone.*"

Paul put his arm around Billy's shoulders. "This is our little secret," he said. "If you play your cards right, we might just do it again too."

Billy nodded. "I'm cool," he said. "Don't worry."

Halfway across the field Paul removed his arm from Billy's shoulders. "This is where I get off," he said. He kissed Celeste one last time. "I'll see you later," he said. He waved at Billy and headed in a diagonal line toward the road. Billy guessed that he had parked his car there so that he wouldn't be seen at their house.

"He's nice," Billy said to Celeste as they continued walking.

"Mostly," Celeste said. "He can be a little fucked up sometimes."

She didn't elaborate, and Billy didn't ask her any more questions.

He was just happy that she was talking to him like he was a normal person and not her kid brother. Something had changed while they were in the haymow. He wasn't the same. He couldn't put his finger on it, but he had a feeling that things were going to be a lot different for him from now on.

CHAPTER 17

1991

"I don't know what to think," Celeste told Nate. She was setting the table for dinner, laying out the silverware while the spaghetti boiled in the pot on the stove. In a separate pot the sauce bubbled, filling the kitchen with the scent of basil and tomatoes.

"She said he never had an affair," Nate responded. "Maybe he didn't."

"Maybe," Celeste agreed, but she sounded uncertain. She counted the place settings. Against her better judgment she'd left yet another message for Billy, inviting him to join them. He'd been AWOL since James's arrival, and although she wasn't thrilled about having him around her kids—at least not in the state he seemed to be in these days—she felt she should at least try, if only for her mother's sake. Despite everything, her mother still believed in her youngest brother. Secretly, though, she hoped he wouldn't come.

"Are you saying you think she's lying?" Nate asked her.

"No," Celeste said quickly. She hesitated. "I mean I don't know. I remember it, Nate. I remember exactly what they said. I guess I could have misunderstood, but I really don't think so."

"It was a long time ago," Nate reminded her. "Sometimes we make things different in our memories."

"Maybe so," said Celeste as she checked the spaghetti and gave the sauce a stir. "But maybe she's the one who's changing history."

"Anything is possible," Nate agreed. "But let me ask you this—do you think your father was the kind of guy who would cheat?"

Celeste removed a loaf of Italian bread from its wrapper and began slicing it into thick rounds. "I want to say no," she told her husband. "But you and I both know that any man can cheat under the right circumstances."

"Or any woman," Nate added.

"No, she was definitely the one who was accusing him," Celeste objected. "I told you, she asked him if there was something going on between him and another woman. Someone he'd apparently known for a long time. I just don't know who."

Nate tapped his fingers on the table. "Why didn't you mention this this morning?" he asked.

Celeste shrugged. "I didn't think of it until I was at Mom's," she lied. She didn't like hiding the truth from Nate, but she had to. If he thought she'd deliberately kept something from him that might influence the investigation, he would be furious. *And he would have every right to be,* she thought. But she had still lied to him, and the truth was that she didn't really know why. Even worse, she suspected that it might be because on some level she'd wondered herself if her mother might have something to do with her father's disappearance. *You've read too many mysteries,* she chided herself. *Or seen too many episodes of* Law and Order.

The sound of children's voices interrupted her thoughts, as Adam and Mary ran into the kitchen. Adam was carrying a toy gun, and Mary was chasing him, squealing. Nate scooped her up in his arms and twirled around, making her screech even more loudly. Adam pointed his gun at them and yelled, "Bang bang! You're dead."

"I wish you wouldn't let him play like that," Celeste said to Nate. "What if he accidentally finds one of your real g-u-n-s someday."

"You spelled guns!" Adam crowed.

Nate grinned at his wife. "So much for using that trick anymore," he said.

Celeste busied herself with putting butter and garlic salt on the bread. She really did hate that Nate let Adam have toy guns. She didn't think her husband would ever be careless enough to leave one of his service revolvers around, but she'd heard too many stories of kids killing themselves like that to not believe it couldn't happen. Her own father had left his guns unattended on numerous occasions, and it was probably due to not a little luck that she and her brothers hadn't killed themselves or someone else.

"All right you two," she said. "Go wash up for supper. Daddy will help you."

Nate took Adam and Mary upstairs while Celeste finished getting everything ready. She drained the pasta into a colander, then returned it to the pot and added the sauce, stirring it together so that the pasta was coated. She put a lid on the pot to keep it warm, then poured drinks—milk for Adam and Mary, iced tea for herself and Nate—and set the glasses at their respective places. There was still one more place empty.

She glanced at the phone, considered giving Billy one more chance to join them, and rejected the idea. He was just too much to deal with right now. She was sort of glad that he'd made himself scarce. With him around she and James would just have one more thing to worry about. Besides, he would be fine. Somehow he always managed.

It was strange the three of them being together again. Although she and Billy lived in the same town she didn't see all that much of him, and James wasn't one to write or call. Unless her mother mentioned them she could sometimes go a week or more without thinking of either of her brothers. Not that she didn't care about them—she did. But they had separate lives now and had become different people. They weren't teenagers anymore, their lives intertwined by virtue of living in the same house. But now they were being drawn together again, and the old dynamics were resurfacing.

Her family came back and took their seats, the kids laughing at some private joke. "Don't tell Mommy!" Mary said, sending Adam and Nate into gales of laughter. Celeste returned fire by putting her hands on her hips and saying, "If you don't tell me, then there's no dinner."

The kids, knowing she was teasing, howled anew. Nate shushed them, then said to Celeste, "Someone only washed *one* of their hands."

"Guess which one!" Adam said excitedly. He waved one of his hands at her. It was pink from being freshly washed. He kept the other in his lap. Mary, however, held up both of her more or less spotless hands.

"I think I know," said Celeste. "And I bet his name begins with A."

"Wrong!" Adam exclaimed, holding up the other hand to reveal that it too had been scrubbed.

"It's Daddy!" Mary yelled, and she and Adam cackled like crazed chickens.

"You said you wouldn't tell," Nate said, frowning.

Celeste dished spaghetti onto the plates, adding salad and garlic bread. When everyone had been served she sat down and they began eating. The kids slurped their spaghetti into their mouths, enjoying the sound and making messes of their clothes. Nate and Celeste employed a less enthusiastic but cleaner approach.

"What did you two do in school today?" Celeste asked Adam and Mary.

"Nothing," said Adam.

"We colored," Mary answered. "And pretended we were zebras."

"Wow," Celeste said. "That sounds exciting."

Mary nodded in agreement. "They have *stripes,*" she said.

Celeste thought about prodding Adam for more information. She knew that "nothing" was his way of describing things he didn't think were worth talking about. It was a trait he shared with his father. Or perhaps with all men, she thought, since she'd met very few that actually answered such questions with anything approaching enthusiasm.

As she watched her family eat, she thought how odd it sometimes felt to her to realize that she was grown up. She was only twenty-six, but she was a wife and mother. When she was around the ages her children were now, she had thought her mother was impossibly old. Her mother had been the same age that Celeste was now, maybe even a little younger. It hadn't occurred to Celeste then that her mother was, well, a person. She was just Mom. Her job was to care for Celeste, her brothers, and their father. Whether she had any dreams of her own was something that never crossed Celeste's mind. Not until much later.

She wondered how her children saw her and Nate. They were too young to really think about it at all, she knew that. And she hoped it would be a while before that changed. Mom and Dad meant safety and love. Once Mom and Dad became people who made mistakes and sometimes acted selfishly, the doubts could creep in. The world became less secure and more dangerous. At least it had for her.

She wanted her children to remain innocent for as long as possible. This thing with her father upset her for many reasons, not the least of which was the worry that it would somehow traumatize Adam and Mary. So far they seemed to view the whole thing as an abstract concept, but what would happen if the investigation uncovered something even more unsavory? She hated to think about it.

When dinner was over, Nate took the kids into the backyard to play while Celeste cleaned up. Looking out the kitchen window she watched them as she washed the dishes. They were chasing fireflies. Nate had found some empty glass jars, and Adam and Mary were running around trying to capture the tiny blinking lights that floated among the flowers. Every so often there would be a joyful cheer as one or the other of them succeeded.

She couldn't imagine life being any different. If Nate or either of her children were taken from her, she didn't know what she would do. They were her heart. She wished James would find someone to give him the same thing. Billy too, although she was pretty sure that would never happen. She had no idea what Billy even wanted from his life. James, though, could definitely have it. She wondered what this girl-friend of his was like. He had yet to bring her home for a visit. *Not that this would be the best time,* she reminded herself. She wondered how much James had even told Charly about what was going on.

She finished the dishes just as the screen door banged open and Adam and Mary burst in with their jars. Adam's held six or seven fire-flies, while Mary's smaller one contained only three. "Look," Adam said. "Daddy says we can use them as night-lights." He shook his jar and the fireflies lit up.

"Okay," Celeste said. "But just for tonight. Tomorrow you have to let them go."

The kids nodded in agreement. "Now upstairs," Celeste said. "It's bedtime. Let's go brush your teeth."

She herded the two of them up the stairs, then monitored them while they got into their pajamas and brushed their teeth. They each had their own room, so she tucked Mary in first, kissing her on the nose and saying, "I love you," then repeating the ritual with Adam in his room next door. Each child had a jar of fireflies on their bedside table, and when Celeste turned off the lights the rooms were lit only by faint greenish gold flickers.

She returned to the kitchen, where she found Nate sitting at the table looking at something he held in his hand. He was turning it over, examining it closely and running his fingers over it.

"What'd you find?" Celeste asked him. "A treasure?"

Nate shrugged. "Maybe," he said. "Do you recognize this?" He held the object out to her, and Celeste saw that it was a ring. She took it from him. It was gold. In the center was a large red stone.

"It's a class ring," she said. She looked at the engraving on it. "From our school. Class of 1984."

"Have you ever seen it before?" Nate asked her.

"Could be," said Celeste. "But there are a lot of Cold Falls High School rings around."

"Not from 1984," Nate replied. "And not with that color stone. What month has a ruby as its birthstone?"

Celeste thought. "July," she said. "I remember that because James's birthday is in July."

"Take a look at the pictures on the ring," said Nate.

Celeste turned the ring around. On one side was a picture of a baseball player; on the other was a panel that said "Debate Club Division 3 Champ."

"Oh my God," Celeste said. "This is James's ring."

"You're sure?" Nate asked.

Celeste nodded. "I remember when he brought it home. He was so proud of it. He never took it off. Then he lost it. He looked everywhere, but he never found it." She looked at Nate, dumbfounded. "Where did you get it? James will be thrilled."

Nate rubbed his head with one hand and sighed. "Maybe not," he said.

Celeste didn't understand. "Why wouldn't he want it back?" she asked.

Nate looked at her, his face stony. "Because we found it inside the trunk your father was buried in," he said.

CHAPTER 18

1982

As James put the milk back in the refrigerator Celeste noticed something on his hand. She looked more closely. "Someone's class ring came today!" she said. "Come on, show it here."

James shut the refrigerator door. "What's the big deal?" he asked. "It's just a ring."

Celeste rolled her eyes. "You know what the big deal is," she told her brother. "For one thing, you don't usually get one until you're a senior. Second, you *did* get one because you're a master debater."

"Ha-ha," said James. "Gee, I haven't heard that joke before."

Celeste grabbed his arm, forcing him to let her look at his ring. "Hey, it's your fault for being the genius in the family," she said. James had recently won a big debate competition. As a reward, their parents had bought him a class ring to commemorate his achievement. Although he was downplaying it, Celeste knew that he was proud of himself.

The ring was beautiful. The centerpiece was a blood red stone. For the two side panels James had chosen to represent his involvement in baseball and debating. Celeste nodded her approval. "Very nice," she said. "When are you going to give it to Nancy?"

"What are you talking about?" said James, pulling his hand away from her.

"Please," Celeste said. "You're going out with her, aren't you?"

James snorted. "Not really," he said. "You know Dad told me I couldn't see her until I get my grades up."

"Yeah," said Celeste. "But you won the competition. That's got to be enough for you to get a get-out-of-jail-free card."

"Apparently not," her brother answered, taking a drink of milk.

"Well, you should give it to her anyway," Celeste told him. "That's what you're supposed to do."

"I don't get that," said James. "You spend all of this money on a ring and then you're supposed to give it to a girl? What the hell is that about?"

"What do you give a woman when you marry her?" Celeste asked.

"A ring," said James. "But come on, this isn't the same thing."

Celeste shrugged. "It sort of is," she told him. "It's a symbol of your love." She made kissy lips at him and batted her eyes. "You do looooove her, don't you?"

James laughed. "About as much as you love Paul Lunardi," he said.

Celeste looked around to see if either of her parents was around. "Shut up," she snapped.

Now it was James who made a kissy face. "What?" he said. "Afraid Dad will take your delinquent boyfriend in for questioning?" He made a stern face. "Son, have you ever broken and entered my daughter's panties? Don't lie to me, boy. I'll know."

"Asshole," Celeste hissed, but she couldn't help laughing.

"Jesus," said James. "Both of us are dating people we're not supposed to see. Now we just need Billy to knock some girl up and we'll officially be white trash."

"I don't think Billy has even figured out he *can* knock someone up," said Celeste. "Have you ever seen him with a girl?"

James shook his head. "No," he said. "And he never talks about them. All he's interested in is his comic books."

"Give him a year or two," Celeste said. "He just hasn't grown up yet."

James was looking at his hand. "You really think I should give this to Nancy?" he asked.

Celeste stood up, taking her empty glass to the sink and rinsing it. "It's up to you," she said. "But if I were your girlfriend I would be expecting it."

"If you were my girlfriend," James replied, "we would most definitely be white trash."

Celeste smacked him lightly on the back of the head as she left the kitchen. She went upstairs to her room and shut the door. Going to her closet she felt beneath the stack of sweaters on the top shelf and pulled out two things that were hidden there. The first was a note-book. The second was a copy of *Playgirl* magazine. She'd gotten it ear-lier in the week from her friend Trish, whose older sister had bought it for her because Trish was too embarrassed to do it. Celeste had yet to look at it.

Lying on her bed, she first opened the *Playgirl.* She skipped imme-diately to the first pictorial, which was of a man with blond hair and a body that looked as if it had been completely waxed. Even the bush between her legs was almost nonexistent. *He looks like a baby,* Celeste thought, although he did have a pretty big dick. Not that she had a lot of experience with those. She'd really only ever seen Paul's. It was big too, or at least she assumed it was. It certainly felt big.

She moved on to the next section. The guy in that one was more to her liking, dark haired and kind of rough looking. In the first pictures he was dressed in a garage mechanic's overalls, the zipper pulled down to show his muscular chest. Then he was shown stepping out of it, his half-hard dick swinging between his legs. Only in the final series of shots was he hard. He lay on his back on the garage floor, his arms behind his head and his cock against his belly.

The pictures excited her. She stood up and removed her jeans, slid-ing them over her hips and stepping out of them. When she got back on the bed she lay on her back and slid her hand inside her panties. She was already wet, and her fingers slid between her legs easily. She found the sweet tender bud hidden among the warm folds and began to massage it while she fantasized about the man in the pictures.

She pictured herself on top of him, riding him slowly while he cupped her ass in his big hands. Paul liked to do that. Sometimes he slapped her butt hard. This always made her tense up for a few sec-onds, and Paul liked that. She did too. He always felt huge inside of her when she squeezed him like that. Sometimes she asked him to spank her and he said no, making her beg him to do it. Then when he finally did do it, she would almost always come.

She wondered what it would be like to make love with Paul and the man in the magazine at the same time. Paul had suggested a three-way once, suggesting they do it with his friend Carl. But Celeste didn't find Carl attractive, and she'd said no. But maybe with someone else she could do it.

She rubbed more quickly, pushing her hips up so that the palm of her hand rubbed against her pussy while she continued to finger herself. In her fantasy the man in the garage was playing with her breasts, teasing her nipples with his fingers. She slid up and down him, moaning as she grew more and more excited.

Then she was moaning in real life as she came, and her pussy tightened around her fingers. Her breath caught in her throat as she arched her back and stiffened, her whole body shaking. The waves rippled down her spine, and for a moment she felt she might explode into a million pieces. Then the sensation subsided, and she lowered her butt to the bed.

She removed her hand, wiping her fingers on her panties. Then she stretched, working a kink out of her leg. She felt sleepy and was tempted to take a nap in the warm afternoon sun that came through her window. But she shook off the desire and instead flipped back onto her stomach and opened the notebook. The first twenty or thirty pages were already filled with line after line of her neat handwriting. She looked at the words, page after page of them, and marveled at the fact that she had written every single one.

It was a novel. Her novel. She'd been working on it a little bit at a time for almost two months. It was a romance. Well, a romance with a lot of sex in it. She didn't like those books where the heroine never got to fuck anyone. She wanted to read a story about a woman who wasn't afraid to get naked with a guy. She and Trish had both read *Endless Love* when it came out a few years before, stealing it from a Waldenbooks because they were too afraid to approach the male cashier with it. Celeste had loved it. There had been some sex in it, those passages making her and Trish giggle with embarrassment but also thrilling them with the descriptions of orgasms and penises and even anal sex.

But even that book didn't have enough sex in it. It was like writers were afraid to admit that people her age—especially girls—had sex. So she had decided to write her own novel, one that was about what it was *really* like to be seventeen and in love. The main character was Susan, a high school junior in a small town. Her boyfriend was Chance, a good-looking boy who seemed like a troublemaker on the outside but who was really sweet once Susan got him to open up.

Susan and Chance had a lot of sex. They did it in the back of his car, in the basement of her parents' house, and in the woods. Chance was Susan's first lover, and he taught her all kinds of things about feeling good. The scenes were very long and very sexy, Celeste thought. She

had let Trish read some of then, and Trish had said that they were better than the ones in Jackie Collins's books.

Celeste tried to imagine what it would be like to be a famous writer.
Did Jackie Collins do all of the things the characters in her books did?
Did she sleep with lots of different men and wear beautiful clothes and
travel all over the world? Celeste imagined that she did. Otherwise
how would she know how to write about those things? Celeste had
tried to write about other places—Paris, for one—but the only thing she
knew about it was that the Eiffel Tower was there. That's when she had
decided to set her book in a town a lot like Cold Falls. It was easier.

She was at the part of her novel where Chance had been arrested
for allegedly setting a house on fire. Susan didn't know if he'd done it
or not, but she loved him and wanted to help him. To do it she would
have to lie and say that she was with him the night of the fire. Her parents hated Chance, and if they found out she was seeing him they
would do anything to make sure she stopped. They had already caught
her with him once and threatened to send her to boarding school if she
saw him again, and she feared that this time they would really do it.
(Celeste had some pretty good ideas for ways Chance could rescue
Susan from the school, but she didn't know enough about boarding
schools to write about them so she was trying to think of something
else.)

Of course Susan had decided to be Chance's alibi. Celeste was writing the scene where she went to the police station to make her statement. Luckily, she had been in several police stations during her life
and she could describe them easily. She just needed to picture one in
her mind and describe it the way she saw it.

She was thinking hard about whether the color of the police station
walls should be white or blue, and whether Susan was wearing red
Converse sneakers or black boots, when someone knocked on her
door. The sound startled her, and she jumped up. She grabbed the *Playgirl* and shoved it under the bed. The notebook she closed and held in
her hand as she went to the door.

"Who is it?" she asked.

"Me," James said. "I want to ask you something."

"Hold on a sec," Celeste told him. "I'm getting dressed." She picked
her jeans up and slid them on, making sure she looked normal. Although there was no way James could know what she'd been doing

over the past hour, part of her was afraid he would know that *something* had been going on.

She checked her hair in the mirror, straightened it a little, then opened the door. "What's up?" she asked her brother.

James came into her room, not giving her a second glance. He turned and looked at her. "Do you really think I should give my ring to Nancy?" he asked.

Celeste could tell by the look on his face that he'd been worrying about the matter. His brow was creased, and he seemed confused. She couldn't believe he was getting so worked up about a stupid ring.

"No," she said. "Don't give it to her. Keep it."

James frowned. "Then she'll think I don't like her enough," he said.

"Very good," Celeste replied. "You've just answered your own question."

James opened his mouth to reply, then shut it again. "That was sneaky," he said. He was smiling now, and Celeste knew that she had helped him make the decision he had wanted to make all along. He'd just needed someone to help him make it.

"You're not the only one who can debate," she said. "Now get out. I have work to do."

James left and she shut the door behind him. Returning to her bed, she sat down, opened the notebook, and began to write.

CHAPTER 19

1991

"Thanks for coming in," Nate said as James sat in the chair opposite his desk. "I know it's late."

"No problem," James told him. "You said you had some leads in the case?"

"Possibly," Nate replied. "You remember I told you that we found Dan's body inside of a trunk?"

James nodded. "Yes," he said. "Did you find something in it that might identify the murderer?"

Nate placed a ring on the desk. "We found this," he said.

James picked the ring up. "This is my class ring," he said. "I lost it. Well, actually, Nancy lost it. I gave it to her."

"Do you have any idea what it was doing in that trunk?" asked Nate.

James shook his head. "Like I said, I—Nancy—lost it. I think she said the chain she was wearing it on broke, but she didn't know when or where it happened."

Nate leaned back in his chair. "So it didn't fall off your finger?"

James looked at him. "What? No. I told you—"

"Nancy lost it," Nate said. "Yeah, I know. But don't you think it's strange that it somehow ended up in the trunk that someone buried your father in?"

James shrugged. "Sure it's strange," he agreed. "But so is that fact that someone killed my father, put him in a trunk, and wrote a fake suicide letter. So far nothing is adding up."

"Well, that's one thing we can agree on," said Nate. "It's just not adding up."

James leaned forward in his chair and placed the ring back on Nate's desk. "Wait a minute. You don't think Nancy had anything to do with my father's death, do you? Because I can tell you she would never do anything like that. Hell, Nate, you know. You lived with her for Christ's sake. Do you think she could do anything even remotely like this?"

"No," Nate said. "I don't think she could. So now we're back where we started—how did that ring get inside that trunk?"

"I don't know," said James. "Maybe somebody found it. I admit that would be a big coincidence."

"Huge," Nate agreed.

"But it's possible," James continued. "Or maybe that spot is where Nancy lost it. We used to walk out there quite a bit and—"

"It was found *inside* the trunk," Nate interrupted. "Again, it would be a mighty big coincidence if she dropped it there, someone came along and decided to bury a trunk with a body in it on the same spot, and somehow before that trunk got buried that ring found its way inside. I don't think even David Copperfield could pull off that trick, do you?"

James didn't like the tone Nate was taking with him. "What do you want me to tell you?" he asked his brother-in-law. "I don't know how that ring got inside the trunk. For one thing, I haven't even seen this trunk."

"I can arrange for that," Nate said.

James shook his head. "All I know is that I gave Nancy that ring, she said she lost it, and that's the end of the story."

"Well, it's the end of *that* story," said Nate. "But it might be the beginning of another one. You see, we found something else inside that trunk."

James said nothing, waiting for Nate to continue. Finally Nate opened a drawer and pulled out a file, which he opened. "Trunk contained a thirty-eight millimeter standard issue Colt revolver," he read. "Serial number matches that of weapon registered to Daniel Adam McCloud."

He shut the folder. "There were two empty chambers in that gun," he informed Nate. "The bullets fired from it were the ones found in your father's body."

"He was killed with his own gun," James said.

"Yes," Nate confirmed. "And since we now know that he didn't commit suicide, that means that someone else used his gun to kill him. Unless you consider the possibility that someone came along after he had already shot himself and decided to bury his body in a trunk. But I think that's highly unlikely, don't you?"

"None of this is making any sense," James said, shaking his head. "My ring. His own gun. What are we talking about here?"

"That's what I've been asking myself all day," said Nate. "And I can only come to one conclusion."

"Which is?" James asked. He was standing up, his hands on his waist, looking at Nate, who seemed slightly anxious, even excited, about something.

"That someone very close to Dan—someone who had access to his guns—decided to kill him," Nate said. "And that someone must have dropped that ring into the trunk when they were putting Dan's body inside of it." He stood up. "But what I still can't figure out," he said, "is why you did it in the first place."

"Why I what?" said James. Then he realized what Nate was saying. "You think *I* killed him?" he said.

"I'm sorry, James," Nate said. "But based on the evidence I've got, you're the prime suspect right now."

"This is insane!" James cried. "You think I murdered my own father? Why the fuck would I do that?"

"Like I said, I don't know," Nate answered. "Maybe you'll tell me. Or maybe," he added, "I'll find out that I'm wrong, in which case I'll offer you my sincere apologies. But right now I have to ask you to come with me."

He stepped toward James, who backed away, turned, and started to leave the room. As he passed through the door he smacked into a deputy who was standing there, apparently posted there for just this reason. The man grabbed James by the arm and spun him around, pushing him against the wall. Seconds later James felt handcuffs snap closed around his wrists.

"Nate, this is crazy," James said as the deputy walked him down the hallway. "You know I didn't do this. You know it!"

"James, I don't know what to think. You're right—this is all crazy. And I hope we get it sorted out so that your mother and the rest of you can get on with your lives."

"I need to call someone," James said angrily. "You know I get to do that."

"Of course I do," Nate said. "But first, let me remind you that you have the right to remain silent. If you choose to speak, anything you say can and will be held against you . . ."

James blocked out the sound of Nate's voice. He was still stunned at the turn of events. He'd come to the station expecting Nate to give him information, not arrest him. Then Nate had blindsided him with the ring and the story about the gun. Now he was being taken to a cell as the suspect in his father's death.

Nate continued with the Miranda warning, informing James of his right to an attorney and so on. When he was finished he said, "Do you understand the rights I have just read to you? And with these rights in mind, do you wish to speak to me?"

"Yes, I understand," James said, his voice cold. "And no, I don't wish to speak to you. I wish to speak to my lawyer."

"I'll be sure you get use of a phone," Nate assured him. "And of course I'll have Celeste phone your mother."

"No," James said. "Don't tell Mom. Tell her anything but that. Tell her . . . tell her . . . tell her I'm staying at your place tonight. I don't know. Just don't tell her about this. Please, Nate. It will kill her."

Nate seemed to think for a long time. "All right," he said. "But she'll have to know tomorrow. There's no way we'll be able to keep this quiet."

"I know," James said. "But just for tonight don't tell her. I'll think of something."

Nate nodded. "Sure," he said. "I'll go arrange for that phone."

He turned and walked away, leaving James alone in the tiny cell. James had been in the cells many times as a kid; his father had let him pretend to be a prisoner. Then it had been fun to imagine that he'd done something awful, committed some crime and been arrested for it. He recalled banging on the cell door and demanding to speak to his lawyer. He'd found that hysterical, especially as he'd known even then that he wanted to *be* a lawyer someday.

Now it wasn't funny at all. This time the door was really locked, and no one was going to come and let him out. His father wasn't there to set things right, and James was being blamed for this fact in the most horrible way possible. But worst of all, when he really allowed himself to be objective about the situation, he couldn't even blame Nate. If what he said was true, then James *was* the logical suspect, and protocol demanded that he be detained. Nate was just doing his job.

But he didn't have to seem so smug about it, he thought. Sure, he had apologized to Nate, but that meant nothing. James was fairly certain that part of Nate had enjoyed making him squirm, and was still enjoying it. After all, wouldn't it be poetic justice if the murderer of former town sheriff Dan McCloud turned out to be his own son, and that son was captured by Dan McCloud's son-in-law, who just happened to be the new sheriff? Christ, it sounded like the plot of a John Grisham novel. *More like Stephen King,* he thought.

He sat down on the narrow bed, which was affixed to one wall. He was a bit surprised to find that he wasn't particularly frightened. Maybe it was because he was sitting in a cell he had played in as a boy. Maybe the reality of the situation hadn't sunk in yet. *Or maybe it's because I didn't do it,* he told himself. Of course that's what pretty much every person in his position said. Suddenly he found himself laughing. The whole thing was completely ridiculous, like a bad episode of any one of the eight thousand law shows that clogged the television networks. When he heard the sound of keys jingling he half expected to look up and see Michael Moriarty or Angela Lansbury standing there, promising to spring him as soon as possible.

Instead it was the deputy who had wrangled him down the hall earlier. This time the man let him out and led him to a small room furnished only with a table and a telephone. "You have ten minutes," he said. "I'll be right outside the door. If you need a phone directory, I can get one for you."

"No," James told him. "I know the number."

The deputy shut the door. James could see him hanging around outside, his large body casting a shadow over the door's glass window. Ignoring him, James picked up the phone and dialed a number. The phone rang three times, and then a voice answered. "Hello?"

"It's me," James said. "I need your help."

CHAPTER 20

1982

"What's the big surprise?"

Nancy looked at James expectantly. They were sitting on the bleachers on the football field behind the school. It was lunch hour, and they had escaped the noise of the cafeteria to enjoy the afternoon sun. It was the first week of October, and the weather was cool but bright. The two of them had just begun their junior year a few weeks before, and although technically they still weren't supposed to be seeing a lot of each other outside of school, they considered themselves boyfriend and girlfriend.

James opened the brown bag lunch he'd brought and pulled out a sandwich. "Surprise?" he said. "What surprise?"

Nancy cocked her head to one side and gave him a look. "You said you had a surprise for me," she said.

"I did?" said James, feigning confusion. He scratched his head. "Are you sure it was me and not one of your other boyfriends?"

"Maybe I should go ask them," Nancy retorted. "I'll see you later."

"Ha-ha," said James. "Okay. I'll tell you." He reached into the pocket of his jacket and pulled something out. "This is for you," he said, handing it to Nancy.

"Your ring!" she exclaimed when she saw what was in his hand. She clapped her hands and wiggled a little. Then she took the ring and slipped it over a finger. It was far too large, but she held her hand up to inspect it anyway.

"I thought you could wrap some yarn around it or something," James suggested.

Nancy shook her head. "I have a better idea," she told him. "I'm going to put it on a chain. That way I can tuck it into my shirt and no one who shouldn't see it will."

"Clever," James said. "I like that in a girl."

Nancy leaned forward and kissed him. James put his hand on her neck and held her there for a long time, letting his tongue slide between her lips. When he did that Nancy pulled back.

"Watch it," she said. "You know I don't like that."

He did know. In fact, Nancy didn't seem to like a lot of things when it came to making out. She would kiss him, but that was about it. He didn't even dare bring up the subject of anything more serious, although he would love to. Sometimes being around Nancy was incredibly frustrating, and he was getting tired of jacking himself off after every time he saw her. He'd hoped she would get over her shyness, but she hadn't.

"I can't believe you're giving this to me," Nancy said, admiring the ring again. "What are you going to tell your parents if they notice it's missing?"

"You mean *when* they notice," said James. "Remember who my father is." He thought for a moment. "I'll probably just tell them it gets in the way when I work out, so I take it off and keep it in my gym bag," he said. "Eventually they'll forget about it. Just don't let them see you wearing it."

"Don't worry," Nancy said. "Can I tell Gina and Meredith though?"

"You're going to whether I say it's okay or not," James answered, knowing that Nancy told her best girlfriends just about everything. "So go ahead."

"Thanks," Nancy said. She slipped the ring into the pocket of her jeans. "I know just the chain I'll put it on. It's one of my mother's. I wish she could see me wearing it."

"But then she'd tell your father," James said.

"True," said Nancy. "But if she were alive I bet she and your mother would gang up on our dads and get them to back off on the whole dating thing."

"Maybe Bess will do it," James said.

Nancy laughed. "Please, she's so busy with plans for the wedding that she can't think about anything else. Wait until you see the dress she's making me wear. Hi-de-ous. I look like a giant pink chrysanthemum."

Right around the start of the school year, A.J. Derry had announced that he and Bess Kunkel were getting married. They'd only been dating a short time and many people—including James's mother—were shocked to hear the news. Nancy, though, seemed happy about it. She told James that she liked Bess a lot, and that she was glad to see her father happy.

"Your dad asked mine to be his best man," James told her. "Maybe you two can walk down the aisle together."

Nancy shook her head. "I'm walking with Nate," she said. "Bess's sister is the matron of honor. Your dad will walk with her."

"You're walking with Nate?" James asked. He couldn't hide the annoyance in his voice.

"He *is* going to be my brother," Nancy reminded him. "He's even changing his last name. Now he's going to be Nate Derry."

"Why?" asked James.

"He says that since his father abandoned him he doesn't need to have the guy's last name. My dad is going to officially adopt him."

"How do you feel about that?" said James.

"It's fine with me," Nancy replied. "I like him. I know you don't, but that's just because you're pigheaded and won't give him a chance."

There was no good response to her comment, so James took another bite of sandwich and just kind of grunted at her.

"See," Nancy said. "You're a pig."

They ate their lunch, talking more about the wedding (Bess wanted a Carly Simon song played instead of the usual wedding march music, and they were going to release doves at the end of the ceremony) and school (James had gotten stuck with ditzy Shannon Gullagher as his chemistry lab partner). As always James was surprised at how easily he could talk to Nancy. He never felt nervous around her, or like he had to prove anything to her. It was a wonderful feeling. He was glad that he'd listened to Celeste and given Nancy his ring. It was a silly thing, but knowing that she liked having it made him feel special.

The bell signaling the end of the lunch period rang. They picked up their trash and dropped the paper bags into the basket at the side of the bleachers. Holding hands they walked back to the main building.

At the door James gave Nancy a quick kiss. "I'll see you after school," he said. "Meet me out front."

His next class was English. The assignment for the day was Shirley Jackson's short story "The Lottery," which to his surprise James had really enjoyed. It was a weird story, and the ending was totally unexpected. He looked forward to hearing what Mrs. Randolph had to say about it.

He got to class and took his usual seat about halfway back in the rows. That was always a safe place to be, as teachers almost always picked students they could easily see to ask questions of. Seated in the middle, James could usually relax. Not that he minded answering questions; he just wanted it to be on his terms.

Just as the bell was ringing James saw Nate enter the room. English was the one class they had together. James wished they didn't even have that, but he was relieved that he at least didn't have to see Nate more often. Besides, Nate almost never participated in class discussions, and it was possible to forget that he was even there.

Mrs. Randolph came in and launched right into a discussion of the story, which was about a group of people in a small town who were gathering for a lottery of some kind. A member of each family drew a slip from a box. The family whose representative drew a slip that had a black dot on it then drew again, this time using only as many slips of paper as there were members of the family. The family member who drew the slip with the black dot was the lottery winner.

"What did you think Tessie Hutchinson was going to win?" Mrs. Randolph asked the class.

"A new car," someone said.

"Money," suggested another.

"A house," a third added.

Mrs. Randolph nodded. "Many readers thought that was how the story would end," she said. "Shirley Jackson once said that she was astonished by how many people thought Mrs. Hutchinson was going to win a washing machine."

The class laughed. In fact Tessie Hutchinson's "prize" was that she was stoned to death by the other villagers, including her own family—apparently as some kind of sacrifice to ensure a good harvest. It came as a total shock, and James had read it three times; each time he couldn't believe that Jackson had written something so strange. It was weirder even than a Stephen King story.

" 'The Lottery' generated an enormous amount of mail to *The New Yorker* magazine, where it was first published in nineteen forty-eight," Mrs. Randolph informed them. "Many people canceled their subscriptions, and Jackson received a great deal of hate mail because of her story."

"Because of a *story?*" someone asked.

Mrs. Randolph nodded. "Don't forget, back then there were no horror movies, no video games, no tabloids. People weren't as exposed to violence as we are now. A story like 'The Lottery' was shocking to a lot of people. Many of them thought Shirley Jackson should be arrested or institutionalized."

"Maybe she should have," someone said.

James looked around and saw to his surprise that it was Nate who had spoken. He was leaning back in his chair, doodling on his notebook with a pen and looking not at all interested in the discussion.

"Why do you say that, Nate?" Mrs. Randolph asked.

Nate looked up. "She's clearly messed up," he said. "You can't think up something like this unless there's something wrong with you."

"That's an interesting suggestion," said Mrs. Randolph. "What do the rest of you think? Do you agree with Nate?"

Nobody said anything. Most of them looked uneasily at the walls or pretended to be writing something down. Finally James said, "I don't agree."

He saw Nate look over at him, but he ignored the stare. "Maybe she was using a story to talk about something else," he said. "Maybe this was just the best way she could tell it."

"That's a good point, James," Mrs. Randolph said. "As a matter of fact, many people believe that Jackson was actually writing about the way she and her family were treated in the small town where they lived. Her husband was Jewish, and most of the town was not. It's possible that she was writing about how she felt living there. She gave several different explanations for the story, so we don't really know what she was thinking."

"If she felt like people didn't like her because her husband was a Jew, then why didn't she just write about that?" Nate said. "Why write some stupid story about people stoning some woman to death?"

"Sometimes it's more effective to put your message into a form that will get people to notice it more readily," Mrs. Randolph answered. "Jackson certainly got people's attention with her story. It's one of the most famous short stories ever written, and here we are talking about it thirty-four years after it was first published. You can't say that about a lot of modern literature."

"I still think she's nuts," Nate said.

"Maybe you just don't understand the story," James said, the words coming out before he could stop himself. He hadn't meant to actually speak his thought aloud. Now that he had, Nate was glaring at him with open hostility.

"I mean maybe *people* just didn't understand the story," James said, trying to salvage the moment. But it was too late. Nate—and everyone else—knew that he had been insinuating that Nate was too stupid to get what Shirley Jackson was saying. A couple of people laughed, and James saw Nate's cheeks flush.

Sensing tension in the air, Mrs. Randolph moved on, asking them what they thought the symbolism of the black dot was, and where else in literature the symbol appeared. James tried to concentrate on what she was saying, but he felt Nate's eyes boring into him from across the room. He knew that he'd touched a nerve. Nancy had told him once that Nate thought he wasn't smart enough. James had secretly agreed with that assessment but had never said anything.

The remaining half an hour seemed to drag by, but finally the bell rang and everyone got up to leave. James looked for Nate, but he had been one of the first out the door. James had sort of been thinking of apologizing to him, but only because he didn't want Nancy to be mad at him if she found out about the incident. But since Nate was gone, he couldn't do that anyway.

He had chemistry next, and had to go to his locker to get his textbook. When he arrived, he saw something sticking out of the crack between the locker door and the side of the wall. It was a piece of paper. Nancy often left little notes for him there, and he pulled it out, assuming it was from her. But when he opened it up all he saw on it was a big black spot. It was completely colored in, with absolutely no white showing anywhere within the dot. Someone had clearly spent a lot of time making it, and he was pretty sure he knew who that person was.

James opened his locker and pulled out his chemistry book. He looked once more at the paper with the spot, then crumpled it up and tossed it into the locker. He slammed the door and began walking to class. If Nate Kunkel had wanted to scare him, he hadn't done it. He had just pissed James off. And when it came time for payback, James was going to be ready.

CHAPTER 21

1991

Billy waited until he saw Nate's car pull out of the driveway and disappear down the road. Then he stepped out from his hiding place among the trees and walked to the side door of the house. He knocked twice, then waited for Celeste to answer. She did so a moment later, looking at him with surprise.

"Where have you been?" she asked as she let him inside. "I left like twenty messages."

"Only seven, actually," said Billy. He sniffed. His nose was running, and he felt a little hot. He hoped he wasn't getting the flu. "Do you have any coffee?" he asked his sister.

Celeste poured him a cup as he sat down at the table. "Are the kids here?" he asked.

"No," said Celeste, setting the coffee in front of him. "They're at school."

Billy spooned sugar into the coffee, then stirred it. It was hot, and the smell made him feel a little better.

"Shouldn't you be at work?" Celeste asked. "Or did you get fired again?"

"I didn't get fired," said Billy. "I called in sick after Mom called me this morning. What's this about Nate arresting James for Dad's murder?"

Celeste groaned. "I told her not to call you," Celeste said. "I should have known she would."

"She wasn't making a lot of sense," Billy told her. "What's going on?"

"They found James's class ring in the trunk with Dad's body. They also found one of Dad's guns. Nate didn't have any choice, Billy."

"James didn't do it," Billy said. "You know that." The coffee had warmed him some, but his hands were shaking. The mug rattled softly against the table until he let go of it.

"I pray he didn't," Celeste answered. "I don't want to think he could do something like that."

"You *know* he didn't," Billy repeated. "We both know it."

Celeste looked at him. Billy knew he looked like shit. His eyes were red. He hadn't washed his hair. His fingernails were dirty. He knew that to his sister he looked like some bum off the street. But that didn't make him wrong.

"Celeste, you know that there were other people who had something against Dad."

Celeste stood up, not looking at him as she went to the counter and retrieved a pack of cigarettes. She lit one and stood by the sink, anxiously puffing on it. "Nate thinks maybe James did it accidentally," she said. "Remember, he and Dad were fighting a lot that year. About Nancy. Nate says maybe they got into an argument and James snapped for a moment and—"

"James did not kill Dad!" Billy shouted. He banged his fists on the table, spilling coffee and knocking over the saltshaker shaped like a miniature Christmas tree. He rubbed his eyes with the heel of one hand. His head was pounding, and he wished he had some crystal. "You know James didn't do it," he said in a softer voice.

"How?" Celeste asked. Her voice was tight, as if she could barely breathe. "How do I know that, Billy? Was I there?"

"I don't know," Billy answered. "Were you?"

"Fuck you," said Celeste, jabbing at him with the cigarette in her hand. "Fuck you. You come in here all fucked up on who knows what, talking about shit you know nothing about, and you dare suggest that I know something about who killed Dad?"

Billy found himself laughing. "But it's okay for you to just accept that James did it, right?" he said.

"It was his ring, Billy," Celeste replied. "I saw it plain as day. And he identified it when Nate showed it to him."

"So that makes him the killer?" said Billy.

"No, it makes him the only suspect we've got," Celeste said angrily. "Unless you can come up with a better one. How about it, Billy—you got someone in your address book you want to tell Nate about? You want to get James out of that jail, you give them someone to replace him with."

Billy turned and looked at his sister. There were dark circles under her eyes, and she looked at him like a dog eyeing an intruder into its yard. *She used to be pretty,* he thought. *Now she just looks tired.* "I think maybe both of us could think of a few people," he said.

"Maybe you can," Celeste said. "But not me."

Billy pushed his chair away from the table and stood up. He looked at his sister. "I'm going to go see Mom," he said. "Anything you want me to tell her?"

Celeste shook her head. "No," she said. "Just tell her I'll be over later."

Billy nodded. "Thanks for the coffee," he said. "It was good seeing you."

Celeste said nothing. Billy let himself out, walking across the lawn and heading toward the center of town. He shook a cigarette from the pack he'd swiped off Celeste's counter as he was leaving and lit it. With caffeine and nicotine in his system he could almost function. He'd also, to his surprise, slept fairly well, not that any amount of sleep ever made him feel refreshed. But at least he didn't feel like a zombie.

As he walked toward his mother's house he thought about his conversation with his sister. She was so full of it, pretending not to know what he'd been talking about. But if she wanted to play that way, he could play too. There was no reason for him to get involved if nobody wanted him to. He would just keep his mouth shut and see what happened.

He wasn't sure how he felt about James being in jail. It was weird all right, but if what Nate said about the ring and the gun was true, then James looked mighty guilty. No wonder his mother had been so upset when she'd called. It was bad enough thinking that one of your own children could do something so horrible. But when it was the *golden* child—the perfect one—that must hurt even more.

It was a nice day. He couldn't remember the date, but he knew it was the end of May. As far north as they were it didn't really warm up until now, but when it did it was like summer just came overnight. He was almost hot, although he considered that it could be the fever that was making him feel warm. Still, he rolled the sleeves of his shirt up to the elbow.

The walk to his mother's house took the better part of twenty min-

utes, during which he smoked two more cigarettes and tried to remember the names of all seven of the dwarves from *Snow White*. He
kept coming up with only six, although they were never the same six,
and he couldn't figure out which one he was forgetting. When he
reached his mother's house he was trying to decide if Fatty was a real
dwarf or one he'd made up. But now that he'd arrived he found he
didn't care, and he forgot the whole thing almost as quickly as he'd
thought of it in the first place.

"Hey, Mom!" he called out as he walked into the kitchen. "You
here?"

Like Celeste, his mother always had a pot of coffee brewing. It was
one of their weird shared family habits. He did it too, at least when he
remembered to buy coffee. He guessed that James probably did too.
Although he probably has an espresso machine, he thought as he
poured himself a cup and went in search of the sugar.

"Billy?" He heard his mother's voice coming from the hallway. "Is
that you?"

"It is," he replied as his mother came into the room. She was still
wearing her bathrobe, and her hair hadn't been combed.

"You look awful," she said to him.

"Thank you," he told her, kissing her on the cheek. "And you look
as beautiful as ever."

"Don't be smart," his mother told him. "I look like hell. Can you
blame me?"

"That reminds me," said Billy. "I stopped over at Celeste's. She said
to tell you that she'll be over later on."

"I don't know why," his mother replied. "It's because of her husband that James is in this trouble."

"Nate's just doing his job," Billy said.

His mother turned on him. "How can you say that?" she asked.
"He's your brother."

"I know he is," Billy said. "But according to Celeste, Nate has an
awful lot of proof that he's also a killer."

"That's nonsense," Ada said. "And we both know it."

Billy smiled to himself. *She sounds like me talking to Celeste,* he
thought. Of the three kids he always had been the one most like his
mother. It was probably why she put up with him when everyone else
wrote him off. He wished he could be a better person for her. *Maybe
someday,* he told himself.

"Have you spoken to James?" Billy inquired.

"No," Ada said. "But I understand he's called a lawyer. We're supposed to hear from him—the lawyer—later today."

"Do you know his name?" Billy asked her.

"No," Ada answered. "I didn't ask, and Celeste didn't say. I don't know if she knows either."

"She didn't mention anything about it when I saw her," Billy informed his mother. "But maybe she forgot."

"Celeste never forgets anything," his mother said. "That girl can tell you exactly what she wore to school on a Thursday in December sixteen years ago. She gets that from her father."

It was true. Celeste had a memory like an elephant's, which made their earlier conversation even more disturbing. *I know she remembers,* Billy thought. But if Celeste wanted to play dumb, that was her choice.

"It doesn't matter what his name is," Ada said, bringing Billy back to the moment. "What matters is that he can get James out of there. Then maybe that jackass Nate will figure out who the *real* killer is."

"I take it you haven't let Nate know your opinion on this matter," said Billy.

"No," his mother said sharply. "And I'm not going to talk to him until he lets James out and admits that he's wrong."

Billy hesitated over asking his next question, but he knew that he had to. "Mom, do you think that there's any possibility that James did do it?"

"No," his mother said quickly. "I know he didn't."

"Are you saying that because he's your son?" Billy pressed her.

Ada didn't turn around as she answered, "I'm saying it because I know," she said.

CHAPTER 22

1982

When the light went on, Celeste nearly screamed. When she saw her mother standing in the doorway, a look of horror on her face, she nearly died. She quickly covered herself with the afghan, which had fallen on the floor, and tried to push Paul off her. As he hadn't yet realized the severity of the situation, he thought she was teasing him.

"Oh, you want to play rough, do you?" he said, and started to pull his belt from around his waist.

Celeste kneed him and jerked her head toward the door, where her mother still stood with her face frozen in shock. Paul, finally noticing her, said, "Hey, Mrs. McCloud. How's it going?"

Ada looked at Celeste. "Get dressed," she said. "And you," she said, looking at Paul. "Get out of my house."

She turned and went back upstairs. Celeste got up and looked for her T-shirt. "Fuck," she said as she searched under the couch. "Fuck, fuck, fuck, fuck, fuck, fuck, FUCK!"

"She didn't seem too upset," said Paul as he put his shoes on. "Don't freak out."

"You have no idea," Celeste told him. "She's going to go nuclear when I get up there. You'd better be at least twenty miles from here by then or you'll feel the shock waves."

Paul shook his head. "I don't get what the big deal is," he said. "It's not like we were doing it. Christ, I hadn't even taken my shirt off yet."

"Yeah, but I did," Celeste reminded him. "And even if you were down here saying the goddamn rosary she wouldn't like you. You know that."

Paul stood up and tried to give her a kiss. Celeste pushed him away. "Go," she said. "Now." She nodded toward the set of steps that led from the cellar to the storm doors at the rear of the house. "Use that door. If she even thinks she sees you she'll probably take a shot at you. And she doesn't miss."

Paul left, opening the storm doors and escaping into the sunlight. Celeste knew that it wasn't going to be so easy for her. She had to go upstairs and face her mother. And the longer she waited, the worse it would be. Readying herself for the storm, she went upstairs.

Her mother was in the kitchen. There was a pile of strawberries on the counter beside her, and she was using a paring knife to cut the stems and leaves off before rinsing each berry under the tap. The cleaned berries were sitting in a white bowl on the other side, so that the whole process looked like a miniature assembly line: cut, wash, bowl—cut, wash, bowl—cut, wash, bowl.

Celeste took a seat at the table, waiting for her mother to say something. For a good ten minutes not a word was spoken, the only sound coming from the water gurgling down the drain and the knife snicking through the tops of the berries. Then, finally, Ada said, "I didn't raise you to be that kind of girl."

Celeste wanted to ask her exactly what kind of girl she meant, but instead she said only, "I'm sorry. Really, though, nothing—"

Her mother held up the hand with the knife in it, silencing her. "It doesn't matter what you were or were not doing," she told Celeste. "The point is that you were doing something your father and I expressly forbid you to do."

Celeste understood perfectly what her mother was saying—it wasn't what she'd been doing (although Celeste knew that it mattered more than her mother was letting on) but that she had been doing it with Paul Lunardi. The only good thing about the situation, if it could possibly be considered a good thing, was that her mother's dislike of Paul seemed to outweigh the fact that Celeste had been on the couch with her tits hanging out.

Despite her relief, she heard herself say, "I don't know what you have against Paul. He's a nice guy." She regretted it immediately, but it was too late. Her mother whirled to face her.

"Paul Lunardi has seen the inside of your father's patrol car on more than one occasion," she said. "He is a liar, a thief, and I suspect a whole lot of other things that make him not a nice guy."

"But I love—" Celeste began.

"You do not!" her mother exclaimed, drowning out the rest of the sentence. "You may think you do, but you're a young, foolish girl. I'm sure that boy has filled your head with all kinds of promises that he has no intention of keeping." She shook the knife at her daughter. "It's about time you smartened up, Celeste," she said. "Sometimes I don't think you have a brain in your head."

She turned back to the berries, leaving Celeste to sit in wounded silence. She couldn't believe her mother had said such hateful things to her. Not liking Paul was one thing, but to call her foolish and to suggest that she wasn't a reliable judge of someone's character was just cruel. She knew Paul better than her parents did, but they acted as if she was some stupid little kid with a crush.

She started to get up.

"Where do you think you're going?" her mother asked.

"To my room," said Celeste. "Unless there's something else you want to say." She tried to make her voice drip with sarcasm, but if her mother sensed it she didn't show it. She simply said, "I'm sure when your father gets home he'll want to talk to you."

Celeste's veneer of bravado suddenly crumbled. "Don't tell Daddy," she said. "Please, Mom."

Ada looked at her. "Why not?" she asked.

Celeste searched her mind for a reason, but all she could come up with was, "You know he has it in for Paul. He'll—I don't know—take him in for something. Lock him up. You know he will."

To her surprise her mother laughed. "And good for him if he did," she said, wiping her eyes with her sleeve. "But he won't. He might let that boy *think* he's going to, but just to scare him."

Celeste felt fury rise in her. Her mother was acting as if this were some kind of game, that she and Paul were pieces that could be moved around at will to entertain her and Celeste's father. Still, Celeste was frightened.

"You don't have to tell him," she said, near tears. "I promise nothing like this will ever happen again. I'll break up with Paul. I won't see him or talk to him or anything."

Her mother snorted. "Of course you'll see him again," she said. She turned and looked at her daughter. "Do you really think I was never seventeen years old?" she asked. "I know how you feel. I know you think this boy is the most wonderful boy in the world. You think your father and I can't possibly understand why he's so special. Am I right?"

She looked at Celeste, waiting for an answer. Celeste, though, wasn't sure if she should agree or not. Either answer seemed like the wrong one. She decided the safest thing to do was just to shrug.

Her mother sighed. "Believe me, Celeste, I *do* know. Which is also why I know that Paul Lunardi is not good for you. You have to trust me on this." She set the knife down and turned the water off. Drying her hands on a dishtowel she turned to her daughter. "I'll make a deal with you. I won't tell your father about today."

Celeste breathed a sigh of relief, and was just about to thank her mother, when Ada continued. "But you have to promise me something."

Oh shit, Celeste thought. *Here it comes.*

"I'm not going to ask you not to see that boy," her mother said. "Because I know you will, at least until you learn the hard way what he's really like. But I am going to ask you to go out with Nate Kunkel."

"Nate?" Celeste said. "Why would I want to go out with Nate?"

"Why would you not want to?" her mother asked.

Celeste groaned. "Look at him," she said. "He's a total dork. Plus, he's like sixteen."

"He's almost seventeen," her mother countered. "Which isn't that much younger than you are. And he's not a dork."

"But you don't even like his mother," Celeste objected.

"Who says I don't like Bess?" Ada demanded.

"Everybody knows that," said Celeste.

"Yes, well, it's not Nate's fault who his mother is," said Ada.

"Mom—" Celeste began.

"That's your choice," Ada interrupted. "You can go out with Nate Kunkel and I won't tell your father, or you can say no and explain to him what you were doing in his house with Paul Lunardi."

"This is so not fair," said Celeste. "How many times do I have to go out with Nate?"

"As many times as he asks you," her mother said. "You're going to ask him to the next school dance. If he says no, you're off the hook. But if he says yes, you're going—and you're going to be nice to him. Then, if he asks you out again, you're going to say yes."

"For how long?" said Celeste. "I mean what if he decides that I'm the love of his life and he wants to marry me? Do I have to do it?"

"We'll cross that bridge when we come to it," Ada answered. "So do we have a deal?"

Celeste hesitated for a moment. Then she imagined her father's face when he heard that she and Paul had been going at it in the basement. "Okay," she said, shaking off the image. "I'll ask him to the next dance. But if he says no, then that's it, right? No more blackmail."

"No more blackmail," her mother agreed.

"Good," said Celeste. "Now can I go to my room?"

"Yes," her mother said. "I believe you have a phone call to make." She wrote something on a piece of paper and handed it to Celeste. "There's the number."

She was right about that. Celeste did have a call to make. But it wasn't to Nate Kunkel. When she got upstairs she took the phone from the hallway into her room and dialed Paul's number. He answered on the second ring.

"It's me," Celeste said.

"Are you still alive?" Paul joked.

"Barely," said Celeste. "I had to make a deal with the devil to keep her from telling my dad."

"What'd she ask for, your soul?" Paul said. "Or maybe mine?"

"Worse," Celeste told him. "She's making me take Nate Kunkel to the next school dance."

Much to her annoyance, Paul laughed. "That's it?" he said. "You have to go to a dance? Fuck, I thought she would at least have told you that you can never see me again."

"She knows better," said Celeste. "Besides, it's not really her that's the problem. It's my father. That's why I agreed to this stupid deal. If she ever tells him about us, then it *will* be all over. He won't just kill me, he'll send me to a convent or something. And you'll find yourself being some Bubba's bitch."

Paul grunted. "That guy's such an asshole," he said. "He thinks he can order everyone around because he has a badge and a gun."

"Yeah, well, that is kind of why he can order everyone around," said Celeste.

"It's not right," Paul said. "Man I'd like to kick his ass."

"Right," said Celeste. "Why don't you just kill him instead. That would solve the whole problem, at least until they catch you and send you to the sizzle chair." She made a sound like bacon frying, but Paul didn't laugh.

"They wouldn't fry a kid though," he said.

"What are you talking about?" Celeste asked him.

"A kid," said Paul. "If a kid shot someone, he'd just get put away until he was eighteen."

"Oh, okay," Celeste said. "So then all we have to do is find some kid to shoot my father and then everything will be perfect. What a great plan. I don't know why we didn't think of it before. I know—why don't we see if we can get Billy to do it? We can tell him that if he doesn't we'll bust him for smoking pot. Oh, except that we're the ones who turned him on to it in the first place."

She laughed at the stupidity of the idea. Sometimes Paul came up with the weirdest shit. But that was one of the things she loved about him. He had a twisted sense of humor.

"You're right," he said. "Besides, the kid probably couldn't hit the side of a barn with a gun anyway. He's such a spazz. With our luck he'd shoot himself in the foot."

Celeste heard footsteps on the stairs. A few seconds later her door opened and her mother peered in. Seeing her on the phone she whispered, "Is that Nate?"

Celeste nodded, then gave her mother a thumbs-up sign as if everything had been settled regarding the dance. Her mother smiled and backed out of the room, shutting the door.

"Ugh," Celeste said to Paul. "Momzilla was here. I should go. See you tomorrow?"

"Sure," Paul said. "And don't forget to ask Billy about being our triggerman." He made a sound like a gun being shot.

"I'll get right on that," said Celeste. "I'll let you know what he says."

She hung up, waited a few seconds, then looked at the piece of paper her mother had given her and dialed the number.

"Hello? Mrs. Kunkel?" she said when someone picked up. "This is Celeste McCloud. Could I please speak to Nate?"

CHAPTER 23

1991

Charly pulled up in front of the house and checked the address. She was definitely in the right place, but it didn't look at all as she'd expected it to. From James's descriptions of his hometown she had expected nothing but farms and dirt roads. In reality Cold Falls was much more modern than that. Some of the houses were in areas that were arguably—she searched for an appropriate word—pastoral, but it was hardly all farmland. It probably had been at one time, as she had definitely seen some fields of cows and horses while driving in and there was still evidence of past agricultural undertakings (the old barn a quarter of a mile behind the house, for instance) here and there, but all in all it was a far cry from the sleepy little burg she'd envisioned.

If her idea of Cold Falls had been so off base, she wondered, what was the McCloud family going to be like? James had described them to her as well, and she had seen some photos, but real life often turned out to be vastly different. Given the peculiar circumstances that brought her to Cold Falls for the first time, she was understandably anxious. James's call had come as a complete shock to her. At first she'd thought he was joking, but she'd soon realized that the situation was very serious. She'd booked a flight, called her employer to say she needed some time off, and packed her suitcase. Now, after an hour's drive from the airport in Utica, she was there. As she got out of the car and retrieved her briefcase from the backseat, she marveled again at how quickly life could change. Yesterday she had been wondering where to take her clients to lunch; now she was on the other side of the country, about to meet her boyfriend's family while he waited in a jail cell for her to come rescue him.

She had spoken to James's sister, Celeste, just before getting on the plane in Seattle. James had told Celeste—curiously, through her husband, who had been the one to arrest James—that a lawyer would be coming to help but hadn't told her who that lawyer was. Celeste had at first not recognized Charly's name, but after a few moments of confusion they had sorted it out. Now, she hoped, Celeste was waiting inside to meet her.

She'd been told to go around the back to the kitchen door, and so she did. She'd barely raised her hand to knock when the door opened and a woman who was clearly James's sister greeted her.

"You must be Charly," she said. "Come in. I'm Celeste."

Charly stepped into a kitchen that appeared not to have been renovated since the early 1970s. Seated at the table was a woman Charly recognized from photos as Ada McCloud. As Charly came in, Ada stood and opened her arms. Charly hesitated, but Ada came and embraced her, kissing her on the cheek. "I'm so glad you're here," she said. "I made up the guest room for you."

"Oh," Charly said. She hadn't anticipated staying at Ada's house and had made reservations at a motel she'd found online. But Ada sounded so relieved to see her that she couldn't say no. "That's wonderful," she said. "Thank you."

"Won't you sit down," said Ada, pulling out a chair. "You must be exhausted."

Charly accepted the chair, setting her briefcase on the floor beside her feet. Ada immediately jumped back up and said, "Can I get you something to drink? Coffee?"

"Actually, tea would be great," Charly said. "If it's no trouble."

"It's no trouble," Celeste assured her as she filled a teakettle with water from the tap. "James dragging you out here is trouble."

Ada, who was looking through the cabinets, turned to Charly with a box in each hand. "Lemon or mint?" she asked.

"Oh. Mint, please," Charly said. She addressed Celeste again. "Now your husband is the town sheriff, correct?" she asked.

Celeste nodded as she adjusted the flame beneath the kettle. "I know it's weird," she said.

"It is that," Charly agreed.

"Is it a problem?" Celeste asked her.

"Not a problem exactly," Charly told her. "It's just that normally it would be a conflict of interest for anyone personally involved with the prosecution—in this case, the police—to be involved in my investigation."

"You'll find out pretty quick that nothing about this family is normal."

Charly looked up as a young man walked into the room. He looked like he hadn't slept—or bathed—in a long time, although when he smiled at her she saw that he was actually very handsome.

"I'm Billy," he said. "The prodigal son."

"Hi, Billy," Charly said. "It's nice to meet you."

"We'll see," Billy remarked, pulling out a chair and sitting down on her right. A moment later Celeste set a mug in front of her, then took the chair to her left. "Cream and sugar are on the table," she said.

Now surrounded by the three members of the McCloud family who were not dead or in jail, Charly looked around at their faces. They were all watching her intently, and she noted with some interest that they all had the same intense eyes that James had. They were looking at her as if waiting for her to perform a magic trick and would be terribly disappointed if she failed to awe them.

"I don't really know much about what's going on," Charly began. "To be honest, James didn't tell me why he was coming here. Last night when he called was the first time I heard about the finding of Mr. McCloud's body. So I'm afraid I only have bits and pieces to go on."

"It's fairly simple," Ada said. "Nate's arrested James for killing his father, but James had nothing to do with it."

"It's not that simple, Mom," said Celeste. She turned to Charly. "They found some things that belong to James with my father's body."

"I'll get all that information when I go to the police station tomorrow," Charly said.

"Tomorrow?" said Ada, sounding distressed. "Can't you get James out today?"

Charly poured some milk into her tea (it was in a china calf and came out through the mouth) and stirred it before answering. "It may take me some time," she said carefully, "depending on the evidence and on whether James is formally charged with anything. Legally they have to charge him or let him go."

"They haven't charged him," Ada said instantly. "Have they?" She looked at Celeste for help.

"No," Celeste said. "Not yet."

Charly found James's sister interesting. She wondered how Celeste was handling being in the middle of the situation. More important, she wondered what Celeste believed to be the truth about what was going on. She would have to find out, but she also had to be careful not to alienate Celeste in any way, or to give her any information she didn't want Celeste's sheriff husband to have. It was going to be quite a balancing act.

"I could call Nate and have him come over," Celeste said. "My husband," she added, when Charly didn't respond.

"I'm sorry," Charly said. "I knew that. No, it's okay. I'll go see him tomorrow. But if you could tell him to expect me around ten, I'd appreciate that."

"This is all pretty weird, isn't it?" Billy said.

Charly looked at him. "Yes," she said. "That about sums it up."

Billy grinned. James had told her that Billy was the family black sheep, and if what she'd heard was accurate she could see why. But there was also something about him that she liked. He was clearly damaged, and that always intrigued her. Just as she'd wondered about Celeste's take on things, she was curious to hear what he had to say. Whatever it was, she had a feeling it would be interesting.

Ada seemed fairly straightforward. Having just found out that her husband had been murdered, and now having her son arrested for it, she was understandably dazed. Anybody in the same situation would be. Charly would talk to her more when her children weren't around, when she would be more likely to speak openly.

"You must be tired from all that flying and driving," Ada said.

Charly looked at her watch. "Well, it's only about four back in Seattle," she said. "But to tell the truth I could use the rest. I haven't slept since James woke me up yesterday, and I can't sleep on planes."

"Billy, show Charly to the guest room," Ada said.

"I have to get my bag from the car," Charly said. "I'll be right back."

"I'll get it," said Billy. "You go upstairs. It's the last door on the left."

"Just what I like," Charly joked as she handed Billy the keys to the car. "Room service."

As soon as Billy left, Celeste turned to Charly and said, "If you have anything in there you don't want to lose, be sure to check your bag when it comes back."

"Celeste!" Ada said.

"Well, it's true, Mom," Celeste said. She looked at Charly. "Billy has one or two little—hobbies—that can get expensive," she said.

"Got it," Charly said. "Thanks for the heads-up."

"Billy's a good boy," said Ada. "He just has some problems. But we all do. It's nothing to be ashamed of."

Celeste put her hand on her mother's wrist. "True, Mom. But some people's problems are bigger than others'." She stood up. "Come on, Charly. I'll show you where your room is. It used to be my room, so I think I can find it."

Charly rose. "I'll see you in the morning, Mrs. McCloud."

"Ada," the other woman said. "Don't make me sound older than I am."

"Good night, Ada," Charly said.

She followed Celeste through the living room and up the stairs. It was fascinating being in the house where James had grown up. On the wall there were pictures of him from infancy through college, and walking up the stairs was like watching a flipbook of his life, each step taking her forward a year or two. She paused at one, a picture of James standing with a pretty girl, both of them dressed in prom clothes. Celeste, seeing her stop, said, "The girl is Nancy Derry. My husband's sister. Well, half sister. His mother married her father."

"She's lovely," Charly remarked. "James, on the other hand, has some seriously big hair."

"It was the eighties," Celeste said. "We all had big hair. That was the winter formal, I think. Nancy left a few months later."

"Left?" Charly said.

Celeste nodded. "She went to spend the summer in Maine with some of her relatives. She liked it so much she never came back. I don't think anyone has seen her since then."

"Did she and Nate date for very long?" Charly asked.

"About a year or so," Celeste said. "My father kind of broke them up. He thought James wasn't taking school seriously enough and wouldn't get into a good college. James was pretty upset when she just up and left." She smiled at Charly. "But clearly he's gotten over it."

They resumed climbing the stairs, then walked down the hall. As they passed one of the doors Celeste said, "That's James's bedroom. It's exactly the way it was when he left for college."

Charly peeked inside for a moment. "I'll have to check it out later," she said. "It will be like walking through the Smithsonian."

"And here we are," Celeste said, opening the door to the last room on the left.

Charly entered the room. "Now this looks like it's had a face-lift," she said. "Not a Prince poster in sight."

"Mom redid it the week after I married Nate," said Celeste. "She said that once I was married I was never coming back home. I guess she'll do the same when James and Billy get married."

She suddenly got quiet. When Charly looked at her, she saw that Celeste had tears in her eyes.

"I'm sorry," Celeste said. "It's just that . . ." She stopped and wiped her eyes. "I'm sorry," she said again.

Charly had an idea about what had made Celeste sad. "He'll get married," she said. "Maybe even to me."

Celeste laughed. "Thanks," she said. "I needed that. And I hope you're right."

"Right about what?" Billy came through the door with Charly's suitcase in hand. He set it on the floor beside the bed.

"About me becoming your sister-in-law," Charly told him.

Billy nodded. "That would be nice," he said. "We haven't had such good luck with in-laws so far." He looked at Celeste as he said this, and Charly saw Celeste stiffen visibly.

"I should go," Celeste said. "I'll tell Nate you'll come by in the morning." She said nothing to Billy as she left the room.

"You sure you want to get involved with this family?" Billy asked as Charly lifted her suitcase onto the bed.

"Looks like I already am," Charly replied. She thought suddenly of Celeste's warning and glanced at the zippers on her luggage. They seemed to be untouched.

"Can I give you a piece of advice?" said Billy. He had taken a seat on the edge of the bed and was rubbing his fingers over the stitching on the quilt.

"Shoot," Charly told him.

He looked up at her, and for a moment his eyes were clear and sharp. "Don't believe everything you see," he said.

CHAPTER 24

1991

Charly returned to the house in the early afternoon. By the time she arrived, Ada was frantic. She'd been waiting all day to find out what the young woman had learned at the police station, and as soon as Charly came in Ada sat her down in the living room. She held her hands in her lap, trying not to show her nervousness. Despite Charly's pleasant demeanor Ada was slightly frightened of her. She could well understand why James had described the young woman as a shark in the courtroom.

"How is he?" she asked.

"Considering everything that's happened, he's doing much better than I had anticipated," Charly told her. "He hasn't slept much, but that's to be expected. He's upset and angry, but he understands why he's there and he's ready to get on with it."

"What does that mean?" Ada asked. "Get on with it. What happens now?"

Although she'd spent most of her life married to a man whose career was enforcing the law, Ada had never really paid attention to the details of what happened to criminals once Dan had arrested them. She'd never even been on jury duty, escaping every time by telling the judge that her husband was a sheriff. Now that her son was the one in trouble she was embarrassed to admit that she had no idea what the legal process involved.

"Tomorrow he'll be arraigned on charges of first-degree murder," Charly told her, walking her through the steps. "Basically that means that they feel there's enough evidence to try him for the offense—in this case, murder. There will be a preliminary hearing the day after tomorrow in county court, where a judge will determine if James can post bail."

"You mean he can get out?" said Ada hopefully. This was the first piece of good news she'd heard, and she grabbed on to it as she would a life preserver in a storm-tossed sea.

"Normally I'd say there was a chance of that," Charly replied. "But in this case I suspect not. Given the peculiar circumstances I think they'll want to keep him in jail through to the time of trial. It's also likely that given the relationship your family has to the sheriff that James will be transferred to a jail somewhere else to avoid any conflict of interest."

Ada sighed as the one spot of hope she had was snuffed out. She hadn't expected Charly to bring her good news, but hearing what was likely to happen made everything seem much more real than it had before. Hearing words like *trial* and *arraignment* upset her greatly. It was as if her son was caught up in the machinery of a system designed to swallow him up, and she couldn't do anything about it.

"There's something else," Charly said. "I'm not licensed to practice in the state of New York. I can assist another attorney, and I can give you my advice, but I can't officially represent James. Also, there's the conflict of interest problem again. As his girlfriend, it's best if I keep my involvement—at least publicly—to a minimum."

Ada's heart sank, and she realized that she'd already been thinking of Charly as the guardian angel who would rescue her son. Now she felt alone again. "So what can we do?" she asked. "Who's going to be his lawyer?"

"Before I left I put a call in to a law school classmate of mine," said Charly. "She practices in Albany now, and she gave me the names of some local attorneys who she thinks might be able to help us out. I'm going to call them this afternoon. Hopefully one of them will agree to work with us."

Ada nodded. Hearing Charly use the word *us* made her feel a little better. "I'm so relieved you're here," she told Charly. "I don't think I could have done this on my own. I have Celeste and Billy, of course, but they're . . ." She didn't know how to finish the sentence. "They're not lawyers," she concluded.

"I'm more than happy to help," Charly told her.

Ada sensed her hesitating. "What is it?" she said. "Is there something you haven't told me?"

"No," said Charly. "Actually, it's something I want to ask you. You received a letter following Daniel's disappearance, correct?"

Ada nodded. "Yes. It came the day after he left," she said.

"And in that letter Daniel said that he was killing himself because he had cancer," said Charly.

Ada nodded again. "He said he didn't want any of us to watch him die," Ada told her.

"But now we know that Daniel didn't kill himself," said Charly. "Which means that the letter was a forgery."

"I hadn't thought about that but yes, it must have been," Ada replied.

"Was it handwritten?" asked Charly.

"It was typed," Ada said. "Daniel had terrible handwriting. He probably typed it on one of the machines at the station."

"But he didn't write it," Charly reminded her. "Or at least we can assume for the moment that he didn't. Did the letter sound like him? Like something he would say or write?"

"Yes," Ada said. "I remember actually hearing his voice as I read it."

"Would it be possible for me to see it?" asked Charly.

Ada shook her head. "I don't have it," she said. "I gave it to the police and never got it back. I didn't think to copy it. Honestly, I wouldn't want it around."

Charly wrote something in a small notebook she produced from her bag. "I'll see if I can get it from the police," she said. "They must have it on file." She clicked her pen closed and set it on the coffee table. She didn't say anything for a long time.

"You're thinking that James could have written the note, aren't you?" Ada asked her.

"It did occur to me," Charly said after a moment. "Who would be better able to mimic someone's voice than someone from his family?"

"James was only sixteen when Dan disappeared," Ada said. "Do you really think a teenage boy could write something like that? Or *do* something like what they're saying James did?"

Charly didn't answer the question. Instead she said, "The letter said that Dan was killing himself because he had cancer. We know he didn't write it, but was he sick? Was that part of the letter true?"

"No," Ada said. "I mean I don't know if he was or not. When I read his letter it was the first I ever heard about any cancer. As I said, we all assumed the letter was from Dan so we accepted that he must have been sick."

"Don't you think that's sort of peculiar?" said Charly. "If he really was ill, wouldn't you know he wasn't feeling well?"

"Dan wasn't the kind of man who complained," Ada explained. "Unless his pains were obvious I never knew about them. I don't think that man ever took anything stronger than an aspirin the whole time I was married to him."

"But surely you would have noticed that he was going to a doctor," Charly suggested.

"We believe he was seeing a doctor in Syracuse," said Ada.

"Based on what information?" Charly asked.

"Credit card charges," Ada explained. "After Dan died I started looking through the credit card bills. Dan always paid them and I'd never looked at them before, so I had no idea what was on them. In the months before Dan's death it seems he had gone to Syracuse four or five times and stayed in a hotel there. Each time it was on a night when he'd said he was working. We don't know anyone in Syracuse, so I imagine that's where his doctor was."

"The police never tried to find out for sure?" Charly asked.

"I don't believe I ever asked," said Ada. "There didn't seem to be any point. I have no idea what the doctor's name could be, so I don't know how they would find out who it was."

"They could call oncology centers," said Charly as she made another note. "It's not really all that difficult to locate a person's physician."

"I never thought of that," Ada admitted. "I suppose I just believed what he wrote in the letter. There's no other reason I can think of for his being in Syracuse so frequently."

"But surely you considered the possibility that the letter either wasn't from him or that it wasn't true?" said Charly. "After all, there was no body. He could have gone anywhere and just made up the story about cancer to throw everyone off his trail."

Ada nodded. "I did consider that possibility," she said. "But as I said, I knew my husband. If something were terribly wrong—if he was unhappy—I would have known. He was able to hide physical pain, but I always knew when he was unhappy about something."

"I don't mean this to sound condescending," Charly told her. "But wouldn't you say that someone who is in enough emotional pain that he decides to end his life is unhappy?"

Ada glanced at the fireplace mantel, where a photograph of her and Dan looked back at her. Dan was smiling, and his arms were around Ada. "I tortured myself about that every day for years," she told Charly. "Why didn't I know? Why didn't he tell me? Why did he just leave and not give me a chance to say good-bye?" A tear slipped from her eye and she wiped it from her cheek with trembling fingers. "You can't imagine what it's like," she said.

Across from her, Charly shook her head. "No, I can't," she agreed.

Ada turned to her. "And now to find out that it was all a lie," she said, shaking her head. "It's like it's happening all over again. Only now I'm losing my son."

"Not if I can help it," Charly told her.

Ada felt more tears forming in her eyes. All of a sudden they burst forth, and she found herself sobbing. A moment later Charly was beside her, rubbing her back and consoling her.

"It's okay," Charly said. "Ada, it will be okay."

"You don't know that," Ada said. "You can't know."

Charly took her hand. "Do you believe James killed his father?" she asked.

"No," Ada answered, shaking her head. "Of course not."

"Neither do I," said Charly. "Which is why we have to do whatever we can to find out what really happened eight years ago."

"Yes," Ada agreed. "That's right. I'll do whatever I can."

Her breathing had returned to normal, and although she was still crying a little bit she felt better. That particular moment had passed, and now she felt silly for having broken down in front of Charly like that.

"I'm sorry," she said. "It's just that I—"

"No need to apologize," Charly assured her. "Believe me, I understand."

Ada smiled at her. "How do you keep yourself so together?" she asked.

Charly laughed. "It's a trick they teach you in law school. Actually, they remove the part of your brain that makes you human. That way you can handle all of your cases completely objectively."

Ada found herself laughing at the joke. "I can see why James loves you," she said.

Charly smiled but said nothing. Watching her, Ada wondered if perhaps she'd said the wrong thing. She'd assumed that James and Charly were serious. After all, he'd dated Charly longer than he had any other woman. But perhaps she was mistaken. *Or maybe she's reconsidering,* she thought with alarm. *Maybe she doesn't really want to be a part of this.* It was a horrible thought, but one that Ada couldn't help but have. Charly was being very helpful, but surely she had her limits, as anyone would. Especially if there was a chance the person they loved was guilty of a terrible crime. Charly said she absolutely thought that James was innocent. *But so did you,* she reminded herself.

"Is there anything else I can tell you?" Ada said, suddenly wanting to change the subject. "About Dan? Or what happened? I think I've told you just about everything, but maybe you have other questions."

Charly shook her head. "Not at the moment," she replied. "There's a lot I need to think through. That letter—what we thought was a suicide note—just isn't adding up. I have to work that around in my head for a while."

"Why don't you go upstairs and lie down," Ada suggested. "Some rest will do you good. I'll call you when it's time for dinner."

"Thank you," Charly said. "I think I will." She stood up, holding her notebook and reaching for her briefcase.

"I'll bring you some hot tea in a little while," said Ada. "That will make you feel better."

She watched as Charly went upstairs. Then she walked into the kitchen, got the kettle from the stove, and ran the tap to fill it. *You almost blew it,* she chided herself. *Of course she would pick up on the cancer business.* She turned the water off and set the teakettle on a burner. Things had come close to unraveling. She had to be more careful. Fooling the men of the small-town sheriff's department was one thing; getting by someone like Charly was quite another. But she could do it. All she had to do was let Charly think that she'd told the whole truth. If Charly did, then everything should turn out all right.

For all of them.

CHAPTER 25

1983

Ada unfolded the letter and read it for what she thought must surely be the thousandth time since she'd opened the envelope an hour earlier.

Ada:

As I'm sure you remember from when you tried to get me to write my own wedding vows, I'm not very good with words. So I'm just going to say this. I love you more than anything in the world, which is why I have to do what I'm doing. I know it will probably seem like I'm being selfish doing it this way, but I hope you can understand why I think it's the best for all of us.

About a year ago I wasn't feeling so good. I went to a doctor, which you know is something I never do, so you also know that it must have been pretty bad. I didn't go to Doc Brennan. I don't know why. I guess something told me this was more serious than just the flu. And it was. It was cancer.

I know you think I should have told you, and maybe you're right. But when they told me it was something they could maybe stop for a little while, I decided to wait. And then when they found out they couldn't stop it, and told me I had maybe another six months before things got really bad, I couldn't imagine making you and the kids watch me go. That's no way for a man to die, rotting away in front of his family.

So I'm going to go out on my own terms. Quick and easy. No pain. No hospital. I'm going to beat this the only way I can. They won't find me. I don't want you to have to deal with that either. And I don't want a funeral. Just remember me the way I was.

I guess there's not much else to say except that I love you and I'm sorry.

Love,

Daniel

The signature was written in her husband's familiar scrawl, in blue ink. *He must have typed this at the station,* she thought. She imagined him sitting at his desk, pecking away at the typewriter with his awkward two-fingered style, his brow furrowed in concentration. Had everyone assumed he was just writing up another report? Had Dan paused midsentence to answer some mundane question, then returned to composing his good-bye?

She folded the letter and held it to her chest. She'd tried over and over again to tell herself that it wasn't real, that the envelope she'd opened had contained nothing but a request to purchase magazines in exchange for the chance to win a million dollars. Or perhaps it had been meant for someone else, and been delivered to her by accident. Some other Ada. From some other Dan. But not her, and not her Dan. It couldn't be.

Oddly, the fact that her husband had killed himself was the easiest part of the letter to accept. Although it was devastating, she understood it. It was everything else that she had difficulty believing. How could Daniel not tell her that he was ill? How could she not have realized that something was wrong? Why had he not at least given her a chance to tell him she loved him one more time?

Somehow something had gone terribly wrong with the connection between them. She had failed to sense something that, as a wife, she should have sensed instinctively. Yet she had known nothing, suspected nothing. Until opening the letter she had believed that it was yet another ordinary Wednesday, one in a seemingly endless stream of Wednesdays that they would share.

Now all of that had been taken from her. Even in her grief she knew that later she would be angry with Daniel, infuriated by his selfishness. She would curse him, perhaps even hate him for a time in the guise of being offended on behalf of their children. But at the moment all she felt was an overwhelming sense of having been left all alone.

She pushed the feeling away. There were things to be done. Something bad had happened, and now she had to go through the appropriate steps one went through in such instances. That would help, or at least put off the inevitable moment when everything came crashing down around her once more.

She made a list in her head, as if she were following one of the innumerable plans Dan had worked up for the family in the event of emergency: fire, flood, even tornado despite the fact that central New York had seen only three in the past century. He had a plan for all of these things and more (automobile accident, snake bite, broken bones) and had gone over them with Ada and the children numerous times.

Now, though, they were all confused in her mind. Although she tried to outline the procedure for dealing with a husband who had committed suicide, she instead found herself repeating bits and pieces of other plans. *Bottled water,* she thought incongruously. *A radio. Designate a central meeting point. Light flares. Establish a line of control. Fifteen compressions followed by two packing breaths. Locate a pulse.* She considered and discarded each new thought, searching for one that would actually help. She understood now why so many people died in seemingly controllable situations; there were just too many possibilities. *Crack the window and allow the vehicle to fill with water so that the pressure equalizes and you can open the door,* she told herself. *If you feel heat behind the door, stay in the room and wait for help. The bite of a black widow is painful but seldom fatal.*

She shut her eyes, attempting to slow the torrent of thoughts. (*The safest place to be is in a doorway. Use a belt and two sticks to splint the leg. If there's the possibility of injury to the spinal column, leave the victim in place unless there's an immediate threat to life.*) One by one she silenced them until only a handful of options remained. *In near-drowning incidents you have four to six minutes until brain*

*damage occurs. Wrap burns lightly with clean cotton cloth. Do not
remove an impaling object from the eye.* And then, finally, there was
only one: *Call for help.*

Yes, that was what she needed to do. She needed to call someone.
Then it would be someone else's worry. She would no longer have to
think about it; she could simply sit and wait for help to arrive.

A.J. She would call A.J. He would know exactly what needed to be
done next. After Dan he was the person she most trusted to make
things all right. If she called him he would be there as quickly as possible, reassuring her with his words and taking things into his hands.
Then maybe she could allow herself to give in to the grief in the way
she longed to give in to sleep after a hard day.

She picked up the phone. Her fingers dialed the number of their
own accord while her mind attempted to make sense of the suddenly
mysterious combination of letters and numbers on the phone's face-
plate. When she heard ringing it sounded to her like the trilling of
some peculiar far-off bird.

And then there was A.J.'s voice, saying hello. Instantly she felt relief
flood through her. She began to speak, not understanding the words
but knowing somehow what information needed to be conveyed. Having received A.J.'s promise to be there as quickly as possible, she hung
up and continued to stare at the phone, marveling at its ability to solve
her problem so neatly and efficiently.

By the time A.J. arrived she had managed to pull herself together a
little. She'd washed her face and combed her hair. She'd also managed
to find her purse, remove some money, and ask Celeste to take Billy to
McDonald's and *Return of the Jedi,* which she knew he wanted to see.
She'd explained the cancellation of dinner on the ruined potatoes and
a subsequent headache, a lie neither of her children questioned. James,
she remembered, was playing an away game with his baseball team
and wouldn't be home until nearly midnight.

Alone in the house, she busied herself with washing up the dishes
from the uneaten dinner. She had just finished drying the last of the
plates when A.J. arrived. He found her in the kitchen and immediately
drew her into an embrace. As soon as his strong arms were around her
she began to cry again. A.J. held her as she pressed her face against his
shirt. He smelled of Bay Rum. It was the same aftershave Daniel used,
and for a moment she convinced herself that he had returned to her

and that everything was all right. Then A.J. spoke and his voice, different from Dan's, broke the spell.

"Can I see the letter?" he asked.

Ada reluctantly broke their connection. Almost immediately she felt alone again, as if she'd been holding on to a life preserver that was suddenly snatched away. She removed Dan's letter from the pocket of her apron and handed it to A.J., watching as he unfolded it and read it, his eyes quickly scanning the page. He then looked at the envelope.

"Utica," he said. "That's where it was mailed from." He looked at Ada. "He's probably heading up to the St. Lawrence."

Heading, Ada thought. *Not headed. He thinks Dan is still alive.*

"He's got his car, right? Not the patrol car."

Ada nodded. "I suppose so," she said.

"I'll call the station and have them send out a description over the wire," A.J. said.

They won't find it, Ada wanted to say. *He's too careful for that.* She didn't know how she knew this, but she was sure of it. Yet she couldn't bring herself to contradict A.J. Nor did she respond when he said, "We'll find him, Ada. We'll find him and get him back here."

She allowed A.J. to reassure her, even as she knew that she was the one reassuring him by letting him believe that everything would be okay. She made coffee and sat at the table while A.J. drank it, leaving her own cup untouched. She listened as he spoke with hope in his voice.

"He hasn't been gone that long," he said. "That letter was mailed not more than a day ago."

She glanced at the clock on the wall. It was just past seven. Celeste and Billy would be finishing up dinner and heading to the Roxy for the movie. She imagined Billy's excitement; he would be beside himself with anticipation at seeing the final movie in the *Star Wars* trilogy. He'd been begging Dan for weeks to take him. That it was his sister taking him, and not his father, would hopefully not make him suspicious. As for Celeste, Ada suspected that Paul Lunardi was even now looking at the selection in the candy counter and choosing something for Celeste to buy him with her mother's money. For once Ada was grateful for her daughter's defiance; it would keep her from wondering why her mother had asked her to play babysitter to Billy, and on a school night.

"Did he tell you?" Ada found herself saying.

"Tell me?" A.J. repeated. "Tell me what?"

"About the cancer," said Ada. "Did he tell you that he had cancer?"

A.J. shook his head. "No," he answered. "Why would he tell me if he didn't even tell you?"

Ada shrugged. "Sometimes men tell their best friends things they can't bring themselves to tell their wives. You know that as well as I do."

A.J. got up and poured himself some more coffee. "That's true," he said. "But usually that involves other women."

"Was there another one?" asked Ada.

"Woman?" A.J. said, sitting down again. "No. Daniel would never do that."

Ada sighed. "I almost wish it *were* another woman," she said. "Then at least I'd have something real to hate. But cancer . . ." She waved one hand in a gesture of frustration. "There's nothing I can do about cancer. I can hate it, but I can't see it or hit it or ask it what the hell it's doing with my husband."

"I don't think you should tell the kids," said A.J., interrupting her.

Ada looked at him. "Why not?" she said. "I can't keep it from them forever."

"Not forever," A.J. said. "Just until the station can check out any reports of . . ." His voice trailed off.

Bodies, Ada thought, finishing the sentence for him.

"And he might just show up," said A.J. "We should give him twenty-four hours."

Ada knew that Daniel wouldn't be coming back, but she was in no hurry to inform the children of his disappearance. That more than anything would make the situation unavoidably real. Until then she could at least pretend that none of it was happening.

A.J. stayed for several more hours, until Ada was sure that the movie must be over and that Celeste and Billy were on their way home. Although there was nothing terribly unusual about A.J. being at their house, even with their father absent, Ada didn't want to give them any cause to worry. *They'll be worried soon enough as it is,* she told herself. After promising A.J. that she would wait for his call before doing anything else, she showed him out and returned to the kitchen. The arrival of dark frightened her somewhat, as if whatever had taken Daniel might come for her next, and the warmth and light of the kitchen made her feel less worried.

A.J. had left the letter on the table. Ada picked it up, returned it to its envelope, and put it once more in her pocket. She knew she would have to give it to the police in the morning, but for one more night it was hers to keep safe. Now all she could do was wait.

I love you, Daniel, she thought as she waited for her children to return to the empty house. *I don't think you could ever know how much I love you. And I'm sorry.*

CHAPTER 26

1991

Charly was amazed by the change that had occurred in Billy. Gone was the slightly tired-looking boy of the previous evening. He had been replaced by a sallow-skinned, red-eyed man who slumped in his chair as if sitting up took more effort than his body could exert. He was wearing the same clothes as he had been during their first meeting, although now they had a slept-in look that gave him the appearance of a vagrant. His hair was messy and his words when he spoke fell thickly from his bruised lips. Charly couldn't imagine what might have happened to him in the preceding twenty-four hours to create such a drastic transformation but it disturbed her, although neither Celeste nor Ada seemed much concerned. *They've seen him like this before,* Charly thought. *So often that they no longer notice.*

Turning her attention away from Billy, she looked at Arthur Peckinpaugh. One of the three attorneys Charly had called on her friend's recommendation, Arthur had been the only one to return her call. They had spoken late the night before, with Charly filling Arthur in on the details of the case. He had been reluctant to sign on to something so serious with so little time before arraignment, but had finally agreed on the condition that Charly do most of the work for him, acting behind the scenes. She had of course agreed, and Arthur had met her that morning at the Onondaga County Courthouse in Syracuse.

She wondered what Arthur thought of Billy. Arthur was an older man, in his fifties and from all appearances quite conservative. He had a formal attitude that Charly appreciated but that she knew could be disturbing for families who wanted a lawyer with a gentler bedside manner. She'd realized immediately that she would have to be the comforter, a role she did not relish but that she took on for the sake of James's family.

Now they were all—with the exception of Nate—gathered around the kitchen table. It was Charly who had suggested the kitchen, thinking that it would be a less intimidating environment than the living room.

"It was very straightforward," Arthur said, explaining the morning's events. "The charges were read. As expected, James has been charged with murder in the first degree. I requested bail, which was denied." He glanced at Charly. "I believe Ms. Trent told you that would likely be the case."

Charly affirmed this with a nod. She knew, though, that Ada had been holding out hope that a miracle would occur and James would return with Charly and Arthur from the court appearance. The look on her face when James failed to emerge from the car had broken Charly's heart.

"I've been given all of the information the DA was given by Mr. Derry," Arthur continued. "I will of course be going through that thoroughly."

"I don't see why Nate can't be here," Celeste interrupted. "He *is* part of the family. And now that the case has been turned over to the county court, I don't see why he shouldn't know what's going on."

Charly waited for Arthur to speak, but he seemed to be deferring to her on the matter of dealing directly with the McCloud family. "I understand your feelings," she told Celeste. "But as the arresting officer Nate will more than likely be called to testify at the trial."

"So?" Celeste said. "It's not like he's going to spy for the DA. He might actually be able to help."

"Possibly," Charly agreed. "However, Arthur and I feel it's best that we involve him as little as possible to prevent the appearance of a conflict of interest."

"It's also important that you not discuss this matter with him any more than absolutely necessary," Arthur added.

"He's my husband," said Celeste. "What am I supposed to do, move out until after the trial?"

"Ideally, yes," Arthur told her. "But we realize that isn't a practical possibility," he added when Charly shot him a look.

Celeste shook her head but said nothing in reply. Charly saw Ada reach out and take her daughter's hand. Celeste pulled away, tucking her hands beneath the table. Ada's hand remained on the tabletop. She didn't look at Celeste.

"The next step is the grand jury," Arthur said. "The prosecutor will present the evidence against James to them and they'll vote to indict him. That will happen in the next week, unless the prosecutor can prove that more time is necessary to present the evidence."

"And if the jury doesn't indict him?" Ada asked.

"Then he's free," said Arthur. "But the chances of that happening are almost nil. Just from the little I know about the evidence, it seems fairly certain that the grand jury will find that there's enough for an indictment."

"You're talking like you think James is guilty too," Billy said suddenly. He was glaring at Arthur with open hostility in his glassy eyes.

"We have to assume the worst, Billy," said Charly. "I know it's difficult for you to hear us say that the case against James doesn't look good for him, but please understand that until we have our own evidence to contradict what the DA has, we have to proceed this way."

Billy gave a snort and hung his head. Celeste turned to her brother. "Besides," she said, "the evidence is pretty strong against him."

Billy's head shot up. "Right," he said, sneering. "I forgot. You have to take Nate's side."

"I'm not taking sides," Celeste objected. "I'm just saying that right now things don't look so great for James."

"Celeste," Ada said. "Billy."

"No, Mom!" Celeste exclaimed. "I'm tired of tiptoeing around Billy just because he's a fucked-up mess."

Charly watched, horrified but curious, as the family drama played out. Ada seemed to have retreated into herself, while Billy was still shaking his head and Celeste, now enraged, continued to rant.

"Maybe no one else around here wants to face facts," she said. "But you'd better start, because it's looking more and more like maybe James—"

"Why don't you shut the fuck up?" Billy said angrily. "Maybe you think Nate is some kind of goddamn saint, but not everyone does. Did it ever occur to you that maybe he—"

"Enough." This time it was Ada interrupting. She looked from Billy to Celeste. "That's enough out of both of you. The only thing that matters now is that we help James."

Silence descended over the kitchen and they all sat without speaking for a long moment. Finally it was Arthur who broke the tension. "While I agree with you, Ada, I think perhaps we should take a moment to discuss what each of you believes about the case." He looked around the table. "If any of you have doubts regarding James's innocence, I need to know."

"Ask Celeste," Billy said. "She's the one who apparently thinks he did it."

"I didn't say that," Celeste retorted.

"Why don't you tell me what you *do* think," suggested Arthur.

Celeste crossed her arms over her chest. "I don't really know what I think," she admitted. "If you'd asked me a week ago if I thought James was capable of killing someone, I would have said absolutely not." She looked up at Arthur and Charly. "But people are always doing things you never thought they would do, aren't they? You read about it in the paper all the time. Someone murders someone else and the neighbors all talk about how he was such a nice guy or how she was a great mother and they never thought she could drown her kids in the bathtub."

"That's very true," Arthur said. "Billy, what do you think?"

"I think it's a bunch of shit," he said. "But what do I know?" He looked at Celeste. "I'm just the fuckup around here. I'm not the legal genius that Nate is."

"Leave Nate out of this," Celeste said. "Christ, he isn't the enemy."

Billy laughed. "Okay," he said. "Whatever you say."

Celeste stood up. "I'm out of here," she said, snatching up her coat from the back of the chair. "Mom, I'm sorry, but I can't deal with this asshole right now."

Charly expected Ada to stop her daughter, but she didn't. She just sat, impassive, as Celeste pushed open the screen door and left. The door slammed with a bang, silencing the chirping of the crickets that, until then, Charly hadn't realized was providing background noise for the conversation in the kitchen.

"I apologize for my sister," Billy said, smiling at Arthur. "She's always been a little bit touchy about the guys she's fucking." He followed his statement with a laugh. "Ever since we were kids."

Arthur shuffled the papers before him and opened his briefcase. "I think that's enough for tonight," he said, seeming to be speaking to Charly. "I'll be in touch in the next day or two."

"Can we visit James?" Ada asked. "While he's in . . ."

"Yes," Arthur told her, his voice gentle. "There are visiting hours. Charly can help you find out what they are. Just remember, it's best if you don't discuss the case with him. You never know who's listening."

He stood up, as did Ada. Billy stayed seated.

"Thank you for taking my son's case," Ada said.

Arthur smiled. "Thank Ms. Trent," he said. "She's a very powerful advocate. I originally said no, but she convinced me." He shook Ada's hand. "Try not to worry any more than necessary," he said.

Charly walked with Arthur out to his car. When they were alone she said, "They're quite a bunch, aren't they?"

Arthur opened the door and set his briefcase on the passenger side seat. "I've seen worse," he said. "But not much. What do you think is really going on?"

Charly leaned against the car. "Honestly? I don't know. I can't really get a firm reading on any of them."

"The son appears to have a serious drug problem," Arthur remarked.

"Billy?" said Charly. "Oddly enough, I think he's the only one who tells you what he really thinks."

"Maybe the drugs make him uninhibited," Arthur suggested.

Charly shook her head. "It's more than that," she told him. "It's like he's the only one who sees what's really going on in the family. Ada is dealing with her husband's death all over again, and she's worried about James. Celeste is torn between her husband and her family. But Billy's different. It's almost like he's so past caring what anyone thinks about him that he's not afraid to be who he is."

"That's an interesting theory," said Arthur. "I'm not sure I agree that he's a reliable source, but maybe I won't write him off quite yet. As for the sister, what do you make of what happened in there?"

"Like I said, she's torn," said Charly. "Her husband is the one who arrested James. That's bound to create friction. But from what I can tell, Nate was just doing his job. Frankly I'd be more concerned about his motives if he hadn't brought James in."

"So you think James did it?" Arthur asked suddenly.

"No," Charly said instantly. Then she shook a finger at Arthur. "That wasn't fair," she told him. "You caught me off guard."

"I wanted an honest answer," Arthur said.

"I think you got one," said Charly.

"You think?"

"I'm supposed to be objective," Charly said. "Open to all the possibilities. You can't defend someone if you can't at least imagine how he might have committed the crime, right? That's first-year criminal defense."

"But you don't think he did it," said Arthur. "I can tell."

"No, I don't think he did," Charly said. "I think he *could* have, but I don't think he did. Then again, I can't give you a reasonable explanation for why I think that. I just do."

"I'll be objective enough for both of us then," Arthur said. "At least as far as James McCloud is concerned. But if you're sure he didn't do it, we're going to have to find some evidence to support it, because what there is now is pretty damning."

"I know," said Charly. "And I'm on it."

"Just remember, we don't have a lot of time," Arthur reminded her. "We both know that grand jury is going to indict, and the longer people have to think about the possibility that James killed Dan, the more sure they're going to be that he did do it."

He got into his car and shut the door. "We'll talk tomorrow," he said. "I'll let you get back to the Brady Bunch in there."

Charly waved as Arthur pulled out of the driveway. She was relieved to have him on her side. At least for the moment. If she didn't come up with some hard evidence to help their case, and quickly, he might not be so willing to stand beside James when it came time for trial. She needed to give him something he could use. But finding it wasn't going to be easy, particularly with the way the McClouds were behaving toward one another. Before she could help James, she was going to have to find a way to work with them.

She turned back to the house. Part of her didn't want to return to the kitchen where Ada and Billy were waiting for her. But then she thought about James, and she knew she couldn't turn away from them now.

"But one of you had better start cooperating," she muttered.

CHAPTER 27

1983

"I love Boy George," Celeste said, reaching over Paul and turning the volume up on the car's stereo. She sang along with the song as Paul tried to kiss her. " 'Do you really want to hurt me?' "

"No, but I wouldn't mind punching that freaky fag in the mouth," said Paul, changing the station. Steven Tyler's rasp replaced Boy George's sultry croon. "Much better," Paul said. "Now *that* is music to make out to."

Celeste giggled as Paul bit her neck. But when he started to suck on it, she hit him on the back of the head. "Knock it off," she said. "If I come home with a hickey my father will be at your house with a shotgun."

Paul sat back. "Fuck him," he said angrily.

Celeste looked out the window. They were parked behind the Stop & Save. The lights in the lot flooded everything with a sickly orange color and emitted a faint buzzing noise that made it sound like a million flies were about to descend. The lot was just about empty, with the few occupied spots taken up by cars belonging to the store's employees. The grocery had closed almost two hours ago, but Paul had insisted on staying there because he didn't feel like driving around. Now the only sign of life was the stock boy who was pushing a long line of carts across the lot.

Celeste turned her attention back to Paul, running her finger along his arm. "Come on," she said. "It's no big deal. You just can't leave any bruises." She leaned toward him and placed her hand on his leg. "Besides, there are plenty of other things we can do."

"Forget it," Paul said. He picked up the pack of cigarettes that was lying on the dashboard. Taking one out he started to light it.

"Not in the car," said Celeste. "He'll smell it on me. I'm supposed to be at Roxanne's studying for the European History test, remember?"

Paul stubbed the cigarette out in the car's ashtray. "For fuck's sake," he said. "Why don't you just tell me what we *can* do?"

"Don't get mad," Celeste said. "I'm the one who has to sneak around. You can put up with a few rules. It won't kill you."

"I'm just sick of it," said Paul. "Who the fuck does he think he is saying that you can't see me. You're almost eighteen. You can do whatever the hell you want."

"I wish," Celeste said. "But as long as I'm living there I have to play by his rules."

Paul reached into the backseat and took a can of beer from the bag on the floor. He held it up to Celeste. "Is this okay?" he asked.

"No," said Celeste. "But do it anyway. When my dad or one of his deputies stops you for drunk driving I can always say you kidnapped me."

"You wish I'd kidnap you," Paul joked as he popped the top on the beer and took a long swallow. "Then I'd take you to my hideout and do horrible things to you. Or maybe I'd demand a ransom from your folks. How much do you think they'd pay to get you back?"

"A buck fifty," Celeste said. "I've been with you, so I'm damaged goods."

Paul took another drink. "You know, it's not a bad idea," he said.

"What isn't?" asked Celeste.

"Kidnapping you," Paul explained. "We could just run off somewhere, and you could call your parents and tell them I stole you away—just pulled up at Roxanne's house and dragged you into the car."

"Sure," said Celeste. "Why don't we just elope while we're at it? They'd have to be nice to their son-in-law, wouldn't they?" She laughed. "They'd shit their pants," she said.

"It would almost be worth it," Paul agreed.

He drank some more beer. Watching him, Celeste thought about what it would really be like to run away with him. Where would they go? "Florida," she said.

"What?" Paul asked.

Celeste, realizing that she'd spoken her thought aloud, said, "Florida. That's where we should run off to."

"Why Florida?"

"It's warm there," Celeste answered. "And Disney World is there. We could go there every day."

"It is the happiest place on Earth," Paul remarked, draining his beer.

"Oh, I know," said Celeste. "We could get jobs there. You could—I don't know—run one of the rides or something, and I could be in a show."

"A show?" Paul said. "What kind of show could you be in?"

"I don't know," Celeste said defensively. "Any kind. I can sing and dance. Anyway, we could get jobs at Disney World, and an apartment. Wouldn't that be great?"

"I guess," Paul said. "At least until your asshole father shows up and drags you back here and throws my ass in the slammer."

"For what?" asked Celeste. "You haven't done anything."

Paul tossed the empty beer can into the back and got a fresh one. Celeste watched him nervously. She hoped he wasn't drinking too much. All she needed was for him to get into an accident while driving her home. As it was she was pushing her luck. If her parents found out she'd lied to them about going to Roxanne's there was going to be hell to pay.

"Screw Disney World," Paul said. He pointed a finger at her. "What we need to do is get rid of your old man once and for all."

"Right," said Celeste. "I know, why don't we just run him down with your car? Or tie him up and throw him in the lake. That should do it."

"Nah," Paul said. "Just a quick shot to the heart. Nothing fancy." He held up his finger, now in the shape of a gun, and pointed it at Celeste. "Bang!" he said.

"That's not funny," Celeste told him, swatting at his hand.

"Who says I'm being funny?" Paul replied, grabbing her hand and pulling her to him so that his face was mere inches from hers. "Don't you want to be with me?"

"Yes," Celeste said. She was looking into Paul's eyes. She could smell the beer on his breath and feel the heat rising from his skin. She wanted him to kiss her.

"Then wouldn't you do anything to make that happen?" asked Paul.

He put one hand on one of her breasts, squeezing it softly and running his fingertips over the nipple.

Celeste didn't answer. Would she do anything for him? She loved him more than anything. She wanted to be with him forever, without having to run around and worry about what her parents thought. How far would she be willing to go to have that?

"I would," she said finally.

Paul kissed her, slipping his tongue into her mouth. After a minute he pulled back. "That's my girl," he said. "I'd do anything for you too."

"Like what?" Celeste asked him.

"What did I tell you?" he replied. "I'd kill your old man."

Celeste looked at her watch. "Shit," she said. "You've got to get me home. It's almost eleven. I told my parents I'd be home by ten-thirty. They'll be calling Roxanne's house if I'm not home in like fifteen minutes."

Without a word Paul started the car and pulled out of the lot, headed in the direction of the McCloud house. Celeste knew he was pissed, and that made her angry. He had no right to be mad at her because of the rules her father made. It wasn't her fault that her parents didn't like Paul. Yeah, she wished they would give him a chance, but it wasn't like Paul was a choirboy or anything. He should understand that not everyone saw him the way she did. *It's just as much his fault as it is theirs,* she thought, although she didn't dare say as much to Paul. That would just set him off, especially since he'd been drinking. He was always nastier when he drank. Not that he'd ever been mean to her or anything. It was just that he could be a little scary.

Paul turned up the volume on the radio and began singing along with Def Leppard. "Passion killer, you're too much," he sang in an off-key voice. "You're the only one I wanna touch."

He leaned over and kissed Celeste on the cheek, making the car swerve into the opposite lane. Celeste gave a little shriek as Paul turned the wheel and brought the Mustang back where it was supposed to be.

"Hoo-ya!" Paul shouted, shaking his head so that his hair flew out like a mane.

Celeste was relieved to see him happy again. Sometimes, she thought, all it took was a little rock and roll and crazy driving to put Paul in a better mood. The sudden swings had confused her at first, but now she was used to them. It was just who Paul was, a wild boy who couldn't be tamed. *My wild boy,* she thought happily.

A few minutes later Paul pulled the car to a stop just down the road from Celeste's house. She'd asked him not to drop her off at her driveway because even though she'd told her parents that Roxanne's older brother would drive her home she didn't want to risk her father recognizing Paul's Mustang.

"I'll call you tomorrow," she said, giving Paul a kiss. He put his hand on the back of her head, holding her in place as he kissed her back. Celeste felt herself becoming aroused, and she put her hand on Paul's chest and gently pushed him away. She knew that if she didn't leave now she wouldn't be able to.

"Tomorrow," she said.

Paul waved and pulled away and did a U-turn in the road, heading back the way they'd come. Celeste watched until his taillights winked out. Then she walked the hundred or so yards to her house. Several of the upstairs lights were on, but the downstairs was dark. She hoped this meant that her parents were already in bed.

"He should really get that muffler fixed."

The voice startled her, and she gave a little yell. Turning around she saw a shadow behind her, and for a moment she thought she was being attacked. Then her father's face emerged from the dark and he was standing in front of her, still dressed in his sheriff's uniform. He regarded her with a grim expression.

"Dad," Celeste said. "Um, hi."

"Hi," her father said, raising his hand as if they were acquaintances meeting on the street. "You have a good time studying with Roxanne?"

Celeste's mind raced as she grasped for an answer. Had her father recognized Paul's car, or did he think it was Roxanne's brother who had dropped her off? Without knowing she wasn't sure what she could say.

"Oh, you know," she said. "It was studying. How much fun can you have?"

Her father sniffed the air. "I didn't know Roxanne smoked," he remarked.

"She doesn't," Celeste said quickly. "Clark does. Her brother. The one who brought me home."

Her father nodded. "It's a bad habit," he said.

Celeste, sensing that she had escaped detection, shook her head in agreement. "I know," she said. "The whole car reeks of smoke."

"I'm not talking about smoking," said her father. "I'm talking about lying."

Celeste's heart seemed to stop. She said nothing, waiting for her father to continue. The longer he looked at her without saying anything the more terrified she became, until finally she realized that she was shaking in fear.

"Your mother called Roxanne's twenty minutes ago," her father informed her. "She apparently gave the wrong brownie recipe to Mrs. Lemmon this afternoon, and she wanted to let her know she would bring the right one over tomorrow. You can imagine she was a little surprised to hear that you weren't there."

Damn it! Celeste thought. Leave it to her mother to screw things up for her. She knew her mother hadn't done it on purpose, but she was still pissed off. If she hadn't called Mrs. Lemmon, no one would have known she'd lied about where she was going.

"I can explain," Celeste said, realizing immediately that actually she couldn't. She'd been caught, and there was no getting out of it.

"Inside," her father said, indicating the door.

They walked into the house, where Ada was waiting for them. She didn't even look at Celeste. "Was she with the boy?" she asked her husband.

"Ask her," Daniel replied.

Celeste felt her mother's gaze fall upon her. She had recovered sufficiently from the shock of being found out and she was now becoming indignant. "I'm not a little kid," she said huffily.

"Which is exactly why I would expect you to have better sense than to go slutting around with Paul Lunardi," her mother snapped.

Celeste's face burned. How dare her mother call her such a thing. Did she really have such a low opinion of Celeste? Celeste began to shake, and clenched her hands to steady herself.

"Answer your mother," she heard her father say.

"She didn't ask me anything," said Celeste. "All she did was call me a slut."

The slap surprised her. She cried out and brought her hand to her face. The stinging brought tears to her eyes, and as the shock of being hit wore off it was replaced by a quickly rising pain. She tried to breathe and found that she couldn't. All she could do was stare at her father, who was standing in front of her with his face contorted in rage.

"I'll make this very simple," he said, speaking in a slow, even tone that made Celeste even more frightened than she already was. "You are not to see that boy ever again. If you do, I will make his life one never-ending hell. Do you understand?"

Celeste nodded, still unable to speak. Her breath had returned to her, but she didn't dare open her mouth.

"Good," said her father. "Now go upstairs. Maybe tonight you'll think about how you're going to apologize to your mother in the morning."

Celeste ran up the stairs and down the hall. Only when she was in her room with the door shut behind her did she allow the sobs inside of her to come out. Even then she buried her face in a pillow, screaming her frustration into it and beating the bed with her fists. She'd never been so hurt, and the fact that it was her father who had hurt her made it all a million times worse.

I should let Paul kill him, she thought. *I should just let him do it.*

CHAPTER 28

1991

Charly was just nodding off—having finally calmed her racing thoughts by lying very still and imagining a series of pebbles being dropped one at a time into a pool of clear blue water—when she heard a tapping. Thinking at first that it must be the sound of rain on the roof (it had been threatening all day to pour) she ignored it. But when it came again she realized that someone was knocking on the bedroom door. Reluctantly she threw back the covers and padded across the room. Opening the door, she saw Ada standing in the hallway.

"I'm sorry to bother you," Ada said. "May I come in?"

"Of course," Charly said. "Is something wrong?"

Ada entered and stood in the center of the room, looking around as if it were the first time she'd ever seen it. "When Celeste was about nine, she asked us if she could paint the walls in here purple," she said. "I didn't want her to. I said it was because I didn't think purple would go with the carpet. But really it was because I didn't want her to cover up the wallpaper I'd put up when she was born. It had little pink and yellow flowers on it." She turned to Charly. "It's very difficult when you realize your children are reaching a point where they no longer need you," she said.

"Do they ever not need you?" asked Charly. She didn't understand why Ada had woken her up. Did she really just want to talk about her children?

"I'd like you to read something," Ada said. She walked over to Charly and handed her a letter. "This is the letter that Daniel sent me."

"I thought you said you didn't have a copy," Charly said, confused.

"I said that I didn't have a copy of the letter that I gave to the police," Ada answered. "And that's true."

"Then I don't understand," said Charly. "What's this?"

"The letter I gave to the police is not the letter that came in the mail," Ada said. She sat on the edge of the bed, smoothing out the blankets. "No one has ever seen this one but me."

Charly opened the envelope and pulled out a single sheet of paper. Her eyes quickly scanned the three typed paragraphs.

Dear Ada:

By the time you read this I will be dead. I've lived for a long time with a terrible secret, and I can't live with it any longer.

What I have to tell you is very hard to say, so I'll just say it. I am the one who killed Rebecca Derry. Why I did it doesn't matter. But I did do it, and now it's time I paid for my sins. I don't want to cause any more pain than I have to, so I'm going to end things my own way.

I know you will have a lot of questions, and I'm sorry that I can't answer them. I don't know that I even have the answers. All I can do is ask you to forgive me. I love you and the children more than I can say. I hope that you can believe that.

Daniel

When she finished reading, Charly looked over at Ada, who was sitting calmly on the bed watching her. "This is the letter you received?" she said.

"Yes," Ada said. "I wrote the one that I showed A.J. and gave to the police."

"Why?" asked Charly.

Ada sighed. "I didn't want to disturb the ghosts," she said. She looked at Charly and her eyes were wet with tears. "Rebecca Derry was a wonderful woman," she said. "And A.J. is a wonderful man. I didn't want to reopen his wounds. It would have been too difficult for him, as well as for Nancy."

"So you invented the story about your husband having cancer?" said Charly, still not quite believing that she was hearing correctly.

"It seemed the most logical," Ada replied. "It really would be like Daniel to kill himself rather than put us through the pain of watching him die. And I thought there would be fewer questions that way."

Charly sat down on the wooden desk chair over which she'd laid her clothes just an hour earlier. She couldn't believe what Ada was telling her.

"Did Daniel really write *this* note?" she asked.

"Until this week I thought that he had," said Ada. "Now I don't know any more about it than you do. That's why I'm showing it to you."

"I can't believe you've kept this a secret for so long," Charly told her.

"Neither can I, frankly," said Ada. "And there have been many times when I've wanted to tell the truth about it. But I always convinced myself that there would be nothing to gain from it but more misery."

Charly read the letter again. The short, perfunctory style was jarring, as if the note had been written hastily. Yet whoever had written it had taken the time to type it out. *Why would someone do that?* she asked herself.

"I imagine you think I'm quite a monster," Ada said, interrupting Charly's thoughts.

"To be honest I don't know what to think," said Charly. "But I can say that I don't think you're a monster."

Ada wiped away a tear. "You don't know how important it is for me to hear that," she said. "I almost talked myself out of coming up here, but something told me you would understand."

"I don't know as I *understand*," Charly told her. "But I'll try. First of all, who is Rebecca Derry? I assume she's somehow related to Nate Derry."

"No," said Ada. "She was A.J. Derry's first wife. Nate's mother is his second wife, Bess, and Nate is from Bess's first marriage. He just took the Derry name. Rebecca died long before Bess ever returned to Cold Falls."

"How did she die?" Charly asked.

She listened as Ada told her about the break-in at the Derry home, about how Rebecca was killed by a shotgun blast to the head, and about how Dan himself had handled the investigation and declared the woman's death the result of being in the wrong place at the wrong time. The telling of the story took only a few minutes. When Ada was done Charly was ready with a list of questions.

She led with, "Why would Dan have killed Rebecca Derry?"

"I imagine because they'd been having an affair," Ada replied.

"You imagine or you know?" asked Charly.

"I suspect it," Ada said. "I don't know. And now they're both dead so I can't ask them."

Charly noticed that a harder edge had crept into Ada's voice all of a sudden. Clearly—and understandably—the direction the conversation had taken was making her uncomfortable. But Charly had to ask the questions if she was going to make any sense out of the new information she'd been given.

"And did you know about this before this letter arrived?"

"No," Ada admitted. "But once I got the letter I started to put things together, and . . . it all made sense."

Charly thought that she would need a lot more information before she could agree with Ada that her hypothesis made sense. But that would have to wait. She was tired, and she needed time to gather her thoughts before attempting to get anything more out of Ada. She decided to change tack slightly.

"Were any parts of the story you told me—and the police—true?" she tried.

"Some," said Ada. "For instance the hotel receipts. Daniel did make several trips to Syracuse in the months before he disappeared."

"But if we now know he wasn't going there to see an oncologist, what was he doing?" Charly asked.

"I don't know," Ada said. "Perhaps he was seeing another woman. To be honest I try not to think about it. There doesn't seem to be any point."

That's the thing, though, Charly thought. *It might be exactly the point.* If Dan McCloud was having affairs, there could be any number of people who might have wanted him dead. Including his wife. Ada had already confessed to forging a note to hide the supposed truth about her husband's disappearance. What else might she be hiding? Things had suddenly become far more intriguing—and far more complicated—than Charly had ever imagined they could.

"This is a lot to take in," she admitted to Ada. "We have a suicide that wasn't a suicide. We have a forged letter that was meant to cover up a letter that was in all likelihood forged in the first place. But if it wasn't forged, we have a dead man who admitted to the murder of his best friend's wife."

She waited for Ada to respond in some way. Finally Ada said, "I used to think that when I grew up I would understand everything. That life would make sense and people would behave according to rules I could figure out. But it doesn't work that way."

"No," Charly agreed. "It doesn't. That was one of the hardest things for me to accept when I started studying law. The law is all about rules. Hell, it's nothing *but* rules. But the people who are supposed to follow those rules, and even the ones who are supposed to interpret them, all have different ideas about how it's supposed to work."

Ada stood up. "I should let you get your sleep," she said. "I just wanted you to have that."

"May I keep it?" Charly asked, holding the letter out to give Ada a chance to take it back. She was curious to see what the other woman would do.

Ada looked at the letter. "Keep it," she said. "But may I ask what you're going to do with it?"

"I don't know yet," said Charly. "Technically it's evidence, and I should turn it over to the DA."

"Which would get me in trouble," Ada said.

"Which would get you in a *lot* of trouble," Charly agreed. "And it wouldn't necessarily help James any. In fact, it might make him look more guilty, because the DA would almost certainly argue that either the two of you conspired to kill Dan or you forged the letter to cover up what James allegedly did. Either way you don't win."

"But not giving it to the DA makes you guilty as well, doesn't it?" Ada asked.

"In the eyes of the law, yes," said Charly. "But sometimes the eyes of the law look the other way," she added.

Ada nodded. "I think I understand," she said. "Thank you."

She walked to the door. "Sleep well," she said as she left the room.

Charly shut the door, then went to the bed and got in. She was no longer even remotely sleepy. How could she be, when Ada had just dropped such a bombshell on her? Part of her felt she should barricade the door somehow, in case Ada changed her mind about revealing the truth. But she thought Ada had probably used up whatever store of guile she'd had. After all, she had lived with her secret for eight years. Worse, she had lived those years believing that her husband was not only an adulterer but a murderer.

There was no doubt in Charly's mind that she had kept quiet for the sake of the children. And not just her own, but Nancy Derry as well. Whatever pain she'd felt, Ada McCloud had buried it beneath her desire to keep life as normal as possible for her family. That it was all a lie almost didn't matter now. What was done was done, and the people they had all become as a result of Ada's decision were now free to do as they would.

Besides, Ada's deception didn't change the fact that Daniel Mc-Cloud had been murdered. *Someone* had killed him. *Someone* had written the note and mailed it to Ada. The questions foremost in Charly's mind were who killed Dan and was the accusation in the letter true or just another red herring. Answering the latter question would lead to answering the first. But where should she begin her search?

She worked her way backward through the riddle, separating out each element until there was no more sorting to be done. And she was left with Rebecca Derry. That was where it all began, and where she herself would begin to look for answers.

Having made a decision, Charly set the letter aside and closed her eyes. Moments later she heard the unmistakable sound of rain falling overhead. It grew louder, and then a deep boom echoed from far off. The storm had finally arrived. Charly lay in the dark, listening as it grew in intensity. Lightning crackled in the world beyond the bedroom window, briefly illuminating the dresser and mirror before the room plunged once more into darkness.

CHAPTER 29

1983

"Mom, the water is boiling over."

Ada looked up. On the stove thick clouds of steam rose from the pot of potatoes. A mound of foam covered the top, and streams of water streaked the sides. As the water hit the burner beneath the pot it sizzled ferociously.

Ada continued to stare at it, not moving. Part of her mind recognized that something was happening that required her attention, but another part was busy dealing with the words she'd just read. That part was in control at the moment, and the overflowing pot seemed nothing more than a dream. Bill too was merely a ghost, one who had appeared out of nowhere to make an announcement of imminent tragedy.

Then he shook her, and she awoke from her stupor. Instinctively she rose from the chair and went to the stove. Turning the burner off, she took up a dishrag and began mopping up the spilled water. It was hot, and burned her hand, but she took no notice of it. She looked into the pile of ruined potatoes as if she were trying to read the leaves in the bottom of a teacup. Surely she would find something there—some sign or omen—that would explain what was happening.

"Mom, are you okay?"

She turned and looked at her youngest son. He was regarding her with a puzzled expression, his face both wary and frightened. She saw that he sensed her confusion and was in turn upset by the change in mood that had come over her and that seemed now to permeate the entire kitchen. She wanted to comfort him—to tell him that everything was fine—but she couldn't. Her ability to protect her child had been stripped away by her own unexpected shock.

Finally she managed to shake her head. "I'm fine," she told Billy. "I just wasn't paying attention."

"You sure made a mess," Billy said. Whatever anxiety he'd absorbed from her had vanished with her assurance that things were back in order. The momentary disruption in his world had been repaired, and for him all was as it should be.

For Ada things were very different. The potatoes were nothing compared to the destruction that was occurring inside of her. Thought tumbled upon thought, each one with claws so sharp that she felt physical pain, a kind of rending of the heart that made her breath catch in her throat.

"I sure did," she said, agreeing with Billy. She hoped her voice sounded normal, although at the moment she had absolutely no idea what normal would be.

Billy laughed. "Wait till I tell Dad," he joked.

"Yes," said Ada. "He'll think it's funny." She smiled, picturing herself as a grinning skull, its lips stretched in a grotesque death rictus.

Billy went out the screen door, off on some personal errand. *He's probably going to ride his bike,* Ada thought. *It's nice out. He should ride for a few minutes before dinner.*

Only she knew that there wasn't going to be any dinner. The roast was done, and although the potatoes were ruined it would take only another half hour to prepare a new batch. But she wouldn't do that. She *couldn't* do it. At the moment she couldn't even remember how potatoes were cooked, or why she would want to do such a thing.

The letter was sitting on the table. She realized with alarm that Billy could easily have picked it up and read its contents. It would have been a natural thing to do, especially for a curious boy such as Billy. He was always asking questions beginning with *why,* and *how,* and *what.* It was one of the things that she loved most about him. The world was a mystery he seemed determined to solve. Unlike James, who saw life as an obstacle course to be conquered, and Celeste, who took the path of least resistance, Billy was an explorer. It was in his nature to test and to try, to sample experiences and see what could be taken from them. She would not have been at all surprised had he read the letter (it was rare that anyone in the McCloud household received actual letters) or at least asked what it was and who had sent it. She was relieved that he hadn't.

You have to do something, she reminded herself. *There isn't much time.*

Billy would expect to return from his bike ride to find dinner waiting for him. Celeste too would be home any minute, under strict orders to not be late. Dan and Ada suspected that she was spending her afternoons with Paul Lunardi, and Dan had made a point out of telling Celeste that she was expected home every evening before six. It was five thirty now.

She found herself walking toward Dan's study. Really it was just a small room in which they tended to collect the bits and pieces of their lives that had nowhere else to go: roller skates and softball bats, winter shoes, boxes of tax returns from the past twelve years (Dan was convinced that they were overdue for an audit and kept every receipt). There was a desk in there, with a typewriter that Dan sometimes used to type up reports and that the kids sometimes used to type reports for school. Ada used it herself to type up recipe cards and the annual Christmas letter.

She sat down at the desk and inserted a piece of paper. She stared at the blank page, wondering how exactly she would get the thoughts in her head to form actual words. An idea had come to her, but she had no idea how to bring it to life. That people could write actual books suddenly seemed the most miraculous thing in the world.

She closed her eyes and composed herself. *It has to sound believable,* she thought. She laughed at the absurdity of the idea that she was sitting at her husband's desk composing his suicide note. It simply wasn't possible. Yet she knew that she had to do it. Some primitive instinct told her that she could not let the truth of what was in the letter come out. No one could know. And if she had to do this to make that happen then she would do it.

She kept the letter short, feeling that the less she said the less chance there was for discovery. Dan had killed himself. But why? What would cause a man like Daniel McCloud to do such a thing? She thought over all the possibilities: financial problems, addiction of some kind, a failure in his career. All of these were plausible—but not when the man in question was Dan. Not only were none of these things applicable to him, they could all be easily disproved.

He was dying, she thought suddenly. *He didn't want you to see him suffer.*

She realized instantly that it was the perfect lie.

Resuming her typing, she worked out the details. They came easily, reinforcing her belief that she'd chosen correctly. Although she still couldn't accept that the situation itself was real, she nonetheless was determined to cope with it. It had of course occurred to her that the letter was a fake, a joke perhaps, or some kind of maliciousness on the part of a disgruntled party. The contents could not possibly be accurate. And she still half expected Daniel to walk through the door and greet her with his customary kiss.

But only half. The other part of her believed that the letter told the truth. She couldn't say why she thought this. That would require reviving some old fears, ones she had tried her best to bury. It would also require admitting certain things about herself, her husband, and their marriage. In the event that these things she feared were indeed at the heart of the letter's accusations, she had to prevent them from tearing what was left of her world apart.

She finished the letter and read it once more. Yes, it sounded like Dan. Not that she was surprised. For years she had written his letters to various civic organizations thanking them for their support. She had even composed his address to the 1979 graduating class of Cold Falls High School, exhorting them to live lives based on the concepts of service and community building. His written voice was more her own than it was his, and whatever annoyance she might have felt while writing thank-you notes to the Elks and the Girl Scouts now paled in comparison to her relief at being able to create a credible approximation of Daniel's thoughts.

Although the real letter had not been signed, she signed hers. Again, years of forging her husband's signature on checks and Christmas cards enabled her to perform this task without hesitation. She then folded the letter in thirds and slipped it inside the original envelope. The letter she'd received she put inside a fresh envelope. She would deal with it later.

Returning to the kitchen she prepared for the next step in her charade. Celeste had come home with only a few moments left before her deadline expired. She stood in front of the refrigerator, the door open, peering inside.

"Are we out of orange juice?" she asked.

"Yes," Ada said, although she knew there was an unopened carton on the shelf, hidden behind a gallon of milk.

Celeste shut the door. "Why's it smell in here?" she said, sniffing the air.

"Dinner burned," Ada explained. "I had to do something in the yard and I just forgot."

Celeste rolled her eyes. "I guess it's pizza then," she said. "I'll call."

"No," Ada said. She located her purse in its usual location at the end of the counter. Opening it she looked into the pocket in which she kept her household cash. There were several bills left over after the week's shopping. She removed two of them. "Why don't you and Billy go get something. Then maybe you can take him to see *Return of the Jedi*."

Celeste eyed her suspiciously. "What's the catch?" she asked.

"There is none," said Ada. "It's just that he's been bugging me for weeks to go, and I don't want to see it. I've got a headache now and don't feel like making anything else for dinner. Here, you can take the car." She handed the keys to Celeste, who immediately put them in her pocket.

"What about my curfew?" she said.

"Don't worry about it," said Ada. "I'll tell your father I said it was all right."

She held her breath, waiting for Celeste to argue. It seemed that more and more her daughter went out of her way to pick fights, even when she was already getting what she wanted. But Celeste simply nodded and said, "Cool. Where's the kid?"

Ten minutes later Celeste and Billy were gone. Finally Ada allowed herself to consider the facts as outlined in the letter she had received. Daniel was dead, allegedly by his own hand. And he had killed himself because he had killed Rebecca Derry and could no longer live with the guilt. Whether the first allegation proved to be true remained to be seen. As for the other, there was perhaps no way of knowing for certain.

That Daniel had had an affair with Rebecca Derry was something she had long feared, although there was no proof of it and Ada could not really say why she thought this. But she did, and for this she felt oddly guilty. Rebecca Derry had been one of the kindest people Ada had ever known. Still, Ada had been painfully aware of the way her husband came alive in Rebecca's presence, as if she sparked in him something that was otherwise dormant. It was something maybe only a wife would notice, as A.J. Derry never seemed to sense the change that came over Dan when he was around his best friend's wife.

Had Daniel killed Rebecca? Ada had long ago been disabused of the notion that there was a living soul completely incapable of murder. Despite her love for her husband, she nonetheless could imagine him being driven to such an act. He had a temper. She had experienced it, and had seen it directed at the children. Daniel was a man with a fierce will, and sometimes this will could explode like kindling when sparked. If provoked enough, he could perhaps kill.

Daniel himself had overseen the investigation into Rebecca's murder. He could easily have hidden or doctored evidence to support his ultimate determination that Rebecca's death was the result of robbery. A break-in was easy enough to stage. With no witnesses, there was no one to contradict the findings. Besides, no one wanted to. That Rebecca was murdered was horrific enough; that she might have been deliberately butchered was too much for anyone to bear.

She tried to think back to that night. Had Daniel been home? She tried to remember. No, she realized, he hadn't. She'd been alone, watching television, when he'd called to tell her of the tragedy. It was one of only a handful of times she'd ever heard his voice break. She'd thought then that he'd been overwhelmed with grief. But what if it had instead been guilt? What if he had called not to inform her of Rebecca's death but to take the first step in a great deception, establishing himself as the bearer of tragic news instead of revealing himself to be the cause of it?

No, she could not let the letter's contents be read by anyone. It would destroy her family. It would devastate A.J., whom she loved almost as much as she did her husband. *And it would give Bess Kunkel something to hold over me,* she thought. It was a bitter admission, but she admitted it nonetheless. She had pride—a great deal of it—and she would not let her family be tarnished by a sin that the head of it might have committed.

She had to call A.J. It was the next logical step, calling the best friend of her husband to ask him to provide assistance. The irony of the situation was bitter. It pained her to use A.J. in this way. But there was no choice. She had to get used to telling the lie she had invented, and A.J. was the easiest one to start with because he was the one who stood to be most hurt by the real letter. If she could get him to believe her version of events then she would come to believe it herself. After that it would simply be a matter of repeating the lie until it eventually became the truth.

I'm sorry, A.J., she thought as she picked up the phone. *But it's better this way. For all of us.*

CHAPTER 30

1991

James stared at Charly for a long time. Then he shook his head. "That's simply not possible," he said.

They were seated in the visiting room at the jail. James, dressed in an orange coverall and wearing the white tennis shoes he'd been issued upon processing, was one of four men receiving visitors. The others were chatting with their families; one had a child of two or three on his knee and another spoke animatedly with a man who from the resemblance between them was almost certainly his brother. The third held the hands of the young woman seated across from him between his own hands. He whispered something to the woman that made her laugh. After hearing nothing but men's voices for the past several days, James was startled by the sound.

"It's not possible," he said again.

"I have the letter," said Charly.

"Show me," James told her.

Charly shook her head. "You know as well as I do that I can't bring it in here. They search everything. The last thing we need is for it to be confiscated or go missing. But don't worry, I memorized it."

She recited the letter word-by-word in a flat, almost monotone, voice.

"You sound like a robot," James remarked.

"I'm trying not to inflect," said Charly. "I want you to hear the words, not what I might think about them."

James understood her point. It was difficult when reading evidence or testimony to maintain a completely objective tone. You tended to stress one part or another, to imbue the words with your own take on them, which might or might not be the original intention of the speaker or writer. Once again he admired Charly's excellent skills as a lawyer, although he would have preferred to see them used for someone else's benefit than his own.

When Charly was done James said, "That's it?"

"Short and to the point," Charly agreed. "What do you think?"

James could only give a short laugh. "I don't know what the hell to think anymore," he said. "Christ, I'm in jail for murdering the father I was told committed suicide because he was sick. Now you're telling me he did it because he murdered the mother of my high school girl-friend and that my mother covered it up. You tell me what I'm sup-posed to think."

"Do you think your father could have killed Rebecca Derry?"

James sighed. "You know as well as I do—anyone can do anything under the right circumstances." The image of his father yelling at him flashed across his mind, a memory of being afraid that he was going to be hit. *Yes,* he thought, *he could do it.*

"It would explain why he was so against your dating Nancy," said Charly.

James looked at her. How had he not thought of that? *Because you're not being objective,* he reminded himself. Once again, his ad-miration for his girlfriend grew.

"It would," he said. He hesitated before continuing. "Her mother's death really did a number on Nancy. She pretended like everything was fine, but it wasn't. I don't think anybody knew how much she hurt."

"Not even you?" Charly asked him.

"I was fifteen," said James. "I was about as sensitive as a steer. But yes, sometimes I could tell. We didn't talk about it too much. I don't think she wanted to for some reason. It was like she had this secret that she kept hidden from everyone else, that only she was allowed to look at or play with. I can't really explain it."

"She never mentioned anything about there being problems be-tween her parents?"

"No," James answered. "But Rebecca had died before Nancy and I started going out. The first time there was another woman in the house was when A.J. married Bess."

"And Nancy liked her?"

"Yeah, she did. It's hard not to like Bess," James said.

Charly raised one eyebrow. "Your mother doesn't seem to care for her very much."

"My father dated Bess in high school," James explained. "I guess my mother didn't like her then either. Dad once told me that Mom was so jealous of Bess that she ran against her for class secretary because my father was the president and she didn't want him to be at council meetings with Bess. Mom won, mostly by promising to help the people who voted for her with their homework. She apparently spent the whole year writing papers for other people."

"But she got her man," Charly joked.

James laughed. It felt good to do it. For a moment he forgot that they were in a jail and that he was a prisoner. Looking at Charly in her blue suit with a white shirt beneath the jacket, her makeup perfect and her nails done, he could easily believe that they were just having lunch at Baxter's, as they often did when their schedules worked out. They were waiting for their food—his a Cobb salad and Charly's a Reuben. She would eat only half of it and bring the other half home, where it would sit in the refrigerator for a week, until James threw it out.

"Time's up."

The voice brought him back to reality. A guard had come to their table to let them know that visiting hours were over for the day. He glanced briefly at Charly, then looked at James as if to say, "How did a guy like you get a girl like that?" Then he turned away and went to break up the family with the child.

"Have you shown the letter to Arthur?" James asked as he stood up.

"Later today," said Charly. She hugged him and gave him a quick kiss. "I'll be back," she said. "Try not to worry."

"Sure," James assured her. He was fully aware that both of them knew he was lying.

As soon as the visitors were gone, James and the other three men were returned to the cell block. Alone in his cell, James lay on his bed, staring at the water-stained ceiling and trying to make sense of things. What was true and what wasn't? Who could he believe? His mother had, according to her own testimony, covered up a horrible crime. But she'd done it when she'd believed that Daniel had killed himself. Those circumstances had changed with the discovery of his body, so now what was to be made of the letter in the first place?

Maybe she made them both up, said a voice in his head. *The first one to cover up your father's death and the second to cover up his discovery.* His blood chilled at the thought, not only because of how shocking it would be if it were true, but also because it made perfect sense. His mother could have written the first note to explain his father's disappearance. Now, with the revelation that he'd actually been murdered she might have forged another one to throw everyone off the track by providing a motive for Daniel's murderer.

And the ring, said the voice in his mind. *Don't forget the ring.*

He'd thought that Nancy had lost his ring. But had she? Now he couldn't remember. Maybe she'd given it back to him and *he* had lost it. Or maybe his mother had taken it and placed it inside the trunk in which she'd buried his father's body. The idea was unimaginable. Still, he had to consider it. If she had killed his father, she was likely not in her right mind. In that kind of a state people could do just about anything. He'd seen women blame the killing of their children on demons and men justify the murders of their girlfriends by claiming the women were into rough sex. The human mind, he'd discovered, was capable of all kinds of perversions of logic, all of which were designed to shield it from the truth of its own depravity.

What if she wasn't your mother? he asked himself. *What if this was just another case study? Would you say she was likely to be the prime suspect?*

He pondered the question. Certainly, if he was being objective, it made sense. A woman finds out her husband is cheating on her. She becomes enraged. She kills him in a fit of passion. It was one of the oldest stories in the book. Then, having killed him, she has to figure out how to get rid of the body and explain its disappearance. You didn't have to be Hercule Poirot to figure that one out.

There was something that troubled him even more (he marveled that it was even possible) than the idea that his mother was a murderer, and that was that she was now letting him sit in jail for something she might have done. If it was true that she had killed his father in a jealous rage, they might have a good defense. But if it turned out that she'd done it and then allowed her own son to be accused of the crime, well, that would put things in an entirely different—and far less sympathetic—light.

She wouldn't do that, he told himself.

Why not? he argued. *If she would murder, why wouldn't she let someone else take the blame?*

She wrote the second letter.

He considered that. He'd thought before that perhaps his mother had concocted the second letter in order to cover her tracks regarding the first one. But what if she had done it for *his* sake. By providing an explanation, hadn't she also provided him with a means of escape?

Or perhaps she thinks that you did it, said the nagging voice. *And she's trying to save you.*

That too was a possibility. Either way the letter, if revealed to the prosecutor, would likely result in his release. But at what cost? His mother would suffer, as would A.J. Derry. When viewed that way it made little sense that his mother, had she written the second letter as a means of explaining away the discovery of Daniel's body, would choose the murder of Rebecca Derry as the rationale behind her husband's alleged suicide.

Once again the pieces scattered and he was left with no cohesive picture. There were too many unknowns, and as long as he was locked up he couldn't help Charly except by thinking endlessly about the possibilities, all of which resulted in misery for him and his family.

What if she wasn't the only one who wanted him dead?

The thought flickered in his head like a neon sign turned on at nightfall, bright and welcoming. He'd been so focused on his mother that he'd neglected to even think about any other possible suspects. But why shouldn't there be any? If someone besides his mother *had* sent the first letter, and she wasn't involved in his father's death, then who was it? And if that were true, then her giving the original letter to Charly wasn't about trying to cover up his guilt at all but was a sacrifice on her part to prove his innocence.

This was a somewhat less disturbing possibility, but ultimately it did little to change his situation. Until Charly and Arthur convinced the prosecutor of the letter's validity, he had no chance of getting released. Even then there would be further pain to his family.

He rolled onto his side, hugging the single shapeless pillow he had to his chest. He had never felt so vulnerable. Always he had imagined that the inhabitants of jail cells spent their time hating the system that put them there. Now he realized that while some of them probably did do that, the majority spent their time just being scared.

CHAPTER 31

1983

James watched as Billy tore out of the room, yelling his head off. *Why can't he just shut up?* he thought.

He and Celeste were sitting on the couch looking at their mother, who had just informed them that their father was dead. James, ignoring the fact that his little brother had just run from the room in hysterics, began questioning Ada.

"How do you know the letter isn't a joke?" he asked.

"I don't," his mother admitted. "And I hope as much as you do that your father comes through that door any minute." She hesitated. "But I don't think he will."

"Why not?" James said.

His mother turned and looked out the window. "I feel it," she said. When she looked back to him he could see that she was trying not to cry. "It's just something a wife knows, the same way I would know if one of you was hurt."

James said nothing, but to himself he thought, *Sure you do. And the horoscope is always right,* He loved his mother, but sometimes she seemed, well, a little bit dumb. No, not dumb exactly. Naive. That was the word. She believed almost anything you told her. That was why Celeste got away with so much bullshit. It was also why his mother didn't seem to realize that there was something not right about Billy.

Beside him Celeste had started to cry. Her shoulders hitched as she tried to keep her sobs inside, but she couldn't hold it in anymore. She opened her mouth and let out a long wail that ended in a series of hiccups. James, embarrassed, moved away from her. His mother came and sat between him and his sister. She put one arm around Celeste and reached out to him with the other, attempting to draw him into her embrace. He stood up, stepping away from the couch and going to stand beside Mr. Derry, who occupied his father's chair beside the fireplace.

"Have you gone to the police yet?" he asked, speaking to A.J. directly.

"Yes," the older man said. "They're handling things from here on out."

James nodded, as if that satisfied all of his concerns. In reality he had no idea how he felt about the news he'd just received. He didn't believe it, which made it difficult for him to form any real opinion. He was sure, despite his mother's confidence in her intuition, that the whole thing was a poorly played joke. Why anyone would do such a thing he didn't know, but it made more sense than the suggestion that his father had killed himself. That was simply not something he could ever accept. His father was too strong a man to show such cowardice.

"James, you should go after Billy."

James regarded his mother with confusion. "Why? He can take care of himself."

"You know how he is," said his mother. "I don't want him out there all alone."

James started to rebut, then felt A.J. Derry's hand on his arm. "Go on, son," he said. "Your father would want you to."

My father would want the little sissy to grow up, James thought. But he did as he'd been asked. Truthfully he was happy to leave the house and leave his mother and Celeste to their tears. He understood that they were upset, but he also resented that they were giving up so easily. His mother in particular seemed almost eager to accept that his father was dead.

He had no idea where Billy might have gone, and so he got on his bike and just rode. It didn't matter to him one way or the other if he found Billy. If he did he would bring him home and let his mother or Mr. Derry deal with him. And if he didn't find him he knew the kid would turn up eventually. He often disappeared for hours at a time. Nobody knew where he went or what he did. Celeste always said that he must be in Oz, a joke that had originated when Billy was eight or nine and they'd found him trying to make a hot air balloon out of a laundry basket and a bedsheet so that he could fly to the Emerald City like the Wizard did.

Wherever it was that Billy went, he never talked about it. Probably, James thought, he holed up somewhere and escaped into the fantasy novels he was always reading. James couldn't understand why Billy wanted to spend so much time in worlds that weren't real. The comic books he collected, for example—they were all about freaks and mutants and places that didn't exist. But Billy loved them. And when they tried to get him interested in the real world—in sports, for example—he just shut himself up and wouldn't participate. James's friends often teased him about Billy, and so James had given up trying to make his brother fit in.

He pushed Billy from his mind and returned to thinking about his father. He didn't believe he was dead, and assuming that he *had* sent the letter, to James the logical conclusion was that he had run away. The letter then was a way to cover his tracks. But why would he want to leave? James didn't buy the cancer story, and he didn't think his mother did either. That left two options: his father had committed a crime, which James believed him to be incapable of, or he wanted to get away from them. In short, his father was having an affair.

That his father might be seeing someone other than his mother didn't upset him terribly. A lot of his friends' parents had split up because one or both of them were having affairs. It was hardly a scandal. And his parents did fight sometimes. Celeste had told him about hearing them quarrel over a woman, although she had been vague on the details and hadn't seemed completely convinced herself that she'd heard everything correctly. Still, it was possible.

He had chosen his route by instinct and now found himself pedaling his bike into the woods that flanked the town. There was a well-worn path there, made by thousands of bikes passing that way over the years. It wound its way through the trees in a serpentine pattern, sometimes going up and sometimes dipping precipitously down into a gully or the embankment of the creek that ran through the woods. James pedaled hard up an incline, then stood up straight as the bike rumbled down the other side, the tires bouncing on the uneven ground. Then it was up the other side and into a long, straight stretch at the end of which he veered from the main path and headed into what looked like a clump of very tall grass.

The grass in fact hid the entrance to a second, wider path. This one ran deeper into the woods for about three hundred yards, where it ended in a clearing. Here the creek spread out and formed what for generations of Cold Falls residents had been a swimming hole. At the edge of the cleared space the bank dropped down sharply to the water's edge. A large elm tree (James had identified it as such using his Boy Scouts handbook) rose up beside the bank, its limbs stretched out over the water. From one of them hung a rope that was just barely reachable from the bank and, once grasped, could be used to swing oneself out over the water to drop into the water below. The current rope was perhaps the fifth or sixth to grace the tree, and it was quite old. The knot tied in it was hard and shiny from the countless hands that had gripped it during the journey creekward, and the end was frayed out like the tail of an angry cat.

While in the warmer months the swimming hole was used for precisely that purpose, at other times it became a gathering place for the town's teens. At any given time there would be three or four young people hanging out there. Adults seldom—if ever—made an appearance, although the spot was known to anyone who had lived in the town for any length of time. It was as if upon reaching adulthood the memory of the place faded, or perhaps it was just that there was an unspoken agreement between the generations that the place was a holy one, to be frequented for a time and then handed over to those who came behind. Whatever the reason, it was a place where James and his peers could congregate without fear of interruption.

What they did there varied from person to person. Smoking was a popular pastime, and many a Cold Falls teen had had his or her first taste of tobacco while sitting on one of the several tree stumps in the clearing. The empty cans and bottles that could be seen in the grass were a testament to another rite of passage to which the swimming place played host, as did the occasional empty condom wrapper. Whether what occurred there was the awakening of the passions or a sacrifice of innocence was a matter of opinion.

When James arrived there were six other boys already there, all of them friends of his from school. They looked up when they heard the sound of his bike, momentarily wary then instantly at ease once more. James leaned his bike against the trunk of an oak and came to sit with them.

"Hey, McCloud," said a large, red-faced boy. "What's up?"

"Nothing," James answered. "I'm looking for my brother. Sort of."

The other boys laughed. One spit on the ground. "Did you try the library? Every time I go in there the kid's there. He must read a hundred books a week."

"Probably," James said. He found to his surprise that he wanted to tell them about his father. But he didn't dare. Although they were all his friends, he knew they would talk. It was just what people did, and he didn't want a bunch of gossip about his family going around town. Still, he wished he could ask their opinions on the situation.

"So, Jimmy, you get into Nancy Derry's pants yet?"

James looked at the speaker, a skinny boy with too-long blond hair and a constellation of pimples on his cheeks. His arms, scarecrow thin, were pink with sunburn, and James could see the remnants of dead skin on his neck where he had begun to peel.

"No, Scooby, but I just got done doing your mom. She says to be home by six. It's Hamburger Helper night."

Despite joking with his friends about sex, James was still a virgin. He suspected most of his buddies were too, although Seamus "Finny" Finnegan claimed to have boned one of his cousin Colleen's girlfriends at a Halloween party the year before. They talked about sex as if they were deeply experienced, but the closest most of them had come to a naked girl was jerking off to the *Penthouse* magazines that were handed down to them from Ray Deschanel's older brother Luke.

The other boys roared with laughter at James's taunt. Scooby—real name Johnson Skoboski—grinned. "Yeah," he said. "I'll be home as soon as I'm done with your sister."

A chorus of "Zing!"s and "Oww!"s greeted the retort. Even James joined in, enjoying the feeling of being part of a group. He fit in with these boys. They shared something, a common background and way of life that he found comfortable and reassuring. He was one of them.

"You'll have to get her away from Paul Lunardi first."

A new voice broke through their revelry. James looked up to see Nate Kunkel walking into the clearing. *Nate Derry,* he reminded himself. Nancy's father had officially adopted Nate a couple of months before. But James still called him Kunkel, as Nate was about as unlike A.J. Derry as anyone could be.

The group quieted as Nate joined them. He was not one of them, in fact hadn't even made an effort to be, as if he prided himself on not being from Cold Falls. James wondered what he was even doing there, as he usually kept to himself.

"I'm surprised your dad hasn't slapped a chastity belt on Celeste," Nate remarked as he sat down. He laughed at his own joke. "Wouldn't want Paul Lunardi's swimmers getting into that ocean. Besides, who knows what all he picked up when he was in the joint. I hear he was quite a little bitch."

"Fuck, Nate, it wasn't like he was in Sing Sing," said Peter Staffway, who was sitting beside James. "He was in for like two months or something."

"Just what your old man wants, eh, James?" Nate said, ignoring Peter. "A con marrying into the McCloud family. He'd probably drop dead of a heart attack."

At the suggestion of his father's death James remembered all too well what had driven him from home. Nate couldn't know, of course. *Unless A.J. said something,* he thought. But A.J. wouldn't do that, or at least James didn't think he would.

"By the way," Nate said. "Nancy says to say good-bye."

James looked up. "What are you talking about?" he asked. "Why would she say good-bye?" Nate was really beginning to get on his nerves. James didn't like the cockiness in his voice or the way he was looking at him, as if he knew something James didn't and found that exciting.

"She's going away for the rest of the summer," Nate informed him. "Up to see some relatives in Maine."

"What?" said James, unable to hide the surprise in his voice. "She didn't say anything about going anywhere."

"Yeah," said Nate. "I was kind of surprised too. But she left about an hour ago. My mom drove her to the airport."

"I didn't even know she had relatives in Maine," James said, completely confused. Nancy could have called him, or A.J. could have said something.

"Her father's sister or something," Nate told him. "I don't really remember."

He couldn't believe Nancy would just leave without saying anything. Things had been a little—awkward—between them lately, and he hadn't seen as much of her as he would have liked, but he hadn't thought it was anything to worry about. Nancy just needed a little space. That's what she'd said. There were a lot of changes going on in her life what with her father marrying Bess and the two families merging, and she just wanted some time to chill out. James had assumed that a week or two would go by and everything would be back to normal. It had been longer than that now, and Nancy hadn't returned his call for two or three days, but still he hadn't worried.

Now he did. "Why is she going?" he asked Nate.

"Beats me," Nate answered. "I guess there's just nothing to keep her around here."

James knew the other boy was making a dig at him, but he forced himself not to say anything. Nate was just being an asshole, and if James responded to him he would be just as bad. It was best to keep his temper. His father had taught him that. *No matter how hard they push you, don't let them see you sweat.* He could hear his father's voice speaking the words. *Don't let them see you sweat.*

"Well, I hope she has fun," James said, trying to keep his voice light. "It's just for the summer, right?"

"Sure," Scooby said, but James could tell that he was just trying to be nice. It was clear that Nancy had deliberately not told him that she was leaving. Why she'd done that he didn't know. And now, unless he could somehow find out where she was, he wouldn't find out until she came back.

"Don't worry about it, big guy," Nate said, clapping him on the back. "There are a lot of girls who'll be happy to take care of you." He laughed. "And there's always Ma Thumb and her four lovely daughters," he added, making an up-and-down motion with his fist.

James looked at his watch. "Shit," he said. "I've got to go."

Pretending to be late for something of great importance, he got up and went to his bike. "I'll see you guys later" he said, waving as he straddled the seat and headed down the path.

As he moved away from the swimming hole he heard laughter follow him. Who had said something funny, and what was it? He was pretty sure that he knew, and thinking about it made him pump the pedals as hard as he could.

Fuck Nate Derry, he thought. *Fuck him right to hell.*

CHAPTER 32

1991

Billy heard the bell tinkle and looked up from the X-Men comic book he was reading. He'd had only three customers all day, and only one had actually bought something. He didn't mind having all of that time to read, but if business didn't pick up he had a feeling Jerry's altruism was going to come to a screeching halt. Then Billy would have to either find another job or move back in with his mother. Neither possibility pleased him.

When he saw Charly walk in, he shut the comic and gave her his biggest smile. "Look who's here," he said. "Did you come in for the latest *Wonder Woman?*"

Charly paused at a rack of comics and picked one up. "I never liked her," she said. "She had a tacky outfit. Batgirl was more my style."

Billy laughed. "Bondage chic," he remarked. "Hot."

Charly scanned the rest of the store. "Is there really a market for this here?" she asked, sounding genuinely interested.

"No," Billy said. "I mean there are a pretty fair number of slackers who live in their parents' basements and spend all their time collecting action figures and trading cards, but they don't have a lot of cash. Then we have a few who buy every issue of two or three titles and don't ever read them. They put them in their attics and hope that in thirty years they can sell them and retire—which they won't because now *everyone* is doing that and so there will be twenty-thousand copies of *Suicide Squad #54* sitting around in places like this."

He tapped a stack of books sitting on the counter. "And every once in a while we get someone who actually knows their shit and comes in here because they love the books and want to find the one or two or three that are missing from their collections. But to answer your question, no, there isn't really a market here for this stuff."

He wondered why Charly was there. She might very well be a Batgirl fan (he had a feeling she'd made that up on the fly to impress him) but he doubted she had come there to talk comics. He decided to call her out. "How's James doing?"

"He's in jail facing a murder charge," Charly said. "How do you think he's doing?"

Good. She wasn't going to play with him. He liked that. He was so used to people thinking he was an idiot that Charly's tack was refreshing. "What do you see in him anyway?" he asked. "Unless he's changed since we were kids he's a self-righteous know-it-all with a giant stick up his ass."

He'd expected to rattle her, and was impressed when she didn't seem upset. "I don't know," she said. "Maybe somewhere along the line he pulled that stick out. You should give him a chance. He might surprise you."

"I doubt it," Billy told her. "Nothing about James would surprise me."

"Meaning what?" Charly asked. She turned her full attention on Billy, and he realized that now he *had* rattled her, if only a little.

"Meaning just that," he said cryptically. "Nothing anyone in my family could do would surprise me." He leaned over the counter. "I'm jaded beyond belief," he added.

"Really?" said Charly. "How about if I told you your father may have murdered Rebecca Derry?"

Billy laughed. "Nice try," he said.

"I'm serious," Charly replied.

Billy looked into her eyes. She didn't blink. *Holy fuck,* he thought. *She really is.*

"Why would my father kill Rebecca Derry?" he asked.

"Because he was having an affair with her," said Charly. "Maybe she tried to break it off. Maybe he was jealous. Things got heated; he shot her. Fifteen years later he can't deal with the guilt anymore and kills himself. End of story."

Billy scratched his chin. "It would make a good comic book plot," he said. "Maybe for the Spectre. He's all about retribution. But for my father? No."

"You sound awfully sure of yourself," Charly told him.

"Because I am," said Billy. "Besides, you're forgetting something— he didn't kill himself."

"So somebody found out and exacted revenge," said Charly. "Just like the Spectre. Who are the supporting cast?"

Billy found himself intrigued by Charly's question. In many ways he hated to go along with her, but populating his very own story was irresistible. "Let's see," he said. "James for starters. He finds out his father killed his high school girlfriend's mother, ruining the girlfriend's life. Or how about the wife?" he suggested. "She finds out hubby had an affair. She gets mad and gets even. Predictable, but a classic." He thought some more. "Oh, let's not forget the dead woman's husband, who also happens to be the dead man's best friend."

"Anyone else?" Charly asked him.

Billy thought for a moment. "I think that's about it," he answered.

Charly nodded. "How about the gay son who didn't like being told he wasn't man enough?" she said.

Billy wagged a finger at her. "Never pin it on the gay guy," he said. "Besides, this isn't *Dynasty* and I ain't Steven Carrington. Anyway, I was thirteen when Daddy went bye-bye."

"James was only sixteen, and you said you wouldn't be surprised to find out that he did it." There was an edge to Charly's voice now, as if she had had enough of the fun and games and was getting down to business.

"James is different," Billy said. "Even when he was sixteen he was thirty-five, if you know what I mean. Celeste may have been the wild one, and I may have been the freak, but James was the grown-up."

"And that's what makes you think he killed your father?" said Charly.

Billy sighed. "James didn't kill my father," he said. "You know that as well as I do."

"Then who did?" Charly asked.

"Not James," said Billy loudly. He held up a hand in apology. "Not James," he repeated in a lower voice.

The bell rang again. This time two girls came in. Both were dressed in goth clothing, including thick-soled black boots, black T-shirts over black miniskirts, and black fishnet stockings. Their lips and nails were similarly colored. The only thing not black was their hair, which on one was a deep purple and on the other a fluorescent pink. Billy nodded at them in greeting. "What can I do for you?" he asked.

Before the girls could answer, Charly said, "I should go. We'll talk later." She didn't wait for his reply before turning and leaving.

"Fuck," said the pink-haired girl. "Rude much?"

Billy helped the girls find what they were looking for (Catwoman T-shirts and an old issue of *First Love* that was older than they were) and rang them up. When they had gone he turned on the television that was mounted in the corner opposite the desk and fired up the VCR. After looking through the collection of tapes beneath the counter, he selected one and popped it in. Moments later the opening scene of *Close Encounters of the Third Kind* appeared. Billy watched, enraptured, as a car made its way through a thick sandstorm in the Sonoran Desert. He'd seen the movie who knew how many times, yet every time was still a magical experience for him. When cartographer David Laughlin, pressed into service as a translator, first saw the fleet of airplanes reported missing in 1945 and now sitting in the middle of the desert looking as new as they had the day they disappeared, Billy was as in awe as the bewildered mapmaker was.

He had been seven when *Close Encounters* came out, arriving in theaters six months after *Star Wars*. For Billy, who had found *Star Wars* to be the most thrilling thing he'd ever seen, *Close Encounters* was completely mind-blowing. While he loved Lucas's western-set-in-space, it was Spielberg's movie that touched his very soul. The idea that not only were there other worlds but that he might actually be able to *go* to them gave him hope. For months afterward he had watched the night skies from his bedroom window, praying for the arrival of a spaceship that would take him away.

Eventually he had given up on the spacemen and found other ways to escape. Drugs became his preferred means, particularly anything that took him out of his body. He experimented with whatever came his way, hoping that each new thing would take him farther than the last and bring him closer to the world in which he longed to exist. Yet each time he ended up disappointed, until one day he woke up with the understanding that while he had been looking for the aliens he had somehow failed to notice that he was one of them himself. He was strange, and he frightened those who tried to know him. He frightened himself too, because he didn't know what he was.

He still didn't. And now he had settled into a kind of half life, existing in a world of fog and shadows made possible by the powders and pills he consumed like candy, washing them down with whatever was at hand. Occasionally he emerged from this toxic mist and saw the world beyond, but so far nothing there had compelled him to remain for any length of time. Sometimes—more and more rarely—he met another who was like him, or who at least seemed to be like him. Then it was as if the spaceships had descended and he was filled with their heart-rattling vibrations, light streaming all around him as he stared, awestruck and joyful, at their beauty.

But the feeling never lasted. After a night, at most a week or two, he would wake up to find his other self gone, disappeared into the ether. Inevitably he would see him again on the street or in the bars and men's rooms that comprised his universe, and he would pretend not to know Billy. In time he became the man that everyone came to but that no one acknowledged. It was a role he was happy to play, as it required little effort, and if the rewards were minimal they were at least fleetingly fulfilling. His own desires were unimportant. As long as he had sugars and chemicals he was more or less content. Love was something he had given up on much as he had given up on being taken by the men from the moon.

He watched the entire movie without interruption. When it was over he looked at the clock and saw that it was close to eight. The store had officially closed an hour before, but neither Billy nor anyone else had noticed. The world outside the window was silver-gilded. *It must be a full moon,* he thought, and walked to the window. Sure enough, the moon hung fat and round just above the housetops.

He closed up the store and locked the front door. He had nowhere to be, and so he walked slowly through the night until he found himself, as he often did when he walked without purpose, at the Engine Room. He opened the door and was greeted by the familiar stale-sweet smell that emanated from every gay bar he'd ever entered, as if the men inside emitted a unique odor composed of beer, poppers, smoke, and lust. It was as heady to him as the purest coke, and he inhaled it with just as much pleasure.

No one greeted him as he walked through the room to the bar. He was pleased to see Cory standing behind it. Billy wouldn't call the bartender a friend, but he was as much of one as Billy had. At the very least he didn't recoil when Billy came near him.

"What'll it be tonight?" Cory asked him as he took a seat on a stool.

"Something different," Billy replied. "Surprise me. As long as it's sweet."

"Coming up," said Cory. He took a bottle from the shelf and poured something brown into a glass. He followed this with a pour from his soda gun, then stirred the drink with a straw and set it in front of Billy. "Seven and Seven," he told him. "Luckiest drink there is."

Billy picked the glass up. "Here's to getting lucky then," he said, and drank. Immediately he recognized the syrupy taste of 7UP, and beneath that the warmer, harsher burn of whiskey. It was good.

"Special occasion?" Cody asked him when he set the half-drained glass down.

Billy chuckled. "Didn't you hear?" he asked. "My big brother has come home for a visit."

Cory nodded. "I heard something about that," he said.

Several people were looking in Billy's direction. He knew that for once they were discussing not his failings but James's sudden and unexpected rise to fame. He was surprised then to find that he was more than a little jealous. Until now he had been the black sheep of the family, a dubious but nonetheless real distinction. But with one blow James had usurped his title. Now he was once again the little brother, always one step behind and forever coming up short. He finished the rest of his drink.

"Let me ask you something," he said to Cory. "Do you believe in UFOs?"

Cory didn't answer right away. He poured a drink for a customer at the end of the bar, tossed several empties into the large plastic trashcan behind him, and took down the bottle of Seagram's to make Billy another drink. As he poured he said, "Once, when I was maybe ten years old, my parents sent me to summer camp. One of those places with a fake Indian name. Gitcheewigwam or something. Anyway, I hated it. I was the new kid. The rest of them had gone to camp together for a couple of years. So of course I was the one they pranked.

"Finally I couldn't take it anymore, so every night I'd sneak out of the cabin and go down to the lake. There was a lifeguard chair there— one of the big wooden things with a roof over the seat. I'd climb up there with my blanket and sleep. Sometimes I'd just look at the stars and try to find the constellations. One night it was clear as anything. It looked like someone had turned on every light in the sky. I was sitting there, trying to figure out where Cygnus was—you know, the swan. All of a sudden this bright light appeared over the lake. It was blue and it was kind of, I don't know, electric. It hung there for a while and then it took off."

Cory moved his flattened palm up and away, miming a spaceship rising into the sky. "I don't know what it was, but I've never forgotten it. I'll tell you this much, it was no airplane or weather balloon or whatever the hell they tell you is up there."

"Did you tell anyone?" Billy asked him.

Cory nodded. "The next morning at breakfast I told the guys from my cabin. I thought they would think it was cool, and that I was cool for seeing it."

"But they didn't," Billy said. In his mind the ending to the story was inevitable.

"Nope," said Cory. "They called me Astroboy for the rest of the week."

Billy smiled and held up his glass. "To Astroboy," he said. "Welcome to the club."

CHAPTER 33

1983

Billy was walking home from school when the red Mustang pulled up alongside him. Paul leaned out the window. "Want a ride?" he asked.

Billy peered inside the window, expecting to see his sister sitting in the passenger seat. To his surprise it was unoccupied. "Where's Celeste?" he said.

"She has something to do," said Paul. "Come on. Get in."

Billy walked around to the other side of the car. He opened the door and got in, and Paul pulled away from the curb. He didn't say anything, and Billy didn't know how to talk to him. He'd never been alone with Paul before; Celeste had always been there too. Now that it was just the two of them Billy found himself feeling anxious.

"How come you're walking home?" Paul asked.

Relieved to have the silence broken Billy told him, "I didn't feel like taking the bus."

Paul looked at him and grinned. "Someone giving you trouble?" he said.

Billy wasn't sure how to respond. The fact was someone *was* giving him a hard time. But did he want to admit this to Paul and risk looking like a little kid? He considered lying, then for some reason he didn't understand he chose to tell the truth.

"Gloria Fitzroy," he said.

Paul laughed. "A girl?" he said. "What? She trying to get you to screw her or something?"

Billy blushed. The idea of Paul thinking that he might actually be having sex thrilled him. It was like he was one of the guys. No one ever talked to him that way. James *never* would.

"Yeah," he said. "That's it."

In reality it was exactly the opposite. Gloria had recently taken to calling Billy a queer. This had quickly spread, and now some of the other kids were following her lead. He didn't know why they'd singled him out to torment, and he hoped it wouldn't last long. But in the meantime he tried to avoid Gloria and her friends as much as possible, hoping that they would find someone else to pick on when he wasn't around.

Paul laughed again. "What's the matter with her? She an ugly bitch?"

Was Gloria ugly? Billy considered the question. He'd never looked at her in that way. Or at any girl for that matter. They just didn't interest him. Sometimes he heard other boys talking about this or that girl and how pretty or not pretty she was, but he never joined in and they never asked his opinion.

"I guess she's okay," he told Paul, unable to find anything in Gloria's appearance to sway his vote either way.

Paul glanced at him. "Just not your type," he said, and winked.

Billy felt something in his stomach jump. Paul had turned away again, but Billy was still thinking about his wink. Something about it excited him. Paul was really treating him like a buddy and not like his girlfriend's little brother. He leaned back in the seat and put his arm on the window's edge.

"Yeah," he said. "She's not my type."

He realized then that they weren't heading in the direction of his house and instead were going toward the lake. "I thought you were taking me home," he said.

"Why?" Paul said. "Are you in a hurry? I thought we'd take a drive. But if you want to go home—"

"No," Billy interrupted. "I was just asking." He tried to sound relaxed. "It's cool."

When they reached the turnoff for the lake Paul passed it and instead turned onto a narrower, unpaved road. He drove slowly down it, maneuvering the Mustang around the deeper ruts. Billy, having no idea where they were going, watched the trees go by. They were newly green, and the sunlight passing through the leaves created shadows that dappled the trunks and ground. The air was warm but not hot.

Finally they came to a stop. They were in a small cleared space in the trees. It was big enough for perhaps half a dozen cars to park side by side, but they were the only ones there. Through the opening in the trees Billy could just see the lake. The sunlight glinted off the dark water and blinded his eyes with its brightness.

Paul reached across Billy and popped upon the glove compartment. His arm brushed against Billy's chest, and again Billy felt something stir in his belly. Paul removed a small plastic bag and shut the compartment door.

"How do you like this place?" he asked Billy as he opened the bag and removed something. "Pretty cool, huh?"

"It's beautiful," Billy answered. "I never knew it was here."

"You know the swimming hole?"

Billy nodded. "Sure."

"Well this is where you come when you outgrow it," Paul said. He was holding a rectangular piece of paper in his hand and pouring the contents of the plastic bag onto it. Billy, remembering the afternoon in the haymow, recognized the process at once.

Paul rolled the joint and licked the paper's edge to seal it. He lit it and took the first drag, then handed it to Billy. Billy accepted it eagerly. This time when he drew the smoke into his lungs he was able to hold it without choking. He waited as long as he could then exhaled the smoke out the window.

"You're a real pro at this now, aren't you?" Paul teased. "We might have to move you up to something else soon."

"Like what?" asked Billy.

"Oh, there's all kinds of good shit out there," said Paul. "It all depends what you want. I can get you up, I can get you down." He looked over at Billy. "I can make you feel any way you want to."

Billy took another hit on the joint. He was already feeling it. The light on the lake was softening and he was feeling less anxious about being alone with Paul. *He likes you,* he told himself. *There's nothing to worry about.*

Paul leaned his seat back and stretched out, spreading his legs. "That's better," he said. "Try it."

Billy copied him, reclining the seat halfway so that he was looking through the top of the windshield at the green leaves and blue sky. It really was much more relaxing. He found himself getting slightly sleepy from the combination of the pot, the sun, and the breeze blowing lightly across his face. He was glad that he'd accepted Paul's ride, that they were spending time together like friends.

He was just about to nod off when he felt something on his shoulders. He opened his eyes and saw that Paul had stretched one arm out across the seats. His hand rested just behind Billy's head, and his fingers lightly touched Billy's hair. When Billy looked to his left he saw Paul's muscled forearm and thick biceps. Dark hair poked over the neck of Paul's wifebeater, and beneath his arm a tangle of hair, wet with sweat, was visible. Billy stared at it, unable to look away.

"You're cool," Paul said. "You know that? I like hanging out with you."

Billy didn't know how to respond. "Thanks," he said, feeling like an idiot. "You're cool too," he added hastily.

Paul ruffled his hair. "So you like me," he said. "Good."

Billy's neck began to hurt, but still he didn't turn away from looking at Paul. A bead of sweat was running from Paul's armpit down his side. Billy watched its slow progress, suddenly longing to reach out and touch it. He saw the muscles of Paul's torso twitch as the sweat tickled him.

Paul's hand moved to Billy's neck, and Billy felt himself tense up.

"Relax," Paul said, massaging his rigid muscles. His fingertips were rough, his motions firm and strong. Billy relaxed into his touch and Paul said, "There you go."

Nothing was said for a few minutes. Paul continued to rub Billy's neck and Billy tried to calm his breathing. He could feel his heart racing. Then to his horror he realized that his dick had gotten hard. He looked down and saw that it was making a mound in his jeans. He prayed that Paul wouldn't notice. *Maybe Gloria is right,* he thought. *Maybe you are a queer.*

The thought terrified him. He was particularly fearful that Paul would see his excitement and hate him for it. Their friendship would end as quickly as it had begun. He would tell Celeste. Everything would be ruined.

He closed his eyes and tried to will his hard-on away. He thought of the most boring thing he could—state capitals—and started to name them in alphabetical order by state. *Alabama,* he began, thinking back to the list in his American History textbook. *Montgomery. Alaska—Anchorage. Arizona—Phoenix.* He stalled, unable to remember what came next. All he could focus on was Paul's fingers on the back of his neck. *California,* he recited silently. *No. Arkansas—Little Rock.*

Tentatively he slipped his hand into his crotch. His dick was still hard. He could feel it beneath the fabric of his jeans, traitorously large. There was no way Paul wouldn't see it if he looked over. *No,* Billy prayed. *Please don't let him see it.*

"Hey," Paul said.

Billy froze, waiting for the inevitable exclamation of disgust he knew was going to follow. But Paul's hand didn't move, and all he said was, "You ever shoot a gun?"

It took a moment for the words to make sense to Billy. When he realized that Paul wasn't freaking out on him he nearly burst with relief. "Just a BB gun," he answered. "Oh, and a rifle once. But that's it."

"I'm surprised your old man hasn't taught you how," said Paul. "He must have a bunch of guns."

"He does," Billy said, thinking about the locked cabinet in his parents' bedroom. "But we're not allowed to touch them."

"Too bad," said Paul. "It's a lot of fun." He turned to look at Billy. "We should do it sometime. I can teach you how."

Billy couldn't look away from Paul's gaze. It was as if a magnet was pulling him in. He swallowed hard, trying to get rid of the knot that had suddenly blocked his throat. "I'd like that," he said hoarsely.

"Of course we need a gun to do it," said Paul. "Too bad you can't get one of your dad's."

Billy heard himself say, "I might be able to." Instantly he regretted it. There was no way he would be able to get into the cabinet and take a gun without his father knowing it. And if—no *when*—his father found out, he would get the whipping of his life.

"I bet you could," Paul said. "You're a smart kid. A lot smarter than your brother," he added.

"James?" said Billy, as if he had a dozen brothers and needed clarification.

"What an asshole," Paul commented. "That guy's so far from cool he's on fire." He laughed at his own joke.

Billy joined in. "Yeah," he said. "He really is an asshole."

"So what do you think?" asked Paul. "Are you up for it?"

No, Billy thought instantly. *No way.* But then he imagined showing up James and, more important, showing Paul that he deserved to be his friend. He pictured Paul and himself standing in front of a target— maybe a beer can on a post or something tacked to a tree—and Paul showing him how to hold the gun. He felt Paul's arms around him, his hands cupping Billy's and guiding his finger to the trigger. He heard the retort of gunfire and felt his body pushed backward into Paul's.

"Yeah," he said. "I can do it."

"That's my man," Paul said. He smacked Billy lightly on the head, then patted Billy's thigh. "I knew you'd be cool with it."

He rested his hand on Billy's leg and Billy was once again overcome with fear as he realized that Paul was dangerously close to his crotch. Then the little finger of Paul's hand lightly grazed the length of his dick. Billy's body jerked in terror, but Paul didn't seem to notice. "When do you think you can get it?" he asked.

"I don't know," Billy stammered. "Um . . . maybe this week?" He knew he sounded like an idiot, and cursed his stupidity.

Paul gave his thigh a hard squeeze and let go. "Fucking A," he said. "Man, this is going to be a blast."

Billy collapsed against the seat in relief. Now that Paul wasn't touching him he could breathe normally. He shifted so that his left leg was slightly above the right, hiding his erection. Paul returned his own seat to its original position. "I should get you home," he said. "You ready?"

Billy fumbled with the lever beside his seat, first throwing himself even farther back and then finally managing to get himself upright. Paul seemed not to notice his incompetence as he started the car and turned on the radio. He backed the car up, turned it around, and drove back to the main road. As they emerged from the trees into the bright light of the afternoon Billy felt the magic of the hour begin to dissipate.

I promised him I'd get a gun, he realized. What was he, crazy? He couldn't steal a gun from his father's collection. *Not steal it,* he told himself. *You're just borrowing it. If you're careful he won't even miss it. Then you can put it back after you and Paul are done with it.*

Paul was singing along with the radio as they drove. Billy listened to it, remembering how it had felt to have Paul stroking his neck. Even the perilous moment when Paul's hand had been on his leg now seemed to him to have been something wonderful. He rubbed the spot where Paul's hand had lain. Yes, he would get a gun for him. He would do anything he asked.

CHAPTER 34

1991

Bess Derry was very pretty. Petite and slim, she had blond hair cut in a short shaggy style that complemented her heart-shaped face. Her features were delicate without being fragile, and her eyes were a shade of brown the color of honey or maple syrup. It was a peculiar way to describe someone's eyes, Charly thought, but that was indeed what the color reminded her of.

"Thank you for seeing me," she said as Bess motioned for her to come into the house.

"It's my pleasure," Bess told her.

The Derry house, like the McClouds' was an old one. It had originally, Charly could tell as she'd driven up, been a farmhouse. Now the farm itself was gone and only the house remained, looking a bit lonely sitting back from the road surrounded by tall pine trees. Inside the house retained its original features. The walls of the living room were painted a pale blue, and the furniture was of the Shaker style. Charly could easily imagine a farmer and his family sitting down to dinner at the big plank table in the dining room, which was visible through a doorway to the left of the entryway.

The day was warm, and the windows of the house were open, letting in a breeze that ruffled the white curtains that hug each pane. Charly smelled the unmistakable odor of narcissus (it always reminded her, unpleasantly, of cat urine, although she found the flowers beautiful), and a quick scan of the living room revealed a pot of them atop a small table. On the wall above the fireplace hung a painting of a brown-and-white spaniel dog holding a dead quail in its mouth.

A moment later a dog very much resembling the one in the painting came bounding into the room, its paws slipping on the wood floor as it rounded the corner. It was followed by a young girl who called out, "Poppy!" as she entered the room.

The dog, seeing Charly, ran to her with its stubby tail wagging. It jumped up, putting its paws on her legs and sniffing at her excitedly.

"Poppy," the little girl said. "Get down." She came over and gripped the dog lightly by the back of the neck, pulling it off of Charly. The dog sat and looked at the girl expectantly.

"You're not getting a cookie," the girl said. "That was bad."

"And this is Becky," Bess said to Charly over the girl's head. "Our resident dog trainer."

"It's for a 4-H project," Becky informed Charly proudly.

Unlike her mother Becky was solidly built, with arms and legs that didn't possess the awkward thinness generally seen in girls her age, which Charly knew to be eight. She'd found out as much as she could about Bess Derry and her daughter from Ada and James before calling to arrange a meeting.

"Becky, take Poppy outside," Bess said. "Charly and I are going to talk for a while."

The girl left the room, the spaniel obediently following behind her. Bess shook her head. "She has a thing for animals," she told Charly. "It doesn't matter what kind. She talked about getting a puppy nonstop for six months until we couldn't take it anymore and gave in. But she's done all the work herself, so I can't complain."

She walked into the living room and motioned for Charly to have a seat on the sofa. "Can I get you anything?" she asked. "Tea? A pop?"

"Pop," Charly repeated. "I haven't heard soda called that in a long time. Not since I lived in Minnesota."

Bess laughed. "My mother was from Ohio," she said. "My sisters and I picked it up from her. Would you like one? I think we have Coke and maybe Dr. Pepper, if A.J. hasn't drunk it all. He must go through three cans a day. He's worse than a teenager."

"No, thank you," Charly answered. "I'm fine."

Bess sat in a chair across from Charly. "It's terrible what's happened," she said.

"It is," Charly agreed.

"I remember the day Ada got the letter from Dan," said Bess. "It's the first time I ever saw A.J. cry."

"I understand he and Dan were best friends," Charly said.

"I don't think two men have ever been closer," said Bess. "They were more like brothers." She paused. "Sometimes I think Dan's death was harder on him than Rebecca's was."

"Why do you say that?" Charly asked her.

Bess shrugged. "Oh, I don't know really. There's just this bond that men have when they've been friends for a long time. They know each other, maybe even better than we do as their wives. Don't get me wrong—A.J. loved Rebecca as much as any man could. But when he lost Dan it was as if part of himself had died too." She looked at Charly. "I don't think I'm explaining myself very well," she said.

"I think I know what you mean," said Charly. "With women, men are dealing with something totally different from themselves. With other men they don't have to work so hard to understand, or to be understood."

"That's it," Bess said, pointing a finger at Charly. "You just said it better."

"What did you think of Dan?" Charly asked her.

"Me?" said Bess. "Oh, I loved him. You probably know that we went together in high school." She laughed lightly. "I don't think Ada has ever forgiven me for that."

"Was that a problem for your husband?" Charly inquired.

"A.J.?" said Bess. "No. He doesn't have a jealous bone in his body." She cocked her head and looked at Charly for a moment. "You think that maybe it was A.J. who killed Dan, don't you?"

Taken off guard by the woman's question, Charly faltered momentarily. She was surprised that Bess had guessed correctly. Now she was unsure of how she should proceed.

"I'm not offended," Bess assured her. "It's a logical question, isn't it?"

"Well, yes," said Charly. "At least it is if you don't believe James McCloud is the real killer."

"I don't know if he is or not," Bess told her. "But let me ask you this—did Ada suggest that A.J. or I had anything to do with what happened?"

Charly shook her head. "No," she answered. "I just have to consider all the possibilities."

"And we're next on the list," said Bess. "Fair enough. What else can I tell you?"

"Did you have an affair with Dan McCloud?" Charly ventured. So far the woman had been very open, so she decided to ask the question that was at the center of this particular explanation for Daniel's murder.

"I wondered when that would start," Bess said.

"Why?" asked Charly.

Bess laughed, but this time the tone was not light. It was harsh, angry. "It's this place," she said. "This town. Oh, I suppose it's every small town. There have to be secrets. They feed on them. I think sometimes that without the rumors and the gossip this place would shrivel up and die."

"What have people said about you and Dan?"

"The usual," said Bess. "I moved back because I couldn't get over our high school romance. Dan had been pining for me for years. I was determined to take him away from Ada. You can guess the rest."

"And none of it was true?" Charly said.

Bess shook her head. "I've made a lot of mistakes in my life, but that isn't one of them," she said.

"Would you tell me if you had?" asked Charly.

"You know, I probably would," she said. "I've never been very good at keeping secrets."

"So if Daniel McCloud was the real father of Becky, you'd acknowledge that?" Charly said.

Bess's face suddenly clouded over. "Why would you say such a thing?" she demanded.

"I'm sorry," Charly apologized.

"I think perhaps you should go," said Bess.

The change in the woman was like night and day, Charly thought. She'd asked the question specifically to see if she could rattle Bess, and she clearly had. But something puzzled her. She believed Bess when she said that she hadn't had an affair with Daniel McCloud. The way she'd spoken of him was with the affection of a shared history, not with the words of a scorned or bereaved lover. True, eight years had passed since Dan's murder, but still Charly believed she was telling the truth. Besides, she wasn't done yet.

"Just one more thing," Charly said. "Does A.J. know that Nate isn't your biological child?"

All the color drained from Bess Derry's face. She began to shake, and her hands gripped the arms of the chair like talons. She stared at Charly, her lips trembling. "How do you know that?" she said, her voice hardly more than a whisper.

"It wasn't difficult to find out," said Charly calmly. "Adoption records are a matter of public record. It came up during a routine background check."

Bess bit her lip. Charly could tell that she was struggling to maintain her composure. She waited patiently, knowing that eventually Bess would have to say something. No matter what it was it was sure to be of interest, whether it helped the case or not.

"No," Bess said finally. "Nate doesn't even know."

Charly tried not to show her surprise. "You've never told him?"

Bess shook her head. "He came to us—to my then husband and me—when he was a baby," she said. "His mother was a friend, a young woman I knew from nursing school. She didn't have the means to care for a child, so Fred and I agreed to take him. Several months later the girl was killed in a car accident. Nate never knew her, and I didn't see any reason to tell him. He had a family. To tell the truth, after a few years I rarely thought about the girl. It was as if Nate had always been mine. Which really he has," she added.

Listening to Bess talk about her son, Charly almost felt guilty about blindsiding her with the adoption question. But now that Bess had admitted to hiding it not only from her husband but also from Nate himself, she found she had more questions.

"You and your husband never had children of your own?" she asked.

Bess nodded. "I was pregnant once," she said. "I lost the baby at six months."

"I'm sorry to hear that," said Charly. "I can't imagine what that must be like."

"I hope you never find out," Bess told her. "It's the most horrible thing I've ever endured. It nearly killed me, both physically and emotionally."

"And yet you had Becky," said Charly.

Bess nodded. "Yes," she said. "Then we had Becky."

"And there were no complications?" Charly asked.

"There were complications," Bess answered after a moment. "There were a number of them." She hesitated a moment and then looked into Charly's eyes. "You asked me before if Daniel was the father of Becky," said. "I was telling the truth when I said that he wasn't. However, you're correct that A.J. isn't the father."

"Who is?" Charly asked her.

"That's the funny thing," said Bess. "I don't know."

"I don't understand," Charly told her. "If it isn't Daniel, and it's not A.J. . . ."

"I didn't sleep around, if that's what you're inferring," said Bess. "I don't know who the father is because, you see, I'm not the mother."

"You adopted her?" said Charly. "But you were pregnant."

"I'll tell you everything," Bess said. "At least as much as I can. But understand something. I'm only telling you because it might—might—have something to do with Daniel's murder. I pray to God it doesn't, but I couldn't live with myself if I didn't at least try to help that boy."

"Thank you," Charly said.

Bess stood up. "If you don't mind, I'm going to get some tea. This might take a while."

CHAPTER 35

1983

"Whose is it?"

A.J. was sitting on Nancy's bed, holding his daughter in his arms. Her face was buried in his chest and she was sobbing violently. A.J.'s face was red with anger. Bess had never seen him look so frightening. Although he looked right at her where she was standing in the doorway, he seemed not to see her at all.

"Whose is it?" he asked again.

"I don't know," Nancy answered. Her voice was soft like that of a much younger girl, and it broke with the occasional sniffle as Nancy continued to cry.

"Is it James's?" A.J. asked her.

Nancy shook her head. "No," she said. "I told you, I don't know his name."

Bess stepped into the room. A.J. looked at her helplessly. She nodded at him to let him know she would take over. Sitting on Nancy's other side she said softly, "What happened, Nancy?"

Nancy turned a tear-streaked face to Bess. Her eyes were red, and her lip bled where she had apparently been biting it. Bess pushed Nancy's long hair out of her face and said again, "What happened, sweetheart?"

"I can't . . ." Nancy said, and began crying again.

"Yes, you can," Bess assured her. "We're not going to be mad. I promise."

Nancy's crying slowed. She pulled away from her father's embrace and just sat between him and Bess, looking at the floor. "I'm sorry," she said.

"You don't have anything to be sorry for," said Bess.

"I went to a party," Nancy said. Her voice was flat and robotic, drained of all emotion. "At the swimming hole."

She's worn out, Bess thought. She wondered how long Nancy had known about the pregnancy. She wasn't showing, but that didn't mean much. Many women didn't show until they were well into their second trimester. Nancy could have waited months to tell them. Or perhaps she hadn't even known herself until recently.

"It was New Year's," she said. "A bunch of kids got together."

"What kids?" her father asked. "Who was there?"

"A lot of people," Nancy said. "Not just from here. Everyone knew about it. We were drinking and stuff, and I guess I drank too much."

She stopped. Bess didn't blame her. The rest of the story was pretty obvious, and there was really no need to tell it. The details would only embarrass them all.

"You don't remember his name?" Bess asked.

"I told you, I don't know," Nancy said. "I don't even remember what he looked like."

On her other side A.J. cleared his throat. "Someone who was there must know who he is," he said. "We'll just have to ask—"

"No!" Nancy shouted. "You can't do that."

Her father bristled. "And why not?" he said. "This boy has to take responsibility for what he's done."

Nancy turned to Bess. "Please," she pleaded. "Don't let him. He can't."

"We can talk about that later," said Bess. "The first thing we have to do is make sure you're okay. You're five months along now, and I bet you haven't even seen a doctor."

"I did," Nancy said. "When I first figured out what was going on. I took the bus to Syracuse, to the Planned Parenthood office." She looked at Bess with sad eyes. "I thought I could get rid of it," she said. "But I couldn't."

"Oh baby," Bess said as she put her arms around her stepdaughter and held her close. "You're a brave girl, that's for sure."

After reassuring themselves that Nancy wasn't going to do anything drastic, they left her in her bedroom to get some rest and went into their own bedroom to discuss the situation.

"I can't believe her," A.J. said. "I didn't raise her like this."

"Like what?" said Bess. "Like a normal girl? Like someone who makes mistakes sometimes?"

"This isn't just a mistake, Bess," A.J. said.

"Yes, it is," she argued. "It's a whopper of a mistake but it's still a mistake. It happens, A.J."

He had been her husband for only seven months, and there were things about A.J. that she was still getting used to. But already she'd learned that he sometimes overreacted, especially when Nancy was concerned. She suspected it was mostly guilt he still felt about Rebecca's death, as if somehow he was responsible both for it and for taking Nancy's mother away from her. She'd tentatively broached the subject, but A.J. always managed to avoid the conversation.

"It has to be James," A.J. said.

"She says it isn't," Bess reminded him.

"She just doesn't want to get him in trouble!" A.J. insisted.

"Honey, if there was any boy you would want to be the father, wouldn't it be James McCloud?" Bess asked. "And don't you think Nancy knows that?"

A.J. put his head in his hands. "What are we going to do?" he said. "This is going to ruin her life."

Bess sat beside him, rubbing his back and thinking. Gradually an idea formed in her head. "Do you remember Patty Ebersol?" she asked A.J.

"From high school?" he said.

Bess nodded. "She was a freshman when we were sophomores. Really sweet girl. Anyway, one day she came to school all excited because she'd won a scholarship to science camp. Some kind of essay contest in a magazine or something like that. It was going to be for the whole summer and she was going to get credit for it and I don't know what all."

"What does this have to do with anything?" A.J. asked her.

"I'm getting to that," said Bess. "So that was in April or May. Then school let out and off she went to Washington, D.C., which is where the camp was. She came back right before school started in the fall, with all kinds of stories about what she did and how much fun it was and how many new friends she'd made. She told the stories so many times that we all got sick of hearing them."

A.J. gave her a look that suggested that he knew exactly how Bess and her friends had felt about Patty's stories. She ignored him.

"Well, that Thanksgiving Louise Thallmaker's cousin Leslie came to visit. She had also gone to science camp, so we asked her if she knew Patty. She didn't, which was odd because only about fifty people got to go and most of them were boys, so she should have at least *heard* about Patty. We thought maybe she just didn't remember, so we had a party one night and invited Patty to come. Leslie didn't recognize her at all, and when she started asking Patty questions about camp and what projects she'd worked on, Patty couldn't answer her."

"And the point of this is what?" A.J. asked.

"It turns out that Patty hadn't gone to summer camp at all," Bess explained. "She'd gone to stay with her grandmother in Poughkeepsie because she was pregnant. She had the baby and then came back as if it had never happened."

"How did you find out?" said A.J.

"She finally owned up to it," Bess said. "I guess she got tired of worrying that someone would find out, so she decided to get it over with."

"And what about the baby?"

"She gave it up for adoption," Bess said.

"I still don't understand what that story has to do with Nancy," her husband said.

"Your sister lives in Maine, right?" Bess said.

"Sarah," A.J. said. "Yeah, she lives in Bangor."

"School is almost over with for the year," said Bess. "If Nancy was to take a little trip to see her cousins, that wouldn't look peculiar, would it?" She counted on her fingers. "October," she said, frowning. "Well, we can work that out. The point is, nobody has to know."

"I'm not ashamed of her," said A.J.

Bess leaned over and kissed his cheek. "I know you're not," she assured him. "I'm not saying you are. I'm just thinking about what's best for Nancy. It would be one thing if we knew who the baby's father is. But we don't. That's going to make things twice as difficult for her if people find out."

A.J. nodded. "But what about the baby?" he said. "I don't want her to give it up, especially after what happened to Rebecca. A child should be with its mother. I don't want to take it away from her."

Bess took his hand. "I think there's a way she won't have to," she said.

Over the next half an hour she outlined her plan. Nancy would go to Maine to stay with Sarah and her family. As soon as she was gone, Bess and A.J. would announce that Bess was pregnant. Nancy would have the baby at the end of September (they would blame her late return on a case of chicken pox contracted from one of her cousins) and when A.J. and Bess drove up to get her Bess would go into labor and deliver "her" baby there. Then the three of them would return to Cold Falls with the new addition to the family.

"That's crazy," A.J. protested when Bess had finished explaining her idea. "How are you going to convince people that you're pregnant."

"They have these suits," Bess told him. "Fat suits, they're called. They use them in plays and movies and whatnot. I'm sure we can get one somewhere. I'll wear that. Nobody will know."

"Then what?" said A.J. "We raise the kid as our own? What about Nancy?"

"What about her?" Bess replied. "She finishes school. She goes to college. She gets married and has more kids. She has a *life.*"

"She'll never go along with it," A.J. said. "I know her."

"Then let me talk to her," said Bess.

A.J. snorted. "What makes you think she'll listen to you any more than she'll listen to me?" he said.

Bess patted his leg. "Because I'm not her father," she said.

A.J. finally relented and Bess returned to Nancy's room. She knocked on the door and heard a faint "Come in" in response. She opened the door to find Nancy standing in front of the full-length mirror that hung on the door to her closet. She was wearing a T-shirt that was far too large for her, and she was pulling it taut against her belly.

"It's starting to show," she said. "Pretty soon everyone will know."

Bess went and stood behind her, putting her hands on Nancy's shoulders and looking at their reflections in the mirror. Nancy's eyes were still pink and puffy, but she'd combed her hair and didn't look quite so distraught. Bess stroked her hair gently.

"They don't have to," she said.

Nancy turned to face her. "I said I'm not having an abortion," she said.

There was a fire in her eyes that surprised Bess. "I didn't say you should abort it," she told Nancy. "There are other options."

"And I'm not giving it away," said Nancy. She placed her hands protectively over her stomach, as if Bess had come to snatch her unborn child from her right then and there.

"Sit down," Bess said, taking her hand. "Listen to what I have to say."

Once again she described her solution to the situation. When she was finished Nancy was quiet for a long time. "I want her to be named Rebecca," she said.

"What if it's a boy?" Bess asked.

"It isn't," said Nancy. "I just know it isn't. And her name is Rebecca."

"I think that's a wonderful name," Bess said. They could worry about choosing a boy's name later; right now she just wanted Nancy to agree to the plan.

Nancy chewed on her thumbnail for a minute. Then she looked at Bess and took a deep breath. "Okay," she said.

Bess hugged her. "You're doing the right thing," she said. "You'll see. There's so much waiting for you out there. This way will be the best for everyone."

"You're sure you can find one of these fat suits?" Nancy asked.

"Yes," said Bess. "I'll get one—even if I have to make it myself."

Nancy eyed her as if sizing her up. "Well I do need to come up with a final sewing project for Home Ec," she said.

When informed that Nancy had decided to go along with Bess's plan, A.J. drew both his wife and his daughter into a hug. "I love you both so much," he told them. "It's all going to be okay. I promise. It will all be okay."

CHAPTER 36

1991

"I know it's been a long time," Charly said. "But I need your help."

She waited—holding her breath—for an answer to come through the phone. For a moment she feared that she had been hung up on. But then she heard the sound of a deep inhalation.

"Okay."

The one little word sent her heart soaring. Trying to keep her voice steady, she said, "Thank you."

But already the line was buzzing like angry bees.

CHAPTER 37

1991

Billy took the towel from his mother and pressed it to the side of his face. Inside of it was a plastic baggie filled with ice, which Ada had just taken from the freezer. At first the shock of the cold stung and made him wince. But he forced himself to hold the bag still, and after a minute the pain subsided.

"How did you say you did this?" Ada asked.

"I tripped," Billy answered. "I was walking home from the store and just wasn't paying attention. Next thing I knew I was facedown on the sidewalk."

"Well just hold that there for a while," his mother told him. "Then we'll clean it up. You don't want those cuts getting infected."

Billy leaned his elbows on the kitchen table, resting his battered cheek against the ice. He closed his eyes and tried very hard to stay in the moment. His mind wanted to take him elsewhere—somewhere where he didn't feel sick to his stomach and his hands weren't shaking. He had to fight the urge to get up and run back to his apartment, where a bottle of Jack was waiting in a cupboard to help him out.

He should never have taken the Ritalin. But it was all he could score, and it was better than nothing. He'd gotten it from Chuck Wentz, who stole it from his kid brother and sold it at a buck a pill to finance his own more expensive habits. Billy had bought six smarties off Chuck, using all the money left in his pocket. He'd downed three of them at once, chasing them with half a can of Bud he'd found abandoned on one of the bar's tables.

Ten minutes later his heart was beating faster and his mind was trying to focus on the song pouring from the bar's speakers. It was vital that he understand exactly what the singer was saying. He concentrated on the words, annoyed that he was having trouble making them out because of the conversations going on around him. All he could remember was the singsong chorus: "La da dee, La dee da. La da dee, La dee da." It had filled his head, repeating and repeating as he tried vainly to make sense of it.

He didn't remember leaving, but he did remember falling. At least, he remembered feeling that the earth was rushing toward him, and he remembered hitting the sidewalk with a sickening thud. He thought he might have passed out then, but not knowing what time he'd left the bar he wasn't sure. At any rate, no one had passed by him, or if they had, they had not stopped to help.

He also didn't remember calling his mother. When her car had pulled up alongside him as he was trying to remember where his building was, he had at first not recognized her. But she had gotten him into the car and then into the house. He'd been sitting in her kitchen for almost two hours, and only now was he able to think at all clearly.

I must have called her from the pay phone, he thought. He had to have dialed purely from habit, as even now he couldn't recall the actual number. Some sort of survival instinct had kicked in and told him to call the one person who he knew would come to his rescue.

"You were drinking," he heard his mother say. She was dressed in her nightgown; he had gotten her out of bed. She was also wearing a pair of battered pink slippers, which he recognized as ones he'd given her for Christmas. He'd gotten them at Target for $4.99. She had given him enough money to pay his rent for three months.

"A little," he told her.

"A little," she repeated, shaking her head. "A little too much."

"What time is it?" Billy asked.

"Two," said his mother. "Time for anyone with any sense to be in bed."

Billy groaned. "Go on," he said. "I'm just going to sit here for a while. I can get myself home. Don't worry about it."

"No," his mother replied. "We're going to clean those cuts and then you're going up to your room and going to sleep."

"Really," Billy objected. "I'd rather sleep in my own place."

"You're sleeping *here,*" said his mother. "Your bed is all made up."

It's always made up, he thought. *You're always waiting for me to come home.*

His mother pulled his hand away from his face and touched his cheek. He pulled away. "Ouch!" he exclaimed.

"Don't be such a baby," his mother said. "I'll get the Bacitracin."

She left him alone as she went down the hall to the bathroom. He heard her open the medicine cabinet and move things around. He was tempted to get up and leave, but his body refused to cooperate. When his mother returned, brandishing the Bacitracin, he was exactly where she had left him.

She turned on the tap and wet a clean dishcloth, which she used to wash Billy's face. The soap she'd added to it stung, but the numbing effects of the ice made it bearable. She followed the cleaning with a thick coat of ointment, which she smoothed over his cheekbones.

"There," she said. "You'll be as handsome as ever in a couple of days."

Billy gave her a kiss on the cheek. "Thanks," he said. "You always know what to do to make things better."

"I wish that was true," his mother said. She sat down and folded her hands on the table. Looking at them Billy saw that she was wearing her wedding band.

"I thought you took that off," he said, touching the ring with his finger.

"I did," his mother said. "I just put it on this afternoon. I don't honestly know why."

Billy didn't say anything. It didn't matter to him if she wore her ring or not. She'd kept it on for the seven years it took before his father had been declared legally dead. Then one day he noticed that it was not on her finger. He never asked her precisely when she had removed it, and she had never brought it up.

"Is it because they found him?" he asked her now.

His mother rubbed her thumb across the ring. "I guess part of me never really believed he was dead," she said. "Now I know for sure."

"It's okay to take it off," Billy told her. "Nobody thought you forgot about him."

His mother gave a sharp cry and brought her hand to her mouth. He knew then that he had hit on the reason for her putting the ring back on. He reached over and rubbed her shoulder. "It's all right," he said.

She took his hand and held it tightly. "They called today to say that we can have the body. We can bury him." She shook her head, and when she spoke her voice cracked. "I can't, Billy. I can't bury him. Not while James is in jail."

"You don't have to," said Billy. "I'm sure we can . . . keep him somewhere . . . until this is all over. Have Celeste call and find out."

He had almost volunteered to do it himself but had stopped himself in time. He didn't want anything to do with arranging for his father's body to be taken care of. The farther he could stay away from what was going on the better. He stood up. "I should go up," he said. "Thanks for coming to get me and"—he indicated his face—"you know."

"You're my son," his mother said. "I'd do anything for you. For any of you."

"I know," Billy said. He gave her another kiss on the cheek.

As he was leaving the kitchen his mother said, "He did love you."

Billy paused but didn't turn around.

"He didn't understand who you are, but he loved you."

Billy knew she was waiting for him to say something. He and his parents had never spoken openly about his sexuality. There had been no big coming-out moment, no drama, no scene. He had simply let them figure it out on their own. Whether they disapproved or not was not something he'd thought much about, and because the subject was never discussed he had simply assumed that it embarrassed them. He considered that their problem, not his.

"Good night, Mom."

As he walked down the upstairs hall he saw that the door to Celeste's room was closed. He'd forgotten that James's girlfriend was still there. He hadn't thought about her since their conversation in the store, when she'd left rather abruptly. He couldn't recall now exactly what they'd talked about. James, of course. Everyone had to talk about James. *It's like he's the fucking baby Jesus,* Billy thought as he went into his room. *And every day is Christmas.*

He flipped on the light and shut the door. As always when he visited his old room it felt like stepping into a time capsule. The shelf above the desk still held his collection of *Star Wars* figures, and on the wall over the bed was a *Raiders of the Lost Ark* one-sheet his father had gotten for him from the owner of the local theater. It had hung there for years, and Billy, when he'd finally started to understand what was so appealing to him about Indiana Jones, had regularly kissed Harrison Ford good night.

The books that filled the bookcase across from his bed still held his favorite titles, all arranged neatly by author. He knelt down and scanned the spines, considering several and finally selecting one and placing it on his bedside table. Then he removed his clothes, stripping down to his boxers and leaving everything else in a pile, and got into bed. He put the pillow behind his head and stretched his legs beneath the cool sheets. The bed was a bit too small for him now that he was a grown man, but he didn't care. Being in it made him feel like a boy again anyway, and somehow his body seemed to follow suit, compacting or shrinking just enough for him to fit comfortably.

He picked up the chosen book and looked at the cover. It was a light grayish blue, with concentric circles of white and black scattered across it. It was a paperback, bought from a school book club, and it had been read numerous times. He opened the book to the first page.

" 'It was a dark and stormy night,' " he read.

The book—*A Wrinkle in Time*—was one of his all-time favorites. He related to the two main characters, the socially awkward and headstrong Meg Murry and her precocious little brother Charles Wallace, who was thought by most of the townspeople to be an idiot but was actually both highly intelligent and telepathic. It was from this book that Billy had learned the term *sport* as used to describe something that was the result of a genetic mutation. Charles Wallace was a sport—genetically different from his sister and twin brothers and therefore both extraordinary and (to those who didn't understand him) frightening.

Upon first reading the book Billy had decided that he too was a sport. It explained his ever-present feeling of not belonging, of looking at his family and wondering how he could possibly be related to these other four people who resembled him in appearance but in no other way. That he had not been given telepathic ability in return for being a genetic abnormality was a disappointment to him, but he was nevertheless pleased to have a term for what he was.

He could probably have told himself the story as easily as read it. He knew large parts of it by heart, and he followed the words merely for the pleasure of losing himself in the book. His head still ached, and he knew that it would be several hours yet before he could fall asleep. The drug was still toying with him, making him feel simultaneously overly tired and overly awake. His mouth was dry, and he wished he'd remembered to bring a glass of water with him.

Just get one from the bathroom, he told himself. He wondered if his mother still kept one of those strange plastic boxes that dispensed tiny paper cups in there. When they were little he, James, and Celeste had used them to rinse their teeth after brushing, or when they needed a drink in the middle of the night and were too scared to venture into the dark downstairs of the house to get one from the kitchen.

He decided to go look. Turning the book over he started to set it on the bedside table. As he did a piece of paper slipped out and fell onto his stomach. He picked it up, assuming it was just a scrap he had used to mark his place the last time he'd read the book.

The paper was folded in half. He unfolded it and saw that it was a list.

1. Go to France
2. Be a writer
3. Meet Steven Spielberg
4. Live in New York

He recognized it immediately; it was the list of things he wanted to do when he grew up. He'd written it just before New Year's Eve in 1982. *Just before everything started,* he thought. *Before everything changed.* He was surprised by how little he'd wanted to accomplish back then. His dreams were not particularly grand. Yet now every one of them seemed impossible. At thirteen he had wanted to achieve something, to leave his mark on the world. Now he lived from one high to the next, not really wanting anything because he knew wanting only ended in disappointment.

"Sorry, kid," he said as he crumpled the paper up and threw it in the trash. "It's just not going to happen."

CHAPTER 38

1991

The cars waiting at the curb all looked alike to her. They were the same size, the same shape, the same color. They each held the same kind of people—happy, laughing, excited to see one another. Caught up in the joy of greeting loved ones or saying good-bye before taking off on vacations and visits with other people who cared for them, they were oblivious to her. She stood among them like a ghost, invisible, yet something about her kept them at a distance, as if they sensed her presence and were naturally repelled by it.

She lit a cigarette. She'd had only two in the past seven hours, one before entering the airport in Baton Rouge and another hurriedly and illegally smoked in the women's room in Atlanta, where she'd had only twenty minutes between landing and getting on the plane for Syracuse. Accustomed to a regular supply of nicotine, she was edgy and slightly nauseated. The ham sandwich she'd consumed on her most recent flight churned in her stomach, and she regretted not making another bathroom stop before leaving the airport.

"Nancy!"

She looked for the source of the voice and saw a woman waving to her from the window of yet another car indistinguishable from the rest. The car pulled up to the curb and the woman got out. "Hi," she said. "I'm Charly."

"Hi," Nancy said, noting the woman's smart clothes and manicured hands. *I already hate her,* she thought.

"Let me get your bag," said Charly, reaching for the battered duffel bag at Nancy's feet.

"I've got it," Nancy said, picking it up before Charly could touch it.

She walked around the car, tossed her bag into the backseat, and got in.

"Would you mind not smoking in the car?" Charly said as she fastened her seat belt.

Nancy took a final puff and tossed the half-smoked cigarette out the window. "Whatever you say," she remarked.

"How was the trip?" Charly asked her as she navigated through the airport traffic and made her way to the thruway.

"Fine," said Nancy. "Does James know I'm coming?"

"No," Charly answered. "Nobody does. I wanted to make sure . . ."

"That I got off the plane," said Nancy. "I get it."

"It's just that you didn't seem sure," Charly explained.

Nancy laughed sharply. "Yeah, well, I'm never really sure about anything. I usually decide at the last second."

"May I ask why you decided to come?" asked Charly.

"You can ask," Nancy said. "But I don't know if I can answer. I guess because I owe it to James."

"Owe him?" Charly repeated. "Why would you owe him?"

Nancy turned and looked at her. "Haven't you heard?" she said. "I broke his heart."

"He told me that the two of you broke up a little while before his father disappeared," said Charly. "But you were teenagers. You don't really think you somehow ruined his life, do you?"

"No," Nancy replied. "I don't give myself that much credit. But I was kind of a shit to him those last few weeks. He didn't deserve that."

"Well, if it helps any I think he'll be happy to see you," said Charly.

"We'll see," Nancy said.

She looked up and caught a glimpse of her reflection in the rearview mirror. She looked terrible. Her skin was too pale, and the makeup that had looked fine in the steamy Louisiana morning light now looked garish in the bright sunshine of a New York afternoon. Dressed in jeans and a red T-shirt under an unbuttoned long-sleeved flannel shirt she'd taken from Brice's closet, she resembled one of the sullen kids who hung out on the porches on her street, their eyes empty and their mouths hard. (And yet, she thought, they looked at her when she passed by and believed themselves above her.)

She wondered what Charly thought of her. She assumed that Charly was James's girlfriend, although Charly hadn't said as much. But Nancy could tell by the way she spoke about him. Even over the phone she had sensed that Charly was more than James's lawyer.

She wanted to ask about Rebecca, but she couldn't bring herself to do it. She hadn't seen her daughter in years. She remained in contact with her father and Bess, but sporadically. It was Bess who had given Charly her number; Bess had always made sure she knew where Nancy was, even when Nancy herself hadn't been sure. She did it for Nancy's father. Nancy knew that the separation hurt her father deeply, but she also knew that it was for the best. It was the sacrifice they both made for the sake of Rebecca.

But now she was coming home. After eight years. It seemed longer. She'd expected to feel more trepidation, but although she was apprehensive she was also strangely calm. It was as if her return was inevitable, had been set even before she left, and now she was simply following a preordained course of action. That explanation made as much sense as the reasons she'd had for doing any of the things she'd done since leaving town in the fall of '83.

The events of those months were buried in the recesses of her memory. Even now, as she went to face the consequences of what had taken place, they hardly seemed real. It was as if it had all happened to someone else, another Nancy in another town, and that she had heard the story somewhere and come to believe it was her own.

"Your brother seems convinced that James killed Daniel," Charly said, interrupting her thoughts.

"Nate?" Nancy said. "I'm not surprised. They never liked each other."

"Why do you think that is?" Charly asked.

"Who knows," said Nancy. "They're guys. You never know what the fuck they're thinking most of the time."

"Are you married?"

"No," Nancy answered. "I'm with a guy, but we're not married. That's not for me."

She thought about Brice. She hadn't told him she was leaving. He'd been asleep when she left, still passed out from the night before. She'd left him a note saying she would be back in a couple of days. He would be okay with that; it wasn't the first time she'd spent a night or two in a different bed. As long as the rent got paid Brice didn't ask where the money came from.

"And no kids?"

"Just the one," Nancy said.

She wondered what it would be like to see Rebecca. Bess sent her pictures from time to time, so she knew what she looked like. But seeing her in person would be completely different. And Rebecca would almost certainly ask questions. She'd been told that her "sister" lived too far away to visit, and she'd accepted that so far. But now she was old enough to know that the world wasn't that big of a place. It was another reason Nancy had decided to agree to Charly's request—it was time to face her greatest fear.

She badly wanted a cigarette, and almost asked Charly if they could stop. But suddenly she found that she wanted to get to Cold Falls as quickly as possible. If they stopped, even just for gas or to get coffee, she was afraid she might find the first car going in the opposite direction and get in it.

"Do you mind if I ask you some questions about Rebecca?" Charly said.

"That's why I'm here, isn't it?" said Nancy.

"Bess says that you don't know who her father is," Charly said.

"That's right," Nancy replied.

"Not even his first name?"

Nancy tapped the window glass with her nails. "Vinny," she said. "Or Nick. Something Italian, I think."

"And you met him at a party?" Charly continued.

Nancy laughed. "If you call a bunch of kids hanging out drinking in the woods in the middle of winter a party then, yeah, we met at a party."

"So he wasn't a local boy then," said Charly. "Was he someone's friend?"

"I'm sure he was *someone's* friend," Nancy said. "He was certainly *my* friend, at least that night. I never saw him again."

"Why didn't you try to track him down?" asked Charly.

"Why would I?" Nancy answered. "So my father could tell him he had to be a man and take responsibility for his kid? So we could get married? Why ruin his life too?"

It had begun to rain, and the scattered drops that had first dotted the car's windshield were now falling more frequently. Charly turned the wipers on and they swung across the glass, efficiently clearing away the water. Nancy watched the mechanical arms go back and forth, silently doing their job. She was very tired, but she feared closing her eyes. If she slept she would dream, and she didn't want to dream in front of this woman who seemed determined to pry all of the secrets from her head.

"Do you think having Rebecca ruined your life?" Charly said.

Nancy didn't answer right away. She fixed her gaze on the windshield wipers, on the hypnotic rhythm of their monotonous motions. As soon as they cleared the glass the rain dotted it again, yet the routine continued without pause, as if the few seconds of visibility it provided far outweighed the effort required to accomplish the task. Nancy, oddly, found herself feeling sorry for the beleaguered wipers, mindless as they were. *So much work for almost nothing,* she thought.

"No, I don't think having Rebecca ruined my life," she said, breaking her attention from the wipers. "But I think it would have if I'd dragged the guy into it."

She looked at Charly, who was staring straight ahead, both hands on the wheel. *Ten and two,* Nancy thought. *Always keep your hands at ten and two.* How often had James said that while trying to teach her how to drive? He'd sounded so serious then, like a real adult. She'd teased him every time, but secretly his carefulness had calmed her. She'd never felt anxious around James. Not until the end.

"Do you have kids?" she asked Charly. She hadn't considered that perhaps James had actually married someone, but why shouldn't he have? And why shouldn't he have a kid or two running around?

"I'm not married," Charly replied.

Right, Nancy thought. *Because you can't have kids if you aren't married.* She almost laughed, but instead turned it into a cough. She really didn't dislike Charly. In fact she seemed more or less okay. Still, the remark struck her as funny. It sounded so old-fashioned. *Next she'll be throwing around words like* wedlock *and* bastard, she thought.

"I want kids," said Charly, surprising Nancy by continuing the conversation instead of asking another question. "It just hasn't all come together yet," she concluded.

She sounded almost sad, Nancy thought. Still, she had a difficult time feeling sympathetic. Charly, as far as she could tell, had pretty much everything she could possibly want. Then again, she'd learned the hard way not to believe everything she saw. The world—and people—were often not what you expected them to be, and especially not what they pretended to be.

"I don't blame Rebecca for anything that's happened to me," she said. "None of it is her fault."

"Who do you blame?" Charly asked her.

I'm supposed to give her a name, Nancy thought. *She thinks that will be the thing that saves James.*

"No one," she said. "I don't blame anyone."

"Not even yourself?" Charly said.

"Especially not myself," said Nancy. "Like I said, it was no one's fault. A tornado isn't anyone's fault. An earthquake isn't anyone's fault. They just happen. Asking how come doesn't change the fact that your house is gone."

She really wanted a cigarette. Instead she reached over and turned on the radio. It crackled with static that was briefly interrupted by the voice of a current pop diva. Nancy turned the dial to a number familiar to her from years before. To her surprise the sound of country western music filled the car.

"It used to be classic rock," she said to Charly as she looked for an alternative. She flipped the dial to the right, racing through the stations, then backing up when some bit of familiar music caught her ear. It was an REO Speedwagon song. She tuned it in and sat back.

"What do you want from me?" she said, asking Charly the question that had been on her mind since receiving the phone call the day before.

"I'd like to say that I know," Charly told her. "But the truth is that I'm not sure. I've collected all of these bits and pieces, but I don't know how to put them together. All I know is that somewhere in all of this is the piece I need to prove that James didn't kill his father."

"And you think I know what that piece is?" said Nancy.

"What," Charly said. "Or where. Or when, or how, or who. I really don't know. But something tells me that your coming back here will help." She took her eyes from the road to look at Nancy and smile. "Thank you for agreeing to give it a try."

We'll see how helpful it is, Nancy thought. *We'll just wait and see.*

CHAPTER 39

1983

Nancy tucked her hair behind her ear. The breeze was strong, and she found herself shivering. Even though it was April and the world had mostly woken up from its winter sleep, the night before it had turned colder and begun to snow, as it sometimes did in the spring. Now the snow had become rain, falling steadily and chilling the air. Nancy was wearing a hooded sweatshirt, which was now very wet and doing nothing to warm her. She didn't care. It wasn't possible for her to be any more miserable.

Yes it is, she argued with herself. *Just wait a few minutes.*

She was standing under the bleachers by the football field behind the school. The seats above her did little to protect her from the rain, which found its way through the openings between the footboards and dripped from the edges in tiny waterfalls. The ground was soaked, and the cigarette butts and candy wrappers that had been discarded there mixed with the softening dirt in a muddy soup that stuck to her sneakers. However, the inclement weather was also the reason for Nancy being the only one at the normally busy gathering spot.

She cupped her hands and blew into them. The warmth lasted only a moment, and then she was cold again. She shoved her hands into the pockets of her jeans, then quickly removed them and tucked them underneath the edge of her sweatshirt, pressing them against her belly. She felt the gentle curve of her stomach, the hill of flesh that had recently begun to swell there as if the spring rains had awakened not only the earth but something inside of her. That thing was growing rapidly, increasing in mass and distorting the shape of her body. She resented its enthusiasm for life, worrying that if it kept up its current rate she would be forced to find new ways to disguise its presence.

Three more weeks, she told it. *Can't you wait that long? Can't you do that one thing for me?*

As if in answer the thing inside of her moved beneath her hands. For a moment she was filled with a bright joy that burst through the cold and rain. Then it was gone. Still, a kind of warmth remained in her hands.

"Hey," a voice said.

She pulled her hands from the sweatshirt and pulled it down, glancing down to make sure that no telltale signs could be seen. Although she knew that the change in her body was slight, she imagined that anyone else looking at her would find her grotesquely distorted. However, she was mostly reassured that she was safe from detection, at least for the moment.

"Hey," she said as James joined her under the bleachers. His hair was wet and plastered to his forehead. She started to reach up and push it away from his eyes, but forced herself to put her hands in her pockets.

"What's up?" asked James. "Why did you want to come out here? It's freezing."

"I noticed," Nancy replied. "But I kind of wanted to be alone."

"Okay," said James. His voice held a hint of suspicion.

I don't blame him, Nancy thought. *Not after how I've been acting.*

She hesitated to begin. This was going to be very difficult, almost as difficult as it was to acknowledge what was happening inside of her. *No,* she told herself. *This is harder.*

"Is something wrong?" James asked after she had remained silent for some time.

"No," Nancy answered quickly. "Well, sort of. But it's not wrong exactly." She looked away from James. *How do I say this?* she wondered. For days—maybe weeks—she had searched for a way to do it as painlessly as possible. She'd come up with nothing.

"This is about us, isn't it?" said James, once again doing part of her work for her. It wasn't fair to make him do what she should be doing, and she knew it.

"Yes," she said. That seemed to unlock something in her, and she began to speak. "I know I've been acting kind of weird for a while," she said. She waited for James to agree, but he just looked at her.

"I've been going through some—stuff," she said. "I can't really explain it."

"Is it some other guy?" asked James.

"No," said Nancy. She found herself a little annoyed that James would think that. Then again she could hardly blame him. She hadn't even let him kiss her for months.

"Then what?" James said. "Come on. Tell me. I'm your boyfriend. You know you can tell me anything. God, you know more about me that anyone else does."

It was true, Nancy thought. She and James had shared so much with one another. But she had discovered that there were things she just couldn't tell him. Not without destroying him, and she wasn't able to do that. It was bad enough that her own life was in tatters. Bringing James into it was a cruelty she simply wasn't capable of, even though part of her very much wanted to ask him to rescue her from her turmoil. She knew he would try. She also knew he would fail. This time it was she who had to rescue him.

"I can't really explain it," she said inadequately. "I'm just—changing."

"Changing how?" asked James. She could hear the frustration creeping into his voice, and it tore at her heart.

"I need some space," Nancy said. "I need to be by myself for a while. Not forever," she added. She knew she was giving him false hope. *But maybe not,* she thought. *Maybe you really can come back to him.* But she doubted it. She didn't think she could face him after it was over, not without feeling like she'd tricked him. That was something she was sure she would feel forever, even if she were able to pretend it wasn't true for his sake.

James reached up and pushed his hair to the side, doing what she couldn't. "You're breaking up with me," he said, as if he was the one giving *her* the bad news.

Nancy nodded, unable to answer.

"I don't get it," James said. "Did I do something wrong? Is it because I wanted to—"

"No," Nancy interrupted. "I wanted it too. You know that."

"But—" said James.

Again she interrupted him. "I told you, it's not you," she said.

"Is it your father?" James asked. "Does he think we're spending too much time together again? Did my father say something to him?"

Nancy found herself tempted to say yes. It would remove the blame from her and point it in a direction that was already familiar to James. Instead of a new pain she would just be reviving an old one. He had dealt with that before and survived; he could do it again. And she would be removed from the line of fire.

She said nothing, compromising with a sin by omission and telling herself it was the best thing for both of them.

James's face clouded over and he kicked at one of the support posts. "Fuck!" he spat. "I don't get it. My grades are okay. Yours are great. What's the problem now?" He puffed angrily, his breath forming clouds in the cold air. Nancy could tell it was taking great effort for him to control his temper.

"It's just a break," she said.

"Sure," said James. "Another fucking break. What is it with them controlling our lives? Why can't they just leave us alone?" He lifted his hand, curled in a fist, and for a moment Nancy feared he was going to punch one of the posts. Then he seemed to reconsider and stuffed his hands in his pockets. "I'll talk to my dad," he said. "I'll fix this."

"No," Nancy said. "Please don't. It will just cause more trouble. Just give it a little while. Summer's coming. We'll be done with finals. I'm sure things will settle down then."

"Maybe," James agreed. "But they'll just do it again. It's like they don't want us to be together." He looked into her face. "We should get married," he said.

"What?" Nancy said.

"Married," James repeated. "Then they couldn't say anything."

Nancy's head filled with panicked thought. James couldn't be serious. Not sensible James, who despite his occasional outbursts was the most level-headed person she knew. He had to be joking. She found herself unable to speak, and she didn't know if it was because she feared he was serious or because she wanted him to be.

"Don't worry," James said. "I won't say anything. You're right. We just need to wait it out. Everything will be okay."

Nancy nodded. "Right," she said. "It will be okay."

She reached into her pocket and drew something out. "You should take this," she said as she handed the object to James.

"My ring?" James said, looking at it resting on her palm. "Why?"

"I just think you should wear it," said Nancy. "It will make them think we aren't so serious." She hated herself for tricking him into aiding in his own deception, but she had already become a person she didn't recognize or like, and this was just another thing she had to do. What worried her was that it was starting to become easy.

James continued to stare at the ring, not touching it. Nancy's hand shook from the cold, and the ring trembled with it. It seemed to weigh a thousand pounds. She wished he would just take it and not make her beg him.

"No," James said. "I don't want it. I gave it to you. I don't care if you wear it or not, but I want you to have it."

"James," said Nancy. "Please. Just take it. If my father finds it or—"

"No," James repeated. He reached out and took her hand, curling her fingers around the ring and covering them with his hand. She felt her stomach jump at his touch. "You're going to keep it," he said. "Just do that for me, okay? As long as you have it I'll feel like we're together."

Nancy fought back the urge to cry. James was breaking her heart even as she was breaking his. "Okay," she relented. "I'll keep it."

James took her in his arms. She put hers around him, pressing her hands against the wet fabric of his jacket. The ring, clutched in her hand, felt like a hot coal.

"I love you," James said.

Nancy forced herself to say, "I love you too."

"It'll be all right," he assured her. "I know it will."

"Me too," Nancy told him. Tears were forming in her eyes, and she fought them back. But they forced their way out, and as they slid down her cheeks she was grateful for the rain that hid them from James.

James let her go. "Why didn't you just tell me?" he asked as Nancy stepped away from him. "I was really worried."

"I'm sorry," said Nancy. "I just know how upset you were the last time. I didn't want you doing something crazy."

"Like telling my dad to fuck off?" James said. "I really should. It's time he realized I'm not a kid anymore."

"They think they're helping, I guess," Nancy said, hoping to dampen James's ire. Despite the success of their "breakup" she knew that the calm was temporary. When James discovered the true extent of her betrayal—which he would in a few weeks—things would be even worse. For both of them. But especially for James.

Until then she'd been given a reprieve. Not that she felt any better, and not that she wouldn't feel worse with each day she spent with James knowing that soon she would leave him devastated. *But you'll come back,* she reminded herself. *After it's over you'll come back. Then it will all be all right again.*

Maybe. Maybe she would be able to convince James that her visit to her cousins really was a last-minute decision. She'd wanted to tell him, but her father had forbidden it. He was afraid that James would ask too many questions, and as he said, the less anyone knew about the situation the better. When she came back—when the problem had been taken care of—they would have the distraction of the arrival of Bess's baby to deflect any questions that people might have.

She was thankful for Bess's help. It was she who had come up with the plan, she who was even now preparing for the more public deception, feigning a pregnancy. Bess—and her father—were the ones who would have to carry on a daily masquerade. She had only to remain in hiding until it was over. Bess was the one who had to be careful every moment of every day, who had to convince everyone that she was carrying a child in her belly. Nancy couldn't imagine what she would have done without her stepmother there to help her.

"We should get inside," said James. "It's really coming down."

Nancy, so relieved to have gotten through this last, and most difficult, lie with relatively little difficulty had not noticed that the rain was falling more heavily. Now she was aware of the water hitting her face and soaking her sweatshirt. *I need to get dry,* she thought. *If I get sick it might hurt the baby.*

As if reading her thoughts James said, "Come on. I don't want you getting sick." He took his jacket off and put it around her. She started to object, but stopped. She liked that he was trying to take care of her. He made her feel important.

Holding his jacket tight around her she ran with him back to the school.

CHAPTER 40

1991

"Hello, Nate."

Nancy looked at her stepbrother as he sat down across from her. He looked different than she remembered. He'd filled out some, the teenage thinness gone. His face was fuller, and he had a mustache and goatee. She couldn't decide whether it suited him.

Nate waited until the waitress, who had approached the table, finished pouring him a cup of coffee and refilling Nancy's. Then he tore open a packet of sugar and said, "Why'd you come back?"

Nancy took a sip of coffee. "What's the matter?" she asked. "Aren't you happy to see me?"

Nate added milk to his coffee and stirred it slowly. "I didn't know anything had changed," he said.

"It hasn't," said Nancy. "Except for the fact that you arrested James and now he's sitting in jail."

"Why do you care what happens to James McCloud all of a sudden?" Nate said. "You haven't cared for the past eight years."

Nancy shrugged. "Maybe it's time to make up for some mistakes," she said.

Nate looked at her over his coffee. "They found the body, Nancy," he said. "And his ring was in the box with it."

"I heard," Nancy said. "That really doesn't look so good for James, does it?"

"No, it doesn't," Nate agreed. "I'd say it's pretty much a done deal as far as he's concerned."

Nancy said nothing. She looked around the café. Some of the people she recognized, and she knew they must have recognized her as well. If they did they showed no indications of it. There were no stares, no whispering, no nods or waves of acknowledgment. *We're all good at pretending,* she thought. *It's how towns like this keep from going crazy.*

"How's Celeste handling it?" she asked Nate.

He shrugged. "She's starting to accept it," he said. "It's hard for her to believe James could do something like this."

"I imagine it is," Nancy agreed. "It's too bad she had to find out."

"She'll get over it," said Nate. "It's funny what people can learn to live with."

"I'll have to come over and see her," Nancy said. "It's been a long time. I'd like to see Mary and Adam too. They probably don't even know who I am."

She waited for Nate to tell her that it wouldn't be a good idea, but all he said was, "They've heard about you."

I bet they have, Nancy thought. She wondered what her stepbrother and sister-in-law had told their children about their absent aunt. Had Nate stuck to the agreed-upon story all this time? Or had he told Celeste some version of the truth? She couldn't imagine he had. There would be nothing to be gained from it.

"Have you seen Rebecca yet?" Nate asked.

Nancy shook her head. "I haven't been to see Mom and Dad yet," she said. "I called them last night when I got in, though. I'll go over there after we're done here."

"She's beautiful," Nate said. "She looks just like you."

"I've seen pictures," said Nancy. "She looks like my mother."

"She's happy, Nancy," Nate said. "She's really happy. We all are."

"So it seems," said Nancy. "That's good. That's really good."

"Is there really anything you can do to help James?" Nate asked her. "Do you really want to get involved in all of this?"

Nancy looked at him. "No," she said. "I don't want to get involved. But I will if I have to."

Nate looked at his watch. "I don't see why you would want to do that," he said. There was a hint of irritation in his tone.

"Sometimes you just have to do the right thing," Nancy told him. "You should know that."

"I do," Nate said. "That's why I think you should have stayed away. Like you promised."

"Maybe," Nancy agreed. "We'll see." She stood up and pulled her coat on. "I have to go," she said. "But it was good seeing you, Nate."

Nate stayed seated. "If I don't see you before you leave, have a safe trip home," he said.

Nancy patted his shoulder, feeling him jump at her touch. "I'm sure we'll get to spend some more time together," she said. "I didn't come home after eight years just to say hello and leave. I plan on being around for a while."

She left him sitting there and walked out of the café. Charly, who had driven to Syracuse to meet with James's lawyer, had dropped her off before leaving. Now she walked down the familiar street, noting the changes that had taken place since her departure. Like Nate the town had aged but was still very much recognizable. She felt sixteen again as she passed by stores in which she'd shopped and restaurants in which she'd eaten. She paused across the street from the library and watched several people enter and leave. Did old Mrs. Flanders still run the place? Did she still shush anyone who dared break the silence of her kingdom? Nancy considered going in and finding out, but part of her feared finding some new face looking at her from behind the desk.

She continued on past the bank and the Lutheran church and the post office. Two blocks after that she turned onto the street where the high school was. It was halfway down the block, a large brick building with rows of tall, multipaned windows that Nancy remembered could be opened only by the use of a hook, fastened to the end of a stick, that was inserted into a recess in the upper frame. When the frame was pulled the entire window slid back and up on hinged arms, creating openings at the top and bottom. Many days she had sat next to one of those windows, sometimes looking out at the falling snow or rain and sometimes enjoying the breezes that cooled the large, stuffy rooms.

The signboard that had stood in the front of the school when she was a student there—a rectangular white affair onto which plastic letters could be attached to inform passersby about school events—had been replaced by a fancy electronic one. Red letters scrolled by on a black background: CONGRATULATIONS LADY BEAVERS STATE CHAMPS DIVISION III SOCCER! GRADUATION IS JUNE 17! BLOOD DRIVE THIS WEDNESDAY! The different pieces of information were repeated endlessly, a news ticker of enor-

mous interest to those with ties to Cold Falls High School. She'd forgotten that the mascot was the beaver. She'd always thought it was a
decision that must have been made long before the establishment of
girls' teams, and suddenly recalled fondly once writing a headline for
the school paper that read LADY BEAVERS STUNG BY HORNETS 12–27.

Those days seemed a lifetime ago now. She'd never graduated from
the school, instead earning her equivalency degree later on, but it had
played a prominent role in her life and had in many ways been the setting for the most important events in her life. As she walked by the
football field she found herself looking at the bleachers and thinking
of James.

She hurried on, not wanting to be late. The elementary school was
on the same street as the high school, built there based on the assump-
tion that most families would at one time or another have children at-
tending both places. Although it was referred to as the elementary
school it actually housed students in kindergarten through eighth
grade, a situation that greatly irritated those in the upper grades, who
hated that they were lumped in with the younger students simply because the lower school was larger than the high school and could
therefore better accommodate them.

Nancy walked along the side of the school to the back. There a playground had been established, a large area containing swings, slides, a
jungle gym, and a square of concrete perhaps twenty feet on a side
where hopscotch fields could be drawn and games of jump rope played.
Beyond this were fields for sports requiring more space.

Because it was Saturday the playground was quiet. Only two figures
were visible on it, one small and one larger. Nancy stood at the fence
that surrounded the yard and watched them for a minute. Rebecca
was on a swing, pumping her legs as she pushed herself higher with
each arc. Bess stood nearby watching her. Neither of them saw Nancy.

For a moment she was seized with panic and almost ran. What
would she say to her daughter? How could she behave like a sister to
the child to whom she'd given birth. This was the very reason she'd
been unable to stay in Cold Falls in the first place. Now she found that
time had not changed anything. The pain was just as deep.

Before she could turn and walk away from Rebecca for the second
time in her life the little girl pointed in her direction. Bess turned and,
seeing Nancy, waved. Nancy waved back and, forcing her hand to

move, opened the gate. As she stepped through Rebecca brought the swing to a stop, jumped off, and ran toward her. She stopped in front of Nancy and looked up at her.

"Hi," she said. "I'm your sister."

Nancy smiled. "I know," she said.

Rebecca cocked her head to one side. "We look alike," she said matter-of-factly. "But we don't have the same mom." She reached up and took Nancy's hand. "Come on," she said, walking back toward Bess. "How come you've never visited us before?"

"I live really far away," Nancy told her.

"Where?" asked Rebecca.

"Louisiana," Nancy answered. "Do you know where that is?"

Rebecca shook her head. "Can I come visit you there?" she said.

"We'll see," said Nancy. "Maybe someday."

They reached Bess, and Rebecca said, "Doesn't she look like me?"

Bess smiled. "She sure does, honey." She then hugged Nancy tightly. "It's so good to see you," she said. "We've missed you."

"How come you came here and not to the house?" Rebecca asked.

Nancy looked at Bess. They'd agreed to meet at the playground because it was neutral ground. For her own reasons Nancy hadn't wanted to first encounter her daughter at her father's house. The playground had seemed like a good alternative, and Bess had agreed.

"Where's Dad?" Nancy asked. She'd of course immediately noticed her father's absence, and hoped that it wasn't the result of some reluctance on his part to see her.

"He's taking Poppy for a walk," Rebecca said.

"The dog," Bess clarified.

"They don't want dogs pooping in here," said Rebecca. "Someone might step in it." She wrinkled her nose, making Nancy laugh.

"Well we can't have that," she said.

"He should be here in a minute," said Bess. "Then we thought we'd walk into town, maybe get an ice cream or something."

"What's your favorite flavor?" Rebecca asked Nancy.

"I'm kind of boring," Nancy told her. "I like vanilla with caramel sauce."

"Me too!" Rebecca shrieked. "And it's *not* boring, it's *good.*"

The sound of a dog barking distracted her, and she pointed in the direction of the gate. "There's Daddy!" she said.

Nancy turned to see her father walking toward her. He looked older. There was more gray in his hair, and his stomach protruded over the top of his belt. But his face was the same, and when he smiled the familiar crooked smile she nearly burst into tears. She hadn't realized until then just how much she'd missed him.

As Rebecca played with Poppy, Nancy and her father embraced. Neither said a word; they simply hung on to one another, as if each wanted to make sure the other was real and not a dream. When they finally let go her father continued to hold her hands.

"Let me look at you," he said. He touched her face. "You look just like your mother."

"She looks like *me*," Rebecca pointed out for the third time. Then she said to Nancy, as if sharing a secret, "But we don't look like Daddy."

Nancy instinctively looked at her father, whose face had darkened. They exchanged glances for a moment. Then Bess came to their rescue. "You don't look like me either, sweetie," she said. "But you're still my little girl."

Rebecca nodded. "Do you want to see the trick I taught Poppy?" she asked Nancy.

Without waiting for an answer she ran off calling to the dog. As she went Nancy's father said, "She's asking more and more questions."

"I gather she's not the only one," Nancy said. "I saw Nate this morning."

At the mention of her stepbrother she saw her father's face stiffen. Bess too seemed to grow stony. "I can't imagine what Ada is going through," Bess said.

"You don't really believe James did it, do you?" Nancy asked.

Her father cleared his throat. "It doesn't look good, Nancy," he replied.

Rebecca called to them, and the conversation was cut short as they all watched her perform her trick with Poppy, which consisted of telling the dog to sit while Rebecca ran some distance off. "Okay!" she yelled. "Poppy, come!"

The spaniel darted toward her, ears flapping and tail wagging. She barked happily as Rebecca knelt and ruffled her ears. "Good dog," she said proudly.

"You don't owe James McCloud anything," Nancy's father said.

"Who says I came back just for him?" said Nancy. "Maybe it was just time."

Her father looked over at her. "You can't change the past," he told her.

Nancy nodded. "Maybe not," she said. "But maybe you can change the future."

CHAPTER 41

1982

"Nathaniel Adam Derry."

Nate looked at his reflection in the mirror over his dresser and repeated his name. His *new* name. As of that afternoon he was no longer Nathaniel William Kunkel. In the office of A.J.'s lawyer they had signed the papers officially making him A.J.'s son. He had surprised A.J. by also changing his name, choosing Adam from A.J.'s given name of Adam John and jettisoning William, which had come from his biological father. He'd asked his mother's permission, which she'd gladly given, and A.J. had been so overwhelmed with emotion upon hearing the news that he'd begun to cry.

After years of having only his mother in his life it was strange to finally have a father, especially one as kind as A.J. was. Nate's biological father—from what little he remembered of him—had been a distant, stupid man, prone to fits of sulkiness and rages in which he accused Nate and his mother of not loving him enough. These were always followed by tears and, inevitably, a gambling binge after which it all began again. Nate had long ago ceased to think of the man as his father, and in fact often pretended that he was dead.

Now he had a father he was more than happy to call his own. He'd liked A.J. from the first time they'd met and had held his breath waiting for his mother to announce their engagement. When she had he'd been so excited that he'd spun her around like a little girl, laughing with joy. He'd impatiently passed the days before the wedding thinking about how it would feel to be part of a family.

Nathaniel Adam Derry. It was a good name. A solid name. It sounded like someone who would discover something, or perhaps win a battle. He had written it out endlessly in the days before the adoption, filling several dozen pages of a notebook in order to get used to the flow of the name beneath his hand and practicing various ways of forming the letters so that his signature reflected the person he was becoming. He could now sign it quickly and confidently, which pleased him greatly.

It felt a little peculiar to be starting his life over at sixteen, but that was exactly what he was doing. He'd decided that, along with his new name, he would become a new man. He wasn't quite sure how this new persona would manifest itself, but he had some ideas. For one thing he would study harder and make something of himself. He wanted to make A.J. proud of him and not give him anything about which to be disappointed. He would become the son A.J. had never had, returning to him the gift which he himself had been given.

"Nate?"

His mother's voice called to him from downstairs. He leaned his head out and answered her. "I'm up here."

"Could you come down and help me with these boxes?" his mother asked.

"Sure," he yelled back. "Just a second."

Although they had moved into the Derry house—*their* house—several weeks earlier his mother was still unpacking and integrating their things with those already in the house. It was a painstaking process, and one the male Derrys were patient with but growing weary of. Several times A.J. and Nate had shared exasperated looks over Bess's back, both trying not to laugh at the shared joke.

Hopefully, he thought, this was the last of the boxes. His own room was completely set up, complete with the new stereo A.J. had surprised him with on the day he and his mother had moved in. Together they had painted the room a dark blue, and with the addition of an Ozzy poster over the bed and some pictures of Lita Ford and Molly Ringwald taped to the closet door it had become his own.

He left the room and walked down the hall. As he passed the bathroom he saw steam emerging from under the door. Nancy was taking her nightly shower. When he'd first discovered her habit of bathing in the evening he had found it a little odd. But she'd explained that she did it because she didn't like the idea of going to bed dirty from the day. He still found it eccentric, but it was also kind of cute.

He noticed that the door was partly open, and instinctively moved to shut it. As he did he bumped against it and inadvertently pushed the door open even farther. He took a step inside, meaning to close it again. Over the sound of the shower running he heard Nancy singing, off-key, the words to a Michael Jackson song. He paused, listening. Then, looking toward the shower, he saw that Nancy was visible through the sliding glass door. The glass was pebbled, and he didn't have a clear view, but her outline was visible and he saw enough that he was both embarrassed and transfixed.

" 'Billie Jean is not my lover,' " Nancy warbled as she ran her hands through her hair.

Nate watched as she bent her head back and let the water cascade down her body. Her hands ran over her breasts, and he glimpsed her nipples for a moment as she wiped soap from them. Seeing this he felt a familiar aching in his groin. He reached down with his hand and found that he had stiffened in just the half a minute he'd been standing there.

He'd always found Nancy to be pretty, long before the possibility of her becoming his stepsister had arisen. But he wasn't the kind of guy she liked. She preferred someone like James McCloud, although Nate really couldn't understand why. James was such a tight-ass that Nate was sure that if he swallowed coal he'd shit diamonds. What Nancy saw in him Nate couldn't imagine.

Anyway, now they were related so she was off-limits. Still, he couldn't deny that she was beautiful. Her being his stepsister wouldn't change that. He just had to start thinking of her as his real sister. That would take care of any lingering thoughts he might have about her.

Apparently, though, his dick hadn't gotten the message. It remained disconcertingly hard despite his attempts to will it down. *All you have to do is leave,* he told himself. *Just get out of here and shut the door.*

He tried to force himself to turn away, but his feet refused to move. Nancy, still oblivious, was continuing to wash her body. She bent over, running her hands up her legs. Then she turned around and faced the showerhead. First she let the spray hit her in the face, tilting her head back and letting it course down her neck. The glass and the steam prevented Nate from seeing her too clearly, and so he found himself pretending that it wasn't Nancy he was watching but some random girl.

Nancy had stopped singing, and now that the bathroom was quiet Nate feared she would hear him breathing or even just sense another presence in the room. It would be difficult for her to see him, as the bathtub was tucked into the area behind the linen closet that was to his left. By standing across from the closet he could see around the corner, but Nancy would have to open the sliding glass door to see him clearly.

The sound of the water hitting the tub floor filled his ears, and the steam that poured over the top of the shower door caressed his face. He had begun to sweat a little, and a bead trickled down his back. It was very hot, and underneath his sweatpants his body felt as if it were on fire. As if in a dream he slipped his hand inside of his sweats and wrapped his fingers around his hardness. He did nothing but hold it, feeling the blood beat beneath his fingers.

He saw the shadow of Nancy's hand reach up and touch the showerhead, making some kind of adjustment. The sound of the water changed from a gentle rain to something more forceful, and through the glass he saw that it now formed a single stream as it poured from the head. Nancy had taken a step back, and she appeared to be arching her back. One hand ducked into the shadowy area that was her crotch and began to move slowly up and down.

Nate held his breath, imagining what might be happening behind the door. The jet from the shower angled down toward Nancy's circling hand, ending in a dull *tup-tup-tup* sound as her fingers broke the force of its trajectory. Nancy's shadow moved behind the foggy scrim, her hips thrusting forward and back again in a steady rhythm.

Nate looked behind him. The door was still slightly ajar. He closed it completely, turning the knob so that the lock slid silently into place. Then he turned back to the shower. Nancy continued to make the rocking motion. Her breasts pointed up as she put her head back, and water splashed from them as her nipples entered and exited the stream.

Nate pushed his sweatpants down, releasing his erection. It sprang out full and aching into his palm. He stroked it slowly, his eyes fixed on the shower door where the pantomime played out as if in a dream. He felt his heartbeat accelerate to match the whirring of the showerhead,

until the blood throbbed in his ears with the same sound: *Tup-tup-tup.*
Tup-tup-tup.

He had, of course, touched his own dick many times, but never had
it felt as hard as it did now. The circumstances of his discovery aroused
him to new heights. He had become a voyeur hiding and watching,
catching a young woman in the most private of moments. That the
young woman was his stepsister didn't matter. He was excited beyond
the point of being ashamed.

He heard a low moaning sound separate itself from the noise of the
water. It was different from the sounds he made when he jerked himself off, which were guttural and raw, almost beastlike. This was more
breathless, more feminine. They grew in frequency and became a series of tiny exhalations, each exploding from the steam like an explo-
sion of fireworks: *Ahh-ahh-ahh.*

He felt a surging beneath his fingers and looked down just as a jet
of cum erupted from his dick. The first blast fell to the floor, where it
lay like a piece of string dropped onto the pink carpeting. The second
and third he caught in his hand, the sticky wet heat filling his fingers.
He forced himself to keep quiet, grinding his teeth as his body
spasmed and his throat burned with the growls he was obliged to swallow lest he betray his presence to Nancy.

When his legs stopped shaking he quickly wiped his fouled hand
on the inside of his sweats and pulled them up to cover his softening
cock. The cum on the carpet he rubbed in with the toe of his sneaker.
Then he opened the door and slipped outside, closing the door behind him just as the sound of the water ceased. He leaned his head
against the door and heard the shower door slide open. Nancy was
singing again: " 'She looked more like a movie queen from a movie
scene.' "

He envisioned her grabbing one of the fluffy pink towels from the
rod and drying herself with it, wiping the water from her breasts and
arms, drying the damp patch between her legs. He wondered if she
was sticky there, as he was, and if her body had trembled as his had
when she came. He imagined for a moment that she *had* seen him and
that she had pretended not to. The idea made him strangely happy.

The sound of a blow dryer scattered his thoughts and he pulled
himself away from the door. The steam had cooled on his skin, and he
now felt cold. He shivered as he crept away from the door and made

his way down the stairs. His mother was in the living room, adding a box to the five already stacked there in a neat pyramid.

"It's about time," she said. "I was about to come up and get you."

"Sorry," Nate said. "I was in the middle of something."

His mother pointed to the boxes. "Well, take these down to the cellar," she told him. "Stack them in the corner against the wall, but not too near the oil tank. I don't want them getting dirty."

"Got it," Nate said, picking up the topmost box. It was fairly light, and he carried it easily.

He descended into the cellar, pausing to pull the string that turned on the single electric bulb that illuminated the room. The shadows retreated into the corners and the things hidden beneath them—the freezer, the shelves of canned goods, A.J.'s workbench—were revealed. Nate took the box to where the others were already arranged in a neat row and added the new one to the stack.

Instead of immediately going back upstairs he leaned against the freezer and closed his eyes. The rush of excitement he'd experienced had dissipated, and now he felt the weight of guilt descend upon him. *That wasn't cool,* he told himself. *What the fuck is wrong with you?* The voice was harsh and filled with disgust.

But she's not my sister, he argued. *And it's not like I did anything. I just watched. And I couldn't even really see her.*

He took a deep breath. It really was no big deal. He just had to calm down. So he'd gotten a little worked up. How was it any different from thinking about some girl from school while he jacked off? He'd done that plenty of times and never felt bad about it. Why should he now just because the girl had actually been right in front of him?

Besides, it wouldn't happen again. It was just a one-time thing, like the time he'd stolen a Snickers from the drugstore. He'd eaten it but afterward had felt so guilty that he'd thrown it all up and buried the wrapper in the woods so his mother wouldn't find it in the trash and ask him where it had come from. He hadn't stolen anything since then.

This would be the same. He'd just made a little mistake, and not such a big one at that. Anybody would have done what he had. *Well, any* normal *boy,* he thought. After all, boys were constantly horny, right? What were they supposed to do when they accidentally saw a naked girl? Walk away and forget about it? No, he'd done the expected thing.

He wondered suddenly if James McCloud had ever seen Nancy like that. *I bet he hasn't,* he thought. The idea made him laugh. What would James think if he knew Nate had seen Nancy playing with herself? *He'd eat his heart out, that's what,* he thought happily. *He probably wouldn't even know what to do.*

But *he* had known. He had known exactly what to do.

CHAPTER 42

1991

The kitchen was different. The buttery yellow paint had been replaced by wallpaper featuring a pattern of cherries, and the cabinets were new—white with beaded glass panes that turned the objects behind them into ghostly shapes, spectral dishes and phantom canned goods haunting the shelves. The refrigerator and stove were also new, their stainless steel surfaces cold and hard.

But the table was the same heavy oak one Nancy's mother had purchased in the early days of her marriage to Nancy's father. She'd found it at what passed for an estate sale in that part of the world, a yard sale held by the children of a farmer in a neighboring town following his death. It had been covered with odds and ends priced at a dollar apiece. Rebecca Derry, uninterested in the clutter that hid the table, had fallen in love with the ill-used piece and bought it from the farmer's harried daughter for fifty dollars. After placing it in her kitchen she'd lovingly rubbed several coats of oil into the dried and cracking wood, restoring it to a beautiful deep golden brown color.

Many of Nancy's memories of her mother centered around the table. She recalled mornings before school when she'd sat before a steaming bowl of oatmeal, stirring brown sugar and milk into it as her mother ran down the checklist of things Nancy needed to remember to take with her: lunch money, books, the dried wasp's nest for show-and-tell. Later she would sit there and recount the day's adventures, telling her mother everything that had happened to her and receiving congratulations or comfort as the situation required. Always after these moments at the table she felt better.

She wished her mother were there with her now. Although the table appeared the same, the changes in the kitchen had altered something about it. It now seemed out of place somehow, as if it were uncomfortable being surrounded by so many new-made things. *Or maybe I'm the one who's out of place,* Nancy thought. *This isn't my house anymore.*

After two nights at the McCloud house she'd moved, somewhat reluctantly, to her father's house at Bess's invitation. Things had gone well with Becky, and so it had been decided that they could all safely spend more time together. Because Becky occupied what had been Nancy's room, Nancy was sleeping in what had been Nate's room. It too had been renovated, and all traces of Nate were gone, replaced by more wallpaper (this one patterned with pinecones and chickadees), green carpeting, and a bed covered in a red-and-black plaid comforter. The overall effect made Nancy think of a hunting lodge, and she half expected to open her eyes and see a mounted stag's head staring at her with glassy eyes.

"It's peculiar seeing you drink coffee," her father remarked as he set a mug in front of her. "Makes you seem all grown up."

"I am grown up," Nancy reminded him. "I'll be twenty-four in November."

Her father sat down across from her. "It hardly seems possible," he said. "You girls are getting so big. It makes me feel old."

You girls, Nancy repeated to herself as she heaped sugar into her coffee. He made it sound as if she and Becky really were sisters instead of mother and daughter. *That's probably how he sees it,* she reminded herself. After all, that was the story they had all agreed on. He was simply keeping up his side of the bargain.

Becky was at school, finishing up her last few weeks of third grade. The night before she had proudly read Nancy her book report on Edward Eager's *Half Magic,* which she had found among the books in Nancy's (now her) room. It had been a favorite of Nancy's when she was Becky's age, and hearing her daughter describe the book reminded her of herself. Later, alone in the guest room, she had herself reread the book, staying up until two in the morning to finish it and loving it every bit as much as she had sixteen years before.

"Your mother wouldn't let you drink coffee," said A.J.

"No," Nancy agreed. "She said it would stunt my growth."

She and her father both laughed. "Becky tried some of mine the other day," he said. "She said it tastes like dirt, so I don't think we'll have to worry about her turning into a three-cups-a-day girl any time soon." He looked thoughtful. "Just as well," he added. "They grow up too fast as it is."

Nancy wondered if he was thinking about her, and specifically about the conditions surrounding Becky's birth. Or had her father come to completely think of Becky as his and Bess's own? When he looked at her did he see his daughter or his daughter's daughter? Nancy considered asking him, but she was afraid of his answer.

She still wasn't sure what she herself saw when she looked at Becky. The resemblance between them was undeniable. Yet she had spent the past eight years pretending—both to others and to herself—that she was childless. Once, when she was twenty-one, she had gotten pregnant again, the result of a short-lived affair with a man in Truckee, where she'd worked for six months as a waitress in a truck stop café. The man, a long-haul driver, came in twice a week, once on his way down to California and once on his way back up. Each time he stopped by for a bowl of chili, a grilled cheese sandwich, and—following three weeks of constant flirting and ridiculously large tips—half an hour in the cab of his truck with Nancy.

Keeping the child had never crossed her mind. She'd been careless (the trucker never had condoms, and one night she'd forgotten to take some from the supply they used to fill the vending machine in the men's room), and knew that it was her fault, but there was no way she could take care of a baby. She'd used the trucker's tip money (he still left extravagantly large gratuities, particularly if she'd allowed him to fuck her in the ass) for the abortion, then ended the relationship by telling him that she'd found Jesus and could no longer commit the sin of adultery. She'd quit that job soon after and moved to Anchorage.

Had she given birth Becky would now have a "cousin." In that case it would of course be necessary to perpetuate the lie begun with her birth. Maybe she and the child would even have grown up together, always thinking themselves related through Nancy but never knowing how intimately. They would share birthdays and holidays, go to the same school, perhaps have the same friends. Yet they would never call one another sister or brother, never know that they were being deceived along with the rest of the world.

"You and Bess have done a great job with her," Nancy told her father. "She's really happy."

"We've done our best," said A.J. "And she keeps us young."

"Please, Dad," Nancy said. "You're what, forty-five?"

"Six," her father answered. "An old man. I can't keep up with you kids."

Nancy laughed. "You look better than I do," she remarked.

Her father stirred his coffee. "Are you taking care of yourself?" he asked her. "Are you okay? You don't tell us much. We worry."

"I'm fine," Nancy lied. "Things are going great at work." She'd told him and Bess that she worked at an insurance office. It was something neither of them knew anything about, so it was a safe choice. They wouldn't ask questions.

"Are you seeing anyone?"

Nancy shook her head. "I don't really have time," she said. Another lie. She thought about Brice. Was he missing her? She knew the answer to that question—he wasn't. Probably he was shacking up with someone else, waiting for her to get back and resume taking care of him. How did she always manage to find guys like Brice? She'd long wondered what about her attracted them, or attracted her to them. They were never cruel, at least not physically; they were more like overgrown children, always needing someone else to solve their problems and make their lives easier. And she was always willing to do it.

"Well, you'll find someone," her father reassured her. "You're a great girl."

How do you know? she thought. *How do you know what I am? You haven't known me for the past eight years.*

Sometimes it was unbelievable to her that she had been away for so long. She and her father had been very close. Then, almost overnight, everything had changed. She'd gone away and never come back. Gradually she had drifted away from him, until their contact was reduced to the occasional letter. She hadn't even dared call, for fear that Becky would answer the phone and she would break down at the sound of her daughter's voice.

She realized that the situation was largely her own doing. She had chosen to run away from the life her father and Bess had worked so hard to create for her. Bess in particular had given up a lot for her. But part of her still blamed her father for not trying hard enough to reel her back in. Had he asked her she might have come home. But he'd seemingly been content to let her go, as if her disappearance from their lives was a welcome relief.

"What would you think if I moved back to Cold Falls?" she heard herself ask her father.

He set his coffee mug down. "Move back?" he repeated.

"Yeah," Nancy said. "Move back. Here. I could get my own place, find a job."

Her father took some time to answer. "Wouldn't that be hard for you?"

"Not really," Nancy replied. "It's not like I'm a rocket scientist or something. I can find a job."

"I didn't mean that," her father said. "I mean Cold Falls is a small town. You know how it can be."

Nancy sat back in her chair. "You mean people might talk," she said. "Don't they already?"

"They will if they're reminded," said A.J. "Otherwise they tend to forget."

Nancy found herself growing angry. "And it's better if they forget all about me, is that it?" she said. "It's better if *Becky* forgets all about me?"

"I didn't say that," her father said, looking up at her. "I'm just saying that stirring things up could make things . . . harder . . . for everyone."

She couldn't believe what she was hearing. Her father didn't want her to come home. "Do you have any idea how hard it is for me?" she asked him. "I think about her every day. She's *my* daughter."

She saw that what she'd said stung her father. He almost winced at her emphasis on the word, as if she'd slapped him. For a moment she regretted having spoken to him like that, but this was soon replaced with righteous indignation.

"You took her away from me," she said.

"We did what we thought was right," A.J. argued. "We talked about it. You agreed."

"I was sixteen," said Nancy. "I was scared. Yes, I agreed to it. But I didn't know what it would mean. Not until . . ." Her voice trailed off, and she sat looking down at the coffee in her mug. An oily slick had formed on the surface of the coffee, and she saw in it the distorted reflection of her face.

"We did the best we could," her father said.

"You're right," Nancy agreed. "You did. But maybe now it's time for me to try."

A.J. looked at her, his brow furrowed. "What are you saying?" he asked.

"I'm saying maybe it's time to tell the truth," said Nancy.

Her father shook his head. "You can't," he said, his voice barely a whisper. "You can't. It would destroy her."

"Would it?" Nancy answered. "Is it better for her to go her whole life not knowing who I really am?"

"Maybe when she's older," said her father. He sounded as if he was speaking to himself. He didn't look at her. "When she's old enough to understand. We always planned—"

"No, you didn't," Nancy interrupted. "You never planned to tell her. You don't want her to think her mother is some kind of whore."

A.J.'s head snapped up. "I never said that," he gasped.

"You didn't have to," said Nancy. "Everyone was thinking it. Even I was thinking it. That's why I wanted to get away from here—from you—from her."

Her father crossed his arms over his chest. "We're all very emotional right now," he said. "This thing with James is terrible. You've just seen Becky for the first time in eight years. It's a lot to deal with."

"You're right," said Nancy. "But I know this is something I have to do. I have to have my daughter back, Dad."

"It would kill Bess," A.J. said.

"Bess got to raise a child," said Nancy. "She had her chance. She has Nate. And you had me. I might have disappointed you, but you had me. I don't have anyone."

Her father scratched his head. He looked dazed, and he wouldn't meet her gaze. "You can't take her just like that," he said. "Uproot her from everything she knows."

"That's why I'm moving back," Nancy explained. "It will give her time to get to know me. Then I can tell her. Of course she'll be upset. She's a child. But kids adjust. Trust me."

"But who's to say you won't . . ." her father began.

"Leave her again?" Nancy said. "I won't. You just have to believe me."

A.J. was shaking his head again. "I don't know if we can," he said. "We love her so much and—"

"I love her too," Nancy snapped. "But I haven't had the chance to let her know that. Now I do."

"I'll have to talk it over with Bess," her father said.

Nancy felt something inside of her give. "If you don't give her back to me I'll tell everyone who her father is," she said.

A.J. blanched, all the color draining from his face. He stared at her, his mouth trembling. "You don't know who he is," he said. "You said so yourself."

"And we both know that was a lie," said Nancy. She looked directly into his eyes. "We *all* know that was a lie," she said. "Don't we? Or haven't you and Bess discussed it?"

Her father said nothing, and Nancy had her answer.

"You talked about how dangerous it would be to stir things up," she said. "And you're right. We wouldn't want that, would we?"

Her father shook his head slowly. "No," he said, his voice dead. "No, we wouldn't want that."

CHAPTER 43

1983

It hurt more than she thought anything could ever hurt, as if her insides were being pulled out by some monstrous force. She gripped the bedsheets in her fists and arched her back, screaming as another contraction seized her and her muscles seemed to tear apart.

"Breathe, Nancy," a voice at her side said. "Just like we practiced."

Nancy tried to answer, but all that came out was a series of high-pitched cries. She felt a hand place a cool rag on her forehead, and looked up into the face of her Aunt Sarah, who smiled gently and wiped the sweat from Nancy's brow. Nancy focused on her aunt's kind brown eyes and tried to calm herself.

Another spasm shook her and she once again howled in pain. This time she felt something inside of her move.

"Good, Nancy," the midwife said. She was at the foot of the bed, her hands resting on Nancy's legs, massaging the straining muscles. She was peering intently into Nancy's crotch. "When the next contraction comes, push hard," she instructed.

Nancy closed her eyes. *I'm having a baby,* she thought. *It's really happening.*

She had been at her Aunt Sarah's house for four months. It was now the first of October. When she'd left Cold Falls she had barely been showing. Once she'd reached Maine her belly had swelled quickly and considerably; for the past month she'd been waddling around like an enormous goose. Her aunt, who had no children, had made the safe arrival of Nancy's child her top priority. It was she who had suggested the midwife, as an at-home birth would make it easier to doctor the baby's birth certificate and list Bess and Nancy's father as the parents.

Both A.J. and Bess were there as well, although not in the bedroom where Nancy was in labor. The midwife had insisted on having only one other person besides herself and Nancy in the room, and Nancy had asked her aunt to stay with her. Her father and stepmother had seemed perfectly happy to stay out of the way and were now downstairs awaiting the arrival of their grandchild.

So far the plan had worked flawlessly. Bess, by some miracle, had managed to convince everyone—even her closest friends—that she was pregnant. Then, when Nancy's due date neared, her father and Bess announced that they were going to Maine to visit their daughter, who they said had elected not to return to Cold Falls for her junior year and instead would stay in Maine and attend high school there. No specific reason for this decision was given, but it had so far gone unchallenged.

The final part of the deception would take place in another month when Bess would return to Cold Falls with her newborn child. A.J., who would return earlier, would plant the story that she had given birth while visiting Nancy and had remained there under doctor's orders while she recovered. It was all going much more smoothly than Nancy had expected.

Except for the minor matter of her actually giving birth to the baby. Although she'd read books, asked questions, and viewed one disturbingly graphic video of an actual birth, none of it had prepared her for the reality of pushing something roughly the size of a canned ham out of her vagina. Now, try as she might to hold it back, the baby seemed intent on coming into the world as quickly as possible.

"Push!" the midwife ordered.

Nancy obliged, and pain shot through her. Before she could recover from it she heard the command to push come again. She thrust her butt against the mattress and did just that.

"It's coming!" the midwife announced. "One more big one, Nancy. Push as hard as you can."

She did, mustering all of her strength and pushing as though to completely empty her body. She was sure that everything—kidneys, heart, lungs, stomach—must all be passing out of her. She could hardly breathe, and red bursts of pain shot across her eyes like sparklers on a summer night.

"It's a girl."

The three words froze time. Nancy looked down to see the midwife holding in her arms a squalling, red-faced creature still connected to Nancy by a slick-covered cord. Everything else fell away as Nancy looked upon the face of her child. The pain abated and the events of the past two hours seemed never to have happened.

"It's a girl."

The midwife's voice—repeating the announcement—broke the spell. The pain returned and Nancy fell exhausted against the pillows. She breathed raggedly as she looked up at the ceiling and listened to the sound of a baby crying. Only when the midwife placed the child on her chest and Nancy took her in her arms did the moment become real: She was a mother.

The baby squirmed, its tiny fists flailing and its features contorted in an expression of bemused indignance. She was wrapped in a white blanket, which further emphasized the redness of her skin. Nancy briefly thought *she looks like a little monkey.* Then she realized that she was looking at the most beautiful face in the world.

"You did it," her aunt said, crouching down so that her face was level with Nancy's. "Congratulations."

"Her name is Becky," Nancy said. "Rebecca."

They had decided on the name months ago. It was Nancy's idea, and had been enthusiastically embraced by both Bess and her father. They had also encouraged her to think of a boy's name, but she had been so sure that she was carrying a girl that she had put no thought at all into the matter and after weeks of nagging finally told them that she liked Peter, only because it was the first name that came to mind.

Now she had her daughter—her Rebecca. She could hardly believe that something so magical had occurred inside of her, this creation of life. It simply wasn't possible that earlier in the day she'd been thinking about something as mundane as maybe walking to the store for some chocolate chip cookies and now she was holding in her hands an actual living, breathing human whom she had in part created.

"Try to get her to nurse," the midwife said. She helped Nancy sit up and showed her how to hold the baby to her breast. At first Rebecca turned her face away, but after a few minutes of coaxing she placed her mouth on Nancy's nipple and began to suck. Nancy felt as if a current had been turned on inside of her, connecting her to her baby. She felt it flow between them, pulled from inside of her by the tiny lips that tugged on her breast. She began to cry.

"It's all right," her aunt reassured her, rubbing her hair. "It's okay. It's all over now."

You don't understand, Nancy thought to herself. *It isn't over. It's just beginning. And I'm not sad. I'm happy. I'm happier than I've ever been.*

She was left alone with Rebecca for the next hour. The baby drank her fill and then fell asleep cradled in Nancy's arms. She feared moving even a little lest she wake the child up, and so she just sat and watched her daughter sleep, marveling at the ability of the tiny lungs to work and at the way the muscles of Rebecca's face moved as she dreamed of who-knew-what.

She was sitting like this when her father and Bess entered the room. They came and sat on either side of her on the bed. Her father reached out and touched the baby's hand, which tightened around his finger and held on even though Rebecca continued to sleep. All three of them laughed, and A.J. gently pulled his hand away and leaned down to kiss Nancy on the cheek. "She's beautiful," he said. "Just like you."

"I can't believe she's mine," Nancy said. "My Rebecca."

She saw her father and Bess exchange a look. Her father put his hand on her shoulder. "She's going to have a good life," he told Nancy. "We'll make sure of it."

Nancy said nothing. She knew that her father was reminding her that he and Bess would be raising the baby. All along she had understood that this is what would be best for the baby—and for her. But until she'd actually held Rebecca it had all been something of an abstraction. She had been "the baby," not "Rebecca." Nancy had been able to imagine holding a baby, but nothing had prepared her for the reality of cradling something with a beating heart in her arms and of looking down into the face of a real person with needs that she could satisfy and who needed her to protect her from harm.

Everything had changed in the instant in which Rebecca had become a reality. All of the sensible plans now seemed terribly wrong, and the logic used to come to the decision that had been made was revealed to be faulty. Nancy saw things clearly, and the conclusion she came to based on this new perspective was that she had made a very great mistake.

"I want to keep her," she heard herself say.

Suddenly all of the air seemed to have been sucked out of the room. Nancy found she couldn't breathe, and every sound was amplified a million-fold. Her heartbeat echoed off the walls like an enormous drum; each thrum of her blood scattered her thoughts like a flock of startled birds. She saw her father and Bess as if through a snowstorm, indistinct and phantomlike, as if she were being swept into the sky and twirled away. When her father spoke it sounded like someone calling to her through a storm.

"Sweetie, we've been over all of this," he said. His voice was gentle, but beneath it Nancy felt a hint of fear.

He wants to take her, she thought. Instantly she felt the need to protect her child. "You can't have her," she said. "She's *my* baby. Not hers," she added, glancing briefly at Bess as if to gauge whether her stepmother was near enough to attack.

"No one is taking her from you." She heard Bess's voice, soothing and calm. Unlike her father's, there was no strain in it. Nancy looked at her again and saw that Bess was smiling at her.

"She's your baby," Bess said. "And we're going to take great care of her for you."

Nancy shook her head. "She needs me," she argued.

"And you'll be there," Bess assured her. "You'll be right there whenever she needs you. But this way you can have your life too. We're not taking anything from you, Nancy, we're *giving* you something."

Nancy shut her eyes. What Bess said made sense, but still something in her couldn't accept it. She was suddenly very tired. She needed to sleep. Maybe when she awoke things would be clearer. Then she could discuss things with Bess and her father. She could make them understand.

She dreamed that she was in a darkened room. Somewhere a baby cried. *Her* baby. She needed to get to Rebecca and comfort her. But the darkness enfolded her in its wings and she could see nothing. She stumbled around the room, hands outstretched, looking for the door, but all she touched was solid wall. The baby's cries grew louder, more desperate, and Nancy began to panic. Something terrible was happening to her child.

She began to scream in frustration. The wall beneath her hands was never-ending. She came to a corner, turned, and found herself against another wall. Another corner and another wall. Then another corner and another doorless surface. There was no way out. Crying she ran to the middle of the room and began to turn in circles. Rebecca's voice came from all directions, rising up and becoming a heartrending howl that shook Nancy's bones and drowned out her own screams of frustration. Faster and faster she turned, arms outstretched, calling Rebecca's name until her throat burned.

She woke up in a sweat. The room was dark, but moonlight shone through the window and illuminated the familiar outlines of the bed, the bureau, the chair. Nancy breathed slowly, making sure she wasn't still dreaming. For a moment she thought perhaps she'd dreamed everything, but then she placed her hands on her belly and remembered. Immediately she sat up. *Where is she?*

"She's sleeping," said a voice in the darkness.

Nancy looked to the corner opposite the window, where her aunt had placed a large rocking chair. Bess was sitting in it, holding Rebecca in her arms and rocking slowly. Her face moved in and out of the moonlight, visible for a moment and then concealed by darkness. But always Rebecca remained gilded by the moon.

She's sleeping. Nancy repeated Bess's words. Her daughter was sleeping, safe in someone else's arms. *She doesn't need me,* Nancy thought. *She has Bess.*

She lay back against the pillows and watched Bess rock her baby. After a moment a tear slid from her eye and traveled slowly down her cheek. She made no move to wipe it away, even when others followed. She let them come. Silently she cried as she watched her daughter sleeping peacefully in Bess's care.

She found her, she thought, remembering the feel of the endless walls beneath her hands. *She saved her when I couldn't.*

CHAPTER 44

1991

"She says she'll tell the truth," A.J. said.

Nate looked at him in disbelief. His father had called half an hour earlier and said he needed to talk to him. But he hadn't wanted to come to the station or have Nate come to the house, instead suggesting that they meet at a bar just outside of town. Bait & Tackle was, as its name implied, a run-down watering hole popular with sportsmen from the surrounding area, or at least with men who liked to down beers and swap fish tales. In the early afternoon it was nearly empty. A.J. was seated at a corner table when Nate arrived, and Nate had been surprised to see that the glass of beer in his hand was more than half empty.

"The truth?" Nate said, not understanding. "About what?"

"Rebecca," A.J. replied.

Nate looked around, instinctively checking to see if anyone was near enough to hear the conversation. When he was confident that no one could he said, "Why would she do that?"

A.J. took a long sip of beer before answering. "She wants her back," he explained.

Nate gave a choked laugh. "It's a little late for that, isn't it?" he said. "What makes her think she can just have her back after she gave her up?"

"It doesn't much matter what she thinks," said A.J. "If she starts talking, people are going to listen, and then they'll start asking questions of their own."

Nate toyed with the saltshaker on the table. It was shaped like a leaping bass, its mouth open to dispense the salt. The matching pepper shaker was a fisherman whose hat was riddled with holes. "No one will believe her," he said. "You saw how messed up she is. Besides, where's she been for the past eight years?"

A.J. leaned in. "You're not thinking," he said. "Maybe they won't believe her, at least not at first. But enough will. All we need is one to listen to her. There's been enough digging up of things that should have stayed buried lately. If this comes out . . ."

He didn't finish the sentence, instead draining the last of the beer from his glass. Nate thought over what he'd just been told. "Even if you let her have Rebecca there will still be questions," he said.

A.J. nodded. "I know," he said. "But not as many as there would be if we don't."

"You're seriously thinking of doing what she wants?" said Nate.

A.J. didn't answer right away. "I don't know," he said finally.

"She can't take care of a kid," Nate said. "She ran away from her in the first place."

"She ran away from *us*," A.J. said. "And I can't say as I blame her any for that. What she went through no girl should have to go through. But," he added, "it's not just Rebecca she could hurt."

"Have you told Bess?" asked Nate.

A.J. shook his head. "She doesn't know anything about it," he said. "It's going to kill her. She's the one people will point at."

Nate leaned back in his chair. "Fuck," he said. "Why couldn't she just stay away?"

"You know why," his father said.

"James McCloud," said Nate, unable to disguise the irritation in his voice.

"She wants to help him," A.J. said. "We weren't enough to bring her back, but he is."

"So much for blood being thicker than water," said Nate.

A.J. rubbed his face with his hands. When he pulled them away his eyes were troubled. "I don't know what to think anymore," he told Nate. "I've asked myself a million times if we did the right thing, and usually I think that we did. But look what it's cost us. And now . . . maybe it's what's supposed to happen. I don't know."

"No," Nate said firmly. "Dad, listen to me. This is nothing we can't handle. But we have to stick together: you, me, and Bess. Do you understand?"

"But Nancy," said A.J.

"I know," Nate said. "Nancy's had it hard. But she chose to go. We didn't run her off. Don't forget that." He put his hand on his father's arm. "We need to talk sense into Nancy," he said. "She's staying with you, right?"

A.J. nodded. "For now," he said.

"Good," Nate replied. "What you and Bess need to do is sit her down and talk to her. Calmly. Don't get hysterical, and don't accuse her of anything. Just make her see that Becky is better off with you. Bess can do that. She's the one who convinced Nancy to let you raise Becky in the first place."

"Nancy was younger then," said A.J. "She was just a girl. Now she's grown. It won't be so easy to talk her into anything."

Nate heard a note of resignation in his father's voice, as if he'd already decided to give in to Nancy's demand. *I have to snap him out of it,* Nate thought. *If I don't he's going to cave.*

"There's something I need to tell you, Dad," he said. "About Nancy." He hesitated, as if wrestling with a decision. "I didn't want to ever tell you, but I think you need to know now. I've been following up on her."

A.J. looked confused. "What do you mean?" he asked his son.

"The last couple of years," Nate said. "I've been keeping an eye on her. Just in case something happened to her."

"Why would something happen to her?"

Nate sighed. "Dad, Nancy isn't exactly the girl you think she is. She's been into some pretty rough stuff."

A.J.'s confusion deepened. "What kinds of things?" he asked. "I don't understand you, Nate."

"Drugs," Nate said. "Some petty theft. Maybe more."

"More," A.J. repeated.

"She's been picked up a couple of times for soliciting," said Nate. "Once in Portland and twice in New Orleans."

A.J. looked at him with a stunned expression.

"Like I said, I never wanted to tell you," Nate said. "I knew it would kill you to know. But now . . ."

"Why would she do that?" A.J. said, seeming to speak to himself. "She knows she can always come to us if she needs help."

"I think she's the one who needs help, Dad," said Nate. "She's sick. We need to get her some help."

A.J. nodded. "Of course," he said.

"Maybe we could get her into drug treatment," Nate suggested. "The university hospital in Syracuse has a good program. Or if she needs psychiatric help—"

"She's not crazy," A.J. interrupted.

"I'm not saying she is," said Nate. "But we have to consider the possibility. Look how she's acting. She has almost no contact with us for eight years and then shows up because she hears that James McCloud is in jail. And she tells you she wants Becky back. Why now? Why all of a sudden? It doesn't make sense, Dad."

A.J. put his head in his hands. "I don't know," he said. "I just don't know."

"I'm not saying any of this to upset you," said Nate. "But I've been thinking about it a lot. Nancy never did tell you who the baby's father is, did she?"

He watched A.J. carefully, waiting for an answer. His father shook his head. "No," he said. "She never did."

"And you said she took her mother's death hard," Nate continued. "Maybe she kept all of that inside her, and then getting pregnant made something snap. Trauma can do that. And if she didn't get help it could have just gotten worse and worse."

"I shouldn't have just sent her away," A.J. said. "I should have kept her here and gotten her some help."

Nate shook his head. "No," he said. "It's not your fault. It isn't anyone's fault, and beating yourself up isn't going to help. What we have to do now is figure out how to fix this."

"We can't just make her get help," said A.J.

"There might be a way," Nate countered. "If we can show that she's a potential danger to herself, we can have her put under observation for forty-eight hours."

His father said nothing, and A.J. knew that he was thinking about the suggestion. He knew too that his father would not agree to having Nancy forcibly hospitalized. But he'd at least gotten A.J. to consider the possibility that Nancy required professional help. That was a step in the right direction.

"Let me and Bess try talking to her first," said A.J., confirming Nate's prediction. "Maybe we can work this out."

"Okay," said Nate. "I think that's a good idea. And if you can't then we'll talk about what the next step should be. And Dad," he added, waiting for A.J. to look at him. "You didn't do anything wrong."

A.J. smiled sadly. "I wish I could believe that," he said.

Nate reached out and took his father's hands in his. "You didn't," he repeated. "You've been a great father."

"Thank you, son," A.J. replied. "I hope I have."

"We'll get through this," said Nate. "Together. All right?"

A.J. nodded.

"Let's get out of here," Nate said. "You need to go home and talk to Bess, and I've got to get to the station."

The two men stood and walked out of the bar. Outside A.J. got into his truck and left, waving good-bye to Nate as he drove off. Nate climbed behind the wheel of his patrol car and started it. Then he sat for a long time, the engine idling as memories he'd thought long dead were resurrected.

He hadn't lied to his father about Nancy. He had kept tabs on her, and she had been in trouble a number of times. Until now, though, there had been no reason to worry A.J. and his mother with the information. There was nothing they could have done for Nancy—not then. Now maybe there was. But they had to do it quickly, before she caused any real damage. If they waited too long, who knew what she might do, especially if she was unbalanced. Nate had dealt before with people who had nothing to lose. They had a look in their eyes, a blankness that came from realizing that they could not be hurt any more than they already had been.

He'd seen that look in Nancy's eyes.

CHAPTER 45

1982

Nate picked a clump of cotton candy from the cloud of blue spun sugar that was attached to the paper cone in his hand. Rolling it between his fingers he turned it into a ball, then popped it into his mouth. He bit down, his teeth compressing the sugar and sticking together as the candy dissolved and formed a tacky paste. For a moment his jaws were glued shut, then he forced them open and licked the crystallized sugar from his teeth with his tongue.

He'd eaten nothing but sweets since entering the fair gates an hour before, and now he was jittery from the accumulated sugar in his blood. His head ached and his heart beat rapidly in his chest. He felt high and sick at the same time, and it was making him irritable. He tossed the remainder of the cotton candy into the nearest trashcan and wiped his sugar-sticky hands on his jeans, leaving behind a streak of blue like the tail of a comet.

He'd lost sight of Nancy and James. He'd last seen them on the Ferris wheel, where he'd stood in the shadow of a booth offering prizes for anyone able to throw a ring over one of several dozen soda bottles arranged in a large square and watched as Nancy and James climbed into a swinging car and the safety bar was lowered on them. They'd risen into the air, laughing and pointing, and Nate had watched as their car ascended.

But something had distracted him (he thought it might have been the shrieks of the girl whose boyfriend successfully landed rings over the necks of two bottles and won an enormous pink stuffed rabbit for his prowess) and he'd lost track of which of the twelve or thirteen cars with a green grinning clown face on the front was theirs. He'd watched closely as each car descended and the occupants got out, but Nancy and James were never among them, and finally he'd given up and gone in search of them elsewhere.

Nancy had invited him to go to the fair with her and James, but he had declined. She had obviously asked only because she felt bad for him. And James had barely concealed his relief when Nate said he had other plans. Nate had waited until they left, then made his own way to the fair. Surprisingly he had spotted them almost instantly, in line to buy ride tickets, and had been following them ever since.

It was a hot night, windless and dry. The fair had opened the night before and so was crowded with visitors anxious for something to do. It was easy to remain hidden by the throngs of people, and the numerous food stalls, arcades, and rides provided convenient hiding spaces when they became necessary. After twenty minutes Nate's fear of being discovered vanished and he followed his quarry with little worry.

Except that now he had lost them. Still he wasn't concerned. They would reappear eventually. He was sure of it. All he had to do was wait. In the meantime he perused the different exhibits, gazing without interest at black-and-white speckled hens and jars of preserved peaches, handmade quilts, and vases of roses. He wandered through a display of wood carvings and photographs, seeing nothing. He stopped and purchased a sno-cone, lime green and pleasantly sour, and ate half of it while watching a demonstration of country line dancing performed by a group of children dressed in matching costumes complete with cowboy hats and boots.

He found Nancy and James again more by accident than by design, which annoyed him slightly. He had decided to look for them in the livestock arena, knowing that Nancy had an interest in horses and thinking that perhaps she had been unable to resist the lure of what was being billed as the largest Clydesdale ever seen in New York State. As he was making his way there he happened to see, out of the corner of his eye, a familiar face. It rushed past him, not ten feet to his left, leaving him dizzy as it receded from view.

She was on the Scrambler. It took him a moment to find her again, as the cars were spinning quickly, moving in and out and around in a pattern he found difficult to comprehend. He would catch a glimpse of Nancy's face only to have it twirl off in an unexpected direction as the car in which she and James sat was hurled first one way and then another. One moment she seemed close enough to touch, the next she was impossibly far away.

He stood at the railing, risking discovery, and watched as the ride went round and round, the eight arms juggling the cars like so many bowls. The motion sickened him but he couldn't look away, as he feared missing even one glimpse of Nancy. When the ride came to an end and the occupants of the cars tumbled out, walking unsteadily to the exit, he fell in step behind Nancy and James and followed as they moved on. When James took Nancy's hand in his, Nate felt it like a slap.

He'd tried not to feel this way. His mother and A.J. Derry were getting married in a few months. Nancy was going to be his stepsister, and he'd even begun considering asking A.J. to adopt him. It wouldn't make he and Nancy brother and sister except in name, but still it wasn't right. He knew that. Yet he couldn't help himself.

Not that Nancy noticed. She was too wrapped up in James McCloud to notice anything—or anybody—else. She was with him almost constantly. Occasionally Nate and his mother did things with Nancy and her father together, a kind of preparation of sorts for the impending blending of their families, and Nancy always seemed to enjoy their time together. But ultimately it was James she wanted, and James who had her.

Nate told himself that he was looking out for Nancy. He didn't trust James, whom he felt was a phony. He was sure that James was using Nancy, for what purposes he could only imagine. He couldn't even allow himself to consider the possibility that Nancy was letting James fuck her. Yet that was exactly what he was convinced was the case.

James and Nancy stopped in front of the House of Screams. It was a run-down ride, the outside painted to look like a typical Halloween haunted castle, complete with a makeshift graveyard and red electric eyes blinking from the shuttered windows. Individual cars shaped like skulls rattled through an entrance hung with strips of black paper and billowing smoke machine fog, disappearing into a darkened interior. A recorded voice promised untold horrors and a grisly death for any who dared enter the cursed place.

James was trying to convince an uncertain-looking Nancy to go on the ride. Nate could tell by the expression on her face that she didn't want to. *She doesn't like to be scared, you asshole,* he thought. How could James call himself Nancy's boyfriend and not even know that about her. Or worse, did he know and not care? Did he think it was funny to see her scared? The thought of it made Nate burn with anger. If Nancy were *his* girlfriend he would treat her better than that.

Nancy, acquiescing to James's persistent demands, allowed herself to be led up the short flight of stairs to one of the grinning skulls. Once she and James were seated she immediately grabbed his hand. He put his arm around her, pulling her close.

That's it, Nate thought. *Get her scared and then make a move.*

As the skull containing Nancy and James approached the entrance and the mechanical bats overhead flittered and screeched, Nate handed a ticket to the bored-looking attendant overseeing the ride and managed to get into the next available skull car, pushing his way past a trio of giggling girls who glared at him and muttered something under their breath. He ignored them, sitting down and pulling the safety bar into its locked position. Evil laughter surrounded him, coming from the car's tinny speakers, and the same voice that proclaimed the evils awaiting those who dared enter the House of Screams said, "Welcome, victim—I mean visitor. For your safety, please remember to keep your hands inside of the car at all times. If you don't, one of my monsters will be happy to take them from you." This was followed by maniacal laughter as the skull lurched forward and slid onto the tracks. The car pitched forward and went down a small hill, headed for the entrance. Just as it appeared about to hit the doors of the castle they swung open and the car passed through the paper streamers and was enveloped in fog.

Nate saw the skull with Nancy and James in it ahead of him. There was perhaps twenty feet between them. Although he could not see into the car from the rear, the track on which the ride moved was filled with twists and turns, and frequently Nate would get a glimpse of Nancy as her car navigated these changes in course ahead of his. Usually these turns were accompanied by some new horror—a witch who descended from the ceiling, a vampire lurching from a coffin, a Frankenstein monster laid out on a slab surrounded by sparking equipment. It was all very silly, and not at all scary, and Nate took it all in with absolute disinterest, simply waiting for it to end.

Finally the cars came to a stopping point. But instead of depositing the riders outside, as Nate had expected it to, the ride ended at another doorway. As he waited for his skull car to reach the platform, he watched Nancy and James disappear through this unexpected entryway. Then it was his turn, and he left his car and followed suit.

He was in a tunnel. All around him a kaleidoscope of lights swirled, painting his skin purple and orange and yellow. The effect was disorienting, and he touched his hand to the wall for balance. It was curved, and he realized that he was in a tube of some kind. There was a white light at the far end, and it was toward this that he made his way.

He emerged into a room with a floor that sank beneath his feet. Caught off balance he fell and bounced on a cushion of air. He struggled to get to his feet, fell again, and finally attempted to reach the other side of the room through a series of rolls and hops that made him feel and (he imagined) look like a spastic jackrabbit. He heard laughter coming from somewhere ahead of him and imagined that Nancy was watching his humiliation, laughing as James imitated his ungainly motions.

Once out of the room he found himself on surer ground. Here, though, the walls of the hallway were painted in black-and-white stripes that seemed to veer off at odd angles. Also, one wall seemed shorter than the other, so that he found himself leaning to one side out of fear of hitting his head. It took him a moment to realize that the effect was an optical illusion and that he could in fact walk upright. Growing more and more irritated he stormed to the end of the hall and pushed open the door he found there.

He was in yet another hallway, this one narrow and painted a garish red. He knew that Nancy couldn't be too far ahead of him. She and James had only a minute or so head start. And he heard her voice, faintly, coming through the walls.

"James?" she called out. "Where are you?"

"Over here," Nate heard James reply.

The voice seemed to come from right in front of him, and for a second he thought that James must be there. But he saw no one. Then James spoke again, and this time his voice was slightly muffled, as if he'd moved away from Nate.

It's a maze, Nate realized.

He walked ahead about ten feet to what appeared to be a solid wall. He expected to find a turn going left or right, but there was nothing. Confused, he turned around, but the only other direction open to him would take him back to where he'd started. Already the girls in the car behind him were making their way into the hallway, and he didn't want to talk to them.

He put his hands on the wall and felt it move. It swung on some hidden pivot and revealed yet another hallway, into which he passed. The wall swung shut behind him, leaving a deceptively flat surface. The new hallway was green.

"Nancy!" he heard James yell. He sounded some way off.

"Over here," Nancy called back. Her voice was nearer.

Nate felt something bump against the wall. Someone was on the other side of it. He traversed the length of his hallway, pushing with his hands. No hidden doors opened. Then the hallway made a right-hand turn. He continued on, feeling his way, and when he came to what appeared to be a dead end he pressed against the narrow final panel and it swung open, admitting him to a blue hallway.

Ahead of him he saw a brief flash of yellow and realized that someone—perhaps Nancy or James—had just found the way out. He hurried to the spot and looked for the door. It took him a moment to locate it, and by the time he made his way into the yellow hallway behind it, the corridor was empty. He heard laughter, but it was impossible to tell from which direction it came.

"I thought I'd never find you," he heard Nancy say.

He searched frantically for some final door that would get him out of the maze. He could picture Nancy and James walking away together, on their way to the next diversion. Meanwhile he felt like a trapped animal. His fists pounded on the plywood walls as he sought an exit.

It seemed to be taking forever, as if the hall were stretching out just ahead of him so that he could never reach the end. He beat the walls on both sides, jerking from side to side as he moved, going so quickly that his shoulders sometimes hit the wall in his haste. Still no door appeared.

A full minute went by, and he began to panic. What if he had somehow wandered into a hallway with no outlet? He would have to go back and work his way through the green, blue, and red hallways until he found the correct route. In the meantime he was wasting precious time. Even worse he felt as if James had tricked him, deliberately leading him into the maze as a way to lose him. Frustrated, he fell to his knees, anger roiling inside him. James had won. Again.

The door at the end of the hallway opened and the three girls entered. They were giggling loudly, having a wonderful time. Nate hated them. He especially hated being trapped with them. It would mean having to speak to them, which he very much did not want to do.

The girls—as he had—felt the walls on both sides as they made their way toward him. They didn't appear to notice him.

"The door has to be here somewhere," one girl said to the others. "We must have missed it."

They began to turn around, then one of them pointed to something. "What about that?" she said.

Nate followed her finger. On the wall was painted a grinning clown's face. He had briefly glanced at it while searching for the door but had assumed it to be simply decoration. He watched as the girl who had spoken reached out and touched the clown's nose.

A door swung open, letting in the electric lights of the midway. The girls exited, once more laughing. Nate followed them, exiting into the purple gloom of twilight. All around him lights twinkled and voices swirled. He heard snatches of conversation and tried to focus on them. At the same time he scanned the passing crowd for Nancy's face. But it was too dark to see anything but the nearest people clearly.

He had lost them. *No,* he corrected himself. *They lost you. James lost you. And he took Nancy with him.*

CHAPTER 46

1991

"In another month the black-eyed Susans will be open," Ada said.

She and Charly were walking through the field behind the house. It was early afternoon and the sun was warm on their faces. The grass was high after the recent rains, and it rippled softly as a light breeze blew through it.

Charly had invited Ada to walk with her both to get her out of the house and so that she could talk to her about something away from Celeste, who had been an almost constant presence in the house over the past two days. She was looking for the right moment to start the conversation.

"The kids used to come out here to smoke," Ada said, pointing to the old barn. She looked at Charly and raised an eyebrow. "They think I didn't know," she added.

Charly laughed. "They can't hide anything from Mom," she said.

"I didn't used to think so," Ada said. "But they've surprised me from time to time."

Charly wanted to ask her in what ways her children had surprised her but she waited, hoping Ada would volunteer the information on her own.

"You have an idea of who your children are," Ada said a moment later. "Even when they're little you can imagine them all grown up. Probably you shouldn't, but you do. Then when they don't turn out that way you have to get to know them all over again."

"What did you think your kids would be like?" Charly prodded.

"Celeste has turned out pretty much like I thought she would," said Ada. "She never wanted much. Not that being a mother isn't something to be proud of," she added quickly. "But she could have done . . . more if she'd wanted to. Like you have."

Charly didn't know how to respond to Ada's remark. She knew it was a compliment but she didn't want to appear to be insulting Celeste's choices by agreeing. Ada, however, didn't wait for a reply.

"Billy was the most difficult," she continued. "He still is. I don't know as I ever have understood him. Just when I think I do he becomes somebody else. Or maybe I'm just not looking at him the right way."

Charly listened with great interest. She'd never had this kind of discussion with someone, not even her own mother, who was Ada Mc-Cloud's polar opposite. A doctor, she was intellectual to the point of frostiness. Where Ada seemed to react, Charly's mother dissected, examining minutely every aspect of a situation in the hope of formulating a logical response to it instead of feeling her way through it. Charly and her brother often joked that they weren't their mother's children, they were her experiments in reproduction.

Charly had inherited (or taken on, her mother would argue, depending on what theory of personality development one ascribed to) some of this clinical approach to life. It was what made her a good lawyer. But she was fascinated by people like Ada who seemed to not be afraid of reacting to life with raw emotion. For Charly, feeling too much meant that she had lost control. She wondered what her mother would say about her if she were in Ada's place.

"A lot of people think I should be disappointed in Billy," Ada said. "I just think that of the three of them he's the one who's looking for himself the hardest. The other two found themselves right out in the open. They didn't have to look too far."

"And James?" Charly asked.

"James grew into himself when he was a boy," said Ada. "Even when he was four or five I could look at him and see the man in him. Now he's just a bigger version of that." A moment later she said, "When this is all over are you going to marry him?"

Charly was surprised by the abruptness of the question. Immediately she felt her defenses go up. "We haven't talked about it," she said quickly.

"Supposing he does ask you," Ada persisted. "Would you have him?"

Charly thought for a moment. "I don't know," she said, surprising herself with her answer. Until that moment she'd more or less assumed that one day she and James would be married. It was the logical (she noted her instinct to use that word) outcome to their relationship as it had progressed.

She worried that Ada would be offended by her answer. If she was she gave no indication of it.

"I don't say that because of anything that's happened," Charly said.

"No," Ada replied. "I don't imagine you did."

Nothing more was said about the subject by either of them. Charly's worries over possibly having offended James's mother dissipated as Ada's demeanor remained friendly. She sensed no change in mood, and was about to ask another question, when Ada spoke.

"I never regretted marrying Daniel," she said. "Even when I thought he'd murdered Rebecca. You think that if someone you love does something terrible that you'll stop loving him because he's become a monster. But then it happens and you find that you still love him. It's a hard thing to learn about yourself."

Charly had seen enough women stand by their men despite accusations (and outright proof) of horrendous behavior to know that it was not an uncommon phenomenon. But she had always assumed that these women were damaged in some way that made them incapable of severing their feelings for these men. She had never considered that they simply accepted that human beings had moments when they were capable of committing terrible acts.

A colleague of hers, a woman who had made the choice to become a public defender instead of accepting an invitation to join a prestigious law firm, had once explained her decision to Charly by saying, "Even Hitler had a favorite ice-cream flavor when he was a kid." Although Charly appreciated the notion that even the worst offenders started off life as innocents, she'd never been able to fully appreciate her friend's point of view. Now she was beginning to understand. Although she was 100 percent certain that James had had nothing to do with his father's death, she had of course considered the possibility and asked herself what she would do if it turned out he was guilty. Would he suddenly be a different James? Would everything she loved about him be wiped away by that one (admittedly horrific) act, committed under unknown circumstances? Would she still defend him, or would the fact that he was guilty preclude her from caring what happened to him after the moment he was revealed to be a murderer?

Something moved in the grass to their right and Charly, startled, turned to look. She saw the grass parting as something sped away from them, headed for the trees.

"Rabbit," Ada said. "Probably a young one. Daniel used to hunt them. I made him dress them himself. I couldn't do it, but it didn't bother him."

Charly pictured Dan shooting a rabbit, then skinning and gutting it. Was it really that much of a stretch to imagine him killing Rebecca Derry? There was a huge difference between a rabbit and a human, of course, but it was possible. It was also possible that Daniel had been murdered as revenge for Rebecca's death, in which case the guilty party was most likely Ada or A.J. Or both.

Or Nancy Derry or James, she thought. Either could theoretically have done it, Nancy to revenge her mother's death and James because he was angry at his father for hurting Ada or possibly because Nancy asked him to. Neither was out of the question. *And then we have Celeste and Billy,* she added. Each had both reason and means to commit the crime.

The final possibility was the simplest—that Dan McCloud had been killed by someone with whom he'd tangled in his work. But the presence of James's ring with the body made that unlikely. On that point she had to side with Nate Derry and his decision to bring James into custody.

And so she was back where she'd begun.

"When they were little the kids played hide-and-seek in the grass," Ada told Charly. "Billy was the best at it. He could stay so quiet that no one could find him. It used to make James so mad."

"I bet it did," said Charly. "I've seen how he gets when he loses at board games."

Ada picked a piece of grass and idly switched it against her leg as they walked. "He always was the competitive one," she remarked.

Charly waited a moment, then said, "I'm getting the impression that he and Nate had some kind of rivalry." It was the topic she'd been trying to find a way to raise since leaving the house. She tried to keep her voice neutral, not wanting Ada to read anything into her question.

"Nate?" Ada said. "Who told you that?"

"No one really," said Charly. "It's just a . . . feeling . . . I've picked up on. Maybe it's nothing."

"Boys are boys," Ada said. "They get jealous of one another. I suppose Nate and James had their differences over the years, but nothing really to speak of."

"It's interesting that James dated Nancy Derry and then Nate married Celeste," Charly commented. "How did James feel about that?"

Ada shrugged. "He never said anything to me about it one way or another," she told Charly. "But that's James's way. Billy's the only one who said anything."

"Billy?" said Charly.

"Billy and Nate don't much like one another," said Ada. "I think it's on account of what Billy is and all." She looked at Charly. "Nate's not exactly what you'd call open-minded."

Charly nodded. "And what did Billy say about Celeste marrying him?" she asked.

"Oh, nothing special," said Ada. "Just told Celeste she was making a mistake. He didn't go to the wedding, which was probably for the best. Billy doesn't hold his liquor too well."

"Why did Nate decide to go into law enforcement?" Charly asked. "Again, it seems a little coincidental that he would marry the sheriff's daughter and then become sheriff himself."

"You mean it sounds like he wanted Dan's life?" said Ada. "Don't think you're the first one to say so."

"And what do you think?" Charly said.

Ada ran a hand over the top of some Queen Anne's Lace. The heads of the white flowers bobbed gracefully, and a bee that had been feeding on them circled lazily and resettled on the largest bloom. "Nate admired Dan very much," said Ada. "A.J. is his father, of course, but I think Dan was the man Nate wanted to be. He spent a lot of time with him, asking questions about the law and whatnot. Sometimes Dan let him ride in the patrol car with him. James and Billy were never interested in that, and I think Dan liked having someone to teach what he knew to. I hadn't thought of it, but maybe that's why James and Nate never really got on."

And maybe why Nate was so quick to pin Dan's murder on James, Charly thought to herself. If Nate thought that James had something to do with the death of his teenage hero, it would make sense that he would do everything in his power to keep that person locked up. That the person in question was also his brother-in-law would be trouble-some but oddly coincidental. No, she didn't think that Nate had acted out of revenge, as convenient as that would be for her.

She had, of course, been speaking regularly with Arthur about her thoughts and findings, and Arthur's immediate reaction was that A.J. Derry was the prime suspect, followed by Ada and then the McCloud children in no particular order. Being that he was completely removed from the family, and therefore could afford to be objective, Charly tried to keep his opinions in mind when thinking about the case. However, her interactions with Ada had convinced her that despite the woman's interference in the matter of Dan's alleged suicide note, she was not the killer. Whether or not she was hiding something to protect one or more of her children was still a possibility, but even that seemed re-mote.

"I wish he'd stayed buried," Ada said, stopping and looking out over the field.

"Don't you want to know what happened?" asked Charly.

"I know what happened," Ada said. "He left me and the children alone. At some point the why doesn't matter, does it?"

"I don't like mysteries," said Charly. "I want to know everything."

Ada looked at her and smiled kindly. "That's why you'll never be sat-isfied," she said. "There are always questions you can't answer."

Can't, or won't? Charly wanted to ask, but she kept quiet. She knew what Ada meant, even if she herself couldn't see the world in that way. To her the most important thing was to find the truth behind every-thing, even at the cost of her own happiness. To live any other way was, in her opinion, a lie.

"Celeste will be wondering where we are," said Ada. "We should head back."

She and Charly walked without talking, following the path they'd made through the grass on their way out to the field. As they ap-proached the house Charly suddenly thought, *If he asked me, I would marry him.* Her certainty was absolute, and having answered the question she felt the momentary thrill that always accompanied such revelations. But this was almost as quickly replaced by fear. She still had not found the answer that would save James. And time was run-ning out.

CHAPTER 47

1985

"Mom?"

Ada looked at her daughter. Celeste was standing in the doorway to the kitchen. Nate Derry was beside her. They had just informed Ada that they were going to be married.

"Are you okay?" Celeste asked her.

Ada nodded. "I'm fine," she said. She forced herself to smile. "It's just that this is a surprise."

"We've been going out for over a year," said Celeste. "Nate is going to the academy this fall, and I've got the job at the market."

And that makes you ready for marriage, Ada thought. She hoped Celeste wasn't pregnant but had the presence of mind not to ask her. That would just make things worse.

"Don't worry, Mrs. McCloud," Nate said. "I'll take good care of her."

"When are you thinking of having the wedding?" asked Ada, trying to remember what kinds of questions one asked in this situation. Her mind had gone blank, and she prayed she didn't sound as upset as she felt.

"We're thinking September thirteenth," said Celeste.

"Your father's birthday," Ada said dully. She was looking at her hands, rubbing her finger over her wedding band.

"Yeah," said Nate. "We thought it would be a nice way to remember him."

Ada nodded. *It would be,* she thought, *if we were sure he was dead.*

Two years had passed since Dan's disappearance and the arrival of the letter. Ada had been surprised at how quickly life had returned to normal, or at least to the semblance of normal. She had tried very hard to make it so, mostly for the sake of the children. Of course they had the advantage of not knowing the truth about their father's disappearance. Although they were naturally distraught they had progressed predictably through the stages of acceptance until their grief lessened and became merely sadness.

Ada however still woke up every morning and remembered that her husband was a murderer. She had gradually come to accept this and had buried the secret deep in her heart, covering it with layer upon layer of love for her family until it became like a fly caught in amber. She'd accepted the condolences of friends and family graciously and had taken on the role of the tragic widow and played it beautifully. No one looking at her would guess that she regularly dreamed that she had been buried alive.

Twice she had come close to telling someone, but both times she had hesitated until the need passed, and afterward she had been enormously relieved not to have spoken. Whenever she felt herself inclined to break her silence she took out Dan's letter and read it, experiencing the pain all over again. The shock was sufficient enough that it usually lasted several months. Now she read it only when she began to pity herself.

"So what do you think?" Celeste said. "Are you happy for us?"

Ada forced herself to smile. "Of course I am," she said.

Celeste bounced like a happy child. "I was afraid you'd be upset," she said. She took Nate's hand. "Now we have to tell A.J. and Bess. Mom, is it all right if we have dinner there?"

"Of course," Ada answered. "I'll tell the boys. Unless you want to," she added.

"Go ahead," said Celeste. "Boys don't care about this kind of stuff anyway. They'll be happy to have me out of the house."

Nate came over and kissed Ada on the cheek. "I guess I get to call you Mom now," he said, grinning.

"Not until the wedding," Ada said, trying to sound lighthearted. "Now get out of here. Go tell your mom and dad the good news."

Once the kids were gone she busied herself with dinner preparations, trying to calm her mind through the making of meat loaf and the cleaning of green beans. But it was a futile effort, as she'd known it would be. All she could focus on was the news of Celeste and Nate's engagement and how it absolutely had to be stopped.

She liked Nate Derry well enough. After all, she was the one who had first suggested that Nancy go out with Nate, back when he and his mother first moved back to town. But Celeste had shown no interest in the boy—in fact had dismissed him with contempt. So when the two began dating it took her by surprise. She'd even questioned Celeste about it. Celeste's explanation—that she thought it was a good idea if she tried dating someone who was the opposite of Paul Lunardi—made Ada hopeful that perhaps her daughter was maturing. She would have preferred that Celeste test her theory on someone other than Nate Derry, but she'd said nothing, mostly because she'd assumed that like all of Celeste's other romances this one would run its course before things got too serious. But apparently it had not. *I should have paid more attention,* she thought. *Now it's going to be a lot harder.*

The "it" of course was the breakup of the relationship. Ada was determined that the proposed wedding not take place. It couldn't. Not if she wanted to retain her sanity. Having A.J. and Bess as friends was difficult enough; having them in her family would be a disaster. If anyone should ever find out about Dan's role in Rebecca Derry's death it would destroy everything. She could live with sacrificing herself, but she had to keep Celeste out of harm's way.

I'll talk to A.J. and Bess, she thought. *I'll tell them the kids are too young. They'll agree with me.*

They had to. She couldn't face the prospect of years of birthdays and Thanksgivings and baby showers planned with Bess, of family gatherings and forcing herself to forget every time she had to be in the same room with A.J. It would kill her, she was sure of it, every interaction eating her apart little by little until there was nothing left.

She finished forming the meat loaf and put it in the oven to bake. As she was shutting the door it occurred to her that most of the bad news she'd received in her life had been delivered in kitchens. It was ironic that the room in which the most basic necessity of life was lovingly taken care of was also the one in which the greatest blows were dealt. Still, cooking eased her mind somewhat, or at least distracted her for a moment. Now, with nothing to do but set the table and boil the water for the green beans, she was at a loss.

To her relief she was not alone for long. Not twenty minutes later

James came home. He had been at baseball practice and was still wearing his uniform, which was stained with grass and mud. When he came into the kitchen he sniffed the air.

"It's meat loaf," Ada said before he could ask. "And your sister and Nate Derry are engaged." She'd added the last bit before she could stop herself, the frustration caused by worrying about the matter proving too strong for her to resist.

James looked at her with a puzzled expression, as if he wasn't sure if he'd heard correctly. "What?" he said.

"Meat loaf," Ada said. "And Celeste and Nate are getting married."

"Oh," said James. His voice was flat and unreadable, and Ada couldn't tell whether he was pleased by the news or simply indifferent.

"They just told me," Ada said, uneasy with the silence that hung between her and her son.

"Oh," James said again. "Um. That's great. I guess." He was nodding and biting his lower lip, a gesture Ada recognized (Dan had done the same thing) as an indication that he was providing an answer because one was expected but was still making up his mind as to how he really felt. She chose not to press the issue.

"Go wash up," she said. "Dinner will be ready soon."

James exited with a distinct air of relief. Ada wondered what he was really thinking about the possibility of having Nate Derry as his brother-in-law. James seemed to have finally gotten over the hurt Nancy Derry had caused him by leaving so unexpectedly two years earlier. She hadn't even answered his letters, given to A.J. and Bess to pass along, and despite the Derrys' assurances that Nancy was simply busy with settling into a new school and would certainly write when she had time, nothing had come. After a year with no word James had begun dating other girls, but none had lasted more than a few months until recently, when he'd started seeing a girl named Karen Redbone, the sister of a fellow Scout from neighboring Burnsville. Karen was a lovely girl, bright and outgoing, and for the first time since Dan's disappearance and Nancy's departure James seemed truly happy.

But would that change when Nate and Celeste married and Nancy became James's sister-in-law? Ada couldn't see any way it could not be difficult for James, particularly as Nancy had left without a word. Ada had never discussed the matter with James but her suspicion was that Nancy—despite her generally positive outlook—had been unable to accept her father's remarriage and had chosen to leave for that reason.

Why she had broken off contact with everyone else could be blamed on embarrassment or shame.

Now, though, she would surely have to reenter their lives, if only to participate in the wedding if there was one (and Ada was still adamant that there would not be). She would be family. Again it was all too horrible for Ada to think about. Yet she didn't feel she could enlist James's aid in the matter, lest he begin to question her resistance to the union too much.

She put on the water for the beans and began to heat it. As she was stirring salt into the pot a face appeared from around the edge of the doorway. It was Billy. He was wearing a plastic Wonder Woman Halloween mask and a cape striped like the American flag.

"Look what I found," he said. He lifted the mask and pushed it back on his head. "There's a whole box of this stuff in the cellar."

Ada remembered the Wonder Woman mask. Celeste had worn it the year she was eight. James had gone as Scooby-Doo and Billy, who was just four, had been dressed as a cat in a hand-me-down costume that both Celeste and James had worn in years past. Somewhere there was a picture of Dan with the three of them standing in front of the house holding trick-or-treat bags.

Billy stepped into the kitchen, put the mask back on his face, and twirled. "Mighty winds that blow on high, lift me up that I might fly!" he chanted, holding his arms out.

"Take that off," Ada told him. "It's almost dinnertime."

Billy laughed as he removed the mask and untied the cape. "I'm going to make her magic bracelets out of tinfoil," he told his mother. "Thank God her invisible jet is, you know, invisible. But I still need a lasso. Do we have any rope?"

"I don't know," Ada said, distracted by the water, which had begun to boil.

"What's the matter?" asked Billy.

He always notices, Ada thought. *The other two don't, but he always does.*

"Nothing's the matter," she said. She added the beans to the water and put the lid on. "I'm just a little . . . Celeste and Nate are engaged."

"Why would she want to marry that asshole?" Billy replied instantly.

"I don't know," said Ada. Then, realizing what Billy had said, she added, "Don't talk like that."

"Why?" Billy replied. "He *is* an asshole."

"She likes him," said Ada. "It's really none of your business."

Billy snorted. "Please," he said. "We're the ones who are going to have to spend every Thanksgiving with him and buy him stuff for Christmas."

Ada wanted to tell him that she had had exactly the same thought. She knew that she had an ally in Billy, and it was tempting to exploit that for her own comfort. But although he was sympathetic, Billy was also unreliable. He talked when he shouldn't, and had never been able to keep a secret. She didn't dare let him know that she shared his feelings about Nate.

"Yes, well, let's worry about that when we get to it," she said.

"Nate Derry is so not going to be related to me," said Billy as he left to wash up. "I don't care if Celeste likes him, the guy is a tool."

Ada had no idea what a tool was, but the venom in Billy's tone was unmistakable. She was actually a bit surprised. As far as she knew Billy and Nate had had limited interactions, and what little she'd seen of them together had left no impression on her whatsoever. Yet Billy definitely had a dislike for Nate. Then again Billy often spouted opinions on things that left her baffled. The process by which he decided that something—or someone—was good or bad was a mystery to her. She wasn't convinced that there actually *was* a process; more often than not Billy's likes and dislikes were as random (or seemed to be) as the shapes of snowflakes, formed instantly based on inexplicable laws that existed only in her son's world. She'd long ago stopped trying to predict his reactions, as she was almost always wrong.

Still his hostility toward Nate intrigued her, and she wanted to explore it more thoroughly. But not now. Now she would put dinner on the table. She would talk to her sons about their days, and of course they would discuss Celeste's engagement. But she would not invite controversy, nor would she let her own true feelings be known. If she was going to keep her secret safe she would have to do it without the help of James or Billy.

She opened the oven door and removed the meat loaf. "Boys," she called out. "Dinner's ready."

CHAPTER 48

1991

When Billy felt someone press up against him he tried to turn around, but strong arms went around him and fingers gripped the two front belt loops on his jeans. He was pulled backward and his ass rubbed up against something hard.

"Hey, Billy Boy," a voice growled in his ear. "How about you and me go into the little boys' room and have us a good time?" The warm tip of a tongue flicked the spot just under his ear, and the hardness at his back throbbed once as one of the hands slipped down to rub his crotch.

Even if Billy hadn't recognized Red's voice the scent of his cologne would have given him away. It was particularly cloying tonight, and the smell of it made Billy feel sick. So did Red's all-too-obvious arousal. Billy extricated himself from Red's embrace and turned around to face him.

"Not tonight," he said.

Red flashed him a lopsided grin. "What's the matter?" he asked. "You find yourself a new boyfriend?"

"You know you're the only one for me," Billy replied sarcastically. "I'm just not looking for any tonight."

Red looked down at Billy's crotch while tugging on his own. "Okay," he said, clearly annoyed. "But next time you want something I might not be so ready to help you out."

Red went in search of another potential customer and Billy drained the last of his beer. He set the empty bottle on the bar.

"Smart move," Cory said as he swept the bottle into the empties can. "Good for you."

Billy shrugged. "Every so often even I get it right," he said.

Cory filled a glass with two pours from the soda gun and held it out to Billy, who looked at the pinkish liquid but didn't take it.

"It's cranberry and tonic," said Cory. "Nothing else. Makes you look like you're having a drink when you're not."

Billy laughed and took the glass. "Wouldn't want to ruin my reputation," he said. "Thanks."

"I live on the stuff," Cory told him. "That way I can watch everybody else get hammered and try to hook up. It's better than any reality show."

"I guess it would be," said Billy. "I'm usually on the other side, though."

"You're not the worst," Cory told him. "But you've had your moments."

Billy feigned offense. "Are you calling me cheap?" he said.

"I'm saying you sell yourself short," said Cory.

Billy didn't know how to respond. Cory had always been nice to him, but he'd never said anything like that before. Why now? Was he just being nice? Or was something more going on?

Don't be stupid, Billy told himself. *Just because you've thought about getting into his pants doesn't mean he wants into yours. Besides, he knows how fucked up you are. He knows you and Red aren't just taking a piss when you're in the men's room.*

"Maybe," he said. "How much do you think I'd go for at auction?"

Cory wrinkled his forehead and pretended to concentrate hard on the question. He counted on his fingers. "At least a buck fifty," he said.

"Asshole," Billy said, shaking his head. "And here I thought you were going to turn out to be Prince Charming."

"Nah," said Cory. "I turn back into a pumpkin at midnight."

Billy looked at his watch. "That gives us about forty-five minutes," he said. "We'd better get to it."

He was surprised by the ease with which he bantered with Cory. They'd always been able to talk, but this was something different. The mood between them had changed slightly. Were they actually flirting? It certainly seemed so, but that didn't make sense to him. What could someone like Cory want with someone like him? Cory seemed to have it all together, but maybe Billy had missed something. *Or maybe he just likes fixer-uppers,* he thought.

Whatever was going on it was making him nervous. He hadn't had anything but a restroom trick in he couldn't remember how long, let alone gone on a date. Nobody wanted him for more than quick relief, nor did he want anything more from anyone else. If he tried he would just fuck it up.

"I've got to go," he said suddenly. He emptied his glass with one final swallow and patted the bar. "Thanks again. I'll see you later."

"Night," said Cory, waving as he went to talk to another customer.

Billy hurried out of the bar. Once outside he lit a cigarette and began to walk. He felt oddly flustered, and for once he couldn't blame it on too much alcohol or too many drugs. True he'd popped a couple of Valium earlier (he'd found a mostly empty bottle in his mother's medicine cabinet, forgotten behind a box of Band-Aids and a tube of hemorrhoid ointment) but they had provided only a minor escape, probably due to the fact that the prescription was three years out of date. So his mind was mostly clear.

He tried not to think about Cory and their conversation. It bothered him in a way he couldn't articulate, and he was afraid that if he examined his reaction too much it would only make things worse. *Just go home,* he told himself. *Smoke a joint and go to sleep.*

Having settled on this plan he began walking more quickly, as if the troubling aftereffects of his conversation with Cory could be relieved by distance. Lost in his confusion he didn't even notice when the police car pulled to a stop at the intersection of Main and Clayton. He was walking around it when the window rolled down and Nate called out, "Hey there."

The tone of Nate's voice made Billy's stomach turn. It was too friendly, as if he were speaking to a child or to someone he thought didn't speak his language. Billy was tempted to just ignore him. He didn't care if he pissed Nate off; it wasn't as if he and Celeste could think any less of him.

"Want a ride?" Nate asked.

Billy shook his head. "No," he said shortly. "I'm good."

He started to cross the street but Nate kept talking. "I've got some news about James. Thought you might want to hear it."

Again Billy's inclination was to keep going. Anything Nate knew, his mother or Charly would also know, and they would tell him without Nate's irritating cockiness. But there was something in the way Nate held out the offer of information that suggested he wasn't just sharing family news.

"Get in," Nate said, jerking his head at the door.

Reluctantly Billy did. As soon as he was seated Nate started driving. "Put your seat belt on," he told Billy. "Wouldn't want to get pulled over by one of these small-town badge monkeys." He laughed heartily at his own joke. Billy left the seat belt untouched.

"What's going on with James?" Billy asked. Whatever Nate wanted, Billy wanted to find out as quickly as possible. He'd already noted that Nate was driving away from his neighborhood, not toward it.

"Well, it's a funny thing," Nate said. "See, I've been doing some thinking. You and I know that James didn't kill Dad. Am I right?"

Billy bristled at Nate's choice of name for Daniel, as if they were actual brothers instead of accidental relatives. As for Nate's statement regarding James's guilt he merely shrugged.

"If James didn't do it then obviously somebody else did," Nate continued. "We just need to find that somebody."

Billy was already tired of whatever game Nate was playing. "Who do you have in mind?" he asked, trying to force Nate's hand.

"See, that's where it gets sort of interesting," Nate replied. "I've been trying to figure out who might have wanted Dad out of the way. I mean, we all loved him, right? So it can't be one of us."

You're not one of us, Billy thought.

"That got me thinking about Paul Lunardi," said Nate.

Billy tried to keep his voice calm. "What about him?" he asked.

Nate kept one hand on the wheel while putting the other arm along the back of the seat. His hand rested behind Billy's shoulders and Billy shifted a little to put as much distance as possible between them. His shoulder pressed against the window, and he was sort of half turned toward Nate.

"Well everybody knows Dad rode Paul's ass like a jockey," said Nate. He laughed. "You know, because of the thing with Celeste. And Paul hated him because of it."

Billy still said nothing. Inside, though, he felt a chill forming in the pit of his stomach. *What does he know?* he wondered. *And what does he want?*

"A guy like Paul, you never know what he might do," said Nate. "You make him mad enough he just might snap." He paused for a long moment. "Too bad he's dead. He might have something to tell us."

The interior of the car seemed to shrink. Billy sensed Nate's closeness. He couldn't breathe. He longed to roll down the window, both to inhale fresh air and to escape.

"It was a shame how he died," Nate continued. "I still think about it sometimes. That was one of the first cases I handled after I became sheriff."

Billy remembered. He didn't want to but he remembered. In many ways the death of Paul Lunardi had brought a number of things to an end. But it was something best left in the past. That Nate was dredging it up made Billy very nervous.

"I don't know if you remember," Nate said, "but there was a lot of talk at the time that Paul wasn't alone when he died. There was supposedly some evidence to that effect."

There was another long silence. Billy knew that Nate was waiting for some kind of acknowledgment from him. "I remember," he said. He cleared his throat, which suddenly felt as if it were choked with sand.

"All kinds of stories went around," said Nate. "Crazy stories." He laughed. "I remember one guy working on the case thought maybe Paul killed himself because he heard he was going to be picked up for dealing and couldn't stand the idea of having to go back to the pen and be some guy's bitch." He slapped his hand on the steering wheel and chuckled again.

"And what do you think?" Billy said. He was tired of Nate's game.

"That's a good question," said Nate. "I'll tell you what I think. I think it's a definite possibility that Paul Lunardi killed himself because he was afraid somebody would find out he killed Dad."

"You'd have to prove it," Billy replied.

"Yes, we would," said Nate. "But if we *could* prove it, James would be off the hook."

"And how would you do that?" Billy asked him.

Nate drummed his fingers on the back of the seat, right behind Billy's head. "The easiest way would be if we had a witness," he said. "Somebody who was there when Paul died, heard him talking about feeling guilty or just plain afraid of being caught. Hell, whoever it is wouldn't even have to have been there *when* Paul died. Maybe he was just there right before and left before Paul decided to kick off."

"Okay," said Billy. "But wouldn't it be weird that this person waited so long to say anything?"

"No," Nate answered. "Maybe at the time he didn't realize what he was hearing. Maybe he didn't make the connection until now. Someone like Paul, you never knew when he was telling the truth or just talking shit."

That's at least true, Billy thought. Paul had been a consummate liar and storyteller, and he was so charming he could convince you he'd been the first man to walk on the moon, particularly if he thought it would get him something. Billy knew that firsthand.

"So if we can find this someone, I think we'd have an open-and-shut case," said Nate confidently. "What do you think?"

"It would make things easier for a lot of people," Billy said.

"Sure would," Nate agreed. "James would get out, Mom would be happy—hell, we'd *all* be happy. Plus, this witness would look pretty good to everyone. Seems to me it's a win–win situation for everybody."

He brought the car to a stop. Billy was surprised to see that they were in front of the liquor store. He'd been so caught up in his thoughts that he hadn't even noticed Nate turn the car around. Now they sat in the glow of the neon signs in the store's window. The light of a flashing Rolling Rock sign turned Nate's face a sickly green.

"So, you think you might be able to help me out on this?" he asked Billy. "You and Paul hung out sometimes, right? Maybe you can ask around, see if anybody remembers anything."

"I guess I could ask," said Billy.

"I thought you might," Nate said. "How about you think it over—see what you can come up with—then let me know."

Billy tried to open the car door and found it locked.

"Sorry about that," said Nate, hitting the button to release the locks. "Force of habit."

Billy pulled the handle again and shoved the door open. He got out without giving Nate an answer. Nate rolled the window down. "Thanks for the help," he said. "Talk to you soon, buddy."

The car pulled away. Billy, his stomach burning and his nerves twitching, turned and walked through the door of the liquor store.

CHAPTER 49

1988

"Come over here."

Paul patted the space beside him on the couch. Billy hesitated a moment, then went and sat. He looked at the television. On the screen a man was fucking a woman from behind while she gave a blow job to another man, who was lying on his back, his arms crossed behind his head. The woman's tits jiggled with the peculiar Jell-O-like motion of overly inflated flesh. Her hand moved up and down the shaft of the man she was sucking off, her red nails bright against his pale skin.

"Man, that's fucking *hot,*" Paul said. He took a hit off the joint in his hand. His eyes, already red rimmed, were unfocused and glassy. He exhaled and coughed.

Billy too was high. He'd snorted two (or was it three?) bumps of meth, which Paul had only recently introduced him to. He loved the shit; it gave him a rush like coke but was a hell of a lot cheaper. At the moment he was wired for sound, as Paul liked to put it. His heart was pounding and he could hardly keep still.

Paul was the opposite. After a couple of beers and just as many joints he had mellowed out to the point of almost complete inertia. Billy liked him this way—he was invariably nicer when he was stoned than when he was jacked up on stimulants.

"Remember when your cunt sister and me used to get you high?" Paul said. He laughed. "That was like fucking twenty years ago."

It had actually been just about six years, but Billy didn't contradict him. He'd been thirteen then. Now he was eighteen—soon to be nineteen. Paul and Celeste had been broken up for almost as long, their relationship ending shortly after the disappearance of Dan McCloud. Now Celeste was married to Nate Derry and had one kid and another on the way. To Billy's way of thinking her life was basically over, and she wasn't even twenty-five. There would be no getting out of Cold Falls for her, nothing except being the wife of a sheriff and the mother of a bunch of kids.

Things would be different for him. He had plans. True, he hadn't gotten into any of the colleges he'd applied to, but that was because he'd basically blown off his last two years, which had brought his grade point average way down. Now he was at community college taking a bunch of lame freshman classes that he knew he could transfer the credits from when he did get to go to a real school in a year or two.

Besides he didn't really even need school. He was going to be a writer. Sci-fi or fantasy novels. Probably fantasy. He liked those best, stuff like Terry Brooks's Shannara books and Tolkien. He could write books like that. He just needed a really good idea. He was waiting for it to come to him. When it did he would be out of town as soon as he could pack a suitcase. Then he'd go somewhere exciting. New York, maybe, or L.A. Somewhere with creative people, not like the dull hicks he was forced to deal with in town.

"Oh shit," said Paul, drawing Billy's attention back to the video. The two men were now lying side by side while the woman alternated sucking on their cocks.

Paul had undone his jeans and pulled his dick out. Now he was stroking it slowly, tugging it to life. He held the shaft in his fist and ran it the length of himself, back and forth, while his eyes remained fixed on the television. He'd pushed his T-shirt up, exposing his hairy stomach. Although he'd gained weight in the past few years it actually suited him. Billy, watching Paul play with himself, found himself getting hard.

It had surprised—and thrilled—Billy when Paul had continued to hang out with him after breaking up with Celeste. At first they had gotten together once a week or so to smoke pot, often in Paul's car and occasionally at Paul's apartment. Gradually they'd spent more and more time with one another, most often Friday or Saturday nights, when Billy didn't have to be at school the next morning. They would get stoned and listen to music or watch television (Paul loved to watch *Star Trek* when he was high). Billy never told his mother he was seeing Paul; he told her he was at the library or with friends.

The first time Paul had put a porn video in—one Saturday after they'd finished watching *Aliens* and getting buzzed on B&Bs (Paul's name for the combination of Budweiser and bud)—Billy had been taken aback. He didn't find watching naked women exciting, and even the men in the films did little for him. But when Paul began jacking off, everything changed. That first time Billy hadn't touched him. Afraid that Paul would freak out if he acknowledged what was happening, he'd sat on the opposite end of the couch from him and stolen glances as Paul stroked himself. He hadn't even touched himself for fear that Paul would be sickened and stop what he was doing. When Paul came, groaning and staining the front of his AC/DC T-shirt with cum, Billy had gripped the arm of the couch to prevent himself from leaning over and touching the sticky drops coating the hair on Paul's stomach.

Paul, though, had been completely unself-conscious about it, simply wiping away the cum with the bottom of his shirt and opening another beer. Half an hour later, as Billy sat with an erection pressing painfully against his pants, he repeated his performance. This time it took him longer to come, and every second had been torment for Billy.

After that the jerkoff sessions became a part of their routine. For several weeks Paul didn't seem to notice that Billy wasn't participating. Then one Friday he'd simply looked over while beating off to a scene of a woman getting eaten out and said, "Don't just sit there. Get it out."

Billy had obeyed with enormous relief. He'd come quickly, not from watching the video but from the thrill of being next to Paul. He'd slowly moved closer to Paul until their legs were touching. Paul hadn't moved, and Billy had gotten hard and come again, shaking as his body rippled with the force of his orgasm. When, a minute later, Paul too came and unexpectedly gripped Billy's thigh as he emptied his balls into the air Billy had been left breathless.

That was as far as things had gone. Now Billy was mostly at ease with what they did. Although Paul never reciprocated the touching, he seemed to like it when Billy touched him, and he didn't pull away when their arms or legs touched. Billy knew how Paul liked his dick played with and had become adept at getting him to the edge of orgasm and then pulling back. Often he could keep the tension going for an hour or more, until Paul couldn't take it anymore and came in hot spurts, his eyes closed as he thrust up into Billy's welcoming hand.

"Man, that looks good," Paul said.

Billy looked up and saw that the woman had the cock of one of the men buried in her throat. Her nose was pressing into his bush and her lips—red with lipstick—were distended around the thick shaft. The man's hands were entwined in her hair and he was moving her up and down his erection. The second man looked on, playing with himself.

Paul had his hand wrapped around the base of his cock. He was slapping it against his stomach, and a thick clear string of pre-cum stretched between the swollen cock head and his belly. His other hand fondled his balls.

Billy, unable to restrain himself, leaned over and placed his mouth over Paul's cock. He tasted salt and stickiness as his tongue traced the edge of the head. Quickly he moved down, afraid Paul would stop him if he hesitated. Paul's dick slid into his throat and he gagged at its thickness. But he didn't stop until, in imitation of the woman in the video, his nose was buried in the thick hair of Paul's crotch. He felt it beneath his lips, scratchy, and he smelled sweat and something earthier. The scent aroused something deep within him and he put his fingers beneath Paul's balls, rubbing and pressing them to his face.

He felt Paul's hand on his head, and knew then that he would be allowed to continue. With that fear removed he began to move his mouth up and down Paul's shaft, sometimes slowly, feeling every inch with his mouth, and sometimes quickly, using his hand as well. Having never had another man's dick in his mouth, he was pleased to discover that he knew just what to do with it. Probably, he thought, it was because he'd fantasized about it so often.

Paul kept his hand on Billy's neck, occasionally pushing down and forcing the engorged head of his dick into Billy's throat. He would leave it there just long enough for Billy to begin choking, then let up on the pressure so that Billy could lift his head and breathe. Rather than making him anxious, this exertion of control excited Billy.

When Paul next pushed him down, Billy expected the usual moment of breathlessness. But this time Paul kept him there. Billy felt the shaft in his mouth swell as something pulsed through it, and then his throat was filled with jet after jet of Paul's load. He swallowed as much as he could. The taste was thick and bitter, and he loved it. Combined with the smell of Paul's body it was too much, and he felt himself release his own pent-up arousal into his pants. The wet heat slicked his leg.

Paul was softening. Billy sucked hungrily at the deflating cock head, milking the last drops of jism from it. Paul flinched at the touch of Billy's tongue.

"Careful," he said.

Billy was reluctant to let Paul slip out of him. He was intoxicated by the smells and tastes of his body. He longed to bury his face in Paul's ass and lick the sweat from the pits of his arms. He wanted to kiss him. But he was afraid. Something told him that Paul's mood would change if he tried to go further. He had been allowed to be Paul's cocksucker, but he didn't yet understand what the boundaries were.

Paul picked his beer up and took a long swallow. He tucked himself back into his jeans and leaned back, stretching his arms out. He didn't stop the video, and seemed to be engrossed in what was happening on the television screen. He didn't look at Billy.

"I always knew you'd be a good little cocksucker," he said after a moment, still not looking at Billy. "A lot better than your sister, that's for sure."

Billy felt his face flush. He was still riding the elation of having given his first blow job. That he'd given it to Paul, on whom he'd long had a crush, made it even sweeter.

"Girls can give head," said Paul. "But only a faggot knows how to really suck a cock. I guess it's just bred into you guys." He laughed and tipped his beer back, emptying it.

Billy couldn't speak. Paul's words felt like a slap. *Faggot.* It was such an ugly thing to say, and Paul had said it so lightly. *You wanted me to do it,* Billy thought. *What does that make you?* But he said nothing.

The longer he sat there, Paul's face illuminated by the television screen, the angrier he got. His mind flashed back to the day in Paul's car by the lake, when Paul had so obviously been trying to arouse him. He remembered Paul's finger tracing the outline of the hard-on beneath his jeans. He remembered too what Paul had asked him to do that day, and what he *had* done.

"What did you do with the gun?" he asked suddenly. It was something of which they had never spoken.

"What?" said Paul. He was digging through the accumulated debris on the coffee table, looking for something.

"The gun," Billy repeated. "The one I got for you from my father. What did you do with it? You said you'd take me shooting but you never did."

"I did?" Paul answered. He had located a small bag filled with cocaine and was opening it.

"Yeah," said Billy. "So what did you do with it?"

"I don't know," Paul said. "Want to do a line?"

Now that he'd brought the subject up Billy was fixated on it. He had often thought about Paul and the gun, and what he thought was sometimes troubling. He remembered the fights between Celeste and their father over her seeing Paul. He remembered Paul saying that he'd love to teach Dan a thing or two but couldn't because Dan would throw him in jail on some made-up charge. He remembered the mutual loathing the men had for one another.

Maybe he did do it, he thought.

Paul had laid out the coke on the cover of a *Muscle Car* magazine and was cutting it with his Blockbuster video card. Billy stared at the pile of white powder being bulldozed into thick lines. *He used me,* he thought. *He used me then and he used me just now. He doesn't really give a shit about me.*

Paul took a dollar bill from his wallet and rolled it into a tube. He held it to a nostril, pressed the other one closed with his finger, and inhaled a line. He shook his head, snorted deeply, and held the dollar out to Billy. "Take a hit," he said. "It'll get the taste of my cock out of your mouth." He laughed.

Billy wished he *could* wash the taste away. He hated that Paul was taunting him, but he hated even more that he liked having Paul's dick in his throat and that, if Paul let him, he would do it again. He was tempted to do the coke just because it would make him forget for a little while. But he was too angry. He shook his head.

"Suit yourself," Paul said. He leaned over the magazine and snorted the second line. Then he lay back against the cushions and shut his eyes.

A moment later his body began to convulse. At first Billy thought that he was having some kind of laughing fit. But then Paul's arms began to shake like the arms of a puppet, mechanical and jerky. His head was thrown back, and blood poured from his nose. His lips were open and something white and foamy trickled from his mouth.

"Jesus Christ!" Billy yelled. "What the fuck?" He started to reach out to Paul, then pulled his hand back as Paul's body slumped sideways and continued to twitch.

He's ODing, he told himself. *He did too much. He's fucking dying.*

Paul's head was turned toward Billy. Suddenly his eyes flew open. All Billy saw was white. Then they closed again and Paul's body stopped moving. He lay perfectly still, his arms at his side. In the silence all Billy heard was the high-pitched cries of the woman in the video as she came.

"Paul?" Billy said quietly.

He knew he would get no answer. There was no movement in Paul's chest, and his face was pale. He already resembled the corpse Billy feared he was. Finally he forced himself to put his fingers on Paul's neck, searching for a pulse. There was none. He recoiled from the still body, nausea sweeping through him.

He knew he should call someone. But any call to 9-1-1 would be routed to the sheriff's office, which would mean Nate would likely come. He couldn't be there if that happened. No one could know he'd been there. Paul's death was accidental, but there would be questions. Too many questions for Billy's liking. He had to get out of there.

He scrambled to his feet, looking for his jacket. He found it on the chair and pulled it on. He tried to remember if anything else of his was in the apartment, but his mind was a fog. He would just have to hope he'd cleaned up his tracks.

He was about to leave when he looked once more at Paul's body. He felt no remorse or sadness. *You got what you had coming,* he thought as he headed for the door.

CHAPTER 50

1991

"Nate wants me to say that Paul confessed to killing Dad."
Celeste finished folding the T-shirt in her hands and set it on top of the pile of laundry. "I know," she told Billy. She picked up a pair of Spider-Man underpants and smoothed them out on the kitchen table.

"Should I?" Billy asked her.

"It would solve a lot of problems," his sister replied.

Billy tried to read her face, but it was expressionless. She continued to fold the laundry as if she were some kind of automated washwoman. Billy had been there almost twenty minutes and she hadn't stopped once.

"Do you think he did it?" he said.

Celeste shrugged. "I wouldn't put it past him," she replied. "He was a no-good loser."

"You didn't think so back then," Billy reminded her. "As I recall there was a time when the two of you were talking about running off together."

Celeste laughed sharply. "Who told you that?" she said. "Paul? The guy was a liar. I don't think he told the truth his whole life."

Billy considered the comment. There was a time when he would have agreed with Celeste, but not now. Paul may have been a liar but the person he lied to was himself. He'd convinced himself that he was a certain way—a certain type of person—and the rest of his life had been based on convincing himself that his vision of himself was true.

He wasn't like, say, Red, who really was just a liar. Paul was something more.

Billy wondered if Celeste was aware of how much he knew about her relationship with Paul. It didn't surprise him one bit that she was so ready to give Paul up. It would, as she'd said, solve a lot of problems. But did she *really* know anything about Paul's possible involvement in their father's death? If so—and if she didn't care what happened to him—why had she never said anything about it? That Paul might have killed their father was something Billy had considered since the beginning, and he'd always assumed that Celeste thought it as well. As for his own reasons for keeping quiet, he was ashamed to admit to them.

"He did have the gun," he said, trying to sound as if this was a well-known fact.

"What gun?" said Celeste. She tidied the creases on a pair of shorts and folded them in half, then in half again.

"Dad's gun," Billy elaborated. "The one he asked me to get for him."

Celeste looked up, startled. "He asked you to get him one of Dad's guns?" she said. "What for?"

Billy tried to gauge the level of sincere surprise in her response. Did she really not know what he was talking about? It didn't seem possible.

"He said he wanted to teach me how to shoot," said Billy. "We were supposed to go into the woods and practice."

"So you took one of Dad's guns?" Celeste asked.

Billy nodded.

"Does Nate know?"

"I assumed you'd already told him," said Billy. "I didn't mention it."

Celeste shook her head. "How could I tell him?" she said. "I didn't know anything about it."

Before Billy could reply, the door opened and he heard Nate call Celeste's name. He had only a moment to exchange looks with his sister before Nate came into the kitchen. When he saw Billy standing there he stopped in the doorway.

"What brings you here?" he asked.

"I was thinking about what we talked about," Billy replied.

Nate looked at Celeste, then back at Billy. "And?"

"What kind of gun was found with Dad's body?" Billy asked him.

"A Colt," said Nate. "Thirty-eight."

"That's not the gun," said Billy.

Nate looked confused. "What gun?" he said.

"The one I stole for Paul," Billy said. "It wasn't a Colt. It was a Smith & Wesson. I remember that. I took one of the older guns thinking Dad probably didn't use it anymore and wouldn't notice."

Nate looked at his wife. "What's he talking about?" he asked her.

Billy ran his hands through his hair. "I stole a gun from my father's gun cabinet," he said, speaking slowly as if to a child. "Paul asked me to get him one. He said it was so he could teach me how to shoot, but really it was because he thought if Dad was out of the way he and Celeste could get married or some bullshit like that."

"How—" Celeste began.

"I heard him say it," said Billy. " 'Things would be easier if the old man wasn't around.' Something like that."

"He was just kidding," Celeste objected. "He would never—"

"You didn't think it was so far-fetched a few minutes ago," Billy interrupted. "Why's that? Did you know what he was planning to do?"

"No!" said Celeste. She glared at her brother. "What a horrible thing to say."

Billy laughed. "I see," he said. "It's okay to think that James might have done it, but not for little Miss Innocent. What a fucking hypocrite."

"Me?" Celeste snapped. "You're the one who was in love with Paul."

Billy stopped laughing and his face hardened. *So she did notice,* he thought.

Celeste, sensing that she had the advantage, continued. "Maybe Paul didn't ask you to get him a gun," she said. "Maybe you gave it to him and asked him to do something for you. How's that sound, Billy? Maybe *you* wanted to show Dad that you weren't such a little pussy after all. Only you couldn't do it so you asked Paul to."

"Fuck you," Billy spat.

"The two of you shut the hell up!" Nate bellowed. He looked from one to the other. "Billy, you stole a gun because Paul asked you to, right?"

Billy hesitated a moment, then nodded. "Right," he said.

"And *neither* of you knew what he wanted it for," Nate continued.

"I didn't even know he—"

"*Neither* of you knew what he wanted it for, right?" Nate repeated.

"Right," Billy said. He understood where Nate was going with his questioning, and although he didn't trust his brother-in-law he felt it would be to his benefit to go along.

"Right," Celeste muttered.

"And Billy, you're not *sure* what make of gun it was." Nate was speaking now as if he were giving direction and not asking questions. "And you never told anyone because Paul had some kind of hold on you." Nate paused for a moment as if thinking of where to take the plot of his story next. "He said he would tell everyone that you put him up to it. Maybe he even threatened to kill the rest of your family if you said anything." He was speaking more quickly now and was clearly excited. "Isn't that right?"

Billy thought. What Nate was saying did make sense. And for all he knew Paul *had* killed his father. The make of the gun was a problem, but maybe he'd just gotten mixed up about that. Or maybe Paul had stolen a second gun all on his own, or gotten Celeste to do it for him. It really didn't matter. The point was that the story *could* be true. All they had to do was tell it convincingly.

"Billy, this all depends on you," Nate said. "You just have to remember exactly how it all happened. Paul asked you for the gun. You were young and wanted to impress him so you did it. He killed your father. You wanted to say something but he threatened to hurt you and the family. He convinced you to come up with the suicide note and send it to your mother. You would have told the truth after he died but you were too afraid of being blamed for his death. And the drugs you were taking made you confused. You didn't mean to keep it a secret; it just happened. But now you remember it all."

Celeste was nodding. "You won't get into any trouble, Billy," she said. "All you have to do is remember what happened."

She and Nate were both staring at him, waiting for him to say something. And he wanted to say something. He wanted to agree with them. If he did then James would be cleared and everything would just go away. All he had to do was say yes and he could be a hero.

"Okay, he said. "I think I do remember."

Nate smiled broadly. "That's my man!" he said. "Now all we have to do is get a statement from you. I've got to go take care of some stuff at the office, but I'll come over to your place tomorrow and we'll write it all out. You're better at that writing stuff than I am. Work something up, okay?" He clapped Billy on the shoulder. "Wait until Mom hears the news," he said.

He sounds like a kid at Christmas, Billy thought as Nate kissed Celeste good-bye and ran out the door again.

Celeste sat down opposite him, pushing the pile of laundry out of the way so that they could see one another. "It does make sense," she said after a moment.

"It does," Billy agreed. "And the only one who gets hurt is a dead man nobody cared about anyway."

"He could have stolen James's ring," Celeste suggested. "He always hated James."

"That's right, he did," said Billy. After a moment he added, "You know the afternoon Mom told us Dad was dead I ran to Paul's house and threw a rock through his window."

"That was you?" Celeste said. "He thought it was some guy he owed money to. So you really do think he did it?"

Billy shrugged. "I did then," he replied. "But I guess somewhere along the line I convinced myself he didn't. Or maybe I didn't want to believe he did. I don't know. I wanted him to like me."

Celeste smiled wistfully. "He had that effect on people," she said. "And it was hard *not* to want him to."

"Unless you were Mom or Dad," Billy said.

"Or James," Celeste added.

Billy looked at his sister. "It seems too easy," he remarked.

Celeste reached out and took his hand in hers. It was the first time in many years she had touched him. "It *is* easy," she said. "All you have to do is say what Nate tells you to. You didn't do anything wrong. Besides, you were a kid. Nobody is going to blame you."

"Not even Mom," said Billy. He knew he was right. His mother loved him with an inexplicably strong love, one that he'd never been able to explain. She had never blamed him for anything, no matter how low he'd gotten. She wouldn't blame him now. The more he considered the idea the more it made sense. It would wrap everything up as neatly as possible and they could all go on with their lives. Only the already-tarnished name of Paul Lunardi would remain stained.

Celeste patted his hand and let go. "I told you Nate isn't a bad guy," she said. "Maybe this will change your mind about him."

"I never said he was a bad guy," Billy countered. "I said he was an asshole. And that was because of what he did to you at that New Year's Eve party."

"What New Year's Eve party?" said Celeste.

"The one the year before Dad died," Billy said. "Eighty-two. At the swimming hole. Don't you remember, he got all grabby?"

"I wasn't there," said Celeste. "I was with Paul that night."

"No, you were there," Billy insisted. "I remember seeing Nate talking to you. Then you kind of pushed him away and he pushed back. You fell down. How can you not remember that?"

"Trust me, Billy, I wasn't there," said Celeste. "I remember that night really well. Too well."

"But I—"

"I wasn't there!" Celeste said loudly. "Jesus, Billy. You want to know how I know? Because that was the night I got pregnant." Her voice softened and she looked away.

"Pregnant?" Billy repeated. "By Paul?"

Celeste nodded. She dabbed at her eye with one of the unfolded T-shirts. "I had an abortion," she told him. "He wanted to have a kid." She sniffed and laughed bitterly. "I guess he thought if I had his baby I wouldn't leave him," she said. "I waited until afterward to tell him that I'd done it. I thought he was going to kill me. But he was actually okay about it. It kind of scared me. I kept waiting for him to do something really awful, you know? That's why I finally broke up with him."

"You haven't told Nate?" Billy asked.

"No," said Celeste. "I haven't told anyone. So don't you go doing it."

"We'll just add it to the box of secrets," Billy told her.

Celeste took a deep breath. "When they found Dad's body the first thing I thought was how angry Paul was when I told him I had an abortion," she said. "I was going to say something to Nate then, but I didn't know how. He's kind of weird about that whole topic. Then he told me about James's ring and I guess I was so relieved that I wouldn't have to tell anyone my secret that I didn't . . . " Her voice trailed off.

"It's all right," Billy told her. He knew that she was feeling guilty for not coming to James's defense when she had the opportunity. But he also knew how difficult it was to tell the truth when you were the one who would come out looking bad. If he wanted to be forgiven for his own sins he realized he would have to forgive Celeste for hers.

"I don't know what you saw that night," said Celeste. "Are you sure it was Nate?"

"I thought it was," Billy answered. "But if it wasn't you then I don't know who it was."

"There were probably a lot of people there," said Celeste. "And you were probably high," she added. "Right?"

"Maybe a little," Billy admitted.

"So you've hated Nate all these years because you thought he was mean to me?" his sister said. "That's kind of sweet in a fucked-up way."

"I thought you were nuts when you married him," said Billy. "Not that I'm crazy about him now," he added. "But maybe I owe him a second chance."

CHAPTER 51

1982

He was fucking *cold.*

There was a fire going but he didn't go near it. If the older kids saw him there they would probably make him leave. The only reason they let him stay at all was because he was James and Celeste's little brother. That and because he stayed out of the way and never gave them a chance to notice him. Not that being invisible didn't have its advantages. He could snag a beer and nobody would notice. And as long as he stayed where he was he could smoke his joint without having to share it or, worse, get a lecture from James or Celeste. Not that he knew where either of them was. Nor did he care.

He could see a lot from the platform in the tree. It was high up, and you could only reach it by climbing a series of branches that were too light for most of the kids to use. In the summer some of the more adventurous swimmers jumped from it into the swimming hole, but now it had been forgotten. It was the perfect place for Billy to sit and watch what was happening.

And there was a lot happening. So far he'd seen David Haycroft, the son of the Lutheran minister, taking a drunken piss and trying to write his name in a snowbank, as well as Ray Deschanel and Tara Berkins making out behind a tree while Tara's supposed boyfriend, Tommy Pendergrast, was over by the fire talking to some girl Billy didn't know. There were a lot of people Billy didn't know, all of them kids from other schools. That's how the New Year's parties always were, people from all over came to them. And that's why they were so interesting.

It had snowed a lot in the previous week and the woods were piled high with drifts. Some of the boys had shoveled the clearing and packed what they couldn't shovel into a hard floor. The snow was banked up around the edges, which helped protect the fire from the wind and the people around the fire from the cold. But many of the partygoers were scattered throughout the trees anyway, especially those who wanted privacy while engaging in more intimate activities. Over the sounds of talking and laughter Billy could occasionally hear groans and the sounds of kissing.

He was particularly pleased that he had managed to score some pot from Paul earlier that day. Actually he had just taken it from the glove compartment of Paul's Mustang while Paul and Celeste were distracted by an argument about Paul's failing to get tickets to a Loverboy concert that Celeste wanted to go to. No one had noticed him slip the baggie into the pocket of his jeans. Not that there was a lot of pot in it, but it was enough to make three or four pretty good joints. He'd already smoked one and was on his second.

He heard laughter and looked down to see a couple of people playing around on the frozen surface of the water. They were pretending to skate, shuffling their feet and sliding as far as they could. Inevitably they fell down, landing in the thin coating of snow that still covered the ice. Billy recognized one of the boys by the red scarf around his neck. It was James. Nancy had knitted the scarf and given it to him for Christmas. She'd made it way too long and so James had to wear it wrapped around his neck twice. Even then the ends hung down past the edge of his jacket. It was a really ugly thing but James claimed to love it. Celeste was down there too. Her puffy purple coat was unmistakable. She'd gotten it for her birthday, and James teased her that it made her look like the Grimace character from the McDonald's ads.

Billy took a hit on the joint and let the smoke work its magic. He was already flying high, and the additional pot just took him higher. He felt as if he were floating on the cold winter air and looking down on the party like some kind of invisible bird. He laughed at the thought of himself with wings and flapped his arms loosely.

He heard a loud burst of laughter and looked toward the fire, where Scooby Skoboski had dropped his pants and was bent over, mooning the people seated on a nearby log. His pale ass reflected the flames, and when he turned around Billy caught a glimpse of the hair around his dick as he pulled his pants up. He kept watching, hoping

Scooby would repeat the stunt, but instead the older boy grabbed a beer from the tub filled with them and sat down between two girls who promptly turned to the people on their other sides and started talking to them.

Poor Scoob, Billy thought. *Too bad you're such an ugly fucker.*

He scanned the faces in the clearing, looking for anyone or anything interesting to follow. Nothing caught his eye until he saw, standing at the very edge of the clearing, Nate Derry. It almost looked as if Nate was hiding. His body was partially concealed by a tree, and he was dressed in a black wool coat and black sweater. He was moving his head from side to side as if he was looking for someone in particular.

All of a sudden Nate turned and his eyes met Billy's. Billy felt his heart stop. The smoke in his lungs seemed unbearably harsh, but he couldn't blow it out. It burned as he watched Nate's face, waiting for him to do something. But then Nate turned away and Billy realized that he hadn't been spotted at all. Nate had simply been looking in his direction. With great relief Billy regained control over his body. He released the smoke, choking as it poured out of him in a thick cloud.

Shit, that guy is like a fucking Ringwraith, Billy thought. He'd recently gotten into the Tolkien books, and now he understood what the writer meant when he described how Frodo and his companions felt when the dark creatures looked in their direction. Nate's gaze held malevolence, an iciness that could be felt across the clearing. Billy shuddered, glad that the exchange was over. He'd always found Nate a little creepy; now he was even more convinced that there was something weird about him.

He leaned back against the trunk of the tree and relaxed. The beer and pot had done their job well, and he was in a state of blissful disconnection. The uneasy feeling Nate had engendered in him quickly faded away under the soothing caress of the drugs and left him sleepy despite the cold. He found his eyes closing, and despite trying to force them to stay open he was soon dozing twenty feet above the heads of the oblivious revelers.

"Happy New Year!"

He awoke to the sounds of cheers and noisemakers. For a moment he didn't know where he was, but a quick glance around him reminded him. In the clearing people were hugging and kissing. From far off he heard the sound of the clock in the tower of St. Agnes's chiming twelve. It was 1983. He celebrated with a long drink from the can of Genny Cream Ale he'd somehow managed not to knock from the platform when he woke up.

He crossed his arms and rubbed himself, trying to warm up. He vaguely remembered something he'd learned in Scout camp about alcohol making you colder, or something like that. Anyway, he remembered that you weren't supposed to get drunk and fall asleep in the cold. He knew he needed to get down and get warm. Even better, he should get home and go to bed. He wondered if James and Celeste were still around or if they'd left. He'd gotten to the party himself, knowing that they would never agree to take him. But surely they would give him a ride home. *If they're here,* he told himself.

Moving unsteadily he inched himself over the edge of the platform. His stomach lurched uncomfortably as he tried to balance, and for a moment he thought he might puke on the people below him. *Happy fucking New Year,* he thought as he steadied himself. He worked his way down the ladder slowly, one step at a time. No one noticed him descending from his hideout.

When his feet touched the ground he stood for a moment, swaying slightly as he tried to focus on the faces around him. They swam in and out of focus. He would identify one and then just as quickly forget the name that was attached to it. This struck him as incredibly funny, and he laughed. *Just find James or Celeste,* he told himself.

He made his way around the clearing, peering at the people standing talking or seated in little groups around the embers of the dying fire. Many people had already left, but there were still perhaps thirty partiers carrying on. Most, if not all, were drunk or stoned or both. Again no one paid Billy any attention.

He saw a flash of red and identified it as James's scarf. But before he could make his way over to it it disappeared into the inky night. Rather than chase after his brother he decided to look for Celeste. He hoped she was around somewhere.

He found himself walking along the edge of the swimming hole, moving away from the chatter of the group. He entered the woods, following one of the trails that snaked away into the trees. He recognized it as the one that would—eventually—lead him out of the woods and end at the road to his house. But home was at least two miles away. Also, it had begun to snow again. It wasn't a blizzard by any means, but it was heavy snow and it would make walking uncomfortable. Already the flakes were sticking to his face.

He kept going, trying not to think about his cold feet and his rapidly chilling hands and face. His head was beginning to hurt, and he regretted not following James and his red scarf when he'd had the chance. Now it was too late to go back. The sounds of the party were growing fainter, and the only light he had was that provided by the moon. Fortunately it was just past full and despite the snow the woods were fairly bright.

He saw movement ahead of him—someone walking. The body passed out of the shadows into the light and he saw the moon reflecting pale purple on it for a moment before the shadows once more swallowed it up. *Celeste,* he thought. His spirits rose and he hurried on.

He turned a corner and saw Celeste not ten yards away. But she wasn't alone. Someone stood with her. He heard voices.

"Come on," said a male voice. "I won't hurt you."

"No," Celeste said. "I don't want to. I just want to go home."

He tried to identify the guy's voice. It wasn't Paul and it wasn't James, the two people Celeste was most likely to be walking home with. But he recognized it. He just couldn't put a name to it. Like the faces in the clearing it came in and out of focus. He fought through the haze in his mind but couldn't get out of it. His vision began to swim and the nauseous feeling grew stronger. He was going to be sick.

"No," Celeste said again.

Now something was the matter with her voice. It didn't sound like his sister. Billy shook his head, trying to clear it, but the fuzzy feeling only increased. He inhaled cold air, hoping it would revive him.

Dimly he watched as the two figures appeared to struggle. The voices grew louder for a moment, then were snuffed out as if a door had closed on them. Billy heard nothing but his own breathing. Where the shadows had been a moment before there was only emptiness.

"Celeste?" he whispered. "Are you there?"

"Please." The voice was faint, like the mewling of a kitten. It came from somewhere to the left, carried through the trees by the wind. Billy strained to hear it, but his stomach wrenched violently and he began to vomit. He fell to his knees in the snow as the beer came up and clogged his throat.

He heaved twice, emptying his stomach. He knew it would come again, and as he waited for the next wave to hit him he took in great gasps of frozen air, trying in vain to rid his mouth of the sour taste of vomit. In the momentary silence he heard the voice again.

"Please," it said. "Stop."

This was followed by the man's voice. "I don't want to hurt you."

That's Nate, he thought just before his insides twisted and sent him falling forward, his hands in the snow, and he retched again. *And that isn't Celeste, it's—*

CHAPTER 52

1991

"Nancy," Billy said.

He sat up. The room was moonlit, and for a moment he thought he was still in the woods, still throwing up into the snow. He peered into the shadows, looking for the figures struggling against one another.

Nancy. It had been Nancy, not Celeste. It all made sense now. Celeste hadn't been there at all. He'd remembered the purple coat but had forgotten that she'd hated it and had passed it on to Nancy, who loved it. It was Nancy that Nate had attacked.

He swung his legs out of bed and sat on the edge of the mattress, his head in his hands. He heard Nancy's voice in his head: *Stop. Please.* How had he been so wrong?

You were drunk and high, he reminded himself. *And you were thirteen years old. You didn't know what you were hearing.*

But what *had* he heard? Why had Nate been pulling his stepsister into the woods? What were they fighting about? And why wasn't Nancy with James? None of it made sense. Still he was sure he was right about it being Nancy. Celeste's reminder that she'd been with Paul that night was what had triggered the memories.

Maybe you dreamed it all, he argued. *Nancy would have been with James. And why would Nate attack her? Besides, you were so wasted you could barely get yourself home that night.*

That was true. After throwing up he'd passed out sitting in the snow and leaning against a tree. He'd woken up later to find the woods silent and himself alone and shivering. His hands were so numb that he'd had to thrust them inside his pants and cup them around his balls to warm them back up. His legs had been all pins and needles as he walked toward the road home. But he'd done it, arriving at his house weary, sick, and cold. Fortunately it was just past two. His mother was asleep and his father was not yet home from his annual New Year's Eve drunk patrol. It had been easy enough to get upstairs and into bed without detection. There, wrapped in his blankets, he'd finally warmed up and fallen into a deep sleep, not waking up until well past ten o'clock.

He forgot about what he saw in the woods until a week or so later. By then all he could remember was that he'd seen Nate Derry arguing with Celeste. He almost asked his sister about it but decided not to. Neither she nor James had said anything about his being at the party, and he was hoping they hadn't noticed. But years later, when Celeste announced her engagement to Nate, Billy remembered.

Only I had it all wrong, he admitted now.

Maybe it didn't matter. After all, it had sounded like just a fight. But something told him that it had been more than that. Now that the memories had come back they seemed darker than he remembered, as if all these years he had been blocking something out.

He had to talk to Nancy. It was the only way he would find out what really happened in the woods that night. He looked at the clock. It was just past four. He couldn't call the Derry house yet. Plus he didn't want to talk about the matter over the phone. If Nancy would talk at all, that is. Probably she'd forgotten all about the incident anyway. While it had seemed like a big deal to his 13-year-old self, maybe the altercation had simply been a minor disagreement.

He got up and searched the bedside table for cigarettes. Finding one he lit it and walked to the living room, where he turned on a light and sat on the couch. He hated being awake in the dark. It made him anxious, as if the night were trying to smother him. But in the circle of lamplight he was okay. He just had to sit there until dawn arrived.

He spent the next two hours reading the newest comic books he'd taken from work. But none held his interest and he flipped from one to the next, hoping something would capture his attention long enough for him to become engrossed in the story. Finally he gave up and just sat there, smoking cigarette after cigarette until the darkness thinned and it was safe for him to go take a shower.

An hour later he was walking toward the Derry house. He still had no idea what he was going to say to Nancy. He hadn't seen her since her arrival back in town, and anyway they had never been close friends. She'd always been nice to him, but James was all they had in common. He understood that she'd come back to help his brother in some way but so far he didn't understand how she was going to do that. For all he knew she wouldn't even talk to him.

To his relief he didn't even have to knock on the door. Nancy was sitting on the porch steps. She was dressed in shorts and a white T-shirt, and was holding a mug of something hot in her hands. Steam rose up from it and disappeared into the morning air. Nancy's feet were bare.

"Billy McCloud," she said as Billy walked up the driveway.

"Hey, Nancy," said Billy, stopping a few feet from the steps.

Nancy looked him up and down. "You kinda look like shit," she said, grinning.

Billy laughed. "Good to see you too," he told her.

Nancy moved over and patted the porch beside her. "Sit down," she said.

Billy did as she asked. Now that he was there he didn't know how to ask her the questions that had been going through his mind since waking from his dream. Instead he said, "You're up early."

Nancy sipped from her mug (he could now tell from the smell that it was some kind of herbal tea) and nodded. "I can't sleep," she said. "It's too quiet."

"Yeah," Billy said, feeling like an idiot. "I like noise. It helps with the voices in my head."

Nancy turned and looked at him. "You too, huh?" she said. "What do yours say?"

Billy sighed. "Oh, I don't know," he answered. "The usual shit, I guess."

"The usual shit," Nancy repeated. "I hear you. So what do you want, Billy?"

"What makes you think I want something?" said Billy.

Nancy put a hand on his knee and squeezed. "I recognize a hustler when I see one," she said not unkindly. "You've got that look. You need something."

So much for the small talk, he thought. Nancy had changed since he'd last seen her. She'd changed a lot. There was something hard about her now, as if the years had sharpened her edges and made her both wary and dangerous. He wondered what had happened to her to turn her from the laughing, happy girl he remembered into this different woman.

"I've just been thinking about something," he said. "I was hoping you could help me figure it out."

"What's that?" asked Nancy.

"I've been having this dream," Billy told her. "It's all kind of mixed up. I'm at a New Year's Eve party at the swimming hole. I see something happen, but I'm not sure that what I'm seeing is real or not."

"It's a dream, Bill," Nancy said. "You came all the way out here to ask me about a dream? All right, I'll see if I can make up some shit. You're in the woods. Maybe that means you—"

"I saw Nate attack you," Billy said.

Nancy's mouth snapped shut. She gripped her mug of tea tightly, and the muscle in her jaw twitched. "Nate never attacked me," she said.

"But I saw him—" Billy argued.

"You said you had a *dream*," Nancy said angrily. "Who knows why the fuck you dreamed that. Maybe it's all the pills you take."

She started to stand up. Billy grabbed her wrist. "It wasn't a dream," he said. "I *saw* it. I was there."

Nancy pulled away from him. "So what if you were?" she said. "What does it matter now?"

Billy shook his head. "I don't know," he admitted. "But something tells me it does."

Nancy turned. "I have to go," she said. "Becky will be up in a few minutes. I need to be there."

"It has something to do with my dad, doesn't it?" Billy said. He watched Nancy's back as she froze, her hand on the door. After a long moment she turned around.

"Come on," she said, walking past him and down the steps.

Billy followed Nancy as she walked around the side of the house, her bare feet leaving prints in the grass, which was still wet with dew. She moved quickly, and he trotted to keep up with her. He wondered where she was taking him.

"We don't have a lot of time," she said, looking over her shoulder. "Nate's going to be here soon. Dad and Bess are already up."

"What does that have to do with—"

"Just listen," Nancy interrupted.

They had reached the small pole barn that was in the backyard. Once it had been home to a pony and some chickens, but now it held only an old lawn mower and assorted gardening tools. Nancy opened the door and pulled Billy inside. It smelled of dirt and grass and oil. Nancy leaned against the workbench that occupied the length of one wall. She crossed her arms over her chest.

"You did see Nate attack me," she said. "Only he didn't just attack me." She pushed her hair out of her eyes. "He raped me."

Billy, stunned, could only stand there and look at her.

"It wasn't the first time he tried something," Nancy continued. "He used to watch me when I was in the shower. I didn't know, of course, but he told me later. Then he started coming into my room at night. I'd wake up and he'd be sitting on the bed, just looking at me."

"Why didn't you tell your parents?" Billy asked her.

"I thought he'd stop," said Nancy. "He said he would. And he never actually touched me. Not until that night in the woods."

"He *raped* you?" asked Billy.

Nancy nodded. "I guess I was a little drunk. I knew what he was doing but I couldn't really believe it, you know? It was like it was all happening to someone else."

"Where was James?" Billy asked her.

"He was still at the party," said Nancy. "Nate told me he needed to talk to me about something. I don't remember what. I went off with him and that's when you must have seen us."

"Didn't you go back and tell James?"

"No," Nancy said. "He already hated Nate. I didn't want him to do something stupid. Besides, I didn't want him to think I'd done anything to, you know . . ."

Billy was thinking. "That's why you left," he said. "Isn't it?"

"Yes," Nancy confirmed. "I couldn't be around him. Or James. Also, I was pregnant."

Billy, truly shocked, sat down on a bundle of old newspapers. "No," he said. He looked up at Nancy. "With Nate's baby?"

Nancy nodded. "Becky," she said. "Bess isn't her mother. I am."

The story was too much for Billy to take in all at once. Nancy had been raped by her stepbrother and had his baby? And then her stepmother had raised it as her own kid? He couldn't believe that.

"They don't know," said Nancy.

"They who?" Billy asked.

"Dad and Bess," Nancy explained. "They don't know that Becky is Nate's. They think it's some guy whose name I never knew."

"Oh fuck," Billy said. "What about Nate? Does he know?"

"He knows," said Nancy. "I wanted him to spend the rest of his life worrying that someone would find out, so I told him. And now I want her back."

"That's why you're here," Billy said. "Not for James."

"I'm here for James too," said Nancy. "Mostly for Becky, but also for James. He was always good to me. He didn't deserve what happened."

"I don't get it," Billy told her. "What do Nate and Becky have to do with James?"

Nancy came and sat near him on a second stack of papers. Her feet were covered in dust from the floor, and she rubbed one against the other as if she were trying to scrape it off. "I did tell one person about what Nate did," she said quietly.

"Who?" Billy asked. "If you didn't tell your parents or James, then who?"

Nancy looked at him, her eyes wet with tears. "Your dad," she said.

A chill gripped Billy. "And what did he do?" he asked.

A tear ran down Nancy's cheek and fell into the dust. "Oh, Billy," she began.

CHAPTER 53

1983

"I didn't know who else to tell," Nancy said.

Daniel McCloud took her in his arms and held her tightly to his chest. "You did the right thing," he told her.

"Please don't tell my dad," Nancy pleaded. "He'll kill Nate."

"Don't you worry about Nate," Mr. McCloud said. "He'll get what's coming to him." His voice rippled with anger, and Nancy found herself shaking.

"He said he'd hurt me if I told anyone," Nancy said.

"He's not going to hurt anyone," said Daniel. "Come on. We're going to go have a little chat with him."

"I can't," Nancy said. Her heart was beating crazily. "I can't see him."

"I want you to hear what I have to say to him," said Mr. McCloud. "And I want him to see that you're not afraid of him. It will be okay, Nancy. You just have to trust me."

Nancy shook her head. "I can't," she said.

"You can," said Daniel. "You're a strong girl."

She allowed herself to be taken to Daniel's car. "Your dad and Bess are out, right?" Daniel asked as he started the car.

Nancy nodded. She'd chosen that night precisely because the house would be empty. Her father and Bess were in Syracuse having dinner with a friend of Bess's. They wouldn't be back until very late. Only Nate was home.

It was raining lightly. Nancy watched the wipers moving back and forth. She put her hands on her belly. In just the past week she had begun to notice that the swelling was becoming obvious. She knew that soon other people would start to notice, and then she would have to tell her parents. She had no idea how she was going to do that.

"I should just arrest him," Mr. McCloud said as they drove. "Slap his ass in jail."

"No," Nancy said. "I don't want anything like that to happen to him. I just want him to stop what he's doing."

She had lied to Daniel McCloud, or at least omitted part of the truth. She hadn't told him about New Year's Eve. But she *had* told him about how Nate watched her when she showered, and how sometimes he tried to touch her when she was sleeping. She'd told him just enough. She didn't want Nate to get into trouble, but she wanted him to be scared. And she knew Mr. McCloud would scare her stepbrother worse than anyone else could.

When they pulled up to her house, she checked to make sure that Nate's car was there. It was. And her parents' car was gone. Everything was working out perfectly.

"Just stay behind me," Daniel told her as the two of them got out of the car and walked toward the house. "And don't be scared."

"I think he's in the basement," Nancy said as she opened the front door. "He usually goes down there to practice his bass."

Mr. McCloud walked to the kitchen and opened the cellar door. A series of low notes floated up from below. Nate was down there playing, picking out the bass line to a song Nancy couldn't immediately identify, although it sounded familiar. It was only as she descended the stairs behind Daniel that she recognized it as Foreigner's "Juke Box Hero." For some reason this struck her as funny, and she found herself stifling a giggle despite the fear that filled her mind.

She had only a moment to think about it. Seeing Daniel McCloud, Nate stood up. Then he saw Nancy. "What's going on?" he said. "Did something happen to my—"

"Shut up," the sheriff ordered. "You don't say a fucking word, do you understand?"

Nate nodded. He continued to look at Nancy, who averted her gaze and stared at the floor.

"I understand you've been giving Nancy a hard time," said Mr. Mc-Cloud. "That's going to stop."

"What—"

"I told you to keep your mouth shut!" Daniel roared. Behind him

Nancy felt herself shaking. *Don't look,* she told herself. *Just don't look at him.*

"I don't know what kind of sick fuck you are," she heard Daniel say to Nate. "She's your stepsister, for Christ's sake."

"What did she tell you?" Nate said. "Whatever it is, she's lying."

Daniel stepped forward, and Nancy saw Nate sprawl onto the floor. He was holding his cheek and his face had turned a deep red.

"Shut. The. Fuck. Up." the sheriff said coldly. He was standing over Nate, looking down at him. Nate tried to meet his gaze but failed.

"Now Nancy doesn't want me to tell A.J. and Bess about what you've been doing," Daniel said. "And for her sake I won't. But listen up and listen good—if she tells me you've so much as *thought* about looking at her again I'm going to beat your ass so hard you'll wish you were in prison instead."

Nate was looking at Nancy now. She could see that he was trembling, from fear or from anger she didn't know. Probably it was both. Seeing him helpless like that made her glad. After what he'd done to her he deserved to be humiliated. He deserved to hurt.

"How your mother ever gave birth to a piece of shit bastard like you I'll never understand," Daniel said to Nate. He kicked at the boy with his foot.

Nate lashed out, grabbing the sheriff's boot and twisting his arms. Mr. McCloud was caught off balance and fell. Nancy watched it all as if it were happening in slow motion. Daniel's body hit the floor hard. Then Nate was on top of him, both of his fists swinging. "Fuck you!" he yelled over and over. "Fuck you!"

Daniel held up his hands to shield himself from the blows. He pushed aside Nate's arms, and his hands closed around Nate's throat. Nate's eyes went wide as his air was choked off, and he began hitting at the older man with frantic slaps. Mr. McCloud ignored him, rolling to one side so that he was now on top of Nate.

"That was a mistake," he said, leaning down so that his face was very close to Nate's. "A very big mistake."

"Let him go!" Nancy shouted.

Daniel ignored her. Nate's mouth was opening and closing like a dying fish. No sound was coming out and his hands scrabbled uselessly at the sheriff's face.

"You're going to learn a lesson here," Mr. McCloud said. "You'll find out what a piece of scum you are."

Nancy had never seen somebody so coldly cruel. Daniel actually seemed to be enjoying making Nate suffer. *And it's all my fault,* she thought with horror. *This isn't what I wanted. I just wanted him to be scared.*

She ran over to Mr. McCloud and pulled at his shoulder. "Don't hurt him!" she cried.

It was as if the sheriff couldn't hear her. He just continued to stare down at Nate, oblivious to Nancy's entreaties and the ever-weakening attempts by Nate to make him relax his grip.

Nancy's mind raced. She had to do something or Nate would be dead. She looked around the cellar for something that might help. There was nothing. Then she remembered her father's guns. He'd moved them downstairs because Bess said she didn't like to see them around the house. But where had he put them?

She ran to a stack of boxes piled in one corner. Most were empty, having once held Bess and Nate's things. But some contained odds and ends that had yet to find permanent homes. Nancy opened them quickly, pawing through the bits of newspaper and packing material that filled them. Then, in the fourth box she checked, she found the guns. There were maybe half a dozen, all of them handguns her father used for target practice. She grabbed one and ran back to Mr. McCloud and Nate.

"Stop!" she yelled. "Let him go!"

The sheriff didn't turn around. Nate's eyes were closed and it looked to Nancy as if he'd stopped breathing. His hands were at his sides, and his chest wasn't moving.

"You killed him," she said, beginning to sob. "You killed him. I told you not to hurt him."

Mr. McCloud turned and looked at her. Seeing the gun he let go of Nate and held his hands up. "Put it down, honey," he said.

Nate's eyes flew open and he started to cough. At the sound Nancy took her eyes away from Daniel and looked at her stepbrother. *He's not dead,* she thought. *He's all right.*

In the instant that she looked away the sheriff sprang at her, reaching for the gun. Startled she jumped back and stumbled over her own feet. As she fell her hand clutched at the gun. She heard a loud roar and her arm jerked violently as the gun flew away from her. Daniel McCloud stopped and fell to his knees. On his shirt a red stain was spreading out like a flower opening its petals. Then he slumped sideways and lay crookedly on the floor.

"Oh shit," Nate said. He had crawled over to the sheriff's body and was looking down at him. "Oh shit," he said again. "What do we do?"

Nancy looked at the gun, which had landed on the floor several feet away. Then she ran to Daniel and knelt beside him. She tried to remember any of the things she'd learned in the first aid section of health class. *Find a pulse,* she thought. *You need to find a pulse.*

She took Mr. McCloud's wrist and pressed two fingers against it, hoping to feel something there. When she didn't she next tried locating a pulse in his neck. Again she found nothing. And he wasn't breathing.

She rolled him onto his back. The red stain was larger now, and drops of blood smeared the cellar floor. The smell of it sickened her, and she tried to pretend it wasn't there as she unbuttoned the sheriff's shirt and put her hands on his chest. She pressed down eight times, counting out loud. After the eighth compression she put her mouth over Daniel's and blew into it while pinching his nose shut. Then she began the cycle again.

Nate had sat down, his legs splayed out like a child's, and was rubbing his throat. He watched Nancy without saying a word, and she in turn ignored him. She focused on counting. "One. Two. Three. Four. Five. Six. Seven. Eight," she called out. *Breathe one. Breathe two,* she continued silently as she blew into Mr. McCloud's mouth. His lips were cold, and she recoiled at their touch.

"Stop," she heard Nate say. "Stop it, Nancy."

He was now squatting beside her. She felt his hand on her shoulder and shrugged it off. "I have to count," she said. "One. Two. Three. Four. Five."

Nate took her hands and pulled them away from the sheriff's chest. "He's dead," he told her.

Nancy shook her head. "No," she said firmly. "He isn't. We just need to call for help."

It was Nate's turn to shake his head. "We can't do that," he said. "Think about what will happen."

Nancy didn't understand. All she knew was that she needed to get help for Mr. McCloud. She stared at Nate blankly.

"You killed him," he said. "He's dead, and you killed him."

"It was an accident," Nancy said. "I didn't kill him."

"Nobody will believe that," said Nate.

"Yes, they will," Nancy objected. "You'll tell them it was an accident."

"Why should I?" asked Nate. "You're the one who set him on me."

"I didn't mean for this to happen," Nancy said. "He just wouldn't stop." As the reality of what she'd done became more and more clear she felt herself beginning to fall apart. She moved away from Daniel McCloud's body. She felt sick. *The baby,* she thought as her stomach lurched.

Nate was looking at her with a strange expression. "What did you tell him?" he asked.

"I told him the truth," Nancy answered. "I told him what you did to me in the woods."

Nate paled. Nancy watched his face closely, hoping he would believe the lie. It was suddenly very important that he did. To make sure she said, "I'm pregnant."

Nate shook his head. "No," he said. "That's not true."

"It is," said Nancy. "I swear it's true, Nate."

Nate looked at the body on the floor. He seemed to be thinking about something. He chewed on his lip the way he did when he was trying to figure out a difficult math problem. Nancy waited for him to say something. Everything hinged on what came out of his mouth next.

"Okay," Nate said finally, looking back at Nancy. "I'll make you a deal."

CHAPTER 54

1991

"I'm ready to make my statement."

Nate, hearing Billy's voice, grinned. "All right," he said. "I'll be right over."

He hung up, relieved that everything would soon be over. He'd started to worry that Billy was going to back out on him. *You never know with a guy like that,* he thought as he grabbed his car keys from the desk and walked out of the station. *Fucker like him could do anything.*

On the drive to Billy's apartment he thought through what would happen next. Billy—hopefully—would have composed his statement. All Nate would have to do was type it up and hand it over to the D.A.'s office. There would be a little back and forth between the lawyers, of course. The vultures could never just let anything go. But with any luck James would be out of jail in a couple of days and all of his problems would be over. Well, most of his problems. Nancy was still making noise about wanting to take Becky. Once the court found out about her past they would never let her have the kid. Still, she could talk, and even though she was clearly a mess it would take only one person to listen to her and believe her story. Then the whole town would hear it, and a lot of them would start believing her too.

It wasn't just himself he was worried about, although certainly he didn't want anyone (especially Celeste) to know he was Becky's father, or how Nancy had gotten pregnant. Mostly he was concerned about his mother. She loved Becky as if the girl really were hers. A.J. did too. If Nancy somehow managed to take Becky away from them, it would break their hearts.

One thing at a time, he told himself. *You'll figure something out.*

He parked his car on a side street by Billy's apartment. He didn't want anyone to see him there, and although it was just getting dark there were still a lot of people on the streets. He walked briskly to the liquor store and then up the flight of stairs to Billy's place. He tapped on the door.

"Hey," Billy said when he answered the knock. "Come in."

Nate entered the apartment. He looked around, noting the comic books on the table and the ashtray full of roaches. He followed Billy into the living room and took a seat on the battered sofa. "You write something up for me?" he asked.

"Yeah," Billy answered. "Here." He handed Nate a sheet of paper.

Nate scanned the page quickly, his expression growing more and more grim as he read. When he looked up at Billy his eyes were stony. "What the fuck is this?" he said.

"It's your confession," Billy told him. "About raping Nancy."

Nate felt his hand begin to shake, and he forced himself to remain still. "What are you talking about?" he said. "That's nuts."

"I saw you," said Billy.

"You didn't see fucking anything," Nate said. "You were just a kid."

"I saw enough," said Billy. "Besides, Nancy will back me up."

Nate laughed. "And who's going to believe a head case and a queer drug addict?" he asked.

Billy nodded. "Maybe they won't," he said. "But I think they'll trust the DNA test Nancy could force you to take. I understand they're using them in court cases now."

Nate saw the hardness in Billy's face and knew he wasn't joking. "What do you want?" he asked.

"An insurance policy," Billy answered. "I'll go along with you on the Paul story, and you'll sign that confession. I'll keep it somewhere safe—just in case."

Nate snorted. "What? You think I'd try to do something to you? I don't give a shit about Paul Lunardi. Nobody does. You say he killed Dan and I'll be as happy as anyone else."

"It's not for me," Billy said. "It's for Nancy."

Nate nodded. "Of course," he said. "Let me guess, if I don't see that she gets Becky back she'll wave this so-called *confession* around and make me look like a bad guy."

"That's about right," said Billy. "All she wants is her daughter. Give her that and she'll go away."

Nate weighed his options. If he went along with Billy then the murder of Dan McCloud would just go away. James would be released, which would make Celeste and Ada happy (not to mention that irritating girlfriend, who was really getting on his nerves). Best of all, he himself wouldn't be implicated.

But what's to stop queerboy or Nancy from talking later on? he asked himself. *What if they decide they want something else?*

He couldn't trust them. No matter what he did he would always be under their control. Sure, he could always claim that the confession was forged. But that wasn't the point. He didn't like that the two of them had him cornered.

"I know how my father died," Billy said.

Nate looked at him. *Of course Nancy told him,* he thought. *Stupid bitch.*

"Personally I'd like to see you in jail for the rest of your life," Billy continued. "But I don't want Celeste or the kids to suffer."

"I'm not the one who killed him," said Nate. "Did she tell you I was?"

Billy shook his head. "No," he said. "She told me it was an accident. But it wouldn't take much to convince a jury you did, would it?"

"I'd take her down with me," Nate said. "I guarantee it."

"I don't think so," Billy replied. "See, accident or no accident you're still a rapist. You know as well as I do that guys in prison don't much like rapists—especially rapists who attack teenage girls." He smiled. "And I don't have to tell you how guards feel about cop killers, do I?"

Nate's fingers curled into fists as he tried to contain his anger. He wanted to grab Billy by the throat and choke the life out of him.

Billy sighed deeply. "So that's where we stand," he said. "You sign this and I'll sign a statement for you. Everyone gets what they want. Don't sign it and I'll make a call and have your ass in a cell. Then nobody really gets what they want."

Nate looked away from Billy. The queer was right. All he had to do was sign the fucking paper and everything would be over. Then he could get on with his life. He turned back to his brother-in-law. "Okay," he said. "Give it to me."

Billy walked over to him and held out the paper. "I'll get you a pen," he said.

As Billy turned to get a pen Nate leaped to his feet and grabbed him. His forearm closed across Billy's throat in a chokehold. Billy struggled, but he was unable to get away.

"Now it's time for *you* to listen," Nate said. He could feel Billy gasping for breath. "I gave you a chance to be a team player. But you wanted to be the big hero instead. So now there's a change of plans."

Billy's hands clawed at Nate's arm, trying to pry it from his throat. Nate tightened his grip. "If it makes you feel any better, you're not the only one at fault here. Nancy should have stayed away. But I think when this is all over I can talk some sense into her. You, though, are a problem. That's always been your problem, Billy boy. You don't have any common sense."

Billy's struggling weakened as the breath in him ran out. It would be only a few more moments before Billy was unconscious. Nate felt the weight against his body increase as Billy's legs gave out.

"That's it," he said as he lowered Billy to the floor. "Just go to sleep. When you wake up again we'll have a little chat about what we're going to do next."

CHAPTER 55

1983

"Take that end," Nate instructed Nancy.

He watched his sister hesitate as she looked down at the body on the ground. It was wrapped in a tarp, tied with rope around the neck and feet. It looked like a mummy.

"I can't," Nancy said. "I can't touch him." She began to cry.

Ignoring her, Nate picked the body up by the feet and dragged it to the hole he'd dug. It had taken a long time, and he was covered in dirt, but he'd gotten it done. Fortunately the ground was soft there in the woods, which had made it easier.

He looked down at the trunk in the hole. He needed to get the body into it, but there was no way to lower it in, especially if Nancy wouldn't pull herself together and help. Finally he resorted to simply sliding the body over the edge of the hole and letting it fall. There was a soft thud as it hit the bottom of the trunk.

He jumped in after it, standing at one end of the trunk as he wrestled the body into position. He had to bend the knees to make it fit. The stiffening body resisted, and for a moment he had the horrible thought that he might have to saw the legs off. But the knees gave way and he was able, with a lot of pushing, to get the body into the small space.

Before he climbed out of the hole Nate reached into his pocket and removed the ring he'd hidden there before leaving the house. He'd thought of it at the last second, taking it from Nancy's dresser as he'd passed her room after grabbing a change of clothes from his own room. At the time he hadn't known why he was doing it, but now he understood. Even in his confusion a part of his mind had been thinking ahead, planning for every possibility. He was impressed with his instincts.

"Just in case," he said as he placed the ring beneath the body's head. The gun was already there, wiped clean, of course, of fingerprints. Another piece of insurance. Another smart move on his part.

Nancy knew about neither the gun nor the ring, and he would never tell her. They protected her just as much—if not more—than they protected Nate. She was the one who had pulled the trigger. She was the one who would be held accountable. He was doing all of this for her.

Bracing himself against the walls of the hole, Nate lifted his feet and closed the trunk's lid. He slipped a padlock, bought at a hardware store earlier in the evening, through the loop of the trunk's closure and secured it. The key went into his pocket. He would dispose of it later, far away from the burial site. Then, his job finished, he hauled himself out of the hole.

"Can you help me fill it in?" he asked Nancy. She was holding the lantern they'd brought for light, and her face was illuminated with a sickly yellow sheen.

Wordlessly she set the lantern on the ground and accepted the shovel he held out to her. "Put the gloves on too," he told her. "You don't want to get blisters."

She obeyed, still saying nothing. Nate took the second shovel and began to scoop soil into the hole. The first few shovelfuls landed on top of the trunk with a hollow thud, but after a few minutes the sound deadened and became a rhythmic *tump-tump-tump* as he and Nancy alternated loads. The pile of dirt grew steadily smaller, until finally the level of the earth in the hole was more or less even with the surrounding ground.

As Nancy stood with the shovel gripped in her hands, as if only by holding on to it could she keep from collapsing, Nate opened the garbage bag full of leaves and sticks he had made Nancy gather from another part of the woods while he'd dug the hole. He emptied the contents and strewed them over the fresh-turned earth so that it blended with the rest of the forest floor. It wasn't perfect, of course, but it would do. He'd chosen a location that was out of the way of normal foot traffic, and he doubted anyone would come across the site accidentally.

"All right," he said as he surveyed his work. "I think we're good."

"How can you say that?"

Nancy's voice, strained and thin, startled him. He looked at her and found that she was staring at him. "Do you know what we just did?" she said.

Nate went to her and put his hands on her arms. Nancy shrugged him off. "Don't touch me," she said. "Don't you *ever* touch me."

"Listen to me," Nate said. "We have a deal. You don't say anything about . . . what happened . . . and I won't tell anyone that you killed Mr. McCloud."

"It was an *accident,*" Nancy objected. "I didn't mean to do anything. He was hurting you and—"

"It doesn't matter why you did it," Nate interrupted. "You *did* it. That's all they would care about. Do you understand me?"

"We have to tell someone," said Nancy, shaking her head. "Mrs. Mc-Cloud. She'll wonder where he is. James."

Nate bristled at hearing her say that name. James McCloud was the last person he cared about. James McCloud, as far as Nate was concerned, could go fuck himself. But Nancy was right—people would of course wonder where Daniel McCloud had gone. Then they would search for him.

"I'll take care of it," he told Nancy.

"How?" she asked. "How can you just make someone disappear?" Her voice was becoming more hysterical, and Nate feared she was going to snap. If she did it would all be over. She *had* to keep their secret.

"A note," he said, thinking quickly. "Some kind of note, or a letter. A suicide note." The idea came to him in a flash, perfectly formed. "He killed himself," he said aloud.

"Why would he do that?" said Nancy.

"I don't know yet," Nate said. "I'll work it out. Right now we have to get home and cleaned up."

Before he got into the car he changed into the fresh clothes he'd brought. The dirty ones went into a plastic bag, which he carefully tied shut. He was surprised by how calm he was. *Then again, I'm not the one who killed him,* he reminded himself. What he *was* he would not allow himself to think about. He'd done nothing to Nancy to be ashamed about. She didn't understand. He loved her. He would do anything for her. Someday—when she was being more rational—she would see this. She would even be happy. Nothing else would matter.

They drove home in silence. Nancy looked out the window, never once turning her face to him. Finally, to break the silence, Nate turned on the radio. "Domo arigato, Mr. Roboto," sang Styx.

"What the fuck is this song even about?" Nate asked, laughing. "It's so fucked up."

Nancy maintained her frozen silence. She was going to be a problem. If she said the wrong thing to someone, it would all be over. He had to keep her quiet. But how could he? After all, it wasn't just anyone they had just buried in the woods. It was A.J. Derry's best friend. Nancy's boyfriend's father. The town sheriff. If Nate had been asked yesterday to name the one person it would be most inconvenient for someone to kill, it would have been Daniel McCloud.

This just makes it more of a challenge. The thought came unexpectedly, and for a moment he was taken aback. More and more he was thinking about what he was doing as a game. He was thinking ahead, trying to foresee potential obstacles. Already he was looking at the events of the past hours with detachment, replaying them in his mind only to see if there was anything he'd missed, any track he had failed to cover.

That's how you have *to look at it,* he told himself. Nancy's right, it was an accident. But telling anyone would just make things worse. It would be one thing if Nancy weren't—he couldn't bring himself to say the word. *If she weren't the way she says she is,* he thought. He still wasn't convinced about that, but he had no way of proving it right now and he had to assume that she was telling the truth. Besides, he'd never known Nancy to lie about anything.

He glanced over at her. She had her hands clasped in her lap, over her stomach. Was there really a baby growing in there? he wondered. He couldn't imagine it. He didn't even really remember the events of that night. But he knew that whatever had happened had happened because *both* of them had wanted it to. He hadn't done anything that Nancy hadn't wanted him to. If she believed differently it was because she was confused. He would explain it all to her later.

When they arrived at the house he parked the car and turned to Nancy. "I think—"

"Don't worry," said Nancy, opening the car door. "I'm not stupid."

She got out and shut the door. Nate waited a minute, then got out, removed the tools from the trunk, and took them into the garage. The bag of dirty clothes he took with him to his bedroom. He would wash them later. As he walked by the bathroom he heard the sound of water running. Nancy was in the shower. He paused and listened, closing his eyes and imagining her body beneath the hot water.

He leaned his cheek against the door and slid his hand into his pants.

CHAPTER 56

1991

Nancy rehearsed in her head what she was going to say to Billy. She'd been thinking about it ever since their conversation, when she'd told him the truth about his father's death. She had told him everything, surprising herself with her honesty. She'd spent so many years being careful never to say anything that could connect her with Daniel McCloud's death that she had almost convinced herself that she hadn't been involved. But once she'd started talking to Billy she'd found the story pouring out.

At the time she had not understood her need to talk about the events of eight years before, at least not to Billy. Now she did. They were the same—damaged goods—and they understood one another in a way that made it possible for them to not hide from each other. Still, Billy had reacted with surprising calm. There had been no shouting, no accusations, no threats. Billy had simply taken her in his arms and told her that everything would be all right. Then he had left.

She'd waited uneasily for several hours, still half expecting to see the flashing lights of a patrol car as it pulled up outside the house. But eventually that fear dissipated and was replaced by a peculiar calm. She had unburdened herself, and it felt good to be free of the pressure that accompanied keeping such a secret for so long.

That feeling too was soon replaced, however—this time with the understanding that, having told Billy the truth, she could not expect him to keep her secret either. She couldn't wish that upon him, or upon anyone. And so she had decided to tell Charly the truth. But first she wanted to let Billy know that he didn't have to protect her.

She reached his building and walked slowly up the stairs. With each step the weight of her decision grew. She found herself stopping near the top of the stairs. Her heart hammered violently, and she felt that she might be sick. She closed her eyes and breathed deeply.

A sound disturbed her—a muffled thud and the sound of breaking glass. She heard a man's voice swear loudly. She almost called out to Billy, but it didn't sound like him. There was something familiar in the tone. And then she placed it.

She scrambled up the last few steps and pushed open the door of Billy's apartment, which to her relief was unlocked. Going inside she walked quietly through the apartment and into the kitchen. Billy was seated in a chair at the table, his arms tied behind him. He looked dazed, and there were angry red marks on his neck, as if he'd been choked. His lip was bleeding. Pieces of broken glass were scattered across the linoleum and splashes of something dark—soda, she thought— pooled around the chair legs.

Nate had his back to Nancy. He was pouring more soda into another glass. Then he picked up a small plastic container that was sitting on the table. Nancy recognized the familiar orangey brown color of a prescription bottle. When Nate tipped the container a stream of white pills fell into the soda.

"This time you're going to drink it," Nate told Billy. "No more fucking around, or I'll have to find a less pleasant way to end this."

He put his hand in Billy's hair and pulled his head back. Billy opened his mouth in pain, and as he did Nate tipped the glass of soda in. Billy choked on the pill-laced drink, spitting some of it back into Nate's face. He whipped his head from side to side, trying to get away. *That's how he cut his lip,* Nancy thought. *He broke the glass with his mouth.*

She didn't know what to do. She could only watch as Nate tried to force the soda into Billy's mouth. For a moment she felt as if she were back in the basement of her old house, watching Nate struggle with Daniel McCloud. Terror gripped her and held her tightly, refusing to allow her to move. She was fifteen years old again, scared and helpless.

But you're not, said a voice in her head. *Now move!*

She did. Acting completely by instinct she found herself grabbing a knife from the holder on the counter. "Stop it!" She screamed.

Nate, startled, turned around. He looked at the knife in her hand.

"Put the glass down," Nancy ordered.

Nate did. He then held up both of his hands, palms out. "Calm down," he said.

"What the fuck are you doing?" Nancy asked.

Behind Nate Billy spit up, a mess of soda and pills spewing from his mouth and onto his shirt. He gasped for air.

"You're making it look like he killed himself," Nancy said. She looked into Nate's eyes. "Aren't you?" Her mind raced as she put the pieces together. "You want it to look like he killed Daniel."

Nate shook his head. "He threatened to tell everything," he said. "I gave him a way out. It would have worked out for all of us. But he"— he pointed at Billy—"he said we needed to pay."

"You're lying," Nancy snapped. "Billy, are you okay?"

Billy coughed. "I'm all right," he said. "I think it's all out of me."

"Untie him," Nancy ordered Nate.

"You know I can't do that, Nance," Nate said. He laughed. "We've gone too far to go back now." He moved toward her.

"Nate, so help me God I'll slit your fucking throat if you come one step closer," Nancy said.

Nate hesitated. Nancy kept her eyes on his, refusing to look away. She'd learned a few things about dangerous men over the years, and now she played her hand carefully. "Untie him," she said.

"You won't hurt me," Nate said. "I'm your brother."

"No, you're not," said Nancy. "And this time I'm not a little girl. Now untie him."

Nate's eyes narrowed.

"You can try it," Nancy told him, sensing what he was thinking. "And you *might* get away with only a couple of cuts. But I guarantee you I'll get out of here before you do and I'll be screaming bloody murder."

Nate stepped back. Nancy could see the muscles in his jaw tightening. *He wants to kill us both,* she realized. But that wasn't going to happen. This time *she* was calling the shots.

"Okay," Nate said. He moved to the chair and began untying Billy's hands. As soon as the ropes were off Billy jumped up and came to stand next to Nancy.

"Sit down," Nancy told Nate.

He obeyed her, folding his hands on the tabletop. He glanced at the now-empty bottle of pills, and a scowl darkened his face.

"It's over, Nate," said Nancy. "All of it. It's over. And here's what's going to happen—you're going to confess to accidentally killing Daniel McCloud."

Nate's head whipped up. "Me?" he said. "I'm not the one who killed him."

"Really?" said Nancy. "Because that's the way I remember it. I also remember you suggesting that we put James's class ring in the trunk. Oh, and let's not forget the letter. I remember that too."

Nate was shaking his head. "You're just as much to blame for it as I am," he said. "Even more. You pulled the trigger."

"Have you forgotten why Daniel was there that night, Nate?" Nancy asked. "Have you forgotten about how you *raped* me?"

Nate's face flushed, but he said nothing.

"Because I remember," Nancy continued. "I remember *every second of it.*"

Her hands were trembling. The knife shook, the tip moving from side to side. Nancy forced her muscles to hold still. "You're going to confess to killing Daniel," she repeated. "And I'm going to testify that it was an accident. That way *maybe* you won't get too much time and *maybe* your wife will forgive you and you won't lose her and your kids. Do you know how that feels, Nate, to lose a child?"

Nate ignored the question. "After everything I've done for you," he said. "After *everything.*" He looked at her. "Why did you come back? Why couldn't you just have stayed gone?"

"No secret stays buried forever," Nancy answered, her voice almost a whisper.

"Is that what you're going to tell Becky?" asked Nate.

Nancy shook her head. "Do you think I want her to know who her real father is?" she said. "That's my end of the bargain—you confess and I never tell anyone else about what you did to me." She paused a moment. "I've done my time for this, Nate. I've done more time than you'll ever do. And I'll keep doing it because I love my daughter."

"And him?" Nate asked, indicating Billy.

Billy laughed. "As far as I'm concerned you can rot in hell," he said.

"But I'll do it for James, and for my mother, and for Celeste and Adam and Mary." He put his hand on Nancy's shoulder. "And I'll do it for her."

Nancy watched Nate's face for a moment. "So, do we have a deal?" she asked.

Nate nodded slowly. "Yeah," he said. "We have a deal."

Nancy turned to Billy. "Call Charly," she said. "Tell her to come over here."

CHAPTER 57

1991

"I heard about your brother-in-law," Cory said as he handed Billy a glass. "I never expected that ending."

"No one did," said Billy.

"How's your family handling it?"

Billy took a sip of the cranberry and tonic. "It was an accident," he said. "Nate was just a kid."

"I didn't ask how *he* was doing," said Cory.

Billy picked a peanut from the dish on the bar. "Celeste is pretty much devastated," said Billy. "But I think she'll get over it."

"Harsh," Cory said.

"I'm serious," said Billy. "People get over worse shit every day. Plus, she has the kids. She might divorce Nate—I don't know. Maybe she'll meet some nice guy while Nate's hanging out upstate. Or maybe he will."

Cory laughed. "You're evil, my friend."

"Not so much," said Billy. "I'm pretty sweet once you get to know me. Anyway, I think my mother is relieved to finally know what really happened. Besides, as soon as James got out he asked Charly to marry him, so now there's all of that happy bullshit to keep her busy." He took another sip of his drink. "Apparently there's nothing like being in jail for a week to get a man to realize that you're the best thing to ever happen to him."

"And how about you?" asked Cory.

"Me?" Billy said. "Oh, I don't know. Maybe it's time to make something of myself. I don't think the strung-out loser thing is for me." He hesitated before continuing, afraid that he might be opening himself up to ridicule. But he didn't think Cory would do that. "When I was a kid I wanted to write stories," he said. "You know, novels."

"Oh yeah?" Cory remarked. "What kind of novels?"

"Ones people like to read," Billy answered. "I want to go on an airplane someday and see every single person on there reading *my* book."

Cory smiled. "And I bet you will," he said. "I know I'll buy it."

Billy emptied his glass and looked at his watch. "I should go," he said. "I'm meeting a friend for dinner."

"Anyone I know?" Cory asked him. There was a funny tone to his voice, which Billy at first couldn't identify. Then he realized what it was. *He's jealous,* he thought. *He thinks I'm going on a date.*

"It's none of my business," Cory said quickly.

"It's a *girl* friend," said Billy. "And she's not nearly as cute as you are."

He got up to go. "Listen," Billy said, speaking before he could change his mind. "Do you want to get together sometime? You know, somewhere other than here?"

Cory rinsed and dried a glass before answering. "That took you long enough," he said. "I was thinking you'd never get around to it."

"You could have asked me," said Billy.

"You would have just thought I was feeling sorry for you," Cory told him.

Billy started to argue, then realized that Cory was right. "How do I know you're not saying yes now because you feel sorry for me?"

"I didn't say yes," said Cory.

Billy, suddenly confused, didn't know what to say. To his enormous relief Cory looked at him and grinned. "Yes," he said. "How about tomorrow night?"

"Tomorrow's good," said Billy. "It's . . . great. I'll, um, see you tomorrow."

Cory wrote something on a napkin and handed it across the bar. "You'll need my number," he said, laughing. "Call me in the afternoon and we'll figure out what to do."

Billy folded the napkin and tucked it into his shirt pocket. Unable to contain his excitement he waved awkwardly at Cory and left as quickly as he could. Only when he was outside and half a block from the bar did he stop and think about what he'd just done. *Holy shit,* he thought. *I have a date.* He took the napkin from his pocket and looked at it. Then, afraid he might somehow lose it, he stuck it in his wallet alongside the fives and tens.

Ten minutes later he walked into the Hare & Hound and found Nancy already there waiting for him. He took a seat opposite her at the table. A glass of beer—Guinness by the look of it—sat in front of her. It was half empty.

"So, how'd it go?" he asked.

"About like Charly told me it would," Nancy said. "Because I was a minor at the time, and because Nate stuck to our deal and said he did it, I got probation. Three years—which means I can't leave the state."

"Which means you'll be staying?" Billy asked.

Nancy nodded. "Yeah," she said. "I'll be staying."

"I'm glad," Billy told her.

Nancy looked at him. After a moment she gave him a small, quick smile. "Me too," she said.

Billy hesitated before asking the next question. It really wasn't any of his business. *Screw it,* he told himself. *After what the two of you have done for each other you can pretty much ask each other anything.*

"What about Becky?" he said.

Nancy put her hands around the glass of beer and tapped her fingertips on it. "I've decided not to do anything," she said. "At least not now."

Billy raised an eyebrow. "I thought all of this was about her," he said.

"So did I," Nancy admitted. "And it still mostly is, which is why I'm not going to disrupt her life any more than it already is. The man she thinks is her brother is in jail—I don't think she needs to find out that her mother isn't her mother. Maybe I'll tell her when she's older. Right now I have to work on me before I'm ready to be there for her the way I should be."

"Any plans for that?"

Nancy shrugged. "School, maybe. A job. I'm not sure. One day at a time, you know?"

Billy laughed. "That's kind of my mantra right now too," he said.

They settled into a temporary silence as they looked at their menus. Then Nancy set hers down. "Did I do the right thing?" she asked.

Billy closed his menu and laid it on the table. "Define right," he answered.

"You know what I mean," said Nancy.

Billy did know. "First of all you mean we, not I," he said. "And the answer is yes, we did."

"How do you know?" Nancy asked. "I mean, how do you know *for sure?*"

Billy reached over and took her hand. Her fingers were damp from the sweat on her glass of beer. "Maybe you can't," he said.

Nancy gave him a look. "Is that the best you can do?" she said.

"Pretty much," Billy replied.

Nancy pulled her hands away. "I might as well have asked a Magic 8 Ball," she said.

"Hey," Billy protested. "It's the truth."

Nancy sighed. "That's the problem," she told him. "I think you might be right."

"That would certainly be a first," Billy said.

Nancy picked up her glass. "Don't let it go to your head," she said.

Billy laughed. "Not a chance," he assured her. "I'm too used to being wrong to change now. I wouldn't know how to handle it."

"I don't know," said Nancy. "Change seems to suit you."

"Yeah?" Billy said. "Well, you too."

"We'll see," Nancy replied. "No guarantees."

Billy caught a waiter's eye and waved him over so they could order. "There never are," he said to Nancy. "That's what makes things so interesting."

WHAT WE REMEMBER

Michael Thomas Ford

ABOUT THIS GUIDE

The suggested questions are included to
enhance your group's reading of
Michael Thomas Ford's *What We Remember*!

DISCUSSION QUESTIONS

1. The novel's chapters switch back and forth between the events of 1991 and the events of 1982–83. Did you find the transitions jarring, or has the author crafted them in such a way that the story flows smoothly?

2. Some scenes in the book are shown from more than one character's perspective. Often what you might believe at one point in the novel changes when you see the same scene from another perspective later on. How did this affect your reading experience? Were there any instances where you were bothered that something you believed to be true turned out not to be?

3. The action in the book often switches back and forth between the world of adults and the world of children. How do these two worlds mirror each other?

4. Billy McCloud at first seems to be the least reliable character in the novel, but as the story unfolds, he in many ways proves to be the most reliable. Did your opinion of Billy change during the reading of the novel?

5. Nancy Derry arguably suffers more than any character in the book. Yet she could have prevented many of the tragic events in her life by telling the truth. Do you think she made the right choices regarding Becky, her pregnancy, and her role in Dan's death? Can her failure to do so be excused by her youth? Do you see her as a victim or as a villain?

6. Do you think Ada McCloud made the right choice in hiding the alleged confession by her husband? How do you think things might have turned out had she given the letter to the police?

7. Charly enters the story as an outsider coming into a close-knit family and a close-knit community. How does this help and/or hinder her investigation? In terms of the structure of the novel, how does she act as a literary device?

8. How do you think the characters' lives would have turned out had Dan McCloud's body not been found? It could be argued that some characters (particularly Billy and Nancy) are "saved" by the revelations, while other characters (especially Celeste and potentially Becky) have their lives turned upside down. Would it have been better if all of the secrets had remained buried?

9. Who did you first think the killer was, and why? Did your guess change as you read the novel? Were you at all surprised when the killer's identity was revealed?

10. The author has said that the book was inspired by an incident in which he and his sister remembered the same event from their childhood in very different ways. Have you ever experienced this? How did it make you feel to realize that what we think we remember very clearly might not be the truth?

11. How would you describe the novel? Does it fit the traditional definition of a mystery?

12. How is this novel similar to and different from Ford's previous books?

*Bestselling author Michael Thomas Ford demonstrates once again
why he is the master of portraying the contemporary gay
experience, in this moving, beautifully told story of love, family,
and finding one's place in the world.*

When a car accident leaves photographer Burke Crenshaw in need of temporary full-time care, he finds himself back in the one place no forty-year-old chooses to be—his childhood bedroom. There, in the Vermont home where he grew up, Burke begins the long process of recuperation, and watches as his widowed father finds happiness in a new relationship that's a constant reminder of everything Burke wants and lacks.

Meeting Will Janks is an unexpected complication. Will is the twenty-year-old son of Burke's high school best friend, Mars. After what transpired between them one summer long ago, Burke had hoped he and Mars might become more than friends, but Mars has always pretended that night never happened. Will, in contrast, makes no secret of his interest in Burke, who can't resist his attraction to the handsome young man.

The burgeoning relationship draws Burke out of himself and into the community he left behind. Exploring local history, he discovers an intriguing series of letters from a Civil War soldier to his fiancée. With the help of librarian Sam Guffrey, he begins to research a 125-year-old mystery that seems to be reaching into the present day. The more Burke delves into the past, the more he's forced to confront the person he has become: the choices he made and those he avoided, his ideas of what it takes to be a successful gay man, his feelings about his mother's death, and the suppressed tension that simmers between himself and his father.

Compelling, frankly funny, and often wise, *The Road Home* is the story of one man's coming to terms with who he is, what he wants out of life, and where he belongs—and the complex, surprising path that finally takes him there.

**Please turn the page for an exciting sneak peek of
Michael Thomas Ford's
THE ROAD HOME
coming next month!**

CHAPTER 1

And there were in the same country shepherds abiding in the field, keeping watch over their flock by night. And, lo, the angel of the Lord came upon them, and the glory of the Lord shone round about them; and they were sore afraid. And the angel said unto them, Fear not: for, behold, I bring you good tidings of great joy. . . .

Burke couldn't remember the rest. It was something about peace and singing. That much he knew. But the exact words escaped him. He closed his eyes and pictured himself standing at the front of the church, just as Mrs. Throckton had told him to do. He was wearing a long brown robe and holding a staff made from a mop handle. Two other shepherds stood near him, while a couple of little kids dressed as sheep wandered around looking lost.

The problem was his beard. Made of cotton balls glued to construction paper and attached to his face with pieces of string that hooked around his ears, it made it difficult for him to speak. He felt himself growing anxious as he cleared his throat and tried again. But the words seemed to be stuck. He couldn't get them to come out of his mouth. All he could do was look out at the pews filled with people waiting for him to deliver his speech—the most important part of the whole pageant.

He opened his eyes. His heart was beating fast in his chest, and for a moment he couldn't breathe. Then he looked around, saw that he was standing on top of the hill, and he began to calm down. *It's okay,* he reassured himself. *It's okay.*

He moved his feet, his boots crunching in the snow. It had gotten colder since he'd come out an hour ago. He looked up at the sky and saw that it was darkening. Night was coming. Soon he would have dinner with his parents, and then his father would drive them to church, where Burke would play his part in the Nativity pageant. If he could say his lines.

He tried not to think about it, concentrating instead on the hill, and specifically on the path he'd made for the toboggan. It was a good path. He'd planned it carefully, first tamping the snow down with his feet and then dragging the toboggan up and down the hill several times, until the path was exactly wide enough and deep enough to keep the sled on track. It had been a lot of work, and he was tired. But the anticipation of a spectacular ride energized him. As he looked down the hill, he could already feel the shaking of the toboggan as it slid over the hard-packed snow.

The best part, of course, was the jump. Admittedly, it wasn't exactly a jump, more of a very large bump. But it would do the trick. He'd chosen the route precisely because it took him over a mound that stuck out of the hill about halfway down. If he could get up enough speed, the toboggan would hit the bump and lift up enough to create the sensation of flying. This was assuming that he'd planned correctly. Toboggans were tricky things and didn't always do what one wanted them to.

He'd waxed the bottom of his, rubbing the paraffin into the wood until the boards were shiny and slick. So far it had performed admirably, sliding over the snow with a satisfying shushing sound. True, it had once or twice attempted to go sideways or break free from the path, but that was the nature of toboggans, and Burke admired its refusal to be entirely tamed.

It had begun to snow again. Thick flakes tumbled from the sky. Although he loved snow, he wished it would stop, at least until he was finished. New snow filled in the path and slowed the toboggan's pace. A clean, almost icy surface was preferable. Still, he had time before the new snow accumulated enough to affect things too badly.

Get going, he told himself. *This is what you've been waiting for.*

Still, he held back, scanning the track for any imperfections, moving the toboggan back and forth across the snow to make sure its underside was still slippery. He knew that he was hesitating because now that the long-awaited moment had arrived, he was afraid of failure. His mind flashed suddenly to the image of himself standing onstage, unable to remember the words of the angel of the Lord.

He pulled the toboggan to the crest of the hill and the start of the track. Positioning it so that the front extended just over the hill's peak, he sat down and took hold of the guide rope. Tucking his feet into the hollow made by the upward curve of the wood, he used his hands to push the toboggan forward until he felt the front tip. Then, giving one final push, he leaned forward and let the weight of his body propel the toboggan into the fall.

Cold air buffeted his face, making his eyes tear up. He blinked, clearing them, and looked straight ahead. The toboggan was gathering speed, and the snow whispered excitedly as Burke sailed over it. Everything was working perfectly. *It's going to fly,* he told himself.

The mound was coming up. Only a few more yards. He pushed against the wind, trying to use as much of his weight as he could to help the toboggan accelerate. *Come on,* he urged. *You can do it.*

The front of the toboggan began to rise. Burke held his breath, praying that it wouldn't bog down in the snow. It didn't, and a moment later he was lifted into the air. He seemed to rise above the toboggan. Below him the snow spread out like a frozen sea, and he appeared to be flying over the tops of the pine trees that lined the edge of the field. Exultant, he threw his arms out wide and shouted with joy.

This spontaneous expression of happiness was his undoing. The toboggan, its balance upset, veered from its intended trajectory and lurched to the left as it descended. The prow struck the edge of the track at an angle, and the toboggan tipped sideways. Burke, clutching the guide rope, managed to remain seated, but the toboggan itself spun so that it was now moving backward down the hill. It was also picking up speed.

Disoriented and unable to control the toboggan, Burke could only hold on and wait for the ride to end. He had no idea where the toboggan was going, but eventually it had to stop. If he could just hang on, he would be fine.

And then there came another lurch. The toboggan, catching in a bit of frozen snow, upended. Burke once again rose into the air, but this time he could not hang on. His body was thrown from the sled. He somehow turned so that he was facing the sky, and for a moment he thought everything would be fine. Then he struck something with great force, and all went black.

When he next opened his eyes, it was dark and he was cold. Snow was falling on his face, and he lifted his hand to wipe it away. The fingers of his gloves were stiff and scratched his skin. When he breathed, a sharp pain exploded in his chest. He couldn't feel his legs.

He was lying beside a tree, but he couldn't recall how he had gotten there. His mind filled with jumbled images—snow, flying, a toboggan. It all began to come together. Then, all of a sudden, a blinding light filled the sky above him. He shielded his eyes with his hand. The light burned like fire and turned the world gold. Then a voice came from within it.

> *Fear not: for, behold, I bring you good tidings of great joy, which shall be to all people. For unto you is born this day in the city of David a Savior, which is Christ the Lord. And this shall be a sign unto you; Ye shall find the babe wrapped in swaddling clothes, lying in a manger.*

The voice ceased, and Burke heard himself speak. "And suddenly there was with the angel a multitude of the heavenly host praising God, and saying, Glory to God in the highest, and on earth peace, good will toward men."

The air was filled with an unearthly sound—high-pitched cries that hurt his ears and shattered the tranquility. The light around him changed, becoming colder. He was racked with pain and heard himself cry out for help.

"Mr. Crenshaw," a voice said. "Mr. Crenshaw, can you hear me?"

He tried to answer, but his throat was filled with something. *Snow,* he thought vaguely. He was choking on snow. He coughed, trying to clear it.

"Just lie still, Mr. Crenshaw," the voice ordered. "You're going to be fine."

The light lessened, and he looked up into the face of a stranger. From somewhere to the side of him came flashes of red, like fireworks. The strange wailing sounds continued to fill his ears.

"I have to get to church," he told the man who was looking down at him. "I have to be in the pageant. I remember my lines now." He tried to sit up and found that he couldn't.

"Lie still," the man said again. "We're going to get you out of here."

"The toboggan," Burke said. "The snow. There's no snow now. Where did it go?"

A second face—a woman's—came into view above him. "How's he doing?" she said.

"He's pretty banged up," the man answered. "But he's alive."

"He's lucky," said the woman. "The way that car looks, he shouldn't be here."

Burke wondered who they were talking about. He started to ask, but then the light came again. This time it refused to be blotted out by the closing of his eyes. It filled his head, exploding as a chorus of voices rang out.

And once more the world went black.

CHAPTER 2

"I thought you said you were okay with turning forty."

Burke opened his eyes. He had been sleeping off and on for most of the morning. His head was still fuzzy from the pain medication the nurse had injected into his IV when, at dawn, he had woken up screaming. He was no longer convinced that he was dying, but his whole body ached, despite the numbing effects of the Demerol. He looked at the face hovering over him and blinked several times, trying to place it.

"Gregg?" he asked, fishing a name from the depths of his foggy memory. He coughed, clearing his throat, and a glass of water found its way into his hand.

"Here," said Gregg. "Drink up."

Burke drained most of the glass, then handed it back to his friend. "How did you know?" he asked Gregg.

"Apparently, I'm still listed as your emergency contact with your insurance company," Gregg replied.

Burke tried to laugh, but it hurt his chest, and he ended up coughing instead. He and Gregg had been broken up for almost three years, yet it had never occurred to him to change his insurance information. Now he was glad he hadn't.

"I always thought the three-in-the-morning phone call would be about my mother dropping dead," said Gregg as he pulled a chair up beside the bed and sat down. "Frankly, I was a little disappointed that it wasn't."

"Did they say what happened?" Burke asked. "All I remember is driving home after the party."

"Raccoon," said Gregg. "Or maybe a dog. You swerved to avoid hitting it and ran off the road. Lucky for you, the guy behind you saw the whole thing and stopped. You should send him a thank-you card."

"My leg's busted," said Burke.

"I noticed," Gregg replied. He nodded at the pulley system that elevated Burke's right leg—which was wrapped in a cast—above the bed. "Your arm doesn't look too good, either."

Burke glanced down and saw the cast that covered his left forearm. "Not the left one," he said. "Fuck me."

"What else did you manage to break?" Gregg asked.

Burke shook his head. "I'm not sure," he said. "I kind of just got here."

Gregg laughed. "Well, we'll find out," he said. He reached behind Burke. "Sit up if you can," he ordered.

Burke tried, wincing at the pain. Gregg adjusted the pillows behind Burke, and Burke lay back against them. "Thanks," he said.

"Yeah, well, I know what a baby you are when you're sick," said Gregg.

Burke nodded. It was true, he hated not feeling well. It made him feel out of control and, worse, dependent on someone else. He'd never been good at being taken care of.

Gregg went to the window and opened the curtains, letting in the bright morning light. Watching him, Burke was reminded of how much of a nester Gregg was. He loved taking care of things—houses, animals, people. Ironically, it had been the thing that had ended their relationship. Gregg had wanted them to move in together; Burke had been afraid the closeness would be smothering. After a year of waiting for Burke to change his mind, Gregg had moved on.

"That's better," Gregg said, looking around the room. "I hear hospital chic is in this year. Martha Stewart just did a segment on decorating with catheters and speculums."

"I understand they make great Christmas ornaments," said a voice from the doorway. A woman in a long white jacket walked in and extended her hand to Gregg. "I'm Dr. Liu," she said. "I assume you're the husband?"

"No," Gregg said. "The ex-husband."

"Oh, I'm sorry," the doctor said.

"Don't be," Gregg assured her. "He was a lousy husband."

Dr. Liu smiled and turned to Burke. "And how are you feeling today?"

"Not as good as I did yesterday," said Burke.

"I wouldn't think so," the doctor replied. "You knocked yourself around pretty thoroughly."

"My leg and my arm," Burke said vaguely.

"Among other things," Dr. Liu told him. "You also broke a couple of ribs and came this close to shattering your pelvis." She held her fingers an inch apart to emphasize how fortunate Burke was not to have done that. "But the leg is the big thing," she continued. "It took a lot to put it back together. Lucky for you, I'm good at puzzles."

"I like her," said Gregg, grinning at Burke.

Burke ignored him. "When can I get out of here?" he asked.

"Let's talk about that," said Dr. Liu. "I want you here for at least a week."

"A week!" Burke exclaimed. "But I've got work lined up. I'm supposed to shoot Angelina Jolie for *Boston* magazine on Tuesday."

"Not going to happen," said Dr. Liu. "You're not walking on that leg for a while."

"What's a while?" Burke demanded.

"Six weeks minimum," the doctor answered. "Maybe longer."

"No," said Burke, shaking his head. "I can't be laid up for six weeks. No way."

"What did I say?" Gregg said, wagging a finger at him. "You. Sick. Big baby."

Burke groaned. "I have to get out of here," he said.

"You're going to need help," said Dr. Liu. "Do you have someone who can stay with you?"

"I don't know," said Burke. He was irritated now and couldn't think. The pain was coming back, and he wanted more Demerol. "Maybe."

"Well, think about it," said the doctor. "As I said, I want you here for the next week. You can make arrangements for when you're released. But I won't let you out of here until you do."

Dr. Liu excused herself to see other patients and left Burke and Gregg alone again. Burke, thinking about what she'd said, stared at the ceiling. After a few minutes he realized that Gregg had grown oddly quiet. He looked over at his former lover, who was sitting in the chair, looking at his hands.

"Hey," said Burke, "could I . . ."

"No," Gregg said quickly.

"How do you know what I'm going to ask?" said Burke.

"You can't stay with me," said Gregg. "I'm sorry, but it's just a bad idea. Besides, Rick wouldn't go for it."

"How do you know?" Burke argued.

"He doesn't like you," said Gregg.

Burke, surprised, looked at him.

"I'm sorry, sweetie, but he doesn't. He thinks you're overbearing."

"I am not," Burke objected.

Gregg gave him a small smile. "You kind of are," he said. "Besides, I have to work. What about your insurance? Maybe they'll pay for an in-home nurse. You might even get a hot one," he added.

"My insurance doesn't pay for anything," said Burke. "I'll be lucky if they cough up anything for this little vacation."

"I can call them for you," Gregg said. "We'll find out."

"I don't want a nurse," Burke complained. "The last thing I need is a stranger helping me to the toilet and trying to talk to me about his life while he's giving me a sponge bath."

Gregg didn't come back with a smart response, which surprised Burke. It also worried him. Gregg's sharp sense of humor waned only when he was trying to avoid confrontation. The fact that he wasn't saying anything meant that he didn't want to discuss the situation.

"Fine," Burke said after a minute or two had gone by. "Call the insurance company. See what they'll do. I'll figure something out." He waited for Gregg to nod in agreement, then added, "I'm tired. I think I should sleep now."

Gregg got up. "I'll let you know what they say. And you're welcome."

Burke didn't look at him as he mumbled, "Thanks."

"I'll be back tonight," said Gregg.

When Gregg was gone, Burke tried to form a plan. He hoped his insurance would come through, although he really doubted it. Having never been really sick, he'd always managed to get by with the bare minimum, figuring he would up his coverage when he got older.

Yeah, well, you are old now, he told himself.

He ran through a list of his friends, thinking about who might be able either to take him in or, better, come live with him for a month or two, if he needed help for that long. He didn't like the idea of having to move in with someone else. He liked being in his own place, even if he couldn't get around it very well.

Gregg apparently was out as a potential nursemaid. But he had other friends. Oscar, maybe, or Dane. But Oscar worked long hours, and Dane was too much of a cock hound. Burke didn't relish the idea of being in Dane's guest room and listening to his host getting it on with one of his numerous tricks.

What about Tony? he wondered. Tony lived alone, and as a writer, he worked out of his house. *But he has cats,* Burke reminded himself. Just the thought of Tony's three Himalayans—LaVerne, Maxine, and Patty—made his throat close up. No, his allergies would never survive an extended stay with the Andrews Sisters.

He continued mentally working his way through his address book. But for one reason or another, nobody fit the bill. Abe's apartment was too small. Jesse was a slob. Ellen was a vegan. One by one he crossed the names off his list until he had run out of options. Then he rang for the nurse, asked for another shot of Demerol, and drifted into sleep.

When he awoke again, it was dark outside and his room smelled like his elementary school cafeteria. Gregg was once again seated in the chair by Burke's bed. He indicated a tray on the table beside him.

"Salisbury steak," he said. "And Tater Tots. Who's a lucky boy?"

He picked the tray up and placed it on the movable tabletop that swung out from the wall beside Burke's bed. Positioning the tabletop in front of Burke, he laid out the napkin and silverware as if he were setting a table.

"And what will you be drinking this evening, sir?" he asked.

"Gin and tonic," said Burke. "Make it a double."

"Water it is," Gregg replied, pouring some from the plastic pitcher that sat on the table beside the bed.

Burke picked up the fork and poked at the meat on his plate. "When I was a kid, I always loved Wednesdays, because it was Salisbury steak day at school," he told Gregg. "I was in college before I realized that it was just a fancy name for hamburger."

"That explains your sophisticated palate," Gregg joked. It was another difference between them—Gregg loved fine dining (Burke called it snob food), and Burke's idea of cooking was opening a can of soup.

Burke was suddenly ravenous. He attacked his dinner with his good hand, managing despite the fact that he was a lefty and the utensils felt alien in his right hand. He wolfed down the Salisbury steak and

Tater Tots. He even ate the green beans, which normally he would ignore. Only when he turned his attention to the small dish of chocolate pudding did he resume talking to Gregg.

"Did you talk to the insurance people?"

"I did," Gregg answered. He cleared away Burke's tray before continuing. "And you were right. They aren't going to be particularly helpful."

"Define 'particularly,'" said Burke.

Gregg sat down. "They'll pay only fifty dollars a day for in-home care," he said.

Burke swore.

"And that's after the five-thousand-dollar deductible," Gregg informed him.

Burke's response brought one of the nurses to his door. "Are you all right?" she asked, looking more than a little concerned.

"He's fine," Gregg assured her. "He's having sticker shock."

The nurse waited for Burke to confirm that he didn't need anything, then left the men alone.

Gregg sighed. "So where does that leave us?" he asked. "I mean you. Where does that leave you?"

"I don't know," Burke told him. "You don't want me, and I can't think of anyone else."

"It's not that I don't want you," said Gregg. "It's—"

"I know," Burke interrupted. "I'm overbearing."

"Just a tad," said Gregg. "And I work. Don't forget that. What about your other friends?"

"Sluts," said Burke, waving a hand around. "Cats. Smokers. Don't eat meat."

"I see," Gregg said. "Which brings us back to square one."

"I have to pee," said Burke.

"What?" Gregg asked.

"Pee," Burke repeated. "I have to pee. Help me up."

"Um, you're not getting up," Gregg said. "Remember?"

Burke glanced at his leg. "What am I supposed to do?" he said.

"This," Gregg said. He held up a plastic container that he'd taken from a shelf beneath the bedside table. It resembled a water bottle on its side, with one end slightly angled up and ending in a wide mouth.

"You've got to be kidding," Burke said.

"Come on," said Gregg. "It's not that hard." He pulled back the blanket on Burke's bed and started to lift Burke's gown.

"Hey!" Burke said.

"Relax," said Gregg. "It's not like I haven't seen it before."

Burke relented, and Gregg hiked up the hospital gown, exposing Burke's crotch. He placed the urine bottle between Burke's legs.

"Ow," Burke said. "Slow down."

He tried to spread his legs, but when pain shot through the right one, he gave up and balanced the bottle on his thighs. Taking his penis in his right hand, he positioned the head at the mouth of the bottle and tried to pee. At first nothing happened. Then, as if a valve had been opened, urine spurted from his dick. Startled, he let go, and the bottle toppled sideways as he continued to pee. He attempted to grab at the bottle and hold on to his penis at the same time, but his left arm was useless, and he could accomplish only one of his goals. He clamped down, forcing the flow of urine to stop, but not before the hair on his legs was covered in drops of piss.

Gregg, who had prevented the bottle from falling to the floor, repositioned it. "Hold it," he ordered Burke, who placed his right hand on the bottle. Gregg took Burke's cock in his hand and inserted it into the bottle's mouth.

"Don't watch," Burke said.

Rolling his eyes, Gregg looked away. After a moment Burke was able to pee freely. He tried to ignore the fact that Gregg's hand was holding his dick as he drained his bladder. He watched as the bottle filled up. For a moment he was afraid it might overflow, but then the stream slowed to a trickle. To his horror, Gregg milked the last few drops out before removing the bottle.

"Thanks," Burke said.

Gregg took the bottle into the bathroom and poured it into the toilet. When he returned, he had a washcloth in his hand, which he used to wipe the spilled piss from Burke's legs.

"I can do that," Burke protested.

"Shut up," said Gregg. "You don't always have to be the big top, you know."

Burke grunted. He wasn't going to get into that particular argument with Gregg.

"There," Gregg said as he put Burke's gown back into place and pulled the sheet and blanket up. "Feel better?"

"No," said Burke. He was already worrying about what he would do when he had to pee and Gregg wasn't there. He certainly wasn't going to ask any of the nurses for help.

"I had a thought," Gregg said.

"About what?" asked Burke.

"About where you could stay."

"Oh yeah?" Burke said hopefully. "Where?"

Gregg paused for a long moment. "With your father," he said.

Burke laughed. "Right," he said.

"I'm serious," Gregg told him. "He has the room. He's home all the time. It's perfect."

"Except that it's my father," said Burke.

Gregg looked him in the eyes. "You don't have a lot of choices, Burke," he said. "This is a good solution."

"I'm not staying with my father for six weeks," Burke said. "I'm not staying in Vermont."

"There's nothing wrong with Vermont," Gregg argued. "It's beautiful this time of year."

"No," Burke repeated. "End of discussion. I'd rather stay in this place than go there. I'll think of something."

"Okay," Gregg said. "Just keep your options open."

"Don't try that on me," said Burke.

"Try what?"

"That thing you do," Burke said. "Whenever you wanted me to do something and I said no, you would tell me to keep my options open. That always meant you thought I would come around and do what you had wanted to do in the first place."

"That's not true," Gregg said.

"No?" said Burke. "Have you forgotten about the vacation in Provincetown? The tile in my bathroom? The Volvo station wagon?"

"That Volvo saved your life," Gregg said. "And I didn't make you do any of those things. I just suggested."

"Well, stop suggesting," said Burke. "I'm not asking my father if I can stay with him."

Gregg nodded. "All right," he said. He looked at his watch. "I should go." He leaned down and kissed Burke on the forehead. "Just think about it."

"Get out," Burke said, only half feigning irritation.

"Good night," Gregg said as he left. "Don't stay up too late. It's a school night."